THE
TRAITOR'S
RUIN

ERIN BEATY

【Imprint】
MAKE YOUR MARK

NEW YORK

REYAN

SEY LAMAN

Border Road

D

CRESCERA

Northern Ro

🛡 Broadmoor

Western
Strong   Garland Hill   Galarick

*Sagitta
Crossing*

Tieganni Ro

Sunset Road

Na River

Span Road

TASMET

*Arrowhead
Crossroad*

For
Jc

🏰 BEY-LISSANDRA

Western Sea

KIMISARA

2016

SQUARE
FISH

An imprint of Macmillan Publishing Group, LLC
120 Broadway, New York, NY 10271
fiercereads.com

THE TRAITOR'S RUIN. Copyright © 2018 by Erin Beaty.
All rights reserved. Printed in the United States of America.

Square Fish and the Square Fish logo are trademarks of Macmillan and are used
by Imprint under license from Macmillan.

Our books may be purchased in bulk for promotional, educational, or business
use. Please contact your local bookseller or the Macmillan Corporate and
Premium Sales Department at (800) 221-7945 ext. 5442 or by email at
MacmillanSpecialMarkets@macmillan.com.

Library of Congress Control Number: 2017958064

ISBN 978-1-250-30906-8 (paperback) / ISBN 978-1-250-14226-9 (ebook)

[Imprint]
MAKE YOUR MARK

@ImprintReads
Originally published in the United States by Imprint
First Square Fish edition, 2019

Book designed by Natalie C. Sousa
Imprint Logo designed by Amanda Spielman
Square Fish logo designed by Filomena Tuosto
Map by Maxime Passe
Map © 2017 by Imprint

10 9 8 7 6 5 4 3 2 1

LEXILE: 800L

CHERISH	MY FRIEND	RAISE A	TO YOUR HEALTH
	THIS BOOK	AND KNOW I	TOAST
MISTREAT	MY FIEND	HOPE YOUR	ALWAYS BURNS

*To Kim, who didn't tell me how terrible that first draft was,
making all this possible.*

THE
TRAITOR'S
RUIN

1

KNITTING NEEDLES WEREN'T very effective weapons, but they were better than fencing with feather quills.

Sage lunged at her pupil, and the princess blocked her smoothly but stopped short of where she ought to have finished the move.

"No, no," said Sage. "Carry that around and force my blade away so you can move in." She took a step back. "Let's try that again."

"Do you mind?" snapped eleven-year-old Carinthia from across the schoolroom. "I can't concentrate with combat knitting in the background."

Princess Rose lowered her "blade" and rolled her eyes, but Sage gestured for her to stay quiet. "Sorry, Cara. How many problems do you have left?"

"Five."

"That's good enough for today. You can go." The princess was out the door almost before Sage had finished speaking.

"Would you like me to look over her paper for you, Sage?" Arithmetic was easy for Rose, but she'd also do anything to delay needlework.

"No, thank you." Sage picked up the page and scanned it. Twelve of the fifteen finished were correct. Carinthia had made a lot of progress in the nine months since Sage had become her tutor.

"Are you going to the training yards this afternoon?" Rose asked, idly twirling her knitting needle.

Sage tried to act like it hadn't been on her mind for hours as she nodded. "They're having a double ring fencing match today. Master Reed says I'm ready." A glance around the room told her it was tidy enough. She offered Rose the knitting needle she still held. "Don't forget this."

The princess made a face before accepting it. Together they walked into the adjacent room, where Rose's mother and sister sat working on an elaborate tapestry near the hearth fire. The queen was a fair-skinned northerner, with bright, wheat-colored curls that Rose had inherited. Sitting by her side, Princess Cara was in her element at last, stitching scarlet designs into the heavy fabric. Rose groaned. Knitting she disliked, but embroidery she hated.

Sage curtsied. "We're done for the day, Majesty," she said. "Is there anything else you need of me?" The queen was slightly farsighted, and Sage had taken on the additional duties as her private secretary a few months ago. "Any new correspondence?"

"I suspect you are really asking if there is anything for you," the queen said. "But no, there is nothing."

Sage frowned. This was the second week in a row there was nothing from Alex. As he was the king's nephew and she was employed in the royal household, their private letters were often included in official dispatches going to and from the capital—more reliable delivery, but still sporadic.

Orianna looked up from her sewing with a gentle smile. "The Tegann Pass has already opened for the year, so communication will increase in the next few weeks. If anything does arrive, rest assured I will forward it to you immediately."

Sage wasn't sure when she'd stopped feeling awkward when members of the royal family showed such consideration for her feelings. "If there's nothing, then Your Majesty will excuse me."

"May I go with her, Mother?" asked Rose.

The queen's tone became more formal as she addressed her elder daughter. "Twice already this week you have skipped embroidery to watch Sage. Both times you promised to make up your work, and both times you have failed to do so."

"But, Mother—"

"The answer is no." Orianna squinted into the magnifying glass over the cloth. Close work and reading strained her eyes and gave her headaches, but sewing was something Her Majesty would not give up. "You need not ask again."

Sage shrugged apologetically at the thirteen-year-old, but privately she was glad not to have an audience today. Rose stomped to her sewing basket and plopped down, slouching against the back of her chair. Orianna glared at her, and Rose immediately straightened. With a sigh, the queen sat back and rubbed her eyes before looking up to Sage with a weary smile. "You've gone down to the training yards every day this week, if I'm not mistaken. If it weren't for Captain Quinn, I'd think you had your eye on someone."

Sage flushed. "It helps me feel closer to him in a way." The conflict in Tasmet had started at the end of last spring and was now entering its ninth month. No amount of writing could make up for all the time they'd lost. "I also enjoy it. And with all the new soldiers arriving lately, there's so much more I can learn."

Orianna's expression clouded over. "Yes, well, I'm sure you don't want to be late today." She turned back to her sewing and jabbed her needle into the fabric.

The mood shift was puzzling, but Sage didn't have time to unravel it right now. She curtsied and departed the queen's sitting room, already mentally wielding a sword. She'd have to hurry if she wanted to claim one of the padded armor suits small enough to fit her slight frame. In her excitement, she'd taken twenty steps before she remembered she was still wearing a dress. Sage whirled around and trotted back in the direction of her room, loosening the laces of her bodice as she went. Five minutes later she was taking shortcuts through the servants' passages, dressed in breeches and a linen shirt.

More soldiers than ever filled the yards, shouting greetings to old friends and making new ones. Sage wove through the crowds, focused on getting to the main arena. She'd long ago cured herself of automatically searching every group of soldiers for Alex's face, hoping against hope he'd returned to Tennegol before he could tell her he was coming.

3

She had been only partly honest with the queen. Coming here *did* help her feel closer to Alex, but her reasons went deeper. Ever since Father died five years ago, Sage's life had been ruled by others. Her aunt and uncle may have had good intentions, but her guardians had set her on a path of relying on a husband for her safety and well-being. When she worked for the matchmaker, Darnessa was better at letting her have independence, and Sage might have found herself after a few years, but last spring changed everything. She'd never felt more helpless, more of a liability than she did at Tegann.

Alex's soldiers had needed to get packets of red blaze—powders that created massive columns of red smoke when burned—to the scouts outside the fortress so they could signal for help. Sage was the only one who could squeeze out of the sewer grate to escape, but she was caught by a sentry. She'd been barely competent enough to defend herself, and it had almost cost her her life.

She would never be helpless again.

Sage managed to snag the last suit small enough to fit her, beating out a palace squire who had wasted time picking out a sword first. She tried not to look too triumphant as she shoved her arms into the sleeves and buckled the top half to the bottom. Even luckier, this particular outfit was designed to also wear on horseback, meaning the rear and back of the thighs were looser and not padded. Frankly, her backside needed the extra room.

Once the practice armor was secure, Sage selected a training sword, opting for one heavier than squires normally worked with. She would tire quicker, but she'd learned the extra weight behind her swings somewhat compensated for her weaker arm strength. It also made her stronger. She pinned the sword between her knees as she tucked her sandy braid inside her helmet and lashed it down. Then she stood straight and hefted the weapon in her hand, trembling with sudden nervousness.

Today she would find out just how good she was.

2

SAGE TOOK A place in the inner circle of fighters, facing outward. A ring formed around them, matching up one-to-one. She saluted her first partner and took a guard stance, idly wondering if she knew the man. With the bulky and often misshapen padding, there were only three or four men she could positively identify once helmets were on—and one of them because he was missing an arm. It worked both ways, however. Due to her size, most assumed she was a squire, which suited Sage just fine. The regular guards had gotten used to her presence over the last few months, but with all the new soldiers lately, things tended to get awkward if they realized she was a woman.

When the bell rang out, Sage and her opponent quickly fell into a rhythm of attacking and defending. As it was the first round, they both were more interested in warming up than scoring points. They lunged and blocked with increasing intensity until the bell signaled the end of the round after seven minutes. Both lowered their swords and saluted each other again. Her partner took several steps to his right so another fighter could move in front of her. She saluted the new man and set her feet for the next round.

After four rotations, Sage was sweating heavily under her armor but feeling confident in her performance. A few fencers slid in or out of the formation, one pair inserting themselves two positions to her right. She didn't recognize either of them, but it felt like the one in the outer ring was watching her. Had he seen signs she was a girl? Hopefully not. As the man rotated closer, she watched him, too.

The scruff of a black beard showed under the padded helmet, so he was likely in his twenties at least. He was taller than her, but most men were, well-built without being bulky—though the padding made him look slightly hunchbacked—and his sword...It was a standard practice weapon, not a personal one, yet he handled it like an extension of his arm, with swift and smooth efficiency. Not a movement was wasted. A clip across her shoulder reminded her to pay more attention to her current opponent. Sage shook sweat from her eyes and refocused on her own match.

At the next bell, the man stepped before her. His helm exaggerated the movement of his head as he looked her up and down. Assessing her, no doubt. Though she couldn't see anything—not even his bearded neck from this angle—when he saluted she got the feeling he was smiling. He plainly did not see her as a challenge. Well, she would show him she was no novice.

But in less than a minute, his superiority was obvious. Master Reed described her as advanced for her time and with promising grace of form, but her new opponent anticipated her every move and countered effortlessly. When he went on the offense, she could tell he moved slowly for her benefit. Part of her felt angry at being patronized; another part was grateful he hadn't merely disarmed her in the first three seconds. After a time, she realized he was testing her, letting her show what she could do, and she began to appreciate him—until she leaned too far to the right in a parry. His sword whipped around and smacked her rear end.

Through the slit in the helm she caught the glint of his teeth as he grinned. Rage flashed through her—he knew she was a girl! Why else would he have done that except to mock her? Nearly blind with fury, she recovered her balance and attacked, which he easily blocked. Sage shoved away and stepped back, and he shook his head in warning. She struck out wildly, but he knocked her sword to the ground and laid the flat of his blade across her backside again.

Tears of humiliation blurred her vision. While she stood clenching her fists and trying to decide what to do, he retrieved her sword and offered it back to her. There was no sign of a smile behind the mask this time, and she understood. He'd warned her not to attack in anger and taught her a lesson when she didn't heed him. Humbled, she accepted her weapon and assumed the guard position. He nodded approvingly, and they began again.

The bell clanged, ending the round, but the man gestured for the next fighter to go around. The other swordsman shrugged and moved past them. Her mysterious partner had taken an interest in her. Given his skill, it was somewhat puzzling—he gained nothing by staying. Then the bell rang again, and she dismissed her confusion to concentrate on the fight before her. After a few exchanges of blows, her partner stepped back and motioned for her to lower her blade. Cautiously, she did, and he shifted his sword to his left hand and approached to stand behind her. Without a word, he placed his hand on her wrist and corrected what she'd been doing, guiding her arm in a more efficient arc and slice. The man's directions were better for her height and arm strength than what she'd learned.

"Thank you," she said, the words echoing in her helm. The man nodded and took up his position again. When he switched his sword back to his right hand, he flexed his left several times, like it was numb. Her eyes widened.

No, it couldn't be.

But the more she watched him, the more sure she became. When the round ended, once again her partner waved for the next fighter to skip them. The man at the bell called out that this would be the last round.

Their sparring changed. Her opponent became aggressive, forcing her back almost constantly. He plainly intended to make her yield by the end, though she knew he could do it at any point.

Winning this fight would require something other than skill.

She waited until the right moment, then faltered. As she knew he would, the man took advantage of the opening, but she was ready to move into it. Making it look like he stabbed her, she collapsed with a cry. Her partner dropped his sword and dove to catch her.

He rolled her onto her back and knelt over her, pushing her helmet off and feeling along her ribs. "Where?" he gasped. "Where are you hurt?"

Sage grinned up at him. "I'm fine, Captain, but you're dead." She jabbed him in the stomach with the dull point of her practice sword, and he glanced down.

Scrambling to take off his helm, he looked back at her with a mixture of pride and vexation in his brown eyes. "You're a cheater, you know that?"

"As I recall, you taught me to use every advantage I could."

Alex laughed. "So I did. I yield to my lady." All the padding made it difficult for him to kiss her, but he managed.

3

CAPTAIN MALKIM HUZAR sat in the corner of the bustling tavern, nursing a pint of ale. It was a weak brew, but he endured it as he endured everything in this country. The rough weave of his cloak hung around him so only his forearms were exposed. From beneath the hood, his eyes tracked the movements of over two dozen other customers, three barmaids, and the establishment's owner—a fat, greasy man who acted like he owned the barmaids as well, the one exception being a pretty girl with lips and nails painted to match the fiery tints in her hair. The barman gave her a wide berth. Two silvery scars under his left ear were likely the reason.

The redhead brought Huzar an ale to replace the one he'd finished. Before taking his empty mug, she traced a fingernail over the swirling tattoo on his bronze arm. "Don't get many Aristelans here," she said in a husky voice.

She mistook him for an eastern Demoran, but that was fine with him. Kimisar weren't welcome in Demora, even before the current conflict. Huzar allowed himself a vague smile. The door to the tavern opened, bringing a gust of frigid March air Huzar could feel even in this corner. Finally.

"Another ale," he told her. "For my friend."

She glanced over her shoulder at the man weaving through the crowd, and turned back to the bar with a sigh. Huzar exhaled in relief. Pretty as she was, the less attention he drew from anyone, the better.

The newcomer swept back his own cloak, made of a fine but sturdy cloth with the Demoran royal crest on the collar, and joined Huzar at the table, bringing with him the strong scent of horse sweat and dung. He sat at an angle so neither man's view of the room was obstructed. Unlike Huzar, he'd spent most of the winter indoors, and his southern complexion had lost some of its copper undertones. The arms he leaned on the table were also scrawny compared to the muscles Huzar displayed.

"You are late," Huzar said in Demoran. He hadn't spoken his native tongue in over nine months; only a trace of his accent remained. He could even say *Jovan* as the Demorans pronounced it, *Shovan*.

"My work has increased with all these arrivals," the stablehand said. "Fortunately also my pay. Riders tip well for extra care of their mounts." He pushed a small bag of coins across the table.

Huzar pocketed the money with a grunt. As much as he moved around, he didn't have time to find steady employment, meaning every man he checked in with had to give him a small portion of his wages. "What news, then? I have seen many soldiers arriving."

The other man nodded. "I hear rumors."

Huzar held up a finger as the barmaid returned with a full mug. The stablehand grinned up as she set it before him, but Huzar didn't dare look at her. Once she left, Huzar lowered his hand and waited for the man to elaborate.

"They say the king will reestablish the Norsari."

Having delivered this incredible statement, the man took a smug drink, letting it sluice over the sides and down his chin. Huzar blinked as he tried to process the news. Demora's elite fighting unit had been disbanded over twenty years ago, as a disarmament condition of the truce after Kimisara's last major campaign to reclaim the region of Tasmet. A weak and foolish move on the part of the Demoran king, but he'd been young and eager to be seen as a peacemaker at the time. The events of last year undoubtedly nullified the terms of the treaty, however.

Huzar tapped the side of his mug but otherwise held himself still. "I would not consider the fuss in Tasmet worth such action. Maybe only another year with the forces they have will be sufficient." He was also surprised the Kimisar were still raiding Tasmet after all these months, but after three years of famine and blight, there was likely little to return home to.

"It would seem the Demoran king expects more trouble."

Huzar had no knowledge of what his own nation planned, but given the state of Kimisara when he left last year, he doubted it had recovered enough to attempt an invasion. Only the alliance with the D'Amiran family had made last spring possible. The agreement had been distasteful from the start, but he'd followed orders. When it became obvious the Demoran duke had no intention of keeping to the terms, however, Huzar had ordered his men to abandon Tegann and return home. Unfortunately, a company of Kimisar had been stranded in Demora, on the east side of the Catrix Mountains, and Huzar had made it his mission to find them.

Once he did, he realized there were too few men to fight their way back, but too many to keep together for long. He'd ordered them to disperse into the Demoran countryside, find work, and lie low until the time was right to either escape or make a stand. To further throw the Demorans off, Huzar had taken a team to the border to make it look as though the group had crossed into Casmun. Perhaps none of it had worked as well as he'd thought.

"Trouble? From where?"

"Casmun. There have been signs of an alliance between our people and theirs."

Huzar snorted. The Kimisar and Casmuni had common roots, but they hated each other even more than Kimisara and Demora. More likely the Demoran king was misinterpreting the trail Huzar had left going south, believing it was Casmuni testing the border as the Kimisar were known to do in the west.

He stroked the stubble on his chin, wondering if this was a positive or negative development. That the Demorans were confused could be an advantage, but once there were Norsari, it was only a matter of time before he and his men were hunted down and wiped out.

A Norsari unit would take weeks to train, though. Huzar probably had enough time to gather the 150 or so Kimisar scattered east and south of the capital and make a plan to get home. Information would be his primary asset until then.

The captain turned his eyes back to the stablehand. "If there are to be Norsari, who will be the commander?"

"I have heard one name more than any other." The man's grin displayed two missing teeth. "And it is one you will recognize."

A few minutes later, the stablehand left to return to his job at the palace. Huzar ordered a third pint and barely noticed when it was placed in front of him. He did indeed know the name. Few in the city did not. But Huzar had special reason to know it.

Captain Alexander Quinn.

He'd long ago discovered the name of the lead soldier who escorted the women to the capital city for last summer's Concordium. In scraping together information in the past months, Huzar was able to paint a clear picture of what had happened at Tegann. D'Amiran had been outfoxed, and Quinn had taken over the entire fortress with only a handful of soldiers. It appeared the Demoran captain would've succeeded even if Huzar and his men had stayed, the plan and its execution had been that solid. Quinn had also personally killed the duke.

An enemy one could respect was far preferable to an ally without honor, and Huzar bore him no ill will. He only wished to go home. It now appeared he would have to go through Captain Quinn to get there.

4

FROM HER SEAT within the giant willow tree, Sage watched Alex pace the garden path, pausing often to look in the direction he expected her to come from. She'd arrived several minutes before him and loosely braided her bath-wet hair as she waited. Maybe it was cruel, but she wanted to watch him for a few minutes, remembering the way he moved, savoring his eagerness. It was only fair, really, since he must have been spying on her in the tilting yards for quite a while.

He flexed his left hand as he walked, probably out of habit more than necessity now. It had taken weeks to recover full movement from the wound Alex had taken in the forearm at Tegann. He'd even admitted in his letters that he feared there was some minor permanent nerve damage. Alex wouldn't want to make her worry, though, and Sage was concerned it was worse than he said. She'd have to ask his best friend, Lieutenant Casseck, for his opinion.

Sage nervously traced the silver-threaded designs on her dress. The blue brocade gown had cap sleeves and a neckline lower than she usually preferred, making her feel exposed. It was much too formal for a walk in the gardens, but everyone said it suited her coloring and played up her better features. Sage had actually come to like skirts in the past year. Well, perhaps *like* was too strong a word. She'd come to a greater appreciation of pretty clothes, even if she felt like a duck wearing swan feathers.

As the edge of the sun dipped below the high walls, Alex went to sit on the bench, bouncing his knees impatiently. Sage decided she'd had enough and called his name.

He jumped up and turned to squint into the thick, drooping branches behind him. "Sage?"

"I'm in here."

Vaulting over the bench, he parted the curtain of leaves with his hands and leaned in. When he saw her, he scowled. "How long have you been here?"

Sage hopped down from the low-hanging limb. "Long enough."

"Oh, you are going to pay for that." He swooped inside the shelter of the tree and lifted her off her feet. She shrieked and flailed as he lowered her gently to the ground, then pinned her arms down so he could kiss her neck. "Say you're sorry," he whispered, his breath in her ear hitting her like a lightning bolt she felt to her toes.

"I can't." She giggled. "That would be a lie."

"How long did I wait there like a fool? An hour?"

"Try three minutes. Five at most."

"The longest five minutes of my life."

"You deserved it after that stunt you pulled in the yards. How long were you watching me there?"

"Two times in as many hours you defeat me with treachery." Alex released her wrists to bury one hand in her hair and slip the other around her waist. "I'm marrying a criminal mastermind."

"I'm hardly—" But he cut her off with his mouth on hers. Sage wrapped her arms around his neck and kissed him back. His hair was still wet, too, and smelled of evergreen soap, like the mountain forest in winter.

He lifted his face to whisper, "I've missed you so much," before kissing her again and again, each time seemingly different, with a separate memory of longing attached. She never wanted it to end, but at last he leaned back to look at her, tracing his thumb over her lips. "Sweet Spirit," Alex said softly. "I'd forgotten how much I'd do for that smile."

Sage pulled one hand back from his shoulder. "You look well, though this will take some getting used to." She ran her fingers over the scruff on his chin.

For a second he looked puzzled, then he laughed. "Would you believe I'd forgotten it was there? It was just easier to manage these last months. Warmer in the winter, too." He studied her face. "Do you like it?"

She pursed her lips. "I'm not sure yet. It looks quite dashing, but I've only seen and imagined you clean-shaven, so it's a little startling. And a bit rough on my face."

"I'll get rid of it tomorrow."

"I can get used to it. Give me a couple days."

Alex shook his head. "Nothing will come between me and my lady—nothing that would cause her to deny my kisses, especially. Besides, I can always grow it back later."

"If you want." Sage shrugged, honestly not caring. "Who else came with you?"

"Cass and Gram for officers," Alex said, rubbing his face where she'd touched him. Lieutenants Casseck and Gramwell were two of his closest friends and had been with the escort group last year at Tegann. "Plus a hundred handpicked fighters."

That was interesting, especially considering how many similar soldiers had been arriving in the past weeks. She took a deep breath. Now came the question she wasn't sure she wanted to hear answered. "How long are you here?"

"Not sure yet. Several days at least."

Not great, but not terrible. "Will you have many daily duties?"

Alex rolled lazily onto his side next to her and stroked her bare arm with one finger, raising goose bumps among the freckles and faint scars. "Cass can handle most of them for me."

"Shame on you, Captain. That's an abuse of power."

"Rank has its privileges. Besides, he'll make captain soon, so he needs the practice."

"Where will you go from here?"

Alex gently tugged her sleeve down and kissed her exposed shoulder. "Not sure about that, either. I have a theory, but I won't know for a couple more days. We got here a little earlier than expected. Can't imagine what drove me to travel so fast."

"Did you come through Tegann?"

Even in the dim light she could see his face pale. "Yes, why?"

"I was just curious how much it had been rebuilt, after all the fires and such."

"I honestly don't know. We didn't stop." The venom in his voice made her recoil a little. "If it were up to me, I'd have burned the whole place down."

How could she have been so thoughtless? Sage turned his face up to hers to find his eyes bright with tears. "Alex, I'm sorry. I wasn't thinking."

He squeezed his eyes shut. "It's all right. I'm sorry I snapped at you."

She searched for something better to talk about. "So what's your theory about your assignment?"

Alex sighed. "Sage, I've spent nine months waiting for this night. Can we please talk about something besides the army?"

His eyes were still closed as she brought her mouth to his. "I don't think we need to talk at all," she said.

5

MORROW D'AMIRAN HELD *Charlie tight against him with one hand, a* *dagger in the other. Alex's brother, barely nine years old, struggled vainly as* *his dark brown eyes begged forgiveness for being caught.*

No, *Alex wanted to tell him.* You did everything right. This is happening because of my mistakes.

"Choose, Captain." D'Amiran smiled as he brought the blade to Charlie's *throat.*

Choose?

From the back room—the bedchamber—stepped the duke's guard captain, *Geddes, dragging a battered and bloody Sage. She was too weak to struggle* *as Geddes pinned her against his chest, but she stared at Alex accusingly.*

"You said you'd come for me," she spat. "But you didn't."

I thought you were dead. *He begged her to understand.* I would've torn this tower down with my bare hands if I'd known you were here.

The hate in her gray eyes did not diminish as Geddes pulled out a knife *and yanked her head back to lay the blade across her slender throat. The ratty-* *eared guard looked back to the duke.*

D'Amiran was still smiling. "Choose," he said again.

❧

Alex reached for his sword but found nothing at his waist, instead striking his elbow on the stone wall next to his cot. A bolt of pain shot up his arm to his shoulder, waking him fully before rendering his arm too numb to use. He tore at the blanket with the other hand and half fell, half rolled out of bed, then stumbled through the pitch darkness to the door and out into the cooler passage of the barracks. The light of the low torch burned his vision, and he squeezed his eyes shut as he gasped for air. When he was sure he wouldn't be sick, he pushed to his feet and felt along the wall to the outer door.

The faint light from the approaching dawn was gentler on his eyes, and he wiped sweat and tears away as he sagged against a barrel of drinking water. It was a dream he'd had before, though not for several months.

Breathe, he told himself. *It wasn't real.*

But so much of it was.

When he'd kicked his way into the window of D'Amiran's private chamber that day at Tegann, it was the only place left she could've been. Alex had fully expected to be forced to choose between Sage and Charlie, and he'd had no idea how he would handle it. But only Charlie and the duke were in those rooms. And Charlie had died.

D'Amiran had made a critical mistake that morning in sending Captain Geddes to imply Sage had been caught in her attempt to escape Tegann. Alex was meant to think she was being tortured, but instead he'd assumed she'd been killed. For the first hour he was too sick to do anything. By the time he and his soldiers realized she might not be dead, Alex had regained control of himself, and he was able to make a rational, though rushed, plan. Had Alex thought from the beginning she was alive, he might have charged in without thinking.

Not might have. Would have.

Alex ran a hand through his damp hair, relieved that feeling had returned to his fingertips, and stood straight. His body pulsed with adrenaline as he strode back into the barracks. In his room, he quietly felt around for his boots and socks. Lieutenant Casseck stirred as Alex opened the door again to step out into the passage.

"Where you goin'?" his friend mumbled. "I thought we had the morning off."

Normally a day began with group exercises, but Alex had pushed the men with him hard to get to the capital early and felt they deserved rest. "For a run," he answered. "It's almost dawn. Best time for it."

"Crazy bastard." Cass rolled into a sitting position and squinted at the torchlight slicing across the floor. "Need company?"

Alex hesitated. He didn't want to wait the ten minutes Cass would need to be ready. "Catch me on my second lap?"

One circuit was a mile and a half. Cass rubbed his face. "Yeah. Second lap. Just make sure you actually wait for me."

"Then don't be late." Alex broke into a run as soon as he was outside again. By the time Cass joined him, all traces of the nightmare and fear were gone from Alex's face.

At least he hoped so.

6

SAGE WAS TO meet him after Chapel Day services so they could go for a ride in the hills above the city. Alex had brought his spare mount with him to Tennegol, intending to leave her behind for Sage. Knowing she'd be reluctant to accept such a gift, Alex planned to frame it as doing him a favor, which wasn't entirely inaccurate. Shadow had been his first horse, and Alex wasn't ready to give her up, but the weight of a fully armed soldier was a little much for the mare these days. She was perfect for Sage, however.

Sage was wearing riding breeches and her father's old leather fowling jacket as she waited outside the barracks, chatting with a short, black-haired soldier. Her own hair glinted with sunlight as she shook her head and laughed. In his dream she'd been angry, and Alex took a moment to soak her happiness in, replacing the false memory with what was real. Sage looked away from her conversation and caught him staring. The soldier she was talking to stood straight.

"It's been a long time, sir," Sergeant Ash Carter said, rendering a salute. Alex tried not to roll his eyes as he returned it. Ash could've been an officer himself, but he'd refused a commission in favor of supporting his half brother, the crown prince. "How've you been?"

"Not too bad," Alex answered. "What brings you here? I thought you were in Mondelea babysitting Rob." When the conflict in Tasmet had become too risky, the prince was moved to serve in a safer region. Robert hadn't taken it well, and Ash had gone along to calm him down.

"You know how it is when something important needs to be done by someone expendable," Ash said with a self-deprecating grin. Born a year after the death of the first queen, Ash was illegitimate but had all the authority and privileges of a royal. Alex was technically only the crown prince's cousin, but he considered Ash just as much family as Robert. They'd all stuck together through page and squire training. It was only in recent years their lives had begun to diverge.

Alex and Robert had high-profile positions in the army, but Ash preferred to work in the background. Due to his invisible nature, he made an excellent spy. Had Alex not reassigned Ash to scout ahead and then taken his place as lead informant, things at Tegann would've been very different. Sage would've met and befriended the real Ash Carter, for one.

At the thought, Alex glanced at Sage, feeling queasy. She met his eyes with concern written on her face, and he smiled back though the nauseous feeling remained.

"So were you called in, too?" Alex asked his friend, keeping his voice low and trying to convey meaning with his tone.

Ash was about Sage's height, and he had to tilt his head up to meet Alex's eyes. "Yes."

"Do you know why?"

His friend smiled slyly. "Maybe."

"Care to share what you know?"

"And miss the look on your face tomorrow? Not a chance."

Alex rolled his eyes. "I think I already know."

"I really think you don't." Ash's joking manner fell away. "Something big is going on."

Alex glanced again at Sage, whose pale face was blank. She was listening, but pretending not to. "I've spent the last months fighting in Tasmet; you think I don't know how big this conflict is?"

Ash shook his head. "No, Alex, it's bigger."

"Bigger how?"

"No offense to Sage here, but big enough that I can't tell you until we're securely in the council chambers." Ash winked at her. "I'll leave you two to spend some time together. After tomorrow you're going to be very busy."

Sage watched Ash go, her lips pursed. Alex slipped an arm around her waist and drew her close. Sweet Spirit, she smelled good. Like lavender and sage and sunshine.

She turned into him. "I see you shaved," she said.

He bent his face down to kiss her. "Feel for yourself."

"I dreamed about you last night," she whispered several seconds later.

Alex suppressed a shudder as he remembered his own dream. "I hope I behaved myself."

"Hardly."

There were six hundred and forty-four days until Alex reached the age at which Demoran army officers could marry. Six hundred and forty-four days he still had to resist her. He sighed. "Let's get going. It's going to rain in a few hours."

Thirty minutes later they were riding up the hillside trail. Alex's thoughts vacillated between Ash's cryptic words and a question that had plagued him for months. He hardly spoke until they reached the spot he wanted and dismounted. Alex tied up the horses in the shade while Sage set out a blanket and a lunch she'd scrounged from the kitchens. She was studiously peeling an orange when he dropped down beside her and stretched out with a sigh. The restless night and morning run were catching up to him.

"Nice view, don't you think?" he asked, gesturing to the spires and roofs of Tennegol spreading out below them. Beyond lay the Tenne Valley, partially covered by rain clouds slowly drifting toward them. It would be only a couple hours before they'd have to head back to avoid getting wet.

Sage didn't look up. "Are you going to tell me what's bothering you?"

"Just wondering about tomorrow. Ash obviously knows something about my assignment, but he won't tell me."

"Hmm." She didn't sound convinced. "It's a bit strange talking to him, given . . . you know."

That she'd fallen in love with Alex while believing he was Ash Carter. When playing the close infiltration part normally reserved for Ash, Alex had gone as far as to tell her much of Ash's life story. He'd been as honest as he could in everything else, though. The sick feeling returned.

Sage lowered the orange and looked at him with raised eyebrows. "I knew it had to do with him. What is it, Alex?"

He wondered if her job with the matchmaker last year had sharpened her insight, or if she'd just always been this perceptive. She wouldn't let go until she worked it out of him, either. Truth be told, he needed to hear her answer. "Can I ask you something?" he said, brushing a speck of dust off her breeches to avoid meeting her eyes.

She placed her hand over his. "Of course."

He took a deep breath. "When you found out who I was . . . were you disappointed?"

"I was furious. Or don't you remember me hitting you?"

Alex couldn't manage a smile. "No, not because I lied. I meant because I wasn't Ash." He threaded his fingers in hers but still couldn't make himself look up. "If I were really him, I could have given you the life of a princess. We could even be married by now."

"Yes, well, I suppose I've resigned myself to marrying the youngest and most decorated captain in the army," she teased. "I only get a national hero who writes letters promising to pull down the moon if it would make me smile. Poor me." When he didn't respond, she tilted his chin up with her other hand, which still held the half-peeled orange. The light in her gray eyes went from playful to earnest. "I'll admit it's a very . . . romantic idea to be loved by a prince," she said, her voice softening. "It probably kept me from seeing what should've been obvious. But no, I was never disappointed."

"Not even a bit?"

She cocked an eyebrow. "Were you disappointed to learn I wasn't a highborn lady?"

Alex finally smiled a little. "I was just relieved you wouldn't be getting married at the Concordium. Then I realized how much trouble I was in."

"Lots and lots of trouble." She leaned down to kiss him, then sat back. "Hungry?"

Alex took the orange from her hand and tossed it away before pulling her down beside him. "Not remotely."

7

ALEX WALKED SLIGHTLY behind Sage as they returned to the palace, brushing his fingers against her hip more often than the natural swing of his arm should have caused him to. It was a good thing the weather made them return when it did. Otherwise they'd still be on the hillside, trying desperately to resist doing something irreversible.

Why couldn't he dream about *that*?

When they reached the receiving courtyard, Sage suddenly squealed and ran across the gravel to a young woman climbing out of a carriage. The pair embraced and danced around each other for several seconds, laughing and chattering. Even in a simple traveling dress with her mahogany curls bound in a single thick braid, Lady Clare Holloway was easy for Alex to recognize.

"When did you get to Tennegol?" Sage was asking when he caught up to them.

"Just now," said Clare, her shoulders drooping in exhaustion. "We rode through the night." She gestured to the stately man who'd helped her down from the coach. "Papa was called by the king, and he said I could come along to visit you."

The man stepped forward, and Clare introduced him. "Papa, this is my friend I've told you so much about, Sage Fowler. Sage, this is my future father-in-law, Ambassador Lord Gramwell."

The ambassador's bronze mustache twitched with amusement as he kissed Sage's hand. "It's a pleasure to finally meet you, my dear. Your appearance is just as I expected."

Sage's already rosy cheeks darkened further. Between their ride and lying on the blanket with Alex, much of her sandy hair had come loose from its coils. Clare extended her free hand to Alex. "Captain Quinn, I didn't realize you would be here, too."

"I arrived yesterday, Lady Clare," he answered, bringing her fingers to his lips.

"Is– Did you bring– I mean– Did the whole company come?" Clare stammered as he released her hand. She was blushing furiously.

Alex grinned. "I came with Lieutenants Casseck and Gramwell, yes." The two officers had been an easy choice. "I'll tell Gram you're here." He nodded to the ambassador. "And you, too, sir."

Lord Gramwell shook Alex's hand in greeting. His son had been one of Alex's lieutenants since the ambassador retired and brought his family back to Demora a few years ago. Someday the younger Gramwell would also serve as an emissary, which was one reason Lady Clare lived with his parents now, learning the role she'd play as a diplomat's wife.

"Come on," Sage said, tugging Clare toward the main doors. "Let's let Her Majesty know you're here and get you settled."

Alex had a few duties he needed to attend to, so it was better that Sage went with her friend now. "See you after dinner, Sage?" he said hopefully. "Same place?"

Sage paused, looking torn, but Clare answered for her. "Of course she will. We can catch up tomorrow after I've had a chance to rest."

Alex thanked her, though he doubted Clare's willingness to part with Sage was completely unselfish. Casseck would end up covering most of Gramwell's duties, too, once the lieutenant knew his own betrothed was here.

Ambassador Gramwell leaned down to kiss the top of Clare's head.

"I can see you're in good hands. I have urgent business, so you must excuse me." He nodded to Alex, catching his eyes with his own for a second. "I'll see you tomorrow, Captain."

Alex frowned at the man's back. First Ash and now an ambassador. Everyone seemed to know more than he did.

8

THE NEXT MORNING Sage woke later than usual and was struggling to tame her hair when Clare knocked on her door. "Late night?" her friend asked with a smirk. "You look tired."

"You hush," Sage said. "I know you and Luke were out just as late." That was a gamble, but she knew she was right when Clare blushed. With her friend's help, Sage managed to get her hair braided and pinned in a few minutes. Together they walked to the queen's apartment, making plans for the next few weeks. Clare had no idea how long the ambassador intended to stay, but he'd acted as if he'd be in Tennegol through summer.

"He retired rather young, didn't he?" Sage asked.

Clare nodded. "Mama was in poor health, so he returned to Mondelea for her. I think he misses his work, though. He jumped at the chance to come down here."

Sage couldn't help but notice how attached Clare was to her future in-laws, referring to them as *Mama* and *Papa* as northerners called their parents. Considering how cruel Clare's actual father was and that her mother had made no effort to shield her daughters from greed-driven matches, Sage was glad her friend had a real family at last, even if it had taken sixteen years to find them.

A servant ushered the pair into the queen's dining room for a private breakfast. Her Majesty already sat at the cozy circular table draped with a periwinkle cloth and laden with an ivy-spray tea set. Though she'd greeted Clare warmly yesterday, Orianna had seemed somewhat irritated by her arrival, and Sage observed Her Majesty for the first few minutes, looking for signs she was still in a foul temper. The queen seemed cheerful, however, even playfully commenting that Sage was supposed to rest on her day off—not roam the corridors until the wee hours of the morning. Little escaped her notice, apparently.

Sage was relieved by Her Majesty's teasing; she'd been half expecting a lecture about last night. It had been too rainy for their usual spot in the gardens, so she and Alex had strolled the palace halls, hand-in-hand, enjoying several minutes of privacy in every secluded alcove they'd passed—and there had been many. Surely such behavior wasn't proper for a royal tutor. As much as Orianna didn't sound bothered by it, Sage had no intention of abusing that allowance. She and Alex would have to be a little more discreet.

"I'm so glad you girls are here," the queen said, holding on to both Sage's and Clare's hands after they'd recited the mealtime prayer to the Spirit. "I need your help."

Sage glanced at Clare. Her friend looked as bewildered as she felt. "Of course, Your Majesty," said Clare. "Whatever we can do."

"Good." Orianna released their hands, sat back, and picked up her fork. "Do you know why Captain Quinn is here, Sage?"

Sage shook her head, before shoving a forkful of eggs in her mouth, relieved the queen had started eating right away so she could. "Not other than that he has a new assignment. Even he doesn't know."

The queen nodded curtly and turned her blue-green eyes to Clare. "And do you know why Ambassador Gramwell has come to Tennegol?"

"No, Your Majesty. He's said nothing to me."

There was a hard gleam in Orianna's eyes. "Then we all have the same problem. We're being left out of something significant." She gestured at the servant behind her, a young woman who was almost constantly at the queen's side. "This is Meadow. Her brother Bryony attends the king as cupbearer."

Sage knew who Bryony was, so that was said mostly for Clare's benefit. As royal cupbearer, he attended the king in all public functions—and most private ones. However, after catching him throwing knives with astonishing accuracy one morning in the training yards, Sage privately theorized the young man was, in fact, the king's bodyguard. She'd never heard him speak, though. It was rumored he had no tongue.

The queen continued, "For years, they've kept me abreast in matters of state that the king does not bother to include me in. Though I rarely seek to interfere, I feel it's my duty to stay informed." She paused and arched a delicate eyebrow. "Would you like to know what they've heard about the king's current intentions?"

Sage nodded, astonished by the queen's casual admission of eavesdropping on very private royal conversations.

"Nothing."

Sage blinked. "Nothing?"

Orianna shook her head. "Not a word. Bryony has been excluded from almost all His Majesty's meetings and councils." She leaned forward again, her food seemingly forgotten. "But Ambassador Gramwell was immediately included on arrival. Today, Captain Quinn will be added."

The queen's intentions were now obvious. "You wish us to learn what we can through our connections," Sage said.

"Yes."

Sage didn't know how to react, but Clare looked horrified. The queen might think it was necessary to pry into the king's secrets, and if caught she would likely be pardoned, but Sage and Clare had no such guarantee. "Your Majesty, with so many others excluded, the secret must be dangerous," Sage said. *As would be pursuing it*, she silently added.

"You have hit on the reason why I *must* know what is going on, Sage," Orianna said, drawing her mouth into a tight line. She suddenly looked much older than her thirty-five years. "When this new unit he's assembling marches, Nicholas is going with them."

Prince Nicholas was fourteen and trained with the palace guards as a squire, rather than with the regular army as his older half brothers had. As a consequence, he was far less skilled than they'd been at that age. He was also behind his peers academically, though Sage suspected he might be like Princess Cara, for whom learning was difficult. Numbers and letters seemed to change their order as she tried to read them. Sage rarely dealt with the prince and so wasn't able to prove it, though, and if he did have the same problem, he hid it under a haughty attitude. In any case, it sounded like the king wanted him to branch out.

"That may only prove this is *not* dangerous," Clare pointed out. "If he's willing to send his own son along."

Orianna rolled her eyes in the way she regularly scolded Rose for doing. "When has Raymond been known to shield his own sons from danger? Robert and Ash have always served on the front lines."

"That's not true," Sage couldn't help saying. Clare looked shocked at her bold correction, and Sage blushed a little. Her Majesty had always encouraged frankness, but even that might have crossed a line. "Robert was moved away from Tasmet last year."

"Because he is crown prince," replied the queen. "He is of age and becomes more valuable every day, both in what he handles and in his closeness to taking the throne himself. Nicholas may be second in line, but to my husband he's always a third son." Orianna shook her head. "But he's the only one I have."

Sage still felt the queen was overreacting. "Majesty, if Captain Quinn is indeed going along on this mission, I assure you there is no one who can better protect him."

"Maybe so, but that doesn't change that I'm being kept in the dark." Orianna's pale hand closed into a fist. "Do you have any idea what it's like to be lied to by the man you love, Sage? To not be trusted to know the truth?"

Sage flinched. She'd never told the queen how Alex had lied about who he was—and more—to protect both her and Prince Robert. He'd been honest as soon as it was safe, and he'd promised to never deceive her again. It was different.

Wasn't it?

Her eyes drifted to Clare, who had held her while she'd cried, then offered to skin Alex alive but settled for silently threatening him instead. Clare shook her head ever so slightly, as if to say there was no comparison.

"I'm not asking you to do anything illegal or deceptive," Orianna said. "I'm only asking you to pay attention, ask questions, and tell me what you learn. Don't you want to know what's going on, too?"

Sage suddenly didn't just want to know.

She *needed* to know.

9

ALEX LOOKED OUT over the columns of soldiers. He'd brought only one hundred men with him, but as he'd led the morning's exercises, more had trickled in to join them. By the time they'd finished, the ranks had swelled to twice what they'd started with. He glanced up to the observation platform, where a lone man stood watching. Alex knew him by his posture alone.

Colonel Traysden wasn't just the minister of intelligence and one of the king's closest advisers, he commanded the Norsari. Or rather, he used to. The battalion had been disbanded before Alex was born. Few outside the army had given them a thought in over a dozen years, but the colonel had been a friend of his father's, and Alex had grown up hearing stories about Demora's elite fighting unit. The word *Norsari* came from old Aristelan *norsar*, which referred to a bird of prey so swift and stealthy most people had never seen one. Many believed they were only a myth. If Traysden was watching the new recruits—all of whom had been handpicked by their commanders—it wasn't hard to guess why.

The Norsari were coming back, and Alex was to be a part of it.

He was very thorough in cleaning up, trying to fill some of the time before his meeting with the king. When the hour finally came, Alex forced himself to walk to the main hall outside the council chamber with measured paces. Lieutenants Casseck and Gramwell flanked him on both sides. They reached the double doors to the chamber, and the pair dropped back to enter the room a step behind him, though the doorway was wide enough to accommodate all of them at once. As with Ash, their deference bothered him, but it was his friends' way of showing respect for his rank around others.

Another lieutenant paced behind the chairs on one side of the long table. Alex recognized him from morning drills. The man had done very well for all his slighter stature. Alex didn't know his name, so he walked up and extended his hand in introduction. "Captain Alex Quinn."

The lieutenant's blue eyes widened in recognition as Alex approached, and he started to salute, then realized he shouldn't in this situation. Instead he seized Alex's hand like a drowning man. "Lieutenant Ben N-Nadira," he stammered. "It's an honor to meet you, sir."

Alex smiled tightly. It felt good when Sage called him a national hero, but facing others who believed it was awkward. After a few seconds, he extracted his hand from Nadira's grip and stepped aside so his friends could introduce themselves.

Cass's blond head towered over Nadira by nearly a foot. "Lieutenant Casseck. Everyone calls me Cass."

"Lieutenant Lucas Gramwell," said Gram, shaking Nadira's hand. "Luke or Gram is fine."

Two more men wearing silver lieutenant bars entered the room. One looked about the same age as Alex, but the other was older by several years.

"Lieutenant Sorrel Hatfield," the younger man said with a nod, looking Alex straight in the eye, as if daring him to comment on the illegitimacy his botanical name declared. Alex didn't rise to the bait, though he made a mental note that this man might feel the need to prove himself more than others. The lieutenant had hair that matched Gram's ruddy brown shade, but otherwise the two could not be more dissimilar—Hatfield was short and stocky with green eyes, and his skin was more freckled than any Alex had ever seen.

The older lieutenant gruffly introduced himself as Zach Tanner, and Alex instantly liked him. With a background as poor as a tanner, he must have had to fight his way into an officer's commission, perhaps—judging from his scarred face—earning it on the battlefield. Tanner and Hatfield had a rapport with each other, a kinship of experience, and there was no question in Alex's mind that they'd both earned their rank. Ironically, his own famous name meant he'd always have to prove his.

Once introductions were finished, Alex moved to stand by a chair near the end of the rectangular table, and the others followed his lead. Normally the table was long enough to seat all twenty members of the king's council, but several leaves had been removed to size it down for ten, making the room feel even larger. After a minute, the herald announced the king's arrival.

"His Majesty, Raymond the Second, King of Demora."

Everyone came to attention as Alex's uncle Raymond strode in, Colonel Traysden, Ambassador Gramwell, and Ash Carter trailing in his wake. At forty-four, the king had hair that was thin on top and somewhere between gray and white, but his step was light and his mind sharp. The ambassador behind him was older, with thick hair much redder than his son's and shot with white streaks. When they came to the table, Alex and the others turned to face the king and bowed as the chamber doors were shut. Raymond pulled his own chair out and sat, then waited for everyone else to be seated. Traysden and Ash were on His Majesty's right and left, and at Ash's gesture, Alex took the place next to him.

The ambassador sat on the opposite end, barely sharing a glance with his son, while the minister of intelligence watched Alex with keen gray eyes set in a weathered face. What little hair he had left was cut so close to his head it was nearly shaved. Raymond looked to each face with bright hazel eyes, settling on Alex last.

"Welcome," the king said. "Time is short so I will get right to business. Most of you have been in Tasmet these past months dealing with the aftermath of the D'Amiran rebellion and their alliance with Kimisara. I'm sorry to say how much the treachery of our own nobility took us by surprise."

Alex's father, General Quinn, had suspected the D'Amirans of some sort of collusion last year, but winter weather had prevented him from informing the king—which was why the Concordium mission in the spring had included discreet reconnaissance. Had it not been for Sage and her insight on the power the duke had planned to draw to himself through the marriages of his allies, Alex would never have figured out what was going on. While the uprising had been stopped, the region was still a mess of D'Amiran loyalists and Kimisar raiders. Whenever the army engaged the enemy, they succeeded, but they were having trouble finding them.

The king cleared his throat. "Many years ago, I disbanded the Norsari as a gesture of peace, believing their existence provoked hostility. Now I know their absence is an invitation. War is once again on our doorstep, and we are less prepared than ever to deal with it." The king nodded to his right. "To that end, I've been consulting with Colonel Traysden on what I'm sure you all suspect." He paused; one could have heard a feather drop. "I am reinstating the Norsari Battalion. Under the recommendations of your superiors, you six are the most qualified men to accomplish this."

A smile Alex couldn't prevent spread across his cheeks until he realized Uncle Raymond had numbered them at six. Other than Traysden, Alex was the most senior officer present. The smile froze and then dropped off his face.

No, it was impossible.

"We're starting with only a company," the king continued. "Once your unit is functional and training protocols have been established and you're experienced enough to lead new recruits more effectively, we will expand to a full battalion."

Alex's mouth was completely dry as his uncle focused on him again, but it was Colonel Traysden who spoke.

"Captain Alexander Quinn, you are hereby offered command of Norsari Battalion One, effective immediately."

∽✢∾

Alex slumped against the wall outside the council chamber after Nadira, Tanner, and Hatfield had disappeared around the corner. "Did that just happen?" he said.

Casseck rolled his eyes. "No one else was surprised."

35

"I can't even tell Sage." Alex ran a hand over his face. The Norsari were to be a secret until they were ready. "How am I supposed to keep this from her?"

"Say you have command of a special assignment," Gramwell suggested.

Command. She'd be so proud. Alex pushed off the wall. "I'll see you two back at the barracks. We've got to get to work."

"Not yet," came a voice. Ash Carter stood in the doorway to the room where Colonel Traysden, Ambassador Gramwell, and the king had remained. The sergeant beckoned with a finger. "It's not over for you, Captain."

10

INSIDE THE COUNCIL chamber, Colonel Traysden unrolled a map and set books on the corners to hold it open before standing straight. "What we are about to tell you, Captain, must not leave this room. Not even your officers may know."

That was disconcerting. Alex didn't know Nadira, Tanner, or Hatfield yet, but if they'd been chosen for this mission, they were already considered loyal and dependable. As for Cass and Gram, Alex trusted them with his life. With Sage's life. He glanced at his uncle, the king, who stood gazing out the window with his hands clasped behind him. "Why not?" Alex couldn't help asking.

"For the same reason we kept a lid on our extra purpose during the Concordium escort," said Ash. "A man looking for ghosts will see them everywhere."

Like all reconnaissance missions, last year's spying on the duke was approached with neutrality; otherwise everything would've looked like treason. Impartiality was difficult, however. Even now, Alex felt his cheeks grow warm at the thought of how he'd first suspected Sage of being a spy. The evidence was fairly damning at the time, enough that it led him to break into her room and go through her private things. He also was honest enough to admit his personal motivations for uncovering her true identity had been as strong as the tactical reasons.

"What kind of ghosts am I looking for?"

Colonel Traysden gestured to the map detailing the southern

boundary with the desert nation of Casmun. "Late last September, a Ranger detachment came across a place where at least fifty men had camped on the north side of the Kaz River." He moved his fingers over several charcoal lines. "Trails of them trickled out from this point and faded, but one—the largest—went as far as the Jovan Road. Then they turned back south, crossed the river, and went into Casmun."

The minister of intelligence paused and looked at Alex. "What would you conclude, Captain?"

Casmun hadn't talked to Demora in generations, but it seemed obvious. "Our border is being tested," said Alex.

All heads nodded, and Traysden continued. "Unfortunately, little information could be gathered. The camp was almost two weeks old when it was found, meaning it had appeared as soon as the Rangers had passed—which also meant they knew the Demoran routine."

Rangers were squads of about ten soldiers who regularly patrolled Demora's boundaries, which had been considered among the easiest and safest assignments. "Sir, are you saying they watched us for months, and we never noticed?"

"We did notice," answered Traysden. "Rangers have been interacting with Casmuni for the last couple years, but it always appeared innocent, even friendly." He nodded to the king. "His Majesty and I had hoped it meant they wanted to talk."

Uncle Raymond came closer. "Then last year the D'Amirans rebelled and the Kimisar joined them," he said. "Our encounters with the Casmuni didn't seem important until word of this reached us here in November. Both passes were frozen for the winter by then. That's a bad time to realize just how few soldiers are east of the Catrix."

Alex's own orders to report to Tennegol had been written in December, but they'd taken almost two months to reach him, then he'd needed another month to gather the men he wanted. So much time had been lost.

The king sat in his chair and folded his hands in his lap. "The question is, does this have anything to do with what's going on in Tasmet? Are the Casmuni working with the Kimisar to create more chaos, or have they just been waiting for us to be distracted? Either way, a group that large sneaking that deep into our territory isn't something we can ignore."

"It can't be the first or last time they've done it, either," added Ash.

Colonel Traysden put a finger on the map where the Kaz River ran southeast. "This is where you will set up your training camp. From here you can send scouting parties all along the border. Find where the Casmuni have been crossing, when, and how many."

"Pardon my asking, sir, Your Majesty," said Alex, "but why not put a full army battalion in the area now? Why only a company-sized unit, and a training one at that?"

"Several reasons," said the king, sitting back and ticking off his fingers. "First, I want the Norsari back. I've wanted it for years, but I was restricted by that damn treaty until Kimisara broke the terms. Even after last spring, I had to fight the council because many said it was only a rebellion, not an invasion, and the Kimisar in Tasmet had technically been invited in by Demoran nobility. It wasn't until Lord Farthingham's son was killed in action last autumn that the tide turned in my favor. Second, you're starting with two hundred fifty of the best soldiers in the realm. That makes you worth at least twice that number. Third, the flexibility and speed of a Norsari unit makes them ideal for this kind of reconnaissance."

Once they're trained, Alex wanted to say, but plainly they were expected to operate from day one.

"Lastly, Norsari don't need support; they live mostly off the land. You know how many supplies a regular unit requires and how much attention that attracts. I can't spare the numbers, I can't spare the supplies, and I certainly don't want the attention."

Alex furrowed his brow. Since when was Demora short on resources?

"Father," Ash interrupted. "I don't think the captain understands how thinly we're stretched."

"I know the army had to occupy much of Crescera to ensure D'Amiran's allies there didn't try anything foolish," said Alex. In the years before his attempted coup, the duke had bound half of his nobles to the richest families of Crescera through marriages. It was Sage who had realized why.

"It's not just that," said Ambassador Gramwell, speaking for the first time. "Almost no grain has come from Crescera in over a year. Now the bulk of it goes to the army or travels by the Northern Road. Once wagons reach Mondelea, they're faced with three more weeks of a rough journey south or selling their loads to coastal merchants, and most choose the latter. Between that and the valley and capital absorbing refugees from Tasmet, food stores on this side of the mountains are nearly exhausted. How do you think people would react to news we're expecting a Casmuni invasion?"

"Which we are *not* expecting," the king insisted. "But people will assume the worst, and I won't have panic. Meanwhile, I want a diplomatic solution, and that starts with a show of strength. Whatever Casmun's intentions, the Norsari's presence will make them think twice. Your job, Captain, is to find out what those intentions are."

Ambassador Gramwell indicated the Vinova Fortress in the southeast corner of Demora. "I'll be setting up an embassy of sorts here, though it's going to take time to gather what I need. Vinova hasn't been properly manned in years. As a consequence, I must gather a great deal more supplies and personnel." He turned to address the king. "My actions haven't been noticed yet, sire, and in retrospect, bringing Lady Clare with me was most fortuitous. The queen has invited her to stay through the summer, so now I have a public reason to have come to the capital."

Alex was glad for Sage's sake. He'd be gone soon, but Clare would be here.

Colonel Traysden focused on the map. "How long before you'll be ready to leave, sir?"

"If we want to maintain our level of quiet, I need time. Not to mention everything is in shortage."

Traysden grunted. "What about your connections in Reyan? Could they help?"

"I've already contacted them, sir. They'll come through, but it'll be weeks." Lord Gramwell stroked his short beard. "I also suggest assembling the traveling party somewhere outside Tennegol to attract as little attention as possible."

"Cambria can serve your purpose," volunteered Alex. His family home lay less than two days south of the capital. "It's off the main road, but still close, and large enough to store what you need and accommodate your retinue."

Lord Gramwell smiled. "Thank you, Captain. I was hoping for just that offer." Alex made a mental note to warn his mother as the ambassador continued. "I should be on my way before the end of April."

"Very well," said Colonel Traysden, though he didn't look pleased, as he studied a calendar. "Captain, in approximately eight weeks Ambassador Gramwell will pass through your area on his way to Vinova. In that time you must fully train the Norsari and find out exactly what the Casmuni are up to."

It would take two weeks to get to the border, leaving only six for everything else—completely on his own and with more work than he'd ever had before. "When can I tell my officers about our secondary mission?" Alex asked.

"Scouting out the Casmuni situation is your *primary* mission, Captain," said Traysden. "And the answer is, not until you have solid evidence. As far as the men with you will know, this is all for training, until it isn't."

Until it isn't?

During the Concordium escort reconnaissance, Alex's lieutenants had known everything he did, and they'd been there to check his impulses, even if he didn't always listen. If Alex couldn't tell them anything during this mission, the burden of judgment fell completely on him.

11

SAGE WAS ON her way to the royal library when Alex appeared and caught her around the waist with one arm. He whirled her off her feet, eyes alight, then pulled her to the side and out of sight. His kiss was brief, but it reignited the fire he'd left smoldering in her last night. "I have my assignment," he whispered.

She couldn't help catching his excitement. "I can tell it agrees with you. Will you be staying here?"

His smile faltered. "Well, no."

Sage had known that idea was too good to be true, so she smiled and slipped her arms around him. "Must be amazing. You look ready to burst."

"You have no idea." Alex paused as they heard someone passing their secluded spot, and he pulled her deeper into the alcove. "Let's go somewhere private. Your hair is far too tidy." He nuzzled her neck.

Spirit above, she wanted to go with him. "I can't," she whispered. "I have lessons in the library. Clare and the girls will already be there."

"Damn. You'd better go, then," he said. "We can talk later, but it'll have to be tonight. Lots of planning to start. See you in the garden? About the eight o'clock hour? I should have some free time before meeting with Colonel Traysden."

Her disappointment must have shown. Alex tilted her chin up and looked her in the eye. "I only have a few days, but every spare minute is yours. I promise."

"I know. I'll be there."

He planted one last kiss behind her ear before hurrying off. Sage straightened her dress and patted down her hair before continuing on her way, an ache in her chest. Alex's duties were already taking over his time. She'd known this was coming—knew this was the way it would always be—but that didn't make it any easier.

She'd also been so distracted by his kisses and excitement she'd gotten exactly nothing useful for the queen.

With a sigh she entered the library. Sunshine poured in from the domelike cap over the massive, two-story room. Several seemingly random windowpanes were blocked out, and the shelves around the library were set at odd angles and heights. Sage had thought the arrangement peculiar until the master of books explained it was so no direct sunlight ever fell on the royal collection. Then he'd shown her and her pupils how much damage sunlight could do to books and documents over time. Even Princess Cara had found it interesting.

Clare looked up from the table where she sat with the two princesses, who were already absorbed in their research project—Carinthia to get it over with and Rose because she loved it. "What's wrong?"

Sage shrugged, trying to act like it didn't matter. "I just ran into Alex."

Clare nodded sympathetically. "Luke found me about an hour ago. He said Captain Quinn was given command of a new unit. He and Lieutenant Casseck and a few others are going with him."

Sage frowned. It was silly to be jealous that Clare had learned more than she had. "Where are they going?"

"He didn't say." Clare stood and put an arm around her waist. "Don't worry, we can be miserable together."

That both Luke and Alex had given so few details was puzzling. The queen might be onto something after all. "Clare, have you ever heard of Colonel Traysden?"

"Papa mentioned him the other day, but I don't know anything about him."

It was the only bit of information Sage had. "Let's ask Sir Francis."

The master of books looked up from his cluttered desk and smiled as they approached. Sage had met him in the very first week of her arrival

43

at the palace, before she knew she'd be offered a job as royal tutor. Thanks to the map he'd drawn for her that day, she'd never gotten lost in the maze of passages. "Can I be of assistance to my ladies?" he asked, his long, white beard bobbing up and down with his words.

"Perhaps," said Sage. "Have you ever heard of Colonel Traysden? I thought I knew all the palace guards, but that name is unfamiliar."

Sir Francis sat back in his chair, his robes flowing down his thin frame like dusty candlewax. "Colonel Traysden isn't a guard. He's the king's minister of intelligence."

The spymaster. "Where does his rank come from?" Sage asked.

"He was the last commander of the Norsari Battalion."

Sage inhaled sharply, but Clare only looked confused. "Norsari used to be Demora's best fighters," Sage told her. There was almost no limit to what they could be called upon to do—fight in traditional battles, go on rescue missions, scout in enemy territory, even commit assassinations and sabotage. Or so Father had told her.

"They were disbanded by my father twenty-four years ago," said Rose from behind them. "As part of the peace in 486. I wrote an essay on the war last month," she explained to Clare as she held out several pages of the day's work for Sage's inspection. "I interviewed Papa for the assignment. He said he wished he'd never agreed to it."

Sage glanced over Rose's work. She knew the terms of that treaty well—the Norsari had been broken up, and Kimisara had ceded Tasmet permanently to Demora. If last year's fighting could be considered an attempt by Kimisara to take the region back, then the agreement was nullified.

That was what was happening—the Norsari was being re-formed. And Alex . . . Sweet Spirit, Alex had been given *command.* No wonder he was excited.

Sage glanced up at Rose. "I'll look this paper over tonight. You can go to lunch; I'll see you in the classroom later." Cara looked up from her seat hopefully. "Yes, you can go, too," Sage called to her. "Leave your work on the table."

Carinthia was out the door before her sister. Sage turned her sweetest smile on the librarian. "Sir Francis, do you have any books on the Norsari for Lady Clare?"

"Of course, my dear." The master of books stood and led the way between shelves, needing no cataloging system to guide him. When the old man passed away, his replacement would have a hell of a time finding anything.

"It can't be just the Norsari, Sage," Clare whispered as they followed. "Why else would Papa be involved? He's a diplomat, not a soldier."

"Maybe they're anticipating a new treaty when this is over."

"Perhaps." Clare didn't look convinced.

Sir Francis stopped at a shelf of military history and ran a bony finger over the spines until he found the one he wanted. "Here you are, my lady. Birley's account is the most accurate, I would say. His grandfather was among the first Norsari."

"Thank you, sir," said Clare, accepting the book. The librarian nodded and returned to his desk, his mind already back on his previous task. As he walked, he passed a nearly empty shelf.

"What used to be there, Sir Francis?" Sage asked.

The master of books paused to squint where she pointed. "Casmuni history and trade. Ambassador Gramwell took them last night."

Sage and Clare exchanged glances and followed Sir Francis. "What are you working on here?" Sage asked, gesturing at the parchments scattered across his desk.

"Trade documents," he said. "They're all over two hundred years old, and many are in Casmuni, which no one can read anymore. I found them when I was helping the ambassador last night. The previous librarian didn't store them properly, and they're mixed up and falling apart." He settled back into his rickety chair and rubbed his eyes. "The ambassador wants them as well, but I must sort them and have a scribe copy them first. My vision isn't what it used to be."

"I can do that," Sage said eagerly. "Lady Clare can help. She assists Ambassador Gramwell in much of his work already."

Sir Francis smiled up at her, his faded blue eyes watery from the efforts of the last few hours. "I'd be glad to let you, but it will be terribly boring work. And I still need to sort the ones written in Kimisar."

"Which Lady Clare and I both speak. We can do it."

"Well, bless me. You're more than welcome to it." He stood again and shuffled to a back room. "Let me get you blank ledgers to copy them into. One for the ambassador, and one for our library records, if you don't mind."

"Of course not," Sage called to his back before smiling at Clare. "Maybe we'll make one for Her Majesty, too."

12

SAGE DANCED UP the path to the willow tree. Not only had she and Clare managed to sort the crumbling pages, they'd realized they came in groups of three—different translations of the same document. With the old treaties, Casmuni words and phrases could be worked out—not well, but it was a huge start. As it now appeared obvious the king expected to open talks with Casmun, what she and Clare had discovered could be invaluable.

She also had an idea Alex was bound to like.

Sage swept aside the curtain of willow branches. Alex was right there, and she jumped into his arms and kissed him before he could say anything.

"Well, hello to you, too," Alex said when she leaned back. "Happy to see you don't want to waste what little time we have."

Her grin was almost giddy. "How long do you have now?"

Alex dropped to the soft grass and pulled her down next to him. "Maybe half an hour." He leaned closer.

"Alex, wait." She held up a hand to block him. "I wanted to talk first."

He ducked around and kissed her neck. It was very distracting. "What about?"

"When are the Norsari leaving?" she asked.

Alex froze for a moment, then sat back, eyes wide. "Who told you about the Norsari?"

"No one. I just picked up enough details to figure it out."

"What kind of details?" He'd drawn his brows down, but he looked more worried than angry. "From whom?"

"Just . . ." Was it that much of a secret? "Clare said you had command of a new unit, and soldiers have been arriving for weeks, and they've all been so skilled, and then you mentioned Colonel Traysden. I know who he is."

Alex exhaled, though whether in relief or exasperation, she wasn't sure. "Forget what you know, then. Don't speak of it with anyone."

"Of course." She could keep a secret. "But why is Ambassador Gramwell involved?"

"Bleeding hell, Sage!" Alex pulled away from her completely. "What else do you know?"

"Nothing!"

"Doesn't sound like nothing to me."

She reached for his hand. "I promise I haven't been sneaking around. I only know who's involved. I asked some questions. It wasn't hard to draw conclusions."

"Don't go around asking any more questions, all right?" Alex said, shaking his head. "People will think I've told you more than I should have. Both of us could get in trouble."

"Well, maybe we can get around that," she said, excitement rising again. "What if I came with you?"

"Came with me where?"

"To the southern border, where you're going to train."

Alex leapt to his feet. "Another piece of information you forgot to mention you had!"

"Alex, calm down!" she said. "Norsari have to be trained first, and all the maps of southern Demora are missing from the library. It's obvious." She'd noticed the maps were missing when she'd gone looking for one herself, to coordinate with the places she and Clare were reading in the trade agreements. As for her work with the documents themselves, mentioning them didn't seem like a good idea now. Nor did the fact that she'd already told the queen everything she'd concluded.

"Obvious to you, maybe." He crossed his arms. "The answer is no. Absolutely not."

She'd expected hesitance, but the finality in his voice surprised her. "Alex, women travel with the army all the time."

"Not this time."

"I know you'll be moving fast, but I can keep up," she said.

"I know you can. That's not the issue." Alex didn't move from where he stood looking down at her.

"Then why not?"

"Don't you have responsibilities here?"

"Yes, but it's only for a few weeks." The queen would be glad to let her go if Sage could serve as her eyes. She sat up on her knees and raised her hands in appeal. "And I can help. You'll be living mostly off the land. I'm sure your soldiers are already good at hunting, but I could teach trapping—"

"No."

"—and edible plants—"

"I said no."

"—and herb medicine. Even fowling if you want to bring—"

"Dammit, Sage. *NO!*" he yelled.

She shrank back a little. Alex had never raised his voice to her before. Not even the times he was angry with her for snooping around dressed as a maid or for letting Clare leave her alone with Duke D'Amiran for a few minutes. He hadn't trusted her to know which risks were worth taking. Of course, it had been difficult to know when she'd been left out of so much.

Which meant as much as she'd learned about this mission, there was far more she didn't know.

"This is my world," Alex said, drawing a long, shaky breath. "You don't understand it."

It was Tegann all over again. "I'll never understand your world if you keep me out of it!"

"There are some things you don't need to understand."

"Alex, just hear me out!"

"Sage." He knelt in front of her and took her face in his hands. "I'm not discussing this. The answer is no."

He wouldn't listen. He didn't even *want* to listen. She twisted her head out of his hands, tears rolling unchecked down her cheeks. Alex reached out to wipe them away, but Sage leaned back before he could touch her. He sighed.

"This isn't about you," he said softly.

She rubbed her face with her sleeve and refused to look at him. "Don't you have a meeting?"

A long spell of silence stretched out between them. "Do you want me to leave?" he asked.

No. "Yes."

Alex sighed again and stood. "All right." He paused at the wall of leaves. "Will you be here later?"

"I doubt it."

"I'll check anyway. Just in case." He pushed the willow branches aside, letting in a flood of light from the moon and a few torches in the garden. "I love you, Sage."

Then the light was gone and so was he.

❖

Sage didn't know how long she sat there, trying to decide which she hated more: that Alex had refused to even consider letting her come, or that she'd reacted by pouting like a spoiled Concordium bride.

He was lying when he said it wasn't about her. He'd admitted she could keep up, and the way he cut her off when she pointed out everything she could bring to the mission proved he knew all that, too. By not allowing her to make her case, he didn't even have to make his—which meant his reasons were weak or inadmissible.

If they were weak, then she'd effectively beaten his argument. If they were inadmissible, it meant the mission was far more than anyone suspected. Either way, she was desperate to go along now, but there was no way in if Alex said no.

Unless.

Sage pushed to her feet and straightened her dress. A few seconds later she was on the garden path, headed for the private quarters of the royal family. The hour was late, but the queen would still be up, waiting for the king to finish his own endless meetings. Sage knocked on the door, and Orianna herself answered.

"Your Majesty," she said. "I have a proposal for you."

13

CASSECK GLANCED UP from oiling his boots as Alex barged through the door and slammed it shut behind him. Without a word he turned to his bunk and pulled his jacket open.

Cass went back to the boot. "It's less than two years, Alex. Just be glad you have it to look forward to."

Alex's shoulders tensed, his arms angled up to remove the jacket. Casseck paused again and squinted at him. "Did you two . . . fight?"

Alex yanked his jacket off. "She's so damn stubborn."

Cass started to laugh but smothered it at Alex's sharp glance. "I thought you liked that about her," his friend said cautiously. Alex didn't respond. "Do you want to talk about it?"

Alex tossed the jacket on the bed and turned around. "She wants to come along. Apparently she's got it in her head that she could teach edible plants and trapping and fowling."

Casseck looked thoughtful. "That might not be a bad idea. We're focusing on physical conditioning, but that stuff could be critical. We also have a few recruits who can't read—she could school them. I bet she could teach Kimisar, too." He furrowed his brow in confusion. "You don't look pleased."

All those things had also occurred to Alex—she had a lot to contribute, and she'd be even happier than she was here, which was why it hurt so badly to tell her no. He'd been counting on Casseck to back him up. "It's a terrible idea!"

Cass jumped a little. "Alex, no one will rib you about her, especially once they see how much she can contribute and how little trouble she'll be. And you'll be too busy for much, um, else."

Alex scowled. "I can't have her around. She's a distraction."

Casseck raised his eyebrows. "I've lived with you for the last nine months, and I daresay she's a distraction when she's *not* around."

"No." Alex shook his head. "And she won't listen to me. She was all upset, and I had to leave before getting it sorted. I couldn't find her later."

Cass folded up his rag. "In that case, I think I'm done with this for the night."

Alex eyed Casseck as he tucked away his kit. "What are you doing?"

"Morning exercises were always hell when you hadn't heard from her in a while. I expect they'll be even worse tomorrow." Cass peeled off his trousers and crawled into his bed. "I might as well get as much rest as possible."

❈

Alex clutched the gaping wound in Charlie's throat. "No! This is all my fault!"

His little brother choked and gurgled as blood leaked around Alex's fingers, dripping onto the stone floor. There was nothing Alex could do but watch him die.

"Such a shame," said a familiar voice. "Would you like to try again?"

Again?

Alex looked up from where he knelt. Duke D'Amiran held Sage against him, her clothes torn and bloody. The knife he'd used to cut Charlie's throat was now pressed to hers.

"Choose," the duke said.

At his side stood the ratty-eared Captain Geddes, holding up a barely conscious soldier with a dagger to his neck.

Casseck.

❈

Cass was shaking him by the shoulders. "Alex, wake up!"

Alex flung his arms out, nearly smacking Cass in the face, but his friend jumped out of the way in time. They were in the dark, in their barracks room.

He sat up, reaching for weapons that weren't there. "What? What's wrong?"

"You were shouting in your sleep. You woke me up."

Alex rubbed a hand over his face and pushed sweaty hair out of his eyes. "Sorry."

He heard Cass plop back on his bed. "Don't worry about it. Go back to sleep. It's way too early to run, even for you."

Alex slowly lowered himself back down on the cot.

But he didn't sleep.

14

SAGE WENT TO the sitting room before lessons, half hoping the queen hadn't had a chance to present her idea to the king. Orianna looked up from her desk with a smile, then picked up the parchment she was writing on and waved it back and forth to dry the ink.

"I could've done that for you, Your Majesty," Sage said. She couldn't remember the queen writing anything since Sage had taken on duties as her secretary, not even personal letters.

"Not this time," said Orianna smugly. "It's a royal order designating you as Nicholas's accompanying tutor. You couldn't write that yourself."

Sage's mouth dropped open in shock. "His Majesty agreed?"

The queen shrugged. "Well, I didn't specify whom I wanted to send."

"You don't think he'll object when he learns?"

"I think he has weightier matters on his mind. I doubt he'll notice." Orianna set the parchment down and peered at her. "Don't tell me you're having second thoughts."

"Well . . ." Truthfully, the anger that had driven Sage last night was gone, leaving only sorrow at the thought that Alex didn't want her along. She should've returned to the garden and tried to talk to him again. Going behind his back like this was unforgivable. "What about Rose's and Cara's studies?" she said.

"Oh posh." The queen set the note down and signed her name with a flourish. "They've advanced so much under you in the past year they can have a break. I'll take them to Mondelea for a few weeks. We can visit Lady

Gramwell—I'm impressed by how much Clare has learned under her. The girls could use some of the same lessons."

Clare. Everything was nearly settled, and Sage hadn't said anything to her best friend.

"Besides, I thought the plan was also to keep me informed as to what is really going on with this mission." Orianna glanced back with raised eyebrows. "Yesterday we agreed that keeping me out of everything was both insulting and dangerous, didn't we? You were particularly passionate about it last night."

Sage nodded, but now the idea of working actively against Alex made her sick. Why hadn't she thought this through?

Why hadn't Alex just listened?

The queen pursed her lips at Sage's silence. "If you're thinking you've changed your mind, I'll wait to send this order, but the girls and Nicholas already know. I told them at breakfast." She rose and walked to stand in front of Sage, taking her shoulders in her hands. "But I've gotten very used to the idea of having your full and honest account of what is happening. Both Nicholas and Rose are old enough to be promised in marriage. I wasn't concerned before, as there seemed to be no candidates or urgency, but opening talks with Casmun could change that." Orianna's blue-green eyes were pleading. "Don't let this take me by surprise, Sage."

Girls couldn't be matched until they were sixteen, but anything without an official matchmaker was legal. Marriages outside the system were typically the very highest and lowest—either royalty or indentured peasantry. Rose was thirteen, and Sage often felt more like the princess's older sister than her teacher. If that was what was at stake, there was no way she could abandon her.

"You may send the order, Your Majesty," she said, then cringed that she'd just given a queen permission to do something.

Orianna kissed her on the forehead. "I won't forget this, Sage."

Now it was time to face Clare. Her friend was waiting for her in the schoolroom, idly flipping through a history book. Her posture told Sage she was angry, which meant she knew. Sage crossed the room and sat diagonally from her. Clare didn't look up.

"I should have said something to you first," Sage said timidly. "I'm sorry."

"You should be. I came down here to be with you, and now you're leaving."

"I'm sorry," Sage said again. "It happened so fast. I didn't think it would really happen anyway."

Clare shoved her book away. "I thought the one good thing about having to wait years to get married was being able to spend time with you, but apparently you'll choose him over me even now."

"That's not true!" protested Sage. "This is about helping Her Majesty. I'd be going even if Alex wasn't involved."

Clare snorted. "Please, Sage. This is about proving yourself and getting back at him for lying to you last year."

That was too close to yesterday's thoughts for Sage's comfort. She felt her cheeks redden.

"The thing is," Clare continued, "you're so busy trying to prove yourself to everyone, you don't realize he's the only one you don't need to prove anything to." She stood with quiet dignity. "The queen asked me to serve as her personal secretary in your absence, and there are all those documents to copy. So if you'll excuse me, I have work to do."

Sage stared at the empty chair. She'd never really had a friend until meeting Clare last year, and even then it had taken time for Clare to break through the walls Sage had erected around herself. Apparently, keeping a friend was as much work as making one. She put her head on her hands and sighed.

Rose and Carinthia arrived on time for lessons and pounced on Sage as soon as they came through the door. "We heard you're leaving!" cried Carinthia, tears brimming in her wide hazel eyes.

"It's only temporary," Sage said wearily.

"What's wrong?" said Rose, taking a nearby chair.

"Just tired. And actually wondering if I should go after all."

Carinthia brightened. "Please stay! You're the best teacher we've ever had!"

"Which is exactly why she *should* go." Rose frowned at her younger sister. "Nicholas needs her more than we do right now. I think it's wonderful."

Sage shook her head. "I thought so, too, but . . ." She hesitated. Her arguments with Alex and Clare felt too raw and personal to share. "I just had so many plans for us," she finished.

"Don't be ridiculous," Rose said. Carinthia pouted from where she stood, but didn't say anything.

"I know what you need," said Rose, rising to her feet and tugging Sage's hand.

15

THE PRINCESSES PRACTICALLY dragged Sage out of the schoolroom and down the passage and several flights of stairs. In one of the workshops on the lower levels, Eleanor Draper listened as Rose explained how Sage would be tutoring the prince while he was in the field with the army. When Rose finished, the seamstress ordered Sage to strip to her undergarments and stand on the small platform in the center of the room before disappearing.

Even Carinthia was getting into the spirit as she and Rose helped Sage undress. Rose leaned in to whisper while Cara laid Sage's dress over a chair. "You *must* go, Sage, for my sake. I am trapped here at the palace, sewing and dancing and smiling sweetly when I want to scratch someone's face, but you can have an adventure, just like in the storybooks."

Sage looked at her student, realizing for the first time that Rose didn't watch her in the tilting yards and constantly ask about Sage's earlier life out of curiosity or boredom. She *envied* her, yet Sage had never seen a definite sign of it until now. She clasped the younger girl's hands and nodded. "I will," she said. "And when I get back I'll talk to your parents about expanding your education outside of the schoolroom, if only a little."

Rose's eyes lit up at Sage's promise, and she hugged her as Eleanor came bustling back in with a bolt of cream-colored fabric and a pile of linen. The seamstress set down her burdens and then shook out a bleached linen undertunic.

Right before she made to toss it over Sage's head, she paused and frowned. With one finger she tugged on the shoulder strap of Sage's lace-trimmed breastband. "I'll have to make you a few of these that are a bit sturdier."

"I'll take notes for you," offered Rose, moving to the table with parchment scraps and charcoal pencils.

"Thank you, Your Highness," Eleanor said, lifting the shirt over Sage. "I think three should be a good number, and this one fits well, so I can use the measurements in Mistress Fowler's file. Now wait here a minute." The last comment was directed at Sage as the seamstress walked back to the fabric bolt.

With the deftness of her profession, Eleanor laid out the cloth and used a wheeled blade to cut a rough shirt in a matter of minutes. She brought it back to Sage and helped her layer it over the white undershirt. Princess Cara dragged the full-length mirror—a luxury afforded by Eleanor's position as personal seamstress to the royal family—to where Sage could see as Eleanor pinned the sleeves and set the hem to the length she wanted.

The long, cream-colored tunic flared out from her waist like a skirt but stopped at her knees. She would still wear breeches or hose underneath. "I envisioned something shorter," said Sage.

"Pah!" Eleanor paused her pinning to brush away Sage's complaint with a dismissive wave. "You don't want to look like a man, do you?"

Sage opened her mouth to say she didn't care what she looked like, but then clamped it shut. She did care. When Alex looked at her, she wanted him to like what he saw.

"This is a good compromise," the seamstress said. "Simple and easy to move in, but feminine. Look." Eleanor stood and wrapped a cord around Sage's narrow waist, crossed it in the back, and brought it around to the front to join at a downward angle. "A belt here like this and it's quite becoming as well as functional." She moved aside so Sage could see the effect in the mirror. Rose clapped her hands in approval.

Sage gazed at her reflection thoughtfully. It almost looked like a short dress, but she would be able to move in it like the breeches she grew up wearing. The more she looked at it, the more this outfit felt like the best of both worlds. After a few seconds she smiled shyly at the seamstress. "I'll need several. Do you have this fabric in dark green or brown, too?"

Eleanor's apple cheeks plumped up as she grinned. "I have both."

The seamstress worked to pin and record what she would need to make more outfits, reminding Sage of the last time she'd been prodded and measured like this. She'd been preparing to meet the matchmaker, enduring everything with an increasing sense of dread. As she peeked in the mirror again, Sage had a different sense entirely. Then she was being wrapped in the role everyone wanted her to play.

This was like finding herself.

16

LESSONS WERE OVER for the day. Sage was in the schoolroom, copying a three-hundred-year-old trade agreement as the late afternoon sun
slanted through the window. Clare sat at the table on the opposite side
of the room, doing the same work and studiously ignoring her. All Sage's
optimism from the morning had faded. She wondered if it was too late to
back out.

There was a knock at the door, and Alex burst in before either Sage
or Clare could answer, the queen's note clutched in his hand. He scowled
at Sage before addressing Clare. "Will you excuse us, my lady?"

Clare looked startled and began to stand.

"Actually, Clare, I'd prefer you stay," said Sage without breaking eye
contact with Alex. Even if Clare was angry with her, Sage felt like she
needed her friend's support in what was coming.

Alex clenched his jaw. "Fine." He held up the queen's order. "What the
hell is this?"

Sage refused to be cowed. "Her Majesty is concerned about the prince's
education and feels a gap in instruction will only do him more harm. She
asked me to serve as his tutor during the mission."

"She asked, or you offered?"

"Does it matter? I'm the queen's choice."

"It does matter, Sage." Alex slapped the parchment on the table.
"I thought we discussed this last night."

"Really?" Sage raised an eyebrow. "I recall you refusing to discuss it at all."

"So this is what you did? You went above me to get what you wanted?"

"I went to someone who listened," she retorted. "If they could see the merit in my coming along, I thought perhaps you might." Sage sat back and crossed her arms. "I'm not sure why you have so much trouble with it. Your own mother told me how she traveled with your father for months at a time. *While pregnant.*"

"Excellent point, Sage. They were *married.*" Alex ran a hand through his hair and gripped it above his neck as he looked down at her. "We're not."

"It's not like we'll be sharing a tent."

Alex flushed and glanced at Clare, who wasn't even pretending not to listen. "I never thought we would. But I can't have you distracting me."

"I have no intention of being a distraction," Sage replied with calmness she didn't feel. "I'll have my own responsibilities to the prince. You'll hardly see me."

He dropped his hand and shook his head. "That doesn't matter. Just having you there—" He broke off.

There it was again, that undercurrent of fear. Why was he so damn afraid? "If you want it undone," she said, "go to the king." She almost hoped he would.

Alex shook his head. "I received this in front of all my officers. There's no way I can without making one or both of us look like complete fools."

One or both of us. He wasn't willing to tear her down. Sage felt her face grow hot. She hadn't even considered how foolish her actions could make him look. "Then the solution is obvious," she said, going back to writing to hide the moisture in her eyes. "Let the order stand."

"I'd rather you came to your senses."

She didn't reply, and there was a long pause, during which Alex picked up the order parchment again.

"Just think about it, Sage," he said quietly.

"I have."

"*Then think some more.*" He stopped and took a deep breath. "Can we talk tonight? Same time and place as usual?"

"I might be busy." Sage still refused to look up. After what felt like a full minute, he left without another word.

When the door closed behind him, Sage heard Clare gathering the papers and books she was working on. Apparently, her friend had had enough of her, too.

But instead of leaving, Clare brought everything to Sage's table and laid it out, then sat next to her.

"Clare," Sage began.

"Hush," said Clare. "We have work to do, especially if you're leaving the day after tomorrow."

17

EMOTIONS WERE EASIER to keep in check when one's mind was fixed on a challenging task. It was the reason Uncle William had made Sage tutor her cousins after Father died—it distracted her from her grief, and the small victories she achieved with her students had helped counter her depression. Sage focused on copying the documents now, refusing to let any other thoughts enter her head. Clare worked alongside her, acting as though their argument of the morning hadn't happened, and Sage was grateful.

They finished around the seven o'clock hour, and Sage sat back with a sigh, rubbing her tired eyes with the back of her hand to avoid touching her face with her ink-stained fingers. Clare set aside the original parchments and the ledger containing the copies for the master of books. "Did you see the similarities between the Kimisar and Casmuni languages?" she asked.

"I saw some at first in several words," Sage answered. "But after a while I just concentrated on getting it all copied. The order I put each set in was Kimisar, Demoran, then Casmuni, which also separated them in my mind."

Clare shook her head. "You should've copied the foreign ones next to each other. When you see them side by side, it's obvious the structure of Casmuni is identical to Kimisar. Verb conjugation, too."

"That makes sense," said Sage. "They share a common history, which makes it a bit odd that for many of the agreements, Demora acted as a go-between for them, like they didn't want to talk to each other."

"I noticed that, too. What is it that they share? I never learned anything about them in my lessons."

Sage rolled her eyes. "I know. Judging by the majority of our history books, you'd think the world began when Demora was united."

"Well, we count our years from then."

"Exactly. Five hundred and ten years isn't long in the scheme of the world." Sage stretched her arms over her head and groaned. She'd been hunched over the table for too many hours. "Uncle William had a set of Kimisar history books, though, which was one reason I got so good at the language. Apparently, both Kimisar and Casmuni came from the same southwest region of the continent. They were a mostly nomadic people, as their land was poor for farming."

"Like Tasmet?" said Clare. "I remember how rocky and almost barren it was when we passed through last year."

Sage nodded. "Yes, like that. They spread over the continent, never settling anywhere, even where the land was better, because it was occupied. The east side of the Catrix Mountains is mostly desert, though, so they ignored it. Then they discovered the Kaz River had an uninhabited fertile area far to the south. Some of their people began settling there."

"Did they simply grow apart?" asked Clare.

"Basically. Over time they felt less and less loyalty to each other. The eastern people grew rich in resources and knowledge, which is how so much of the history was recorded. An explosion in population and sea trade in the north here pushed the Kimisar back south, where they struggled." Sage pointed to the map of Demora on the wall. "Back then, Demora didn't exist, and everything south of Jovan on both sides of the mountains was considered Kimisara, but it wasn't really a nation. The Casmuni, as they now called themselves, battled the Kimisar along the Kaz River, culminating at a place called Yanli. It was a horrible, lopsided defeat for the Kimisar due to some kind of weapon the Casmuni had developed, and they retreated back into the lands they occupy now. All that was over a hundred years before Demora was united."

"And they still hate each other to this day?"

Sage shrugged. "Who knows now? We used to be friendly with Casmun, as you can see by these agreements, but the D'Amiran royal family refused to provide military aid in 291 when Kimisara tried to invade Casmun, and they haven't spoken to us since. If they're still holding a grudge over two hundred years later, it's not hard to imagine the same long feelings toward Kimisara."

"Fascinating." Clare ran her fingers over a copied page. "And what we learn from these documents could be critical in our reconciliation."

"That might be overstating it," said Sage. "But it could help with the first step, maybe speed up the process."

"Did you tell Captain Quinn about this?"

Sage frowned. "Judging from how upset he was that I knew *anything* about the Norsari, I decided not to, yet. Have you told Ambassador Gramwell?"

"He knows about the trade agreements and that I've been copying them for Sir Francis," said Clare. "I didn't want to mention what all we could learn until I was sure it would be anything useful."

"Good idea, though we can tell the queen everything." Sage's stomach abruptly growled loud enough for Clare to hear. "I'm starving. Let's call it a night."

"Can we have something brought here? I'd like to keep working."

Sage raised her eyebrows. "I figured you'd be wanting to walk with Lieutenant Gramwell tonight. He's leaving the day after tomorrow."

"This is more important right now," Clare said. "*You're* more important."

Sage was suddenly close to tears for the third time that day. "Clare, I really am sorry I didn't talk to you first."

"I know." Clare smiled softly. "You do tend to act before you calm down, but I think I was mostly jealous. You'll see the captain every day. And Luke, too."

"I think it will be much less fun than it sounds," said Sage. "I don't know why he's so against having me with him." She glanced at the darkening sky outside the window. "He'll be waiting for me soon, wanting to try to talk me out of it again."

"Sage?" Clare smirked a little. "Let him wait."

18

ALEX SPRINTED TO the garden, though he knew it was much too late for Sage to still be there. The king had called him up to discuss the rules of engagement for this mission, and after that he'd been caught in a conversation with Colonel Traysden on training methods. He reached the willow tree and pushed into the branches, calling her name, but got no answer.

He was almost glad not to see her. Waiting over two hours wouldn't have done anything for her temper. By now she would have gone to bed.

Alex made his way to her room, taking a longer route through the corridors so he could rehearse what he wanted to say. Though it would be motivated mostly to get in her good graces, he'd apologize. He *was* sorry, but he had to figure out how to get her to listen to him. By objecting outright to her coming, he'd set her on it like a fighting dog. Alex had to calm her down and make her see reason, which was difficult when the thought of her coming along made him panic and forget his own logic.

Her door was in front of him before he was ready. After glancing around, he bent over to look under the door. Completely dark. She was asleep.

He should wake her up, he decided, and had his fist in the air to knock when he imagined her answering the door, dressed in nothing but a shift, her sweet-smelling hair tumbling over her shoulders and down her back, eyes bleary from sleep and possibly red from crying. It would be like the day after he'd told her who he really was, when he would have done anything to take back what he'd put her through. Sweet Spirit, he'd be on his knees begging her forgiveness in a matter of seconds.

And if she forgave him, he'd be in her room, kissing her in the dark, holding her while she wore next to nothing, wanting nothing more than to lose themselves in each other.

The night would end with them in bed together.

Alex stepped back from the door. No, not now. Not while they were both so unable to think clearly.

Tomorrow. First thing.

19

SAGE DIDN'T REGRET a single minute of working with Clare late into the night, but she still needed to sort things out with Alex. Tomorrow would be the last day before the Norsari left Tennegol, and he'd be busy from dawn till midnight. She didn't want to have their argument hanging over and interfering with what he needed to get done. Fortunately, she knew where to catch him in the morning.

All 250 Norsari recruits exercised as a group at sunrise before going for a long run in the hills behind the palace. Sage was sitting on the fence post of a horse pen as the soldiers began straggling back, most carrying their shirts and all looking as though they'd rinsed off in the icy brook outside the gate. Alex was last, his shirt draped over his neck. She'd known he wouldn't have left anyone behind.

Sage hopped to the ground and picked up the waterskin she'd brought with her. "Thirsty, Captain?" she called.

He jumped and turned at the sound of her voice. Without waiting for his reply, she tossed the waterskin at him, and he caught it. After a wary look, Alex tilted it up and let the stream wash his face before aiming for his mouth.

Sage couldn't resist staring. She'd seen him shirtless before, when he was wounded and unconscious at Tegann, but then she'd been too busy cleaning away blood, terrified he'd never wake up. This was different.

Spirit above, he was beautiful.

A pair of tattoos on his left bicep declared his acceptance into the brotherhood of cavalry officers and also his position as a company commander. Those and the scars across the muscles of his arms and torso begged to be touched and explored, while black hair spread across his chest to pour in a narrow stream down to his navel . . . and lower. She suddenly felt warm all over, imagining her body next to his, with nothing between them.

After a couple of swallows, Alex lowered the waterskin and wiped his face with his shirt. That was when she saw the color inked into his upper right arm—his *sword* arm—and in a design as large if not larger than those on the other side. He caught her looking and twisted his shoulder so she could see it better. Rather than the black, blue, and red used for the army symbols, this one was soft shades of green and violet. It was a sprig of leaves and flowers.

Sage.

She raised her eyes to find him smiling shyly. He took a couple steps toward her and offered her back the bag. "Thank you. My lady."

Sage reached for it automatically, and his eyes roved over her, lingering on the curve of her hips accentuated by her breeches. Their fingers brushed, but he didn't let go. "I'm sorry about last night," he said. "There were matters that had to be dealt with. I hope you didn't wait too long."

He hadn't even shown up. All her guilt at not going evaporated. "I suppose it doesn't matter, seeing as we have the next few months."

Alex's expression changed so fast it was like a door slamming in her face. "We need to talk about that."

His tone made it clear he intended to do all the talking. Sage yanked the waterskin out of his hands. "What is there to discuss? I'm going at the request of Her Majesty."

"Sage, I love you, and I want to be with you as much as possible." Alex closed his eyes and pinched the bridge of his nose. "But this is not the way to do it."

Fury and embarrassment hit her like a blow to the stomach. Her free hand balled into a fist. "You think I'm doing this just to spend time with you?"

Alex moved his hand and looked down at her. "Aren't you?"

"I am going as the prince's tutor," she said slowly, through gritted teeth. "I am also willing to assist you in any other instruction you wish your soldiers to have. *That* is my purpose."

At least as far as he was concerned.

Alex's mouth pulled into a tight line. "I can't have you there," he said tersely. "I don't . . . *want* you there. Don't make me . . ."

"Don't make you *what*?" Sage struggled to keep her voice quiet. "I'm not one of your soldiers, Alex. You can't order me around."

He drew his brows down. "Oh, but I can. Did it ever occur to you how I'd have to treat you as your commander? I can't have anything undermine my authority. Everything would be strictly professional. No affection, no favoritism."

He still thought she only wanted to be with him. "I'm not some love-sick schoolgirl following you around like a puppy."

"That's not what I meant, Sage."

"Yes, it was." She crossed her arms. "If you're my commander, then why don't you *order* me to stay?"

"I shouldn't have to. That I don't want you along should be enough for you to say no."

I don't want you. He'd said that twice now. "You don't want to look weak," she spat. "You're afraid people will think you couldn't handle being around me. This is about your precious image as a commander."

Alex flinched; she'd hit a nerve. He shrank back and pressed his palms into his eyes. In that moment he looked so vulnerable she felt a stab of regret. "Please, Sage, just stay here," he said. "I can't do my job if I have to look after you, too."

They were arguing in circles. "It's a good thing I can take care of myself, then, isn't it?" She pushed past him, heading back into the palace, but he hooked an arm around her waist and pulled her against him.

"Please, don't leave like this," he whispered in her ear. "We have so little time, Sage. I don't want to spend it fighting."

She very nearly melted as he pressed his lips to her neck. Water from his hair dripped down her shirt collar. "Me neither," she breathed.

"I'll make it up to you, Sage, I promise."

Her half-closed eyes snapped open, and she twisted around to face him. "You don't have to make anything up to me, because I'm going."

She shoved him away, spraying him with water as the skin was squeezed. The surprise hit to his face enabled her to slip from his hold. "Now if you'll excuse me, *Captain*, I have preparations to make."

∞◦

The princesses didn't even bother showing up for lessons. Instead, Sage and Clare continued working on the list of Casmuni terms and phrases they'd connected to Demoran ones, but the only words Sage heard in her mind were Alex's.

I can't do my job if I have to look after you, too.

He saw her as a burden. Was that what she'd been at Tegann? More than once he'd insisted she couldn't take care of herself.

Did it ever occur to you how I'd have to treat you as your commander?

She didn't want favoritism. She wanted to help. But keeping Her Majesty informed—*spying* for the queen, she might as well call it what it was—didn't feel so much like lying to Alex if she had other reasons to be there. Now it was her only purpose. All that was left was the lie.

"What is wrong with you?" demanded Clare from across the table. "You're acting like you don't want to go anymore."

"Maybe I shouldn't," mumbled Sage.

"Why not?"

I don't want you along.

"A hundred small reasons that add up to this being a ridiculous plan."

Clare didn't look convinced. "Name one."

Sage had been fiddling with the end of her braid. "My hair. It'll be impossible to keep it clean out there."

"That's a pathetic excuse," said Clare.

"No," Sage insisted. "It'll always be in the way. I never kept it this long when I was younger."

"So cut it."

Sage blinked at her friend. "What?"

"Solve the problem. Stop dithering and commit." Clare shook her head. "This isn't like you." She stood and marched into the queen's empty sitting room next door, returning with a large, sharp pair of scissors. Clare set them on the table and folded her arms. "Tell yourself you're going."

It was ridiculous to think Sage wouldn't still be able to back out if she cut her hair, yet somehow she felt it would end the argument within. Or at least silence one side of it.

"You're right," Sage said, pulling the leather tie off the end of her braid. "Let's do this."

20

THE TAVERN WAS crowded with soldiers, and Huzar recognized the feeling permeating the air. They were leaving tomorrow. It was time for one last hurrah before the work began.

They were all serious, well-built men, and they were silent about their mission, even after a few rounds. One who drank enough to start boasting was immediately removed by his companions. Quinn had chosen his Norsari well. Huzar slipped outside after several minutes' observation from the corner. There was nothing to be gained from watching them, and he didn't want to be a face they recognized later.

His man met him in the street and followed Huzar silently to the leather shop several turns away. Inside was another of their country-men, manning the store for his employer. Huzar waited for a last patron to finish his business and depart before signaling his companion to draw the shades and bolt the door. He settled on a stool and placed one tattooed arm on the counter as the stablehand returned to his side, idly admiring a pair of gloves laid out on the counter.

"What news?" Huzar asked in Demoran. He'd ordered that even when alone, no conversations would be in Kimisar. Just commenting on the weather in their own language could mean death if overheard. Better to be heard—and likely ignored—while speaking Demoran.

The shopkeeper swept a few leather scraps into his hand and tossed them in the stove behind him. Unlike Huzar, his complexion was paler than the materials he worked with, and his eyes were a lighter shade of brown—almost amber. Between that and his accent, he was able to blend seamlessly into the tradesmen of Tennegol. He'd even gained the affections of a girl who worked in the palace laundry. Huzar appreciated the extra source of information, but the relationship made him uneasy. "We've been nearly cleaned out by those soldiers—gloves, jackets, belts, pouches," the man said. "But no orders placed beyond what was ready today."

Huzar nodded. "As I expected." He turned to the stablehand. "What have you heard?"

The man whistled through his missing teeth. "Lot of hushed preparations. Very little information to be had." He flicked the gloves away and leaned on the counter with a smile too smug for a man with so little to tell. "The amount of supplies is massive for that number of men."

"They must be going somewhere without local or army support." Huzar frowned. "Which direction?"

"If I had to guess? South."

Not good. The Kimisar were scattered east and south. Huzar had spent months contemplating ways to get them all home, and he kept circling back to part of their original mission. Last spring, the group was supposed to have led much of the Demoran army on a chase through the Jovan Pass to this side of the mountains, using the crown prince as bait. After bringing him back through Tegann, Huzar was to negotiate a ransom that would feed his starving people, but D'Amiran had taken the prince for himself. The duke then had the temerity to blame Huzar when the hostage escaped.

Having a fat, rich nobleman as prisoner might guarantee his men's safety on the long journey across Jovan and Tasmet. The only other way home was through hundreds of miles of Casmuni desert and another narrow, heavily guarded pass to the south. At best, he would lose half his men. Kidnapping may have shown little imagination, but it offered far better odds.

He'd hoped the Norsari would choose a training spot far away, giving him time to gather everyone, take a hostage or two, and race to the border. Were the Demorans already on the alert? He tapped his fingers on the counter and turned back to the leatherworker. "We need to call everyone—"

"You haven't even asked who's going," interrupted the stablehand.

Spirit, grant him patience. Huzar threw a scowl at the man. "That Quinn is in charge is confirmed by Filip's girl in the castle." He jerked his thumb at the man behind the counter. "Also going are two officers who were with him at Tegann."

"Is that all she said?" The man smirked. "Any barmaid in the city could've told you that."

Huzar's hand snapped out and grabbed the stablehand by his scrawny neck. He held him there, not bothering to bring him closer. "I do not play games with information that could mean life or death, and neither shall you."

The Kimisar choked and gurgled for several seconds. "The prince," he gasped when Huzar loosened his grip a little. "The prince is going with them."

Huzar dropped him. "Idiot. Prince Robert is in Mondelea."

"And the bastard prince is worth little," added Filip.

The stablehand gasped as he knelt at Huzar's feet. "Not Robert or the other. Nicholas. The youngest."

"He's just a boy," said Filip.

The stablehand rubbed his neck as he stood straight with a triumphant grin. "He is a squire. He and three others are assigned to each of the four platoons."

Huzar frowned thoughtfully. Demorans took officer training very seriously—something he admired—and their squires were expected to handle many independent duties. Even a prince would not be exempt from the rigors.

One of the most valuable hostages of all, out in the open. Close to the border.

Maybe, just maybe, this was the opportunity he'd been waiting for.

21

THE NORSARI RECRUITS assembled on the plain outside the city gates in the early morning light. Alex led his two mares along as he looked for Sage. She'd skipped yesterday's mission brief, though he'd sent her an invitation. He was actually glad not to see her. The whole time he'd spoken about the training patrols, Alex was conscious of how much he was omitting, how many outright lies he told his own men. Sage would've seen right through him.

A few townsfolk had come to see them off, and several of his men were engaged in quiet talk with sweethearts. Most enlisted soldiers didn't have the money or constant enough location to be properly matched. As a result, they either married low without a matchmaker or waited until they'd saved enough to buy their own land—and rare was the soldier who managed that—or they aimed for a commission, like one of his new lieutenants. Tanner had achieved his rank on the battlefield, having been denied squirehood because he couldn't read until he was past twenty.

That only reminded Alex of how he'd met Sage, and how she'd been eager to teach him to read when she thought he couldn't. She hadn't even been motivated by guilt from their initial misunderstanding; Sage simply wanted to help him be the best he could be. It wouldn't just be Prince Nicholas who benefited from her attitude, either. With everyone she met, Sage unconsciously teased out what they needed to become better people, whether it was learning to read or—in his case—remembering who he was under layers of duty and responsibility.

He continued along, still not seeing Sage in the crowd. Since he hadn't had a chance to ask her what horse she was taking, he'd gone ahead and saddled Shadow for her and arranged another horse from the stables for his baggage. Though horsemanship would be part of Norsari training, only the officers would be riding as they traveled. Every other horse would carry supplies while the enlisted men marched.

After several fruitless minutes of searching, Alex scanned the women watching from off to the side. Could she have changed her mind? If she had, he'd drop the whole captain act in front of everyone and kiss her senseless. To hell with discretion.

His optimism faded into confusion as he still didn't see her. He tugged the horses along until he found Cass, making marks on a checklist. "Have you seen Sage?"

Casseck glanced up in surprise.

"Do you think she changed her mind about coming?" Alex asked hopefully.

His friend stared at him like he didn't know what to say.

"Where is she, Cass?"

Casseck slowly raised his hand from the board he held and pointed.

Alex pivoted to look, but standing behind him was only one of the four squires. He wore a sort of oversized tunic that came to his knees as he secured the load on a packhorse.

Then the boy turned around.

22

SAGE THOUGHT SHE would be sick. Yesterday, cutting her hair had solidified her resolve; she'd never had another moment of doubt. Now everything felt overruled by the shock on Alex's face, but it was too late.

He took several steps in her direction, then without a word, he dropped the reins he carried at her feet and turned away, leaving her with Shadow and a horrible, empty feeling.

Once they were on the road, her hurt evolved into anger. She was coming along. Alex might as well accept it.

The capital city dropped away behind them until the last glimpse of it was covered by the hills. Casseck rode beside her, dispensing advice on leading her packhorse and filling her in on some of the plans they'd made. Maybe he was avoiding Alex, but he kept his thoughts and reasons to himself. There were only so many benign topics they could cover, though.

"How long have you known Alex?" she asked finally.

Cass answered cautiously. "Since we were ten. I arrived after he'd been in page training for a few months. He had a bit of a reputation as a fighter. Did he ever tell you that?"

"Some," she said. "He said he had a rough first couple of years."

"That's an understatement," Cass said dryly. "He got on the wrong side of some bad people right away, and every time new boys arrived, he'd get in a fight over how they were treated. Took a beating for me my first night."

"Is that how he made friends? By taking their initiation licks?" Sage tried to sound disdainful, but in truth she found it admirable. And unsurprising.

"Pretty much, though I don't think making friends was his goal. He was only doing what he saw as right. After a while he had a whole lot of us standing up for the new boys. Strength in numbers." Cass smiled. "Picking on anyone involves finding their weak point. For some of us it's more obvious than others."

"So what was yours?" He was thin now, and Sage had little trouble imagining a young Casseck as all elbows and knees capped with a mop of blond hair. "Were you skinny?"

"I was, but my biggest sore spot was my first name." He raised an eyebrow at her.

Sage suddenly realized she didn't know it. "It must be awful."

"Alex is the only one I won't punch for saying it," Cass said. He turned his face to gaze down the gentle slope of the valley to their left. "Bit surprised he never told you, though."

Sage didn't want to think about things Alex left out. "You can tell me. I won't laugh or tease you."

He didn't look back. "Don't make promises you can't keep."

"Now I feel challenged." It felt good to smile.

He sighed, his expression settling into something she couldn't decipher. Finally he closed his eyes and took a deep breath. "Ethelreldregon."

"Merciful Spirit!" She looked away, putting a hand over her mouth.

He waited several seconds as her shoulders twitched. "You can laugh already."

"I . . . don't . . . want . . . to," Sage managed in a strangled voice. A few titters escaped.

"Yes, you do."

She shook her head, looking at the trees and the mountain peaks to the west, then down to the ground. Everywhere but at him. "Did your parents hate you? Is that why you ran away and joined the army?"

"Well, even a traveling circus wouldn't have me with that name."

That did it; she burst out laughing. "I'm sorry," she gasped. "I promised I wouldn't!"

"Don't fret, I knew you were doomed to fail."

Sage wiped her eyes and yanked Shadow back onto the road before she could get to the patch of grass she'd been aiming for. "So how did that happen?"

"My older brother was named after our father, and it was another eleven years before I came along," he said. "My parents assumed there would be no more opportunities, so I was saddled with a combination of both grandfathers: Ethelred and Aldregon."

"Well, they had to be honored. Understandable."

"And ironically unnecessary. I have three younger brothers, remember?"

"Oh, no!" Sage put her hand to her face and giggled.

Casseck shrugged. "I'm over it now, but it was hell to live with as a kid until I met Alex. Anyone who tried to make fun of me caught his fist. My weakness became his own, and he conquered it." Cass paused and looked out over the columns of marching soldiers. "And that's the way he is with everyone."

Sage glanced ahead. Alex rode stiffly, like he couldn't relax. Had he heard them laughing? He didn't have to be jealous; she'd rather talk to him than Casseck. She reached up to brush hair away from her face and remembered with a jolt how much of it was gone. Her stomach rolled over. "What's his weakness, Cass? Is it me?"

His blue eyes followed her gaze to Alex's back. "You are his greatest source of strength." Cass smiled sadly. "But yes, that also makes you his weakness."

❖

It was an odd mixture of memories to travel as they did. Being in the woods and sleeping outdoors reminded Sage of her father's work as a fowler. Often the pair of them had gone for days without seeing another person, but that was the way Father liked it. He said animals were more predictable when they weren't around humans.

In riding on horseback with a company of soldiers on a road, however, it was more like the journey to Tennegol with the Concordium brides last spring. Except this time Alex wasn't at her side. Back then, the man she'd thought was the captain had kept his distance as Alex did now.

So much the same, and so different.

Alex pushed to get at least thirty-five miles per day at first, often marching the men till it was nearly dark. Without stopping long enough to hunt, they relied on their food supplies, but the pace would slow once they left the main road. The weather was fair, so in the evenings they slept under the stars, not bothering to set up tents. Sage puzzled over Casmuni pronunciations while sitting by the fire late into the night. Her list of translated words and phrases grew steadily, and she wondered how much progress Clare was making.

Spirit above, she missed her. Why couldn't she have thought of a reason for Clare to come along, too?

Most of the time Sage rode with Nicholas. She didn't know him well, so the first few days were spent getting past his haughty attitude. When she finally resorted to the threat of an unsatisfactory progress report getting him sent back to Tennegol—which she was sure Alex would approve, if it got rid of her, too—the prince shaped up. A little.

It wasn't long before she understood why his Kimisar language instructor and other tutors had made so little progress. The majority of his lessons had been based on written material, and as she'd suspected, things became muddled between reading and remembering, just like with his sister Carinthia. Fortunately, after almost a year of working with the princess, Sage had a good idea of how to reach Nicholas.

"What's the point of learning a language no one on this side of the mountains speaks?" he complained at first. "It's not like I can use it."

"That's been the problem," she snapped. Alex's cold shoulder and the prince's whining made her short-tempered. "You can't remember anything because you've never spoken it. Besides," she continued a little more calmly. "It often falls to the younger royals to meet with other nations. You could be negotiating treaties in a few years." Sage decided not to mention that often included marriage.

"Really?" He sat a little straighter in the saddle.

"Of course," said Sage. "But only if you've mastered the language."

Nicholas made much quicker progress after that. It felt good to succeed at something.

The Norsari left the Jovan Road on the eleventh day and headed south, toward the Kaz River. Two mornings later, Alex skipped exercises at dawn and let everyone rest. After breakfast he called Ash Carter and two officers to saddle up to ride ahead with him.

"Why?" she asked Cass, since Alex never looked at her.

To her surprise, Alex answered, "There's someone out there." He nodded to a thin line of smoke in the distance.

Sage frowned. "And you need to investigate?"

Alex shook his head. "Should be Rangers." He exchanged a knowing look with Ash Carter.

Men stationed on the border with Casmun. "May I come?" asked Sage. "Please?"

She expected him to say no, but he instead he paused in preparing his horse to look at her, as if really seeing her for the first time in days. Sage was suddenly conscious of her short, messy hair and how long it had been since she'd bathed.

His face softened a little. "All right. You have ten minutes to be ready."

23

THEY TOOK A narrow path in the direction of the smoke, Lieutenant Hatfield bringing up the rear. Ten solid days of travel would've tested anyone who didn't already live in the saddle, and the backs and insides of Sage's thighs were not only sore, the skin was raw where her weight had rested and chafed. Even with the extra padding she'd swallowed her pride enough to add, Sage fought to keep her grunts and winces to a minimum. Shadow picked her way over the rocky hillside, but without the noise of over two hundred other travelers to cover for her, Sage knew all four men were well aware of her discomfort.

Alex finally halted the horses and called an army greeting. Sage relaxed her legs a little, relieved to not have to clamp them just to stay upright, even if it was only for a few minutes. The response came quickly, and too soon they continued down the hill. Sage tried to direct Shadow where she wanted the mare to go, but it was difficult with her aching body and the mouthwatering scent wafting toward them. She hoped they had enough to share; the Norsari hadn't had fresh meat since leaving Tennegol.

They came upon a group of ten men seated and standing around a fire. Bedrolls were spread about, though a few had been rolled up, indicating they'd spent the night here—which was also obvious from the doneness of the boar roasting on the spit—and they intended to move on before sunset.

Sage swung her leg painfully over Shadow's back to dismount. Her foot hit the ground before she was expecting it to, and her knee buckled as her inner thighs screamed. She only stayed semi-upright because her left foot was still in the stirrup.

Hands at her waist lifted her up, taking the pressure off her trembling muscles. "Are you all right?" Alex murmured in her ear.

He wanted to be gallant *now*, after over a week of ignoring her? "I'm fine," Sage snapped. She eased her other leg to the ground, eyes watering, but he didn't let go.

"Give yourself a minute," Alex whispered. He moved a little closer, his body warm against her back. Without thinking, Sage was leaning into him. Alex turned his face into her cropped hair, his lips brushing the shell of her ear.

"Captain?" Ash Carter called.

The hands and heat vanished. "Right here, Sergeant," Alex said. "On my way."

With the sudden loss of support, she had to grab Shadow's mane to keep from collapsing. The horse looked back in concern, and Sage patted her in reassurance. When her legs felt steady enough to walk, Sage pulled the reins around and looped them on a tree limb. By the time she joined the others around the fire, introductions had already been made. The men, who must have been a Ranger squad, merely glanced at her. Sage felt too weary to explain her presence and was thankful her name was often used for boys.

High-rimmed camp plates were loaded with roasted pork and passed around. Sage accepted one gratefully and eased herself down onto a fallen tree that served as a seat for several men. Without waiting for utensils, she shoved a piece of steaming meat in her mouth. She was licking grease off her fingers and considering how to ask for more when she noticed Alex and Ash had taken the squad's leader off to the side, where they compared maps.

"We're glad to have more troops here," said the Ranger on her right. "Given what happened last year."

Sage glanced at the man before looking back to Alex. "This Tasmet business has everyone on edge, seeing as it all started from within this time."

He nodded. "And now the Casmuni. Can't help wondering if it's all connected."

The soldier now had her full attention. "You've seen Casmuni around here?"

"Well . . ." He tilted his head. "Not exactly. The only Casmuni I've actually *seen* were across the river."

"Really?" said Sage. She sat up, thoughts of a second helping forgotten. "Where exactly?"

"They come to the Kaz River for water, though both sides of it belong to Demora around here." He shrugged. "They never appear to be looking for a fight, so we don't begrudge them a drink. Sometimes we wave and they wave back."

Sage had gained a sense of the importance of water and water rights for the Casmuni, which made sense for a desert people. Several documents referred to "sharing water" like it was a gesture of trust or friendship. The Rangers probably didn't realize just how diplomatic their allowance was.

"How often do you see them?" Sage asked.

"Just in the spring and early summer. Last year and the one before." It was what these men were seeing that had the king so secretive.

"What do they look like?"

"They dress for the desert, covering everything, even their heads and sometimes their faces, to protect from the wind and sun. Brown as Kimisar, they are, like your captain and sergeant." The man jerked a thumb at Alex.

His tone implied a question about Alex's and Ash's heredity. Both had their coloring from their Aristelan mothers—as did Prince Robert— but her companion's mind had plainly gone elsewhere, to soldiers with different origins. "Tasmet had been part of Demora for decades," she said. "Its people aren't Kimisar anymore."

"So you say," the man replied. "But out here you learn to be cautious."

"*Cautious?*" Sage frowned. Even growing up with a fear of Kimisar raiders—remote as that threat had been in Crescera—she'd never judged a person's intentions based on the color of their skin, but the man's attitude implied such prejudice was common in the army. Having only seen Alex among those who knew him, it hadn't occurred to Sage how often he must face hostility in strangers, let alone other soldiers. Casseck never said what weakness Alex had as a boy that was so mercilessly preyed upon, but now she knew.

Those children were probably only imitating the mindset they'd observed in adults but with an extra layer of cruelty. She was sure if she asked Alex about it he'd say it didn't matter. But it *did* matter. Her fingers gripped the metal plate harder as she thought of the page who fought for everyone else when no one fought for him. "It sounds more like *judgment* to me."

"It's not judgment," the soldier insisted. "It's experience."

That he'd spent probably half his life skirmishing with Kimisar in Tasmet had shaped this dangerous attitude, but that didn't excuse it. Sage gritted her teeth. "I wonder how *their* experience with bias like yours affects their judgment."

"Well, I—"

"And when someone gets killed because of those judgments, what will you say? That you mistrusted a man appointed over you—an officer of the king—because he didn't *look* like you?"

His cheeks flushed as he stared at his plate. "It's difficult, you know, when you're out here year after year, fighting. You get in the habit of seeing things a certain way."

And that was the problem. Sage didn't think the man was necessarily a bad person—after all, he didn't harbor the same automatic suspicions of the Casmuni. He was just reacting to what he'd always known. "Much of Tasmet was easily convinced to join the D'Amiran family's plot against the crown," she said softly. "The people there didn't feel loyalty to Demora, even after all this time. I guess they were in the habit of seeing things a certain way, too."

"I don't suppose the fighting now will help much, either," her companion said.

"Probably not." Things were likely set back another generation at least. When she returned to Tennegol, Sage would write her old employer,

Darnessa Rodelle, to discuss the ways she and the other regional match-makers intended to foster healing after the war. Surely they had a plan already. Maybe she could help somehow.

"We're leaving," said Alex, interrupting her thoughts. He stood over them, frowning, before moving away. Sage wondered how much he'd heard.

"I'll take that for you," the man said politely, lifting the empty plate from her hand. Sage was still hungry but felt their conversation was worth far more than a full stomach.

"Thank you," she said. "I didn't catch your name."

"Corporal Dale Wilder," he said, offering his free hand.

She shook it. "I'm Sage Fowler."

"Now, Sage," called Alex.

"Coming." Sage hopped up, then took extra time to brush off her clothes so she could recover from the pain of the movement. "I hope to see you again," she told her new friend.

The corporal smiled. "Oh, I guarantee it. We'll be reporting to your captain fairly regular."

Sage puzzled over Wilder's last words as she hurried to catch up to Alex. "Why will the Rangers be reporting to you?" she asked. "Aren't they a completely different entity?"

"I'm the closest superior. It's a courtesy." His speech was clipped, like he didn't want to be caught talking with her. "And we'll be going out for exercises later. They know the area."

"Will you go across the river?" she asked casually.

Alex looked down at her. "Of course."

Sage struggled to find a way to ask what he would do if he ran into Casmuni, but she probably wasn't supposed to know that was possible, let alone likely. "It's only a few miles to the edge of the desert. Will you train there?"

He narrowed his eyes. "What makes you think we'd do that?"

"I just thought it would be a unique opportunity." She shrugged, trying to look casual. "It's uninhabited, right? They'd never notice."

Alex looked away. "I don't know. I hadn't considered crossing the border."

Oh, but he had. The way he refused to meet her eyes practically screamed it.

It wasn't until they were halfway back that Sage realized they'd left Ash Carter behind.

24

THEY RETURNED TO the Norsari group in the afternoon, but as far as the river still was, Alex felt it was impractical to march today. He left again as soon as he'd gotten something to eat, wanting to scout the best place to set up permanent camp. Cass insisted on accompanying him. Much as he wanted to be alone, Alex knew his friend was right. The squad they'd met today hadn't seen recent signs of Casmuni, but it was better to be safe.

The spot suggested by Sergeant Starkey wasn't difficult to find. An almost-clear slope rose up from the river to a flat plain large enough to build a training ground and hold group exercises. It would also be visible from a significant distance. If the Casmuni crossed the river again, they would do it knowing what waited on the other side.

He and Cass returned around midnight, and Alex was up again before dawn, itching to finally begin his mission. The weight of what he carried in his jacket was also a constant reminder of a particular task he had that day. All the tension made him short-tempered, and he struggled to keep from shouting orders.

Sage ignored him as she readied her gear, which was really as he deserved, seeing he'd barely said ten words to her until yesterday. She probably thought he'd forgotten what today was, and over the course of the morning, Alex never had an opportunity to correct that. Or, in his cowardice, he never made the opportunity.

They were on the move within an hour, and the goal was to reach the campsite by dusk. The men were fresh from their day of rest, so between that and following a major path, they made good time. They reached their destination as the sun set.

Tents started going up to shelter them from the cool wind flowing along the river from the mountains. Alex ordered Sage's set up before his, and it was ready before she was done brushing down and caring for Shadow. When everything was finally settled for the night, he still hadn't had a chance to speak with her. Alex stood outside her tent, watching the silhouette made by a single candle inside.

It was now or never.

Alex took a deep breath and opened the flap to duck inside. He'd given Sage a tent large enough to stand in—an officer's tent—with a cot and a chair and table. She sat at it now, writing what looked like a letter, and when he entered, he brought a breeze that nearly extinguished her light. Sage cupped her hand around the flame to protect it and glanced up, annoyed. Her eyes widened as she recognized him.

It was suddenly like the night they'd met, when he'd brought her supper as she worked in the library of Galarick. When he'd been disguised as a common soldier. Alex hesitated before taking another step. Only then did he remember he should've asked before coming inside.

"Why are you still up?" he asked, inching closer. "You must be exhausted."

Sage went back to her writing. "I have a lot to do, and very little could be done while on horseback."

He stopped on the opposite side of the table. "We'll be setting up everything tomorrow, so Nicholas won't have time for lessons yet. You can relax and recover from the journey."

"I'm fine, sir."

He stiffened. "You don't have to call me that when we're alone."

"My apologies. It's such a rare occurrence." Her quill scratched across the paper.

Alex said nothing but tapped his fingers gently on the wood.

"Do you need something?" She still wouldn't look up.

Alex cleared his throat. "I have something for you. A present."

Her quill stopped, and he heard her catch her breath. He pulled the cloth-wrapped object from his jacket. "I was going to give it to you in Tennegol before I left, but since you came, I decided to wait for your actual birthday." Alex laid it on the table between them, and she hesitated before reaching out to pull the cloth away, revealing a sheathed dagger. "I had it made for you," he whispered. "Months ago."

The dagger's black-and-gold hilt was almost identical to the one she carried, the one Alex's mother had gifted him when he left home for page training. He'd given it to her last spring for protection, but also because any of his men would have recognized it with its inlaid letters *AQ*.

Sage tilted the handle to see the initials in the candlelight. *SF*. "There's no *Q*," she said.

Alex nodded. "I had them leave room for it, if you want to add it later, or . . ."

"In case I change my mind?" She raised her eyes.

He felt the blood drain from his face. There was a flash of guilt in her gray eyes, and she looked down. "I guess this means you want yours back." She reached for the knife at her belt.

"No," he said quickly.

She unhooked it anyway and held it next to the new one. "I suppose it's too small for you anymore," she said.

"Even if it wasn't, I gave that to you to keep. I want you to have it."

Sage pursed her lips. "Will you teach me to fight with two knives, then?"

Alex flushed. "Given the way our last lesson ended, that's not a good idea right now." It had been the night he finally admitted to himself how much she meant to him. His internal defenses suddenly breached, Alex had been unprepared to resist the desires that swept over him, and within minutes he'd been ready to throw everything away for what he wanted. Then she'd called him Ash and brought him to his senses.

"No," she said. "You wouldn't want to say anything you'd regret later."

"I don't regret anything about that night."

Sage blinked at the daggers, silently tracing the initials on both with her thumbs.

"Well," Alex said finally. "Happy birthday." He turned to go.

She dropped the knives and jumped to her feet. "Wait."

Alex eyed Sage warily as she came around the table to stand in front of him. She held out her hands, palms down, in the royal gesture of gratitude she must have picked up from living at the palace. Without thinking, he reached back.

"Thank you," she said softly, squeezing his fingers.

He held on longer than he should have, then pulled her a half step closer. Sweet Spirit, she smelled good. He'd forgotten how good until yesterday morning, when he'd stepped up to help her, and every rational thought had vanished at her touch.

Just like now.

The color of her hair had already lightened a few shades from two weeks outdoors. Her skin, too, was sun-kissed, and more freckled than ever. Alex released her fingers and slowly raised a hand to brush hair from her eyes. Once he'd gotten over the shock of that first day, he kind of liked the way it looked.

"Is there anything else you wanted?" Alex whispered. *Ask me to kiss you*, he begged silently.

Her mouth twisted up a little on one side. "For my birthday or in general?"

"Either." His fingers closed on a few strands of her hair. *Ask me to kiss you.*

Sage shook her head. "I can't have what I want."

"Maybe you can tonight." He leaned forward to close the gap between them. *Ask me to kiss you.*

"Cass told me you didn't want anyone here to know about us." Her voice was suddenly bitter.

Alex froze, his mouth only inches from hers. "That's for your reputation more than mine," he said. "I'm not ashamed of you."

The heat of her hand left his. "You can't have it both ways, Alex."

It wasn't fair of him to do this to her. He couldn't make the rules and disregard them whenever he felt like it. Alex took a step back. "You're right," he said. "I'm sorry."

He turned away and pushed out of the tent, but not before hearing her whisper, "Me, too."

25

REVEILLE WOKE HER from a restless sleep. Everyone was assembling on the flat and clear area for morning drills. Sage rolled from her cot and stretched. Back in Tennegol she went to the tilting yards nearly every day, and she rather missed it. Why not join in here?

After throwing on an overtunic and yanking on her boots, Sage jogged to the exercise area and took a place in the back. The morning calisthenics were brutal on the muscles sore from riding but only made her determined to participate from then on. When the routine ended, Lieutenant Casseck announced everyone was to line up and fill sandbags needed to build the training ground. Sage had written her first report for the queen last night and had nothing else to do, so she saw no reason not to help. Alex—and everyone else—ought to see she was willing to do whatever work needed to be done.

Three hours later, Sage was more sweaty and filthy than she'd ever been in her life. Everyone began straggling to the river to clean up. Sage took a few steps downhill, but then shirts began coming off, and she hesitated. Soon all the men passing her were shedding clothes. She heard a belt buckle being worked a second before she caught sight of the first bare bottom plunging into the river.

Face flaming, Sage ran back to her tent and stayed there for a full hour. How was she supposed to get clean herself? Would she have to bathe in the river fully clothed?

A sloshing sound made her look up, and she peeked out of the tent to see Nicholas setting two wooden buckets of water just outside. She called her thanks to his back and brought them inside, then scrubbed herself thoroughly with the water from one, trying not to get the ground wet. If this was how it was going to be, she'd have to think of something to prevent mud. The second bucket she used to rinse her clothes. When she finally felt it was safe to come out, she wrung the water from her tunic and undershirt and hung them to dry on the line outside. Her underclothes she left spread on her cot.

She was separated from the row of officers' tents by a larger, peaked canvas structure. Sage wasn't sure it could be called a "tent" as the sides were either nonexistent or rolled up. It must be for large assemblies and noncombat instruction, such as Tanner's lecture on battlefield medicine scheduled for that evening. With a start she realized the long table inside was too heavy and bulky to have been carried on the journey. Puzzled, she went to inspect it. The top was fairly flat, but the bottom was much rougher. The sawdust and shavings on the ground coupled with the earthy scent of wood hewn before drying told her it had been *made*. This morning.

Lieutenant Tanner approached with a nod of greeting. "How are you settling in, Mistress Sage?"

She stood straight and rapped her knuckles on the wood. "When did this happen?"

The scars on Tanner's face pulled one eyebrow so they didn't quite rise evenly. "You didn't hear the work this morning? I called out them with carpenter and tree-felling experience, and they did this instead of bagging sand."

"Impressive," Sage said, meaning it. "Is this where you'll teach bonesetting tonight?"

"This is the place," he answered. "And I was supposed to, but Captain Quinn wants me to scout with him tonight, which is why I came to find you. He suggested you'd be willing to talk about foraging and edible plants instead."

Alex wanted her to do something. Was he asking as an apology for last night or just offering her a way to occupy her time? Either way, after all the odd looks she'd gotten on this journey, she was eager to show the soldiers she had something to offer. "Of course, Lieutenant. I'd be happy to."

Tanner smiled as crookedly as he'd quirked his eyebrows. "Thank you, ma'am."

When Tanner was gone, Sage realized she should've asked him more about where he and Alex were going. She'd work the question into a conversation later.

In any case, if she was going to give a lesson tonight, it would be better with examples of plants rather than just descriptions or drawings. The sun was almost at its peak so there was no time to lose. Sage went back to her tent and dumped her pack out onto her cot, then settled it over her shoulders. Her stomach growled as she stepped outside again, reminding her she'd not eaten in hours, so she headed to one of the supply tents first. A few minutes later she entered the woods, an apple in one hand and a hunk of dried venison in the other.

26

NO ONE HAD seen her for an hour. Alex prowled around the camp, getting more anxious with every second that passed. Finally he barged into her tent, searching for a clue as to where she'd gone. A stack of books lay on her desk, including what looked like a journal. Several outfits and personal items sat in a pile on one end of her cot, while some *very* personal items were spread out to dry on the other. Alex flushed and focused on making sense of the stack of clothing.

She'd emptied and taken her bag.

She was going to get something. It must have been urgent. Then he remembered he'd told Tanner to ask if she'd take his place in tonight's lecture so he could scout with Alex. Even if Sage was angry with him, it was safe to assume she'd agree.

Shit. She'd left camp to collect edible and poisonous plants. His left arm ached as he clenched his fists. *Dammit, Sage.*

He was already wearing his sword—he felt naked without it—but he'd need more than that. Things were still being unpacked and sorted, and it took several precious minutes to locate the crossbows. Alex slung one over his shoulder and walked the perimeter of the camp, looking at the ground. She was so lightweight he almost missed her footprints heading into the woods.

Her path wandered quite a bit but went steadily north. It was a good quarter hour before he became fully accustomed to the faint signs she left behind. He was used to tracking much heavier men and beasts. Often the only trace was the fresh divot where a cluster of mushrooms or another plant had been pulled up. Once he found an apple core she'd tossed several feet from her trail.

After about two miles he found several strands of light-brown hair draped over the branch of a low bush. How had that happened? Was she crawling? He crouched down to peer at them, puzzled. It almost looked as if they'd been laid there.

A twig snapped, and Alex jumped up, swinging the crossbow around. Sage stood about twenty feet away, watching him. Relief spread through his chest. She was safe.

The two ends of a broken stick were in her hands. "You're dead," she said coolly.

She'd set a trap for him and gotten close enough to have done serious damage before he could react. Alex dropped the bow, more impressed than he wanted to be. Sage tossed the pieces of twig aside. "You look lost," she said.

"No more than you," he replied. Only then did he realize how thirsty he was, and he'd neglected to bring along a canteen. He'd dropped every responsibility to himself and the Norsari to find her.

She walked past him, headed north again. "I'm heading for the lake."

Alex took a few running steps to catch up. "How do you know there's a lake this way?"

Sage jerked a thumb over her shoulder. "I saw a furlong eagle's nest about a half mile ago. They nest close to water, hence the name."

"That's much farther than a furlong."

"I didn't name it," she said, staring straight ahead. "But anyway, they usually stay within a mile, especially during hatching season."

Alex frowned. "How do you know the direction?"

She finally turned her face up to look at him. "Because I saw the eagle fly over with a fish in its talons. Big fish, too, so it's a decent-sized lake." She smirked. "Honestly, Captain, you soldiers should look up as often as you look down. You walked right under me."

That was where she'd been—in a tree, after effortlessly leading him on a chase for over a mile. Part of him wanted to turn her loose and see how many Norsari could track her down, but that was far too risky. "You shouldn't be in the woods alone," he said. Sage snorted, and he grabbed her arm to make her stop. "Have you forgotten how dangerous it is out here?"

"What are you talking about?" Her forehead wrinkled.

She didn't know about the Casmuni. It wasn't like he could tell her, either. Alex searched for something that would serve as an excuse. "Remember that boar the Ranger squad had? They roam all over this region. Don't tell me you don't know how aggressive they are this time of year."

"I haven't seen signs of any." She looked dubious.

"That doesn't mean you won't run into signs in five minutes," he insisted.

Sage shrugged and turned away. "I can take care of myself. But in any case, you're here now. Keep an eye out."

"That's not all," he called to her back. "You left the camp without telling anyone. No one knew where you were or why you left. You're part of an army unit now; you can't just wander off whenever you feel like it. Do you know how much time I lost looking for you?"

Sage stopped and lowered her head. "I'm sorry," she said to the ground at her feet. "I wasn't thinking. I only wanted to be ready for tonight. I'm not used to keeping you informed." She took a deep breath. "I won't do it again."

Her apology was genuine, and he could tell she realized how in the wrong her actions had been. It took everything he had not to pull her into his arms and tell her it was all right, he was just glad she was safe. If he did, though, more than kissing was likely to start.

"Come on," he said instead. "Let's find that lake and then head back. I'm parched."

27

THE SHORT DISTANCE to the lake was silent, as was the walk back to camp. Sage felt guilty at how much of Alex's time she'd wasted, but that he'd come after her fully armed spoke volumes. Something was out there, and it wasn't wild boar. Coupled with Corporal Wilder's information, it wasn't hard to make theories.

Alex fully expected to run into Casmuni—*in Demora*—yet no one else knew anything about it, except maybe Ash Carter, and he was gone. Was Alex supposed to meet with them? That might explain the secrecy and Ambassador Gramwell's involvement, but if so, Alex obviously didn't trust them.

Sage made herself two promises: she would double her efforts in her translation project, and she'd continue training in combat while she was here. The second might be tricky—all the recruited soldiers were far beyond her in both strength and skill. She'd probably be stuck with the squires, but it was better than nothing.

The lecture on edible and poisonous plants went well, and she didn't even have to ask Alex if she could teach more—he'd already added her to the schedule. When she started Nicholas's lessons, she included the other squires as often as possible, both for their benefit and to create a little competition to get the prince to put in more than a nominal effort. Sage quickly fell into a routine of teaching and training, becoming a camp authority in the classroom and everyone's adopted little sister in the training grounds. Both roles felt comfortable. She rarely saw Alex, as he led back-to-back training patrols that often lasted two or three days. At first she thought the trips had some other purpose, but none of the men she talked to on their return described seeing anything unusual.

As promised, the Ranger squad stopped by the Norsari camp a couple weeks later, and Sage wasn't surprised to learn Ash Carter had taken charge of them. She sat up late into the night, listening to their descriptions of the land along the southern border, including the Beskan and Yanli Gorges the Kaz River flowed through. Both were narrow with sheer walls, but the Yanli was far more dangerous.

"The sides ain't just steep." Corporal Wilder was deep into his wine-skin, gesturing grandly with his hands to emphasize his descriptions. "They're smooth as glass except where it's broken and jagged. Nothing grows down there. We call it the Demon's Alley for the black color and the sharp rocks. The stones make good cutting tools, though. We've used it as a quarry—at least what we could reach."

"What could've created something like that?" Sage asked in awe.

He shrugged. "Never heard a theory that made much sense, but it's a deadly place. A few guards rode a boat through it on a dare two years ago, but half of them didn't make it. Stupid way to die." The corporal spat into the fire.

Sage looked across the flames to where Alex sat with Ash Carter, watching and listening. There was no jealousy on his face over her speaking with another man, but his eyes had a glint of sadness. Their gazes met, and she issued a mental challenge: *Come over here and talk to me if you want.*

Alex looked away. A few minutes later he left the circle of firelight with Ash.

"So, Corporal," she said, keeping one eye on Alex. "Have you seen any Casmuni in the last few weeks?"

Wilder shook his head. "Not a one, but Sergeant Carter has us searching."

"Did you cross the river?"

"Not yet, the water's been high and temperamental. We've stuck mostly around the area from last year."

A chill went up her spine. "What happened last year? I thought you said you'd only ever seen Casmuni on the other side of the Kaz River."

"Around September we found a place where they crossed and camped and scouted about. The thing is"—he shifted to speak to her in a more confidential manner and lowered his voice—"I'm not sure I agree. Our Sergeant Starkey was new at the time—I been out here going on four years. No one listened to me, though, they just followed Sarge."

Sage could barely breathe with excitement. "Why do you think he's wrong?" she whispered.

"Well, it seemed a bit large and obvious, like whoever was there wanted the signs to be found. That always makes me suspicious." Sage nodded in agreement, and he continued. "Second, they had horses. I've *never* seen a Casmuni horse."

"And you'd think if they came to the river for water, they'd bring them," she said.

"Right." Corporal Wilder was getting more excited. "And third, they were there in September. Much later than I've ever seen Casmuni appear—they only come in spring and early summer."

According to the documents Sage had studied, there were two trade routes between Demora and the Casmuni capital city of Osthiza: a circuitous path that went around to the fortress at Vinova and south, and a shortcut through the desert following a network of springs. However, the desert route could only be used a few months of the year, as many of the water sources dried up in the summer. She'd wondered why they didn't just follow the Kaz River all the way, but after hearing Wilder describe the Yanli Gorge, she understood.

The corporal was right: If the Casmuni were to come here, they'd only do it when the desert could be crossed.

"Anything else?" she asked.

Wilder shrugged. "It looked like they went into the desert, but tracking them was impossible. Wind blows everything away after a day."

"So if it wasn't Casmuni, who do you think it was?"

"Who else but the Kimisar?"

That sounded like a rather far-fetched theory, even for someone who had already shown a hatred for the Kimisar. "Here? I've never heard of them going beyond Tasmet."

Wilder's already-flushed face reddened. "I have a, um, girl in a village up by the Jovan Road. She told me last year a number of 'em come through the south pass last May. They raided a string of farms, and disappeared. The army caught a few, but she said there were *dozens*."

The Jovan Pass had been buttoned up by the army around that time. What if those Kimisar had been trapped on this side of the mountains? "Are you thinking that's where they went? Into Casmun?" she asked.

"That's my guess." The corporal took a swig from his wineskin.

Sage glanced over at Alex, who was talking quietly to Ash Carter, far out of earshot. "Have you told your opinion to Sergeant Carter?"

"I doubt he'd listen. Sergeants stick together, in my experience." Wilder shook his head. "It probably don't matter anyway. Desert likely swallowed the bastards up."

Sage only nodded, but she couldn't help wondering if all the Kimisar had truly left.

28

ALEX STARED AT the group around the fire, where Sage was again deep in conversation with one of the Rangers. They were mostly discussing the local geography when Alex had left, and in true Sage fashion, she was happiest when she was learning something. Her smile never quite reached her eyes, however, which made Alex realize how little Sage had smiled at all in the past few weeks. The one time she'd looked across the flames at him that night, he could almost hear her daring him to say something.

After tracking her down on the first day, he'd worried about her constantly, but she'd obeyed his order and never strayed from the camp, even when he was gone. Whenever the Norsari had returned from a training patrol, Sage peppered them with questions, mostly on flora and fauna they'd seen. Probably she was feeling cooped up, hence her interest in talking with those who'd seen more of the area. He felt a little bad about that, but keeping her here was safer for everyone. Safer for him.

Cass, Gram, and Ash still trusted him, though that would change if they ever realized the horrible truth of what Sage's presence meant. Keeping his distance from her was agony at times, especially when he could see she was unhappy, but it was bad enough that his friends knew about their relationship. Though Alex had never entered her tent after that first day, he'd spent several minutes of nights past watching her silhouette as she sat up late, writing. When Alex's first report left for Tennegol, she'd added her own thick packet to the dispatch. A pang had gone through him at the thought that none of it would ever be for him.

"Who are you writing to?" he'd asked. "You realize this mission is a secret, right?"

Sage tossed her head, which she still did despite her lack of hair. "Some of them are progress reports on the prince for Their Majesties. The rest are private letters for Clare, who already knows I'm here."

"What in the world could you have to discuss in such detail?"

She smirked. "Are you worried they're about you?"

That was exactly what he was afraid of.

"Read them if you want," Sage said, waving her hand like it didn't matter. "I know you've never fully trusted me."

That was a low blow, and Alex's first instinct had been to leave them alone. An hour later, he realized that she'd rather skillfully manipulated him, and he broke the seal and read her letters without any feelings of guilt. After all, a commander was expected to closely monitor all communications, especially during sensitive missions.

Her writing was witty and entertaining but carefully neutral in describing camp workings and routines, which would give no enemy significant information if it was intercepted. Everything was so benign Alex couldn't believe there wasn't some kind of code within. Through the night he read them several times over, forward and backward, but try as he might, he could find no pattern, even in the passages about him. Those rather painfully described her loneliness and confusion at his keeping her at arm's length.

He remade the seal and gave Sage no sign that he'd read her correspondence. Later an equally thick package arrived for her from Clare, and though he had every right to read the letters, he passed them on without comment. When Sage brought another bundle to be sent with the weekly dispatch, he managed to resist opening it for two hours. He craved her voice and her insight and her humor, even if it was tinged with sadness. Most of all, he needed the reassurance that she still loved him.

Another dispatch would go out in two days. He was already looking forward to tomorrow night's reading.

Outside the circle of firelight, Ash followed his gaze to the gathered soldiers. "How is Sage doing out here in the rough?" he asked quietly, though they were out of earshot of anyone.

"Never complains," Alex said. "At least not that I've heard."

Ash pushed his black hair out of his eyes. "You say that like you haven't talked to her."

"I haven't."

His friend sighed. "Alex, I don't want to get in the middle of this—"

"Then don't." Alex tore his eyes away from Sage and focused on the sergeant. "You're here to report."

Ash shook his head. "I already told you everything, which was nothing."

A pit formed in Alex's stomach. "I thought you went to where the Casmuni had camped."

"I did. It wasn't helpful."

Alex hadn't expected much after eight months of exposure to the elements. "But they showed you where they found what they did. What are your thoughts?"

"It's not the place I would've picked to set up camp," said Ash. "Visibility was limited in most directions, and it was a poor place to cross the river, even in August." The Kaz was currently running high and fast with melting mountain snow. Alex hadn't ventured across it yet, hoping it would calm in the next couple weeks. "What it did have was a fairly clear path to the Jovan Road."

"Which must have been their goal." Alex folded his arms and turned away from the fire to resist looking in its direction.

"Maybe." Ash shrugged. "I'm going to head upriver tomorrow and see if I can get us a few boats from one of the villages. Could be handy."

Alex nodded. "Sounds like a good idea. Quick communication and travel, at least in one direction."

"Exactly."

Neither spoke for another half minute, during which Alex's eyes wandered to the fire again. "The new moon is in two days," he said finally. "The ambassador had aimed to leave by then. It takes about ten days for our dispatches to reach Tennegol. He'll cross paths with my second and third reports of nothing. It won't look good."

The sergeant leaned against a tree trunk, making him appear even shorter. "I'm as frustrated as you. We still have at least three weeks before he gets here, though."

"Ash?" His friend looked up. "What if there's nothing to find?"

Ash shook his head. "No one comes in like that for no reason. They'll be back."

It felt strange to hope for a foreign invasion to repel, but somehow Alex felt like his career depended on it.

29

SAGE ENTERED THE command tent when bidden, a bundle of letters in hand. Alex looked up from where he sat, writing his report. "It's getting late," he said. "I was wondering if you were going to make this dispatch."

She shrugged. "It doesn't leave until morning."

"So it doesn't." Alex went back to his work, but not before she noticed the eager gleam in his eye. "You can put them in the satchel with the rest."

"Thank you." Sage knelt down and lifted the flap of the leather bag sitting on the ground. There wasn't much in there. She frowned. This could be problematic. She tucked hers in and stood. "Not much this week," she said casually.

Alex gestured to the stack on the corner of his table. "Oh, I'm about to weigh it down some more."

Sage relaxed. He must be adding what Ash had learned while he was away. Alex was also much more cheerful than usual. No doubt because he'd have something to read tonight. Maybe now was a good time. "Captain—" she began, and he glanced up sharply. "Alex," she continued. "I heard you're going across the river with a team tomorrow."

Alex narrowed his eyes in suspicion. "I am."

"AndIwaswonderingifIcouldgowithyou," she said quickly.

Alex shook his head. "Sage, we already discussed this."

Like hell they'd discussed it. "But I can keep up, and I won't be in the way. Please?"

"You won't be in the way because you won't be there."

"But—"

"I said no." Alex went back to writing. "You're not to leave the camp. Do not ask again."

Sage hadn't expected him to say yes, but the curt rejection still stung. She left without another word, and went two rows over to watch and wait. It was late, and most in the camp were down for the night. Alex was the only officer still awake. After ten minutes, the lantern in the command tent moved. Alex came out, the light in one hand and Sage's packet of letters in the other. She edged behind a wall of canvas and waited until he was settled in his own tent for several minutes before creeping back.

The key to a convincing deception, as Sage had learned last year, was to be honest wherever possible. Not only did it reduce the number of lies one had to keep track of, the vulnerability that often came with truth generated empathy in those being deceived. Her letters to Clare were genuine in observation and feeling, even when it came to describing her frustration with Alex and being trapped within the camp perimeter. Part of her hoped he would actually listen to her complaints. The best decoys weren't fake all by themselves.

Inside the dark command tent, Sage dropped to her knees and felt around for the satchel. Alex had moved the courier's bag when he added his last letters and removed hers, but it wasn't far from where she'd last seen it. Quickly, she stuffed the bag's contents into her tunic, then located Alex's commander's seal and tucked it in her sleeve. After a quick listen for anyone nearby, she slipped back out and walked casually to her own tent.

She had to hurry. Not only did she have to read everything in the dozen small packets and reseal them, she had to add what was relevant to her already thick report to the queen. Then she had to return everything to the command tent and leave the satchel a little fuller. Hopefully Alex wouldn't notice the extra contents when he replaced her letters in the morning. So far he hadn't.

30

THE NORSARI DID indeed move south. They traveled so swiftly that Huzar had trouble keeping up, but he also lost time seeking out several Kimisar in the region. His tactic of scattering the soldiers had paid off— all were alive and accounted for, and he was able to assemble a nebulous reconnaissance picture along the way. The most helpful information came from the men who knew the area. Demora had doubled its roaming detachments since he'd left a trail south last summer. That would make what Huzar planned trickier, but ironically, the increased movement of Demoran troops would enable him to better cover the tracks of his own force.

When the Norsari began to set up what looked like a permanent camp, Huzar ordered his second-in-command to draw the rest of the men together by the next fading quarter moon. The Demorans would be focused on training for the next few weeks, but the longer Huzar waited, the more the Kimisar risked discovery. Also the more likely the Norsari would be ready to respond, which meant certain death for his men.

Huzar found a hot spring high in the hills west of the Norsari camp and made his observations from there. The area smelled foul due to the sulfur vents in the rocks, but that meant it was less likely to be diligently patrolled, and without the spring he wouldn't have been able to bear the cold, fireless nights. His biggest challenge was boredom. The days were long when all he could do was wait and watch. As with everything men did, there was a pattern to be exploited. All he needed to do was find it.

The more he observed, the more urgently he wanted to act. Every day the Norsari below grew stronger. Quinn was rather clever to have put his camp where he did—the variety of landscapes made for excellent training. Huzar watched groups of them leave the main camp for days at a time, always going east into the marsh—perhaps as far as the Beskan Gorge—or south across the river, though they hadn't appeared to venture beyond the trees and into Casmun. Once they came toward him in the west, but never too close for comfort. The stench was his ally. He'd have to remember to bathe or they would smell him coming.

Huzar had several options brewing in his mind. The Kimisar were outnumbered not quite two to one, and his men hadn't worked together in months. They weren't nearly cohesive enough to take on those kinds of odds, especially against Norsari. Though it was risky, Huzar planned to divide his men and attack in a way that drew most of the Norsari away from the camp. The squires would be left behind with a smaller force, the prince among them.

Once they had the boy, Captain Quinn might be willing and able to arrange Huzar's passage himself. His father was the commander on the other side, so he'd certainly know who to talk to over there.

The Kimisar could be home by midsummer.

Home.

31

ALEX SAT IN a rowboat, drifting with the current. The day was cool and breezy, but sweat oozed from every pore on his body. He shivered violently with cold and fear, waiting for what he knew was coming. Shouts and crashes echoed off the rocks around him, growing louder as he approached a bend in the river. He gripped his sword in his right hand while the left steered the boat with an oar.

Almost there.

But he knew what he would see. He saw it every night.

The clash of swords drew his attention to the left bank, where Casseck battled three Kimisar, his back to Alex. Though Cass fought well, he was losing ground, and he'd retreated within a few steps of the river. He had nowhere to go.

Alex directed the boat to help him. He could get there in time, except—

A hoarse cry came from the opposite bank, and Alex turned to see Suge struggling with Duke D'Amiran. It was no use, though—her hands were tied, her face bloody and bruised, a knife held to her throat.

Charlie's small body lay at her feet, his blood staining the sand.

⋘⋙

Alex forced his eyes open and jerked to a sitting position on his cot, gasping. He swung his legs down and put his head between his knees and took several deep breaths, trying not to be sick. It was one of the few times he'd managed to wake up before the dream got worse, but he knew from experience he couldn't go back to sleep or it would pick up where it left off.

Sometimes Sage and Charlie were reversed. Sometimes it was Gramwell or Tanner or another of his men fighting on the other side. But the choice was always the same.

He always chose the same side, yet it never mattered—everyone ended up dead.

Except him.

32

THE SIXTH DISPATCH had left two mornings ago, and Sage was beginning work on the seventh. It was hard to believe she'd been here for that long—and had so little to show for it. Each day that passed made her more antsy. Alex was obviously looking for something with all his patrols, but no one else seemed to know what he was finding, if anything. Without a sense of where to start, Sage had very little to investigate or report to Her Majesty. Most of her writing was to Clare, discussing what she'd learned from studying her copy of the trade agreements. A courier from the capital was expected any day now, and Sage was eager to hear what her friend had concluded in her own examination.

Also, she felt like she was being watched.

Not by the soldiers—they knew she was restricted to the camp and so kept an eye on her, but that wasn't it. She often caught Alex watching her, at least when he was around. He was always busy, working directly with the Norsari in their combat training and leading almost every overnight mission. She often didn't know when Alex left, but she always knew when he returned because the first thing he did was look for her. He rarely spoke to her, just seemed to want to assure himself that she hadn't snuck away in his absence. But it wasn't his eyes she felt, either. She couldn't explain it.

Sage pressed the wax seal across the binding string and set the packet aside. The courier would leave at dawn, so she'd wait until late evening to add it to the dispatch. Though the actual reports would be added separately, she still didn't like giving Alex long to read the safe letters. She'd written a great deal about him this time. Her words were as much to him as to Clare.

Spirit above, she missed her friend.

"Mistress Sage," came a voice from outside her tent. It was Prince Nicholas, sounding annoyed at being an errand boy.

She went to the opening and stuck her head out. "What is it, Highness?"

"Captain Quinn requests your presence at the command tent." The prince turned and sauntered off before Sage could ask why. Someone really needed to tell him he had to learn how to follow orders before he could start giving them.

Sage took a moment to straighten her long tunic. The green one was her favorite, though the dark brown one hid dirt and stains better. On her belt she always carried her two daggers now; she felt off balance with only one. She stepped outside and made her way to the center of the camp. It was nearing time for the evening meal, and the delicious scent of venison stew met her at every turn.

Outside the command tent stood a group of soldiers and horses wearing royal livery. Not just messengers, either, from the look of it. Someone important. She quickened her pace and strode inside without asking permission—her presence had been requested, after all.

It took a moment for her eyes to readjust to the shade of the tent, but she recognized Ambassador Gramwell right away. He smiled broadly. "Here's who we've been waiting for!"

Sage was confused until he stepped aside to reveal who was with him.

Clare.

33

IT TOOK SEVERAL seconds for Sage to comprehend her friend was truly here, and wearing clothes in a style similar to her own. She'd never seen Clare in anything other than a long dress fit for royalty—even her nightgowns were embellished and trimmed with lace. For a moment Sage felt sick, thinking her friend had cut off her own hair, but it hung in a thick braid down her back, interwoven with ribbons that matched her knee-length red tunic and thick hose.

Clare jumped forward, looking just as happy as Sage felt to see her. They embraced and began talking over each other with how-have-you-beens and when-did-you-get-heres until someone cleared his throat.

"If you ladies would excuse us," Alex said. "We have military matters to discuss."

"Of course, Captain." Clare grabbed Sage's arm and dragged her out of the tent before she could object. "We have some catching up to do."

Once they were outside, Clare asked Sage to take her to the river, and they walked down the slope together. Sage headed for an area near the edge, by the trees, but Clare steered her to a spot in the middle of the bank.

"There," her friend said. "No one can sneak up on us while we talk." She sat on a wide, flat rock and began unlacing her riding boots. "My feet are dying for a soak."

Picking a place where they couldn't be overheard and now exposing her bare legs to over two hundred men? Clare was getting more astonishing by the second. "I never thought to see you in such a short skirt," said Sage, pointing to the gold embroidered hem lying across Clare's thigh. "Though yours is much fancier than mine."

"Riding in a long skirt every day for three weeks is tiresome," said Clare. "And we likely have two more weeks to go until Vinova."

Sage inhaled sharply. "You're going all the way to the outpost?"

"Papa is." Clare dipped her toes in the frigid mountain water and sighed a little. "I convinced him to take me along."

"How did you manage that?"

Her friend smiled impishly. "By making myself valuable. Mama sent a letter asking me to make sure Papa remembered the details he usually left to her. So I took care of those and many others until I was indispensable."

Sage shook her head in awe as she removed her own boots and sat. "And you rode all this way?"

"Well, not quite," Clare admitted. "At first I could ride only for a half day at a time, but I was able to sit in a carriage when I got too sore." She leaned forward to whisper. "As often as not, I even rode astride, rather than sidesaddle."

Sage toned down her smile for her friend's sake. "Good for you." She put her own feet in the water. "So Vinova, then."

"Yes, of course." Clare sat up straighter. "You were right about everything we suspected before you left. The Norsari are here not only to train, but as a deterrent against the Casmuni coming across the border again and to fight them if necessary. Papa is here to open talks, assuming the Casmuni want to talk, once their invasion is discouraged or defeated."

"He told you all this?" Sage asked in surprise.

Clare shrugged. "Just that we intend to reach out to Casmun, but I've been reading his correspondence." She lifted a dainty white foot out of the water and inspected a blistering spot on her little toe. "I think you've had a bad influence on me." Clare lowered her foot again. "I haven't seen any of the latest report yet. We passed three couriers on the way—the last one yesterday—and they gave us what was meant for Papa and me. I didn't keep most of what you sent, just forwarded it to Her Majesty. I figured you could tell me everything yourself."

"There's very little to report," said Sage with a sigh. "The Norsari constantly go out and come back, but no one has ever seen anything suspicious, even in the times they crossed the river. I think Alex is feeling a lot of pressure to find something. From the looks of it, he doesn't sleep much."

"You haven't seen anything?"

"I haven't left the camp since we arrived."

Clare's mouth dropped open. "I thought you only said that in your letters to throw the captain off. Do you mean to tell me you've learned *nothing* on your own? Why did you bother coming?"

"Keep your voice down," Sage said. "It's not that simple. I'd probably sneak out of camp if I had any idea where to go. Besides"—she glanced around—"I don't think it was the Casmuni."

"You said that in your third report, but I'm not sure I understood why."

"You're still working on all the trade agreements, right?" Clare nodded. "Remember the one that talks about caravans crossing the desert?"

Clare pursed her lips as she searched her memory. "They could only travel in the spring. Otherwise caravans were to go through Vinova."

"Exactly," Sage said. "All the springs dry up. The disturbance that has everyone worked up was in late summer."

"Yes, but there's a difference between a trade caravan and an army, Sage."

Sage sat back a little, her confidence fading. "True, but no one has ever seen Casmuni after the summer solstice."

"But they *have* seen them. They've been coming to the Kaz River for years now."

Sage frowned. "Just the past two."

"And if it's May now, they're due, aren't they?"

"Yes." Sage nodded. "They are."

34

ONCE CLARE AND Sage were gone, Alex invited Ambassador Gramwell to sit while he moved to a chair on the opposite side of the table. "I was expecting you, sir, but Lady Clare was a surprise," he said.

"Ambassadors are always married men for good reason." Lord Gramwell poured himself a cup of water from a pitcher. "Women open doors that would otherwise be shut in our faces. I was already feeling the loss of Lady Gramwell, who is too ill to travel all the way to Vinova, and Clare took care of matters I wouldn't have even thought of. In the end it made sense to bring her." The ambassador raised his cup before taking a drink. "Never underestimate the value of having a smart woman by your side, Captain."

"I won't, sir." Alex had no doubt that was Sage's influence at work, but she'd looked so happy to see Clare. Maybe he could convince her to travel on to Vinova with her friend.

"I met your latest dispatch the other day, Captain." Lord Gramwell set the chalice down and looked at Alex sternly. "It was rather distressing to see you've learned nothing after six weeks."

Alex tried not to fidget under the ambassador's gaze; it was nearly as powerful as his own father's. "Sir, I've almost come to the conclusion that there's nothing to find. Perhaps we were mistaken in our assessment."

"Are you willing to stake your career on that?"

"Not yet," said Alex, trying to sound calm and confident. "I need a couple more weeks of scouting to be certain."

"You have one."

One? Alex fought back panic. "You mean with my next dispatch?"

Lord Gramwell shook his head. "No, Captain. I mean when Colonel Traysden arrives. The courier from Tennegol that caught up to us this morning carried this for you." He reached into his traveling jacket and pulled out a sealed note. "I have my own, but I imagine it says the same thing."

Alex cracked the seal as a cold sweat broke out over him.

> Captain Quinn,
> In light of your findings, or lack thereof, I have turned my full attention to your mission. If your fourth report, which by now has already been sent, does not contain any new information, I will leave for your position within a day, and you may expect my arrival a fortnight after that. If I deem it necessary, I will take command of the Norsari Battalion at that time.
>
> Respectfully,
> Colonel K. Traysden

Alex dropped the note and pulled a calendar toward him. If dispatches took ten days to reach Tennegol, the fourth one would've arrived seven days ago. One day to prepare and tie up necessary matters, and the Colonel would be five days into the journey south by now. No doubt he'd met the fifth report already, and he'd have the sixth in a few more days. Alex had eight or nine days before the colonel arrived. Ten if he was lucky.

Ambassador Gramwell watched him calmly. "I feel the need to remind you that Colonel Traysden handles all intelligence reports from the realm, and the issue here, though significant, is only one of his many national concerns. Your lack of progress has monopolized his attention at a dangerous time."

Alex felt like he would be sick.

"I'm on your side, Captain," said the ambassador. "I hope to the Spirit this is all a mistake and a conflict is not imminent." He stood and looked down at Alex. "But whatever your assessment of the situation, I suggest you be ready to defend it when Colonel Traysden arrives."

35

CLARE AND THE ambassador left early the next morning. It would take them the whole day to get back to the Jovan Road, where their caravan waited. Sage was saddling her friend's horse when Lord Gramwell approached. "You're still welcome to come along, Mistress Sage. I know Clare would love to have you with us."

Last night Sage had dined in the command tent with the officers and their guests. Ambassador Gramwell had invited her to travel with them to Vinova as Clare's companion. She'd politely declined the offer with a side glance at Alex, who she suspected was the source of the idea. Clare slept on a cot in Sage's tent, and in their late night talking she admitted Lieutenant Gramwell had asked her to persuade Sage to go.

"I'm afraid I have too much work to do with His Highness," she told the ambassador. "Her Majesty is depending on me to bring him up to the level he should be at."

Prince Nicholas stood behind Lord Gramwell, holding his horse's lead. He stuck his tongue out at Sage, but she kept a straight face.

"Very well," said the ambassador. "Where is my daughter now?"

"I believe she's taking care of some last-minute feminine issues, Ambassador," Sage answered, knowing very well Clare was in her tent, saying good-bye to Luke in private.

"Say no more, Mistress Sage," he said, looking uncomfortable.

A minute later Clare came walking over with Lieutenant Gramwell carrying her bag. Sage helped her friend mount her horse as Luke shook his father's hand good-bye. "I imagine Alex will send dispatches to both Tennegol and Vinova now," Sage said quietly. "I'll send my reports to you, and you can forward them to the queen. It will take longer, but I don't dare send her anything but progress reports."

"Of course," Clare said, taking the reins and looking quite comfortable sitting astride, despite its unladylike position. "I just hope you have something to actually say next time."

Sage scowled. "I did plenty of work translating. More than you."

"Well, it's not as if you have anyone else to write to," Clare said, then blushed. "I'm sorry, Sage, I didn't mean it that way."

"I know," Sage said. She didn't regret coming, and she'd never considered abandoning her mission for the queen, but if she wasn't here, Alex would be writing to her. Ironically, Sage would be communicating with him more than she did now in camp.

The ambassador had mounted and was leading the small retinue out of the camp. Clare looked down at Sage one last time. "*Bas medari*," she said, using the Casmuni phrase of greeting and farewell.

"*Bas medari*," Sage replied.

When the party had disappeared up the trail into the trees, Sage turned back, thinking to skip morning training and recover from staying up so late with Clare, sorting out the Casmuni words and phrases, and arguing over which syllables to emphasize in pronunciation. Sage was lifting the flap on her tent when she realized the assembled Norsari didn't sound like they were exercising. Curious, she headed for the open area they normally gathered on.

The men were standing at attention as Casseck called out names. When the lieutenant finished, Alex stepped forward. "Those called are excused from duties today and will report to the quartermaster for supplies. We leave at midnight."

A ripple of surprise went through the ranks. Patrols had always been made by established platoons, but the men selected had been drawn from all four. They'd also always left at dawn, so this was either a rush, or something that required the cover of darkness. Or both. Had the ambassador given the Norsari a special mission?

Alex stepped back. "Carry on," he told Casseck, who took charge. The designated soldiers fell out of formation and headed for the supply tents.

Prince Nicholas folded his arms and pouted. "I never get picked."

Sage waited until nearly noon before seeking out Henry, one of the squires whose name had been called. He was in his open tent, sorting his gear while his tent mate, the prince, sulked from where he sat mending a tear in his tunic.

"Hello, Henry," Sage called as she approached. "I heard you won't be coming today." The squire had eagerly joined the prince's lessons with her, though it was probably less for learning and more to avoid cleaning out the horse pen in the afternoons.

Henry looked up. He was the scrawniest of the four squires—about her height and weight—and she was often paired with him in sparring. "Good morning, Mistress Sage. I was just telling His Highness that these patrols are less fun than he thinks."

"He doesn't take into account how his being gone adds to my workload," said Nicholas peevishly.

"I've never been on one," Sage replied, "so I can't say." She surveyed the issued gear laid out on Henry's bedroll. "What have you got there?" she asked, pointing to a shapeless bundle.

Henry held up a long, wide strip of cloth. "I'm to make this into some kind of head scarf. Supposed to cover my face, too." He glanced at the prince. "But someone is using my needle and thread at the moment."

"Hold your horses," the prince snapped. "If you're taking the kit with you, I need to do this now."

"Or you could just borrow Harold and Elliot's," said Henry.

"Harold's using it to make his own head scarf."

Henry rolled his eyes at Sage. "Have you ever tried to argue with a prince?"

"Only every afternoon," she replied. She would've offered her own mending kit, but if the two squires were down to only one needle between them, it didn't bode well for getting hers back. "Do you know where you're going?"

"No one ever thinks to tell the squires, but they gave everyone an extra canteen and one of these." Henry held up a water sling, which was basically a large waterskin that was carried across the back.

Water was plentiful in this area, so the need to carry extra water could only mean one thing: they were going into the desert.

Into Casmun.

36

SNEAKING INTO THE company was easier than Sage had expected. Henry had been agreeable to letting her go in his place once he realized it meant he could spend several days skipping duties and catching up on sleep. Rather than her usual belted tunic and hose, Sage wore a pair of torn, discarded trousers that had just enough serviceable fabric left to tailor into something that fit her small frame. The new breeches coupled with the loose squire's tunic hid her shape rather well. She worried about standing out with the scarf wrapped around her head, but the night was cold and windy, and half the men assembled wore theirs already.

The trickiest moment came before they left. Sage was standing in her tent, loading Henry's borrowed pack, when Alex came to see her. Fortunately, he didn't just walk in like he had that first night.

"Sage?" he'd called from just outside the tent flap. "Are you dressed?"

"Yes," she said without thinking, because she *was* dressed, then she'd nearly shouted, "No, wait! Don't come in!"

The shadow of his hand dropped. "I just wanted to say good-bye."

Sage crept to the entrance. "Where are you going?"

"Just on a training patrol." He sounded tense and distracted. "It will be a longer one."

He'd never bothered to say good-bye before. She didn't know how to respond. "Be safe," she finally said.

His fingers pressed against the canvas. "I love you," he said quietly.

Sage reached out to touch the same spot, but he moved his hand. "I love you, too." She never knew if he heard her.

They forded the river and headed downstream about a mile before Alex made everyone pause and drink from their canteens before refilling them. Then he led them south, away from the water, for another couple miles until they came to where the trees ended and the sands began. By the light of the half-moon, the dunes looked black and white, the edges of the shadows sharp and distinct.

Alex turned to face the men behind him. Sage ducked behind a soldier, not wanting to chance his noticing her. "Everyone will remain vigilant and alert," he said. "If you see any sign of people, report it immediately. The area is uninhabited, but always be prepared to defend yourselves." He nodded to Lieutenant Gramwell beside him, pulled his head scarf up to protect against the sand, and turned and walked into the desert without another word.

No one spoke for the first few hours, just focused on walking in the shifting sands. By sunrise, Sage could barely tell any of the Norsari apart, they were so coated in dust and grit. Alex led them south—or at least she thought it was south—for an indeterminate distance, then turned southeast. She wondered if Alex actually knew where he was going—she certainly couldn't see any landmarks. The squires were generally ignored, except when the group stopped to rest, and they passed out provisions and refilled canteens from the "mules," large bags of water carried by some of the bigger men. By midafternoon, when they stopped to pitch tents and rest through the hottest hours of the day, Sage was feeling fairly confident she'd be able to keep up this ruse, especially if everyone always kept their heads wrapped.

Complications arose on the first night.

They'd stopped again at sunset, to rest and wait for the moon to rise so they could see where they were going. She was bedding down in the small tent she shared with Harold, the other squire, when she caught a glimpse of red-gold hair on the head next to hers. Knowing exactly who she'd find, Sage tore the scarf away from his head. "Highness!" she hissed. "What in the Spirit's name are you doing here?"

"Like you can talk." The prince wore a sleepy grin as he rolled onto his back. "Let's just say I was inspired by my admirable tutor."

"You can't be here!" she whispered furiously. "Do you have any idea what Captain Quinn will do when he finds out?"

"You didn't seem worried about the consequences."

"That's because I have no intention of getting caught." Sage punched him on the shoulder, hard.

"Ow! Neither do I." Nicholas rubbed the spot she'd hit. "Besides, what can he do? Confine us both to the camp? How is that any different from the last six weeks?"

"He can do a lot more than that."

"Then don't get caught." Nicholas shrugged and rolled to his side again, facing away from her.

If only it were that easy. Sage smacked his head for good measure and threw his scarf back at him. "You'd better wear this even in your dreams."

37

ALEX HAD TWO objectives in the desert, besides not dying.

The first was to find Casmuni and ascertain what they were doing. Estimates from last year's intrusion were approximately one hundred, so he brought forty men—handpicked from each platoon—plus Lieutenant Gramwell and two squires, figuring they could handle two-to-one odds fairly well. If the Casmuni numbered significantly more, it was better if none of the Demorans survived.

In the event the Norsari encountered no one, Alex's backup plan was to have the first few miles into the desert charted out when they returned. Then at least he'd be able to present Colonel Traysden with something tangible.

The desert had disturbingly little to map, however. There were no rock formations or permanent hills among the rolling dunes. If Alex hadn't had years of practice orienting himself by the sun and stars, the Norsari would've been completely lost by the first night. On the second morning, Alex led the group west, intending to have completed a wide triangle when he returned. He was doubly glad he'd chosen to travel on foot. Horses would've needed to drink the extra water they could've carried, and the deep sands might have caused them injury.

There were no signs of Casmuni.

The waning crescent moon rose later every night, giving them less light each time. He'd told Casseck to expect his return after the new moon, but unless the Norsari found water soon, they'd have to head back early. Alex tried to tell himself the mission wasn't a complete loss. Just the experience of traversing the sand and learning how easy it was to become disoriented and dehydrated was valuable. None of the men along would ever underestimate the desert.

The wind picked up on the third morning, and visibility was so bad Alex ordered everyone to stay put until the hottest part of the day was over, a move that also conserved water. Weeks of sleepless nights were taking their toll on him, too, but the heat made sleeping damn near impossible. He only managed an hour or two before nightmares put an end to the attempt. Instead he lay in his sweltering tent, thinking. When they broke camp, he would lead the Norsari northeast. They'd be back at the river in two days with nothing to show for it.

He needed to see her.

Casseck would make Sage's protection a priority, Alex had no doubt of that. Even so, her presence at the camp always tugged at him like a rope under strain, trying to drag him back to make sure she was all right. Now he wondered if he'd unconsciously played it safe in the last few weeks, not wanting to risk having to make the choice he always faced in his dreams. If so, he deserved his failure.

He should've told her, should've tried to explain, but doing so admitted he was unfit for duty. As long as he never said it out loud, he could hold on to the hope that it wasn't true.

Did it even matter anymore? He was about to lose his command.

There was so much sand in the air that the time of day was impossible to tell. Around sunset, the Norsari headed back toward the Kaz River, marching in the ever-deepening gloom. Every hundred yards or so Alex stopped to orient himself by the Northern Wheel. Sometimes it took a full minute to find the right stars, the dust was so thick.

Alex gave up and ordered the men to stop again and set up camp sometime around midnight. He was standing on the windward side, trying to decide if he wanted more guards on the perimeter, when he heard it: a voice carried on the wind, speaking a language he didn't recognize.

He grabbed Lieutenant Gramwell. "Do you hear that?"

Gram listened for a few seconds, then nodded. "Doesn't sound like Demoran. Two voices at least."

"Keep setting up, but post more sentries. I'm taking a squad to investigate."

"Do you want a big tent up?" The two-man tents they carried were designed to be combined into larger ones. The unspoken question was whether any "guests" Alex returned with would be held there.

Alex nodded. "Make one out of four." With so many sentries posted, there would be less need for shelter among the men.

Gramwell saluted smartly but added, "Don't get lost."

Alex returned the salute. Fear of getting lost was first in his mind, too; with the wind, tracks in the sand disappeared in a matter of minutes. He selected and briefed eight men, then signaled for them to maintain silence, though the wind appeared to be in their favor for carrying sound. Alex counted his paces, keeping one eye on the wheel to the north.

After about a quarter hour, the voices stopped for a few minutes, but then were heard again, much louder this time, definitely not speaking Demoran. Alex checked his weapons' readiness and headed toward the sound.

A voice suddenly called out. Alex stopped and looked around, catching the faint flicker of a light about thirty yards away.

"Uncover the lamp," he whispered to the man next to him, who promptly lifted the shutter on the lantern he carried. "Wave it around."

At the signal, two shapes came running toward them, at least as much as men could run in the wind and sand. Alex kept his hand on his sword but didn't draw it.

"*Wohlen Sperta!*" the man without a lantern said, reaching out to clasp arms with one of the Norsari. Too late, he and his companion realized they were not among friends.

Nine against two wasn't a fair fight, but Alex didn't care.

❖

The crescent moon was barely visible through the haze when Alex returned.

"Set a level-five perimeter," he told Gramwell. It meant fewer men to guard the captives, but the pair had obviously been searching for lost companions. They'd come running toward the Demorans without hesitation, so it was safe to assume at least ten more Casmuni were still out there.

The combined tent Gram had set up was large enough to keep a clear space around the prisoners. Alex waited for the men to be tied up. He had no way of communicating with them, and both Casmuni looked as exhausted as he felt. Alex guessed they'd been wandering alone for a long time. Once the men were secure to his satisfaction, he left the tent.

Both squires were standing outside, watching from a safe distance. The pair had avoided him for the past few days, which wasn't unusual under normal circumstances. All the boys were a little afraid of him, even the prince, but curiosity had apparently gotten the better of their fear this time. He'd had just as much awe for captains when he was their age—officers always seemed so sure of themselves. Now he knew commanders were stumbling through their duties as much as any squire, trying not to fail or get somebody killed. Alex suddenly envied the boys. Their lives and duties were so much simpler.

The prisoners would be impossible to hide from them. Alex figured it was better to let the boys see more, rather than let their imagination add details where they had none. He also knew what it was like to be in their boots, desperate to see one of their enemies for the first time—under safe conditions.

Alex smiled a little. "Get these men some water and camp biscuits," he called, jerking a thumb over his shoulder. For a few seconds, he considered supervising the encounter, but decided against it. The squires were old enough to handle themselves, and they needed the confidence boost of their captain's trust.

Also, he needed a nap.

38

SAGE ENTERED THE tent with quaking knees. Nicholas slipped in behind her, and the soldier on guard left to wait outside. Even the large tent couldn't contain the five of them comfortably. Undoubtedly the man thought the squires were fine alone with two restrained and exhausted men.

The Casmuni sat back-to-back, resting bound wrists on their legs, which were stretched out with ankles also bound. Judging from the creases in their short, robelike shirts, they'd been wearing belts, but Alex must have taken them. Sage estimated the age of the man facing her to be about thirty. A long white scar ran across the deeply tanned skin of his forehead, and black stubble of about four days' growth covered his face and neck. His hazel eyes were bright with intelligence as he studied her. She pushed her head scarf back and tugged it away to let him take in every detail of her face and hair. He sniffed a little but said nothing.

Sage took a deep breath. "*Bas medari*," she said.

The man's eyes widened. Too late she realized how ironic it was to wish a captured man "good fortune," but then the man bowed his head slightly and replied, "*Basmedar.*"

He made it sound like one word, which could be the difference between spoken and written Casmuni or three hundred years of language evolving. Or he had a sheep herder's accent or something. But he understood her. Nicholas remained silent as she'd instructed.

After water has been shared and good will established, said every document she'd studied, *then shall negotiations begin*.

Sage reached under her tunic and pulled out a small chalice, counting on its formality to distinguish it from anything the man might have already received. Turning to Nicholas, she gestured for him to fill it from his canteen. When he was done she pivoted back to the prisoner and took a slow, deliberate sip, knowing the Casmuni was watching her every move. Then she knelt and offered the cup to him.

After a long, silent moment, during which Sage's courage nearly failed her, the man licked his lips and held up his bound hands to accept the chalice. He grasped it awkwardly but brought it to his mouth and drank all the water down. Sage motioned for Nicholas to fill it again, which he did. This time the Casmuni took a deliberate sip and offered it back to the prince. "Drink it," she whispered, her voice barely carrying above the wind outside.

"I'm not stupid," he muttered, taking it and doing as she said.

The Casmuni tilted his head toward his companion behind him, who watched everything over his shoulder. Nicholas rushed to fill the cup for him.

"*Pala wohl seya*," the man before her said. *I thank you*.

"*Pala wohlen bas*," Sage replied. *I am well thanked*. She sat back on her heels and put her hand on her chest. "Sage Fowler."

"Saizsch Fahler," he said gravely, then gestured to himself. "Darit Yamon." He tipped his head to the man behind him, who had a green scarf still over his head. "Malamin Dar."

She repeated the names, and he nodded. So far, so good.

"*Sey basa tribanda?*" she asked. *Are you well accommodated?* At least that's what she hoped she said.

Darit's eyebrows shot up, the white scar disappearing into the wrinkles on his forehead, and a hint of a smile tugged at the corner of his mouth. He raised his hands. "*Palan pollay basa hastinan*."

She struggled to pick out and understand his words. *Palan* meant *my* or *mine*, *basa* was good or well. Darit was showing her his hands,

137

so *pollay* likely referred to them. She filed the word in her mind and searched for anything that sounded like *hastinan* and found *hastin*—an animal pen.

My hands are well confined.

Darit had a sense of humor. He would need it—and patience—if they were to understand each other.

"You lose your friends in the sands?" she asked.

He shook his head. "No, in the *sera*."

"*Sera?*" she asked. It was a word she didn't know.

Darit blew air out of his mouth in imitation of the wind raging outside the tent. Ah, wind. He was distinguishing that the storm had separated him from his companions, rather than the sand, which was interesting.

Sage was sure she would muddle conjugation, so she stuck to simple sentences. "Where travel you?"

The Casmuni considered the question for several seconds, then answered, "North."

"Travel you in Demora?"

Darit's expression hardened. "No, I stay in my own country."

His point was obvious, and Sage couldn't blame him for being angry. She wanted to ask more, but her time was running out. Sage gestured to Nicholas. "Give them the food."

The prince moved forward and gave them each a dry biscuit. Darit chewed his slowly, screwing up his face, plainly not impressed with the taste. When both he and Malamin had finished, Sage and Nicholas gave them more water, this time from their canteens.

As they prepared to leave, Sage paused to face Darit. "Speak nothing," she told him, putting her finger to her lips. Darit brought his eyebrows together and frowned, but she ducked out of the tent before he could speak.

39

THE WIND WAS finally dying down, thank the Spirit. Alex broke camp in the morning, wanting to get as far from where they'd found the Casmuni as possible. By sunset, the storm of sand had abated, leaving the land completely quiet other than the sounds of the marching Norsari. The silence was unnerving after going so long with the constant whistle of the wind. Alex walked near the front, close to the captives, hoping to catch their reaction if they saw or heard something. The scarred one kept looking around behind him at the column of men. Counting and assessing, no doubt. Alex would've done the same.

What he'd done nagged at him. Alex had fully expected to take prisoners when the Casmuni ventured back into Demora, and the Norsari would've been justified in doing so, but these men had been taken from their own land. It wasn't right.

Alex needed answers, though, and not just for Colonel Traysden's arrival. With so much of the army tied up in Tasmet, a force could march all the way to Tennegol virtually unchecked. If the Casmuni were working with the Kimisar, it could be the end of Demora.

How was he going to talk to these men?

Sage would be able to read the silent Casmuni like a book. Languages were one of her many strengths, too; if anyone could communicate with them, it was her. That meant bringing her into the circle of information, which until now had been him and Ash, and Alex welcomed her insight more than anyone else's. He could also finally include his officers. It was no longer a secret he had to carry alone.

Now that he had these men, however, things were also bound to get more dangerous. When Alex sent his report to the king, he would try to convince Sage to be the courier. The royal family trusted her, and it was important enough that she wasn't likely to refuse. Maybe he should send the prince as well. Uncle Raymond wanted the boy to grow up, but at some point the risk was too great.

They walked through the day and into the night until the moon rose. With its light, he felt safe enough to set up camp, and as the men had been walking for almost twenty hours straight, rest was imperative. Alex couldn't be sure of his location, but he suspected he had only another thirty or forty miles to the river.

Almost there.

40

SUNRISE WASN'T FOR another hour, and Sage swayed with weariness, but she had to talk to the Casmuni while most of the Norsari were asleep or otherwise occupied. Nicholas himself was snoring inside their low tent.

She worried how she would get the man on guard away, but the Casmuni were alone in the tent, both asleep with their hands and feet bound. "Darit," she whispered, nudging his shoulder gently.

Darit opened his eyes and blinked a few times. "Saizsch Fahler?"

"Yes," she answered in Casmuni, pulling her scarf under her chin. "Water?"

He nodded, and she gave him a sip from her canteen. Darit sat up on his elbow. "Why are you here?" he asked.

"Here with you, or here in Casmun?"

Darit smiled ironically. "Both."

Only desperation—or orders—could have driven Alex to be so reckless, but neither explanation reflected well on Demora. "I know not why in Casmun," she said. "I wish help for you. But you must first speak answers."

He studied her for a moment. "Where did you learn Casmuni speech?"

"I learn words from old treaties," she answered. "Is it well?"

Darit's eyes sparkled with amusement. "You speak like a child."

Sage grinned. "Understanding is most important."

"Yes." The humorous expression vanished. "What are your questions?"

Sage took a deep breath. "Why Casmuni come in Demora last year?"

"We did not."

"We see proof," she insisted. "Casmuni come and go ten months past."

"Close to here?" She nodded, and he shook his head. "Impossible. The desert does not allow it."

Just as the trade agreements had said. "How know I this is truth?" she pressed.

Darit's lips twisted up in a half smile. "Try to cross the sand after the solstice, and you will see for yourself."

The extra words in his answer overwhelmed her, and it took him repeating them twice for her to understand. Sage glanced around nervously. A guard could come in at any moment. "Then who come? Kimisar? Are you allies?"

A look of disgust crossed Darit's face. "Zara will grow in the desert before Casmun allies with Kimisara."

Zara had been something much traded in the documents. Sage's best guess was that it was a type of grain. "Can you prove?" she asked. "If yes, I make my friends give you freedom." It was a bold offer she wasn't likely to be able to honor, but she made it anyway.

"I have friends who can take my freedom." He leaned forward. "Many more friends than you have here."

Darit was likely part of a patrol sent from a larger group, meaning that group was probably days away, so that was a bluff, at least for now, but Sage played along. "What do you when free?" she asked.

He shrugged. "Report to my king. He has interest in your country. That is why we visit the border."

"To spy?" It was becoming easier to understand him, partly because he spoke so she could tell his carefully chosen words apart.

"To assess manners. Not so nice, I think."

Sage's mind raced. If the desert was impassable after the solstice, Darit didn't have much time to get back. "Your friends wait for your return?" she asked.

Darit must have been thinking along the same lines. "In several days.

After that I will not be able to meet or follow them." He stopped suddenly, seeming to realize he'd admitted he did not expect a rescue.

"They abandon you if late?"

The Casmuni swallowed and nodded. "Yes. They must return. The springs are fading."

"Until next year," she said, not making it a question that his friends would come back for him.

Darit looked her in the eye. "Yes. Until next year."

The Norsari coming into Casmun like this was tantamount to an act of war. Taking these men captive only made it worse. Sage had to undo the damage before Demora had a real invasion on its hands. She had to tell someone what she knew—that the Casmuni hadn't scouted into Demora and had no intention of invading. Holding these men now risked provoking the very war Alex was trying to prevent.

Sage rose to her feet, intending to go straight to Alex, but the sudden vision of trying to explain everything stopped her cold. He wouldn't listen. Not only had she spoken to the Casmuni, she'd gone behind his back for weeks—essentially spied against him, but that would all be eclipsed by the fact that she was here now. Alex would be so furious she wouldn't get ten words out. Within hours of returning to camp, she'd be on her way back to Tennegol. Going through Lieutenant Gramwell or waiting until she could plead her case to Casseck wouldn't help. At least not in time.

Darit watched as she paced, silently arguing with herself. The Casmuni king was approaching Demora cautiously, testing their "manners," as Darit said. Sage had no doubt they'd be back next year. Whether they crossed the desert with an angry army or with the intention to talk depended on the release of these men.

If they were to be freed, she would have to do it. Alone.

Sage sank to her knees in front of Darit. "Time is little," she said. "If I give you freedom, will you speak well of Demora?"

Darit looked skeptical. "Is that in your power, Saizsch Fahler? I have watched you, and you are lowest among these men."

"I act without permission."

He narrowed his eyes in suspicion. "Why would you do this?"

"This is all bad understanding," she said. "I repair mistake."

Darit struggled to sit up straight. "It will be trouble for you."

Alex's anger didn't frighten her nearly as much as the consequences of holding these men too long. Her actions would go all the way to the king himself, but at least he'd listen, especially with the queen on her side. Sage set her jaw. "I am more than you see."

"That I believe," Darit said dryly.

Sage stood again and dusted sand off her trousers. With the new moon coming, tonight would have several dark hours. She had to start planning. "I must go," she said, pulling her head scarf around her face, leaving only her eyes exposed.

He reached up for her hand with his bound ones. "Good fortune, Saizsch Fahler."

She squeezed his fingers back, trying to ignore the sick feeling in her stomach. What she planned to do bordered on treason. "Be ready."

Sage ducked out of the tent and slammed full force into Alex.

41

SAGE STUMBLED BACKWARD, but Alex caught her arm before she was fully off her feet. "Easy, kid," he said, pulling her upright.

When she was steady, he let her go. Sage cowered away from him, her mind scrambling for traction. Henry usually avoided Alex's attention, but he would've said something. "Sorry, sir," she rasped, trying to imitate the way the squire's voice had begun to crack and break.

"No harm." Alex sounded tired. "Henry, isn't it?"

She nodded, staring at the ground. Whatever she did, she could not let him see her eyes. Thank the Spirit it was still fairly dark.

"What were you doing in there, Henry?" Alex asked sternly, though he sounded slightly amused.

Sage raised the canteen so he could see it. "Giving them water," she squeaked.

"Good initiative." He patted her shoulder and moved around her to the tent where Darit and Malamin lay. Sage edged away as Alex lifted the flap to look inside. "Already asleep," he said. "They'll need it. We're marching through the night again tonight. I want to get to the river by noon tomorrow."

Sage had managed to take several steps, trying to look like a boy who really didn't want to be there right now.

Alex dropped the fabric and turned away. "Get some rest, kid."

Then he was gone.

Sage was still shaking when she reached her low tent and crawled in beside Nicholas. That had been too close, but now she knew it had to be tonight. She nudged the prince. "Harold, wake up."

Nicholas grunted and rolled away. She punched his shoulder until he rolled back. "What do you want, *Henry*?" he groaned.

"I need your help."

⌘

The Norsari broke camp an hour before dusk, Alex giving all the men a chance to sleep several hours between sentry rotations. Sage and Nicholas kept their backs to most of the activity as they packed tents, surreptitiously pouring lamp oil on the fabric before rolling it up. They couldn't risk their fire being put out before it provided the distraction they needed.

Alex stayed near the prisoners while they marched, meaning she and Nicholas would have to wait until the group stopped to rest, and he moved away from them. Sage also kept an eye on the bundle that contained the weapons Darit and Malamin had been carrying when they were captured. If she could get them to the Casmuni, she would, but it was a secondary goal.

The wind picked up, bringing a thick bank of clouds that completely covered the sky. Alex tied a strip of cloth to the top of a spear and used it to orient them, as the wind came reliably from the west. Even so, the pace was almost as slow as it had been during the sandstorm.

Maybe it was her tenseness or her inability to see the stars, but Sage began to feel like they were never going to stop, that Alex would push the men straight through the night without a break. How was Nicholas to start the fire if the gear wasn't in a pile? She wasn't willing to light up a pack if someone was wearing it, though she had to admit it would be quite the diversion.

The man in front of her stopped, and she ran into him, then was immediately crushed from behind by the prince. There were grunts and muffled thuds as everyone realized a halt had been called. No one could see anything.

"Twenty minutes to rest," Lieutenant Gramwell called.

Finally.

The squires' job now was to pass out a small ration of dried venison and fruit. Sage lit a lantern with shaking fingers and passed the flame stick to Nicholas. "Give me fifteen minutes," she whispered.

He grabbed her elbow. "Are you sure you want to do this?"

"I have to. Are you still with me?"

"Of course. Tell Darit I said good luck." He turned away and disappeared into the darkness.

Sage dug around in her ration bag until she found the wrapped packet she wanted. As she walked along the line passing out handfuls, she held the open cloth between her eyes and the lantern, keeping her face shadowed. When she got to Alex, she nearly fainted when he grabbed her leg. "Is Lieutenant Gramwell back the way you came?"

"Yes, sir," she gasped through the scarf over her mouth.

Alex hopped up from where he was sitting. "Make sure the prisoners get a bite and some water."

He was gone before she could answer. Sage stumbled away in the opposite direction, trying not to run. She reached the group at the head of the line and raised the shutter on the lantern higher, hoping to ruin their night vision. Then she continued forward, cranking the light down again. The Norsari paid her no attention as she felt around the stack of gear she knew the Casmuni weapons must be in, searching for the distinctive curved blades. Luck was with her, and she found them on the windward side of the pile, opposite of where men were stepping away from the small gathered circles to relieve themselves. She eased the wrapped bundle from under a bedroll and set it on the edge so it would look naturally placed if anyone found it. Then she set the lantern nearby and lowered the shutter almost completely.

Darit and Malamin were on the other side, and she made her way to them, keeping one eye on the dark shapes of the Norsari barely distinguishable only a few yards away. The Casmuni pair sat unmoving, and she nearly tripped over them.

"Saizsch?" Darit whispered.

"Yes," she answered. "The time is here." Sage dropped to her knees and pulled a dagger from her belt with one hand and groped around for the ropes that bound him with the other. A sudden gust of wind made several Norsari groan in frustration, the sounds providing extra cover.

"The Spirit has blessed us; I have never seen a night so black." His wrists free, Darit rubbed them and stretched his arms while Sage got to work on Malamin's bonds.

"You must hurry." She shoved her ration bag and water sling at him before scooting back to slash through the ropes on their ankles. Sage unhooked the sheath from under her tunic and slid her dagger into it before holding it out to Darit. "Your weapons are with the light, but take this also, that Demorans will know you when you return in friendship."

The phrase about returning in friendship was one she'd seen in several documents. She hoped she said the words correctly.

Darit's warm hand wrapped around hers for a second as he took the knife. "You do not need it?"

"I have another." At her waist, the worn handle of Alex's dagger dug into her ribs. Before sneaking into the mission, she'd wrapped strips of leather around both hilts to hide their distinctive gold letters.

Darit set his right hand on her right shoulder. "Go with fortune, Saizsch Fahler."

All agreements shall be sealed with the clasping of shoulders, so that sides are exposed while no weapons are in hand.

Sage placed her hand on his shoulder in return. "*Basmedar*, Darit Yamon."

42

SAGE SHUFFLED BACK to the circle of Norsari, hoping to draw any wandering eyes from the shadows now crawling around the stack of tents and bedrolls. "My lantern went out," she said. "And my flint is back down the line. Can I borrow yours, Corporal?"

Not knowing whom she was addressing, three men stood at once, patting themselves down, digging in pockets for their own flints. One was passed to her in the darkness. She took it and pretended to fumble through several unsuccessful lighting attempts. One of the soldiers nudged her. "Turn around, kid, you're in the wind."

She also didn't have anything to light, but it didn't matter. At that moment a small bonfire went up near the end of the line. Nicholas had dropped his own lantern on the oiled tents. Men shouted and ran toward the light. Those not close enough to help stood to watch their companions pull the flaming pile of gear apart and stomp on the flames, turning their back on the desert.

Keep looking. Keep looking. Keep looking.

Alex strode around the crowd, giving directions. With the wind, it took a while to get things under control. Just before the fire was extinguished, he spun around and called for everyone to arm up. "We've just announced our presence! Form a perimeter. Sergeants, account for your people and report."

The last flames went out, and the air was filled with curses as men blundered about in the sudden darkness. Every second was needed for

Darit and Malamin to get as far away as possible and for the wind to cover their tracks, so Sage tried to encourage confusion in little ways. Someone asked where the Casmuni were, and she called out that Lieutenant Gramwell had taken them. It was only a few minutes before chaos became order, even in the pitch darkness.

Alex was coming. "Who has the prisoners?" he called.

"Lieutenant Gramwell, sir," someone answered.

"No, he doesn't. I just left him."

"Henry was feeding 'em last I knew."

"Then where's Henry?" Alex said. He sounded worried.

Men called up and down the line for the missing squire.

Sage crept around the back of the pile of gear, keeping it between her and the sound of Alex's voice. The searching became more frantic.

"A torch!" Alex bellowed. "I need a torch!" A flame sparked and grew in the direction of the smoldering fire. Someone must have used the embers. A soldier came running with it.

She should have taken the cut ropes; Alex would find them as soon as he had light. Sage had to do more to slow down the discovery and chase. She turned and sprinted blindly into the desert, making messy tracks she hoped weren't in the direction the Casmuni had gone. She ran over and down several dunes until she was out of breath. Then she scaled one last hill hunched over, digging her fingers into the sand. When she came to the crest, she threw herself over the top and rolled down to the bottom of the other side and lay there, sprawled.

It was many long minutes before a glow appeared over the rise, accompanied by shouting. Sage turned her face away and closed her eyes. Hopefully she'd given Darit and Malamin another twenty minutes while the Norsari tracked her down. Now she'd give them even more time.

"Here! I found him!"

Men came running down the hill, weapons and torches held high. They spread out, some going over the next rise to set a wide defensive circle around her. The more footprints disturbing the area, the better. Alex was on his knees next to her, gently rolling her toward him and pulling the scarf away. "Henry, are you all right?"

She groaned as she turned to her back but kept her eyes shut, partly to make him think she was unconscious and partly because she didn't want to see his face when he recognized her. The hand on her shoulder froze.

"Captain, that's Mistress Fowler!" a voice gasped.

"*I know who it is!*" Alex's hands felt along her neck, head, and shoulders, checking for injuries. Sage moaned and fluttered her eyelids but kept them closed. He moved down to her arms and her ribs, then lower until he had checked her whole body. "Bleeding hell, Sage," he muttered. "What are you doing here?"

"No tracks we can follow, Captain," came a voice and the bright light of a torch. "But the wind covers everything real quick. We were lucky to find him. Her."

"Gather everyone, we're going back." Alex bent low over her and stroked her cheek. "Can you hear me, Sage? Wake up. Please."

She couldn't help opening her eyes at the note of hysteria in his voice, but the light was too bright, and she shut them again almost immediately. His face was stricken, terrified. Though she would've done it over again, the fullness of her betrayal hit her. "Alex," she mumbled.

Sweet Spirit, I'm so sorry.

"Yes, it's me. I'm taking you back." He slipped his arms under her shoulders and knees and lifted her up, cradling her against his body.

She grabbed his jacket and sobbed into his chest. *Oh, Alex, I'm so sorry.*

He held her tightly as he climbed up the dune and began the long walk back to camp. "You're safe now. I've got you. It's all right," Alex whispered.

No, it wasn't.

43

THE SUN WAS several hours above the horizon and the air stuffy with heat when she woke. Sage pried her eyes open with difficulty; they were swollen and crusted over from crying herself to sleep. She must not have even woke when Alex set her down.

Alex.

Sage lifted her head and looked around, finding him immediately. He sat cross-legged on the other side of the double tent, elbows on his knees and hands folded under his chin, watching her.

"Good morning," he said.

His tone was as dead as his face. Alex waited for her to sit up, then nodded to the bowl on the ground beside her. Sage avoided meeting his gaze as she dipped the cloth lying next to it in the warm water. He remained as still as a statue as she wiped grime from her eyes and face.

When she finished, Alex tossed a canteen across to her and went back to his silent position. Sage was so thirsty she'd been ready to drink the dingy water left in the dish, and she chugged half the contents of the canteen without taking a breath. Then she cleared her throat and wiped her mouth with the back of her hand and waited for him to speak.

"I told you to stay at the training camp," he said flatly.

"Yes, you did," she whispered.

"You disobeyed a direct order."

"Yes, I did."

"You almost got yourself killed."

Sage rubbed her nose with her knuckles and sniffed.

"Do you understand now, Sage? Do you realize this is not a game?" His voice began to rise. "Do you have *any* idea what could've happened?"

He was wrong in so many ways, but that didn't change that she'd disobeyed and deceived him. That she'd scared him out of his mind last night. He had every right to be angry. She looked down, fresh tears coming to her eyes. "Alex, I'm s—"

"Save it, Sage," he said coldly.

There was a long pause while she studied her hands in her lap.

"Guess who else I found with us?" he said finally.

Nicholas. She wondered if he had been discovered or if he'd given himself up.

"He swears he acted on his own," Alex continued. "But I find that hard to believe, given how the pair of you worked together to hide for so long. I wonder if the Casmuni would've abandoned their hostage had it been him."

Alex didn't know she and the prince were responsible for their escape. Yet.

His next words were so low she could barely hear them. "Did they hurt you?"

She shook her head. "No."

"Well, thank the Spirit for that." The relief in his voice threatened to break her.

Sage took a deep breath to stay in control. "Have you found them?"

"No, they're gone. They took their weapons and your knife." Alex rose to his feet. "And now that you're awake, we need to leave before their friends come looking for revenge." He reached for the tent flap. "Get your things together."

"Alex." He stopped and looked back at her. "I really am sorry," she said.

There were so many emotions in his eyes, she couldn't begin to separate them.

"So am I."

44

HUZAR WAS READY. The moon was waning, but every day increased the risk of being caught. They couldn't wait for a fully dark night, just the next time part of the Norsari went on patrol. He would divide his men and attack the group when they were a few miles away from the camp, forcing the rest of the soldiers to come to their assistance, and take the prince while he was relatively unguarded.

A diplomatic party was traveling down the Jovan Road, and was no threat, but it caused a delay when part of the group left the road to visit the Norsari camp. Another company of soldiers was coming south from Tennegol as well, but Huzar suspected they were headed into Tasmet. When the diplomat stayed only a day and camp activity immediately picked up, indicating a patrol, Huzar told his men to be ready. Quinn himself led the expedition, and it was larger than all the others before. Perfect. It was astonishing how quickly everything fell apart.

First, the Demoran prince disappeared. He'd never been known to go on a patrol, but the morning after Quinn left, the boy wasn't seen going to the river as he did every morning and evening. Huzar decided to wait a day, on the off chance the prince had gone along. If so, the Kimisar could attack just them, and it was better to let them get farther away in that case.

Then Quinn went into the desert. Huzar wasn't willing to follow him where there was nowhere to hide. Plans changed to attack the regular roaming detachment when it approached instead, but the prince still did not appear. By the third day, Huzar concluded the boy had gone with Quinn.

Shit.

The delay wasn't a disaster, but the Kimisar were getting anxious. Many grumbled at how the lives they'd built in Demora the past year were preferable to returning home. If Huzar dispersed them temporarily, he wasn't sure he'd get everyone back. Far be it from him to force men who had been otherwise abandoned to return, but it risked exposing them all.

Then the army company on the road turned east rather than going through the Jovan Pass. Whether it was on the way to the Norsari camp or following the diplomat didn't matter. It was close enough to change the numbers that were already against the Kimisar. The regular roaming detachment came and went. Dispersing was rapidly becoming the better option.

Huzar was one hour from giving the order when an observer from the far side of the river came running. Quinn had returned.

The roaming squad was still within reach, and the company on the road was at least two days out. The prince was spotted among the returning platoon, which looked exhausted. The night would be solidly dark with the new moon.

Now.

45

THE NORSARI GROUP made it to the river as the sun sank behind the mountains. Sentries from camp met them at the tree line and walked with them to the water, giving Alex a few updates on what had happened in his absence. It was a short list.

Colonel Traysden hadn't arrived yet, which gave Alex at least a day to explain everything to his officers and piece together what exactly had happened in the desert.

Lieutenant Casseck waited on the riverbank. Alex stepped off the row-boat and wearily returned his friend's salute. "Sergeant Carter passed through two days ago, and he'll be back probably tomorrow," Cass informed him as they walked up the hill together. "He said to tell you 'Not a ripple.'"

Ash had found nothing. Alex kept it to himself that there might be waves coming soon. He took time to clean himself up, shave, and get a bite to eat before summoning Sage, Nicholas, and the officers to the command tent. He hadn't discussed the events in the desert with anyone yet, but now he'd bring Casseck and the other lieutenants into the loop. Gramwell came in last, his shaggy bronze hair dripping onto his fresh shirt.

Sage and the prince stood at attention. Cass raised his eyebrows when Alex put them at parade rest rather than direct them to sit when the officers did. Sage was silent, her face blank. She'd also washed up and was now wearing breeches and a clean, light-brown overshirt that came to her knees. Her remaining dagger was hooked to her belt on the right side. The thought of her being dragged across the sand with her own knife to her throat made Alex sick. He didn't know what he would've done if she'd been hurt or kept as a hostage. Or maybe he did know, and he just didn't want to think about it.

Full explanation of the situation could wait until Sage and Nicholas had told their stories and were dismissed. The prince started, once again insisting Sage had nothing to do with his sneaking into the desert mission. He also asked that Harold not be punished, as the other squire had been afraid of disobeying a royal. Alex believed him but still considered Sage to be his inspiration. However, as the prince had so rarely accepted responsibility for his mistakes before now, perhaps not all her influence had been bad. Sage said little other than that she'd also acted on her own in coming along.

Alex took over the conversation then, telling Cass and the others how they stumbled across the lost Casmuni pair and held them after a brief fight. "They acted compliant until last night, when the wind blew a lantern over and set a bunch of tents and bedrolls on fire, and the Casmuni took advantage of the chaos. Mistress Fowler happened to be near them, and they managed to get her knife and free themselves—"

"That's not what happened," Sage said abruptly.

Something in her tone—or rather what it lacked—frightened him. There was no trace of emotion whatsoever. Alex frowned and sat back in his chair. "Then by all means, please describe what happened, Mistress Sage."

She raised her gray eyes to look straight at him, fully meeting his gaze for the first time in weeks.

"I cut their bonds and set them free."

46

FOR A MOMENT he was sure he hadn't heard her correctly. She *couldn't* have said what he heard, but then Casseck's and Gramwell's jaws dropped in shock. Tanner, Hatfield, and Nadira glanced at one another in confusion. The prince didn't look surprised at all.

Alex jumped to his feet. *"YOU WHAT?"*

"She wasn't alone," said Nicholas. "I set the fire as a distraction."

Alex was around the table and towering over her before he knew it. "Why in the name of everything holy would you do that?"

Defiance sparked in her pale eyes. "Because holding them was wrong."

"You don't know what you're talking about!" Alex stormed back and forth in front of her, throwing his arms out and trying to keep his voice down. "You don't have half the information I have."

"Half of your information is wrong."

She spoke with such conviction that he stopped to stare at her. "Explain."

"You think Casmun scouted into Demora, looking for a place to invade," she said. "*That* is why we're really here. You came to investigate and do some scouting of your own. To catch them in the act and find out what they're up to."

The lieutenants and Nicholas were all staring at him now.

"Except there was no one to catch," Sage continued. "You patrolled for weeks and found nothing, so you took matters into your own hands.

You were so obsessed with getting answers to the wrong questions that you invaded another country and kidnapped two men."

Her summation was harsh but completely accurate. "I'm trying to prevent a war, Sage!"

"No," she said. "You're provoking a war. *I'm* preventing one."

Before he could respond, she rushed on. "It wasn't the Casmuni who came here last year. They've never been seen in these parts after the first day of summer. The invaders also had horses, which the Casmuni have never been seen with."

Apparently she and the Ranger had discussed more than geography. "Just because something hasn't happened before, doesn't mean it can't start happening now," he said.

Sage shook her head. "The desert can't be crossed after summer because the chain of springs they have to follow dries up. Nor can they follow the river—the Yanli Gorge forbids it. If I hadn't freed those men, they would've had no chance of getting home this year. When their countrymen came to retrieve them, it would've been with an army."

"And how do you know releasing them won't bring about the same?"

She took a deep breath. "I've been studying old Casmuni trade agreements and treaties for weeks. I've come to understand what is important to them and . . . how to speak with them."

"You talked to the prisoners." He gaped at her. "In their own language."

"Yes."

Alex had thought nothing she could learn or do would astonish him anymore, but he was wrong. Part of him swelled with pride. But none of her investigating had started with what she'd observed here—she'd come prepared and with purpose. Alex turned his head to address the silent officers behind him. "Everyone but Lieutenant Casseck is to leave now."

As one, the group stood and came to attention. "You will discuss nothing of what you heard tonight," said Alex. He would handle them after he got to the bottom of this. "Dismissed." They filed out of the tent, Nicholas trailing. Casseck came to stand behind Alex, off to the side.

159

"Who are you working for, Sage?" Alex demanded.

She hesitated. "Myself. You were hiding something. I wanted to know what."

"Don't lie to me!"

Sage shrank a little, showing regret for the first time since yesterday. "Her Majesty," she whispered finally.

He couldn't decide if that was the worst or best answer she could have given. "Bleeding hell, Sage. You could be charged with treason." Alex gripped the hair at the back of his head. "Why would you agree to something like this?"

"The queen knew there was more to this mission, but the king wouldn't tell her what. He put her only son in danger and wasn't honest about it." Deeper color rushed to her sunburned cheeks, and rage flashed in her eyes. "Do you have any idea what it's like to be lied to like that? To not be trusted to know what's important?"

"I know the importance of following orders, Sage." He let that hang in the air for a long moment. "And so do you."

She looked down at her feet. "I'm not sorry for what I did, but I'm sorry it was necessary."

Alex had a sudden vision of standing before her last year, apologizing in the same way for his own deception. *I regret nothing except that you were hurt.* It had taken a long time for her to forgive him, but maybe she hadn't fully forgiven him after all.

"Pack your things," he said. "You're leaving as soon as I can figure out how."

To her credit, Sage raised her head and met his eyes. "Yes, sir."

"Dismissed."

47

MINUTES AFTER SHE was gone, Alex still couldn't breathe.

"Alex," said Casseck quietly, making him jump. He'd forgotten his friend was there. "Sending her back may not be the best idea right now. We might need her if the Casmuni return."

"No," said Alex, pivoting away.

Cass stepped around to face him. "Alex, she can talk to them. They'll trust her, and she knows much more that could help us."

"*I don't care!*" Alex roared.

"Be honest with yourself! She wouldn't have done this if you hadn't been pushing her away for weeks. She knew you wouldn't have listened."

"Whose side are you on, Lieutenant?"

"Your side, dammit! But you aren't even on your side right now." Casseck grabbed his shoulders. "What is this really about, Alex?"

The memory of rolling the limp body toward him, realizing it was her, thinking for a split second that she was dead. Carrying her back as she sobbed into his chest and swearing to himself he would revisit the Casmuni with a hundredfold of what they'd done to her.

He should have done whatever was necessary to keep her from coming, just as he never should've let her attempt to escape Tegann last year. Everything was compromised, like it had been that night.

It wasn't about her lying. It wasn't about her betrayal. It was about him, what she did to him.

Alex looked up at his oldest friend. "I can't have her here, Cass. I can't," he whispered.

Realization dawned on Casseck's face. "This is about Tegann, isn't it?"

"You were there, Cass. I thought she was dead, and you saw what it did to me." Tears flooded his eyes.

Casseck shook his head. "Anyone would've broken in that situation—"

"But I'm not just anyone, am I?" Alex flung Casseck's arms away. "What if I'd thought she was alive? What if instead of tossing that damn bloody knife at me and letting me draw my own conclusion, D'Amiran made me think she was being tortured or taken to his bedchamber for his own special revenge? What *should* I have done? Nothing. Leaving her there would've been the right thing to do. And I wouldn't have been able to do it."

"Alex—"

"I would've gotten everyone—you, Gram, everyone else—killed. I would've lost a war. Over her."

Alex sank to his knees and pressed his palms into his eyes. "How can I be fit for shoveling shit, let alone command," he whispered, "when I know I'd let every one of you die if she was in trouble?"

He'd finally said it out loud. Because it was the truth.

Cass knelt in front of him. "Alex," he said quietly. "It's not weakness to love someone that much."

"Then what is it?" Alex sobbed.

"I don't know." Cass pulled Alex's head into his shoulder, holding him tightly as he wept. "But it's not weak."

48

NICHOLAS WAS WAITING in Sage's tent, reading through her Casmuni notes by candlelight when she returned. She raised an eyebrow at him. "Just because you're a prince doesn't give you the right to go through my things, Highness."

He looked up. "Nicholas."

She frowned. "What?"

"After what we've been through, I think you've earned the right to call me by my given name." He shifted to face her. "I also owe you an apology. I never acted like it, but Mother told me to follow your instructions as if they were her own. I never understood why until now."

"None of that matters anymore." Sage dropped wearily onto her cot. "The captain is sending me back. You, too, probably."

"How can he do that?" the prince said, sweeping his hand over her ledger. "Doesn't he know what you have here?"

Sage looked down at her hands. "It's more complicated than that. I've broken a dozen promises, and I undermined him as a leader in front of everyone. No apology will ever be enough. Frankly, I don't deserve his forgiveness."

"He still loves you, you know."

She glanced up in surprise. "You know about us?"

"Everyone knows, Sage." Nicholas grinned impishly. "Well, maybe not *everyone*. Just those of us with eyes."

Sage smiled a little before shaking her head. "I'm not sure love is enough to fix this."

"You didn't do any of it to hurt him. If he can't see that, he's an idiot. I'll tell him that, if you like."

She snorted. "I'll pass."

"It's an open-ended offer, so let me know if you change your mind." Nicholas stood and stretched. "With that, I think I'll go to bed. Never thought I'd look forward to sleeping on dirt and grass again. I've got sand in places I can't explain."

"Nicholas." She waited for him to pause. "Thanks. For everything."

He saluted her. "Good night, Mistress Sage."

When the prince was gone, Sage dragged herself to the table and sat staring at her ledger. She'd leave it for Alex. He wouldn't be too proud to use the information. After several minutes of leafing through pages, unable to focus on any of the words, she flipped the book shut. The small trunk at her feet was open, and Sage leaned down and shifted the contents around until she found what she wanted.

She hadn't taken the letter on the desert journey, not wanting to risk ruining it. Now she spread it out beneath the candle and read the words she'd missed, but this time they only spoke of something she'd lost, perhaps forever.

> During the day I miss your laughter and your wit and your
> smiles and the sharpness of your mind. In the evenings
> I think more of your kisses, sighs, and understanding ways.
> Then some nights I lie awake consumed with thoughts of
> the day I can love you in every way. On nights like this,
> my hunger for you overwhelms me. I can dwell for hours
> on the taste of your mouth and the scent of your hair and
> the touch of your skin.

"Sage?" came a voice from outside the tent. "It's Cass. Can we talk?"

She folded the letter and shoved it in the ledger, then wiped her eyes. "Yes, come in."

Casseck ducked inside and hunched over comically, his blond hair brushing the ceiling. He gestured to her cot. "Mind if I sit?"

"Go ahead."

Casseck eased down onto the bed and folded his hands awkwardly. "How are you?"

"I've been better."

He smiled sheepishly. "Haven't we all."

"Did Alex send you?"

"No, he's asleep. He'd probably be furious if he knew I was here." Cass stared at the ground. "Look, Sage, I'm not going to take a side in this. You've hurt him pretty bad, but I know you wouldn't have done what you did without a damn good reason. He's just not been thinking clearly lately. I think you should know why."

"I'm listening."

"Do you know what happened at Tegann after the night you escaped?"

"Clare said everyone thought I'd been caught."

"That was later in the day, Sage. For the first couple hours, Alex thought you were dead." Casseck took a deep breath. "You don't know what it did to him. I've been his friend for twelve years, and I'd never seen him lose control, not like that."

Sage had. She'd held Alex as he cried over Charlie's death through the night, wiping his face after every time he was sick. Had he been like that over her?

She looked into Casseck's eyes and realized that was exactly what had happened.

"But then we learned you might actually be alive," Cass continued. "We started everything early, though it was riskier. Alex searched the whole keep for you. By the time he got to the duke's rooms, they were the only place left you could've been."

Sage felt all the blood drain from her face. Alex, climbing down a rope from the top of the keep and kicking in the window, knowing Charlie was in there and suspecting she was, too.

"He thinks I don't know, but he has nightmares all the time," Cass whispered. "Especially since seeing you again. It wasn't until today that I realized what they were about."

But Sage understood. "They're about choosing between me and Charlie."

Casseck nodded. "And choosing between you and me. Or you and any of the men he commands."

Alex hadn't tried to stop her from coming, confined her to the camp, and kept her at arm's length to protect *her*, he was trying to protect *himself*. She'd been too wrapped up in using her own mission to get back at him for last year to see it. But then, as now, it wasn't about trust. It was about the one threat to Alex's ability to lead men into death.

Her.

And then she'd snuck into the desert mission and made his worst nightmare into reality.

Sweet Spirit, what had she done?

"I have to go," she whispered. "It's the only way he can do his job."

"Maybe, yes, but I also think we need you now." Cass shook his head in disbelief. "Did you really learn to speak Casmuni?"

Sage smiled weakly. "Not well. Just enough to be understood."

"Still impressive."

"Thanks." She twisted her hands in her lap. "Cass, are we broken beyond repair?"

Casseck sighed. "I don't know. If it weren't for Charlie, I'd say you two could get through this, but—" He broke off, cocking his head to the side.

She heard it, too. Shouting. People calling for arms. There was growing light outside the tent walls. Sage leapt to her feet the same time Cass did, and when he ducked to keep from hitting the ceiling, their heads nearly collided. She let him run out ahead of her and skidded to a halt behind him when he stopped.

Henry went running past and Casseck grabbed his arm. "What's going on?"

"We just got a runner from Sergeant Carter, sir," the squire said. "He's engaged a hostile force about a mile east of here. Captain's called every-one to march."

Alex was striding around several yards away, wearing light armor and buckling his sword belt as he shouted orders.

"Casmuni?" said Casseck.

"No," said Sage and Henry at the same time. "Kimisar."

49

NICHOLAS JOGGED TOWARD Alex through the chaos, leading Surry, already saddled and wearing her armored breastplate. "I have your horse, sir!" he called. "The other squires are getting the rest for the lieutenants."

As soon as the prince was close enough, Alex put a hand on his shoulder and used it to help him mount. Nicholas handed him the reins and saluted before running off again. From Surry's back, Alex surveyed the activity with satisfaction. Organization was taking over; the Norsari were forming into lines and the rest of the officers would be mounted within a few minutes. He found Sage weaving through the ranks with a makeshift oxbow on her shoulders, balancing two buckets of water on either side from which men were taking last-minute drinks. Good thinking.

Units were calling out their readiness, and Casseck came trotting up to him on his own dun-colored stallion. "All ready and accounted for, sir!"

"Fourth platoon will stay behind to guard the camp," Alex said. "Have them spread out along the perimeter." Cass passed the order, and Lieutenant Gramwell's men fell out, most frowning in disappointment, though Gram looked exhausted and relieved.

The night was pitch black with no moon. "Have the squad leaders get torches," Alex ordered. "We'll need all the light we can carry if we're going to get there in time." Three precious minutes went by. When Casseck signaled they were ready, Alex didn't hesitate. "Move out!" he bellowed.

The first platoon plunged into the woods, following the wide path along the river. Alex swung Surry around to look for Sage again. She stood watching on the other side of the marchers. Their eyes met.

"Stay here," he mouthed across the stream of men between them before turning and kicking his horse into a run.

◈

The Norsari ran at a trot, making good time on the path, and they reached the area of fighting in about a quarter hour. Ash and the Ranger squad stood in a semicircle, facing the forest with their backs to the river. Several held low-burning torches.

"Thank the Spirit," Ash said, rushing up to Alex as the Norsari poured around them, taking a defensive stance. "We're outnumbered, and they've been coming at us in waves, pushing us back. We had nowhere left to retreat."

Alex looked around at the disheveled and sweaty men. "What are your casualties?"

"None," said Ash, shaking his head in disbelief. "I know we dealt a few, but it's like they were more interested in moving us than fighting us."

The runner had said the attackers were Kimisar, but what Ash said made more sense if they were Casmuni, trying to get back to the river or to make way for someone crossing it. Alex shook his head in confusion. What the hell was going on?

"Here they come!"

Men appeared out of the trees, dressed in Demoran-style clothing. They ran at the Norsari formation, and then, seeing the increase in numbers, slowed down and began to back off. Many turned and fled. "After them!" Alex shouted.

The Demorans pursued the attackers through the woods, clashing occasionally, but it was mostly a chase. Alex couldn't get a solid count on the numbers he was fighting, but the weapons he saw bore no resemblance to the light, curved swords he'd taken from the Casmuni. The Norsari leapfrogged through the trees, passing the torches to keep them in the third ranks so the first two could always see, but their prey kept moving out of the light.

169

Something was wrong, he could feel it.

Ash's men were bringing up the rear, and Alex dropped back to talk to them. "Who are they?" he asked Ash.

"I heard Kimisar words being thrown around, but also Demoran."

"Where the hell did they come from?"

Ash jerked a thumb behind him. "Corporal Wilder's got a theory."

"Yes, sir." A man took a few running steps forward. "I heard a bunch of Kimisar came through Jovan last year, before it was closed up by the army. They raided some and disappeared. I guess with the war on the other side of the mountains, everyone forgot."

The idea of Kimisar hiding in Demora for months was chilling. Could they have been trying to escape into Casmun last year?

And what the hell was this about? Showing up and pushing methodically to the river only to fall back in the same manner? These men seemed intent only on getting and keeping the Norsari's attention.

He hadn't seen a single casualty, nor had he seen the oft-used Kimisar tactic of taking and retreating with hostages.

It was a diversion.

Before Alex could say anything, a bright orange fire suddenly lit up the sky in the direction of the Norsari camp.

The Kimisar *were* after a hostage.

Nicholas.

50

THE NORSARI WERE gone with a swiftness that left Sage in awe, even after spending weeks with them. Lieutenant Gramwell, whom Alex had ordered to stay behind, dismounted and directed the remaining platoon to take defensive positions. He looked fatigued, and Sage knew many of those who'd marched had just returned from the desert, yet none had hesitated, including Alex.

In addition to Gramwell's men, a half-dozen soldiers had remained due to some injury. The lieutenant instructed them to clean up the mess left behind in the rush to arms—weapons racks and crates were overturned and a few tents were down. Fires had been scattered, and several soldiers were assigned to make sure all were out or contained. The remaining horses were skittish in their pens, and Gram handed his mount off to a squire and ordered him to saddle a few more horses in case they were needed.

Sage shrugged the quarterstaff off her shoulders and set the now-empty buckets on the ground. "What can I do?" she asked him as she rubbed her neck.

Lieutenant Gramwell looked at her warily, and she didn't blame him for not quite trusting her now. Finally he said, "There will be wounded. Go ready things in the medical tent."

Sage wouldn't have argued if he'd told her to dig a fresh latrine, but this sounded truly helpful. "Right away, sir."

The deserted army camp was an eerie place. Sage shivered and fingered the knife on her belt as she walked between the rows. She hadn't realized how much noise and activity still went on even in the quietest hours until there was none. A low fire burned in a pit outside the medical and supply tents, and she paused to find and light a lantern before entering the infirmary.

She hung the light from a hook inside and began opening trunks and laying things out on the tables: bandages, witch hazel, tourniquets, suture needles, thread, splints. She was setting out basins for water when the shadow of someone running past her tent made her look up. Whoever it was stopped near the entrance, but didn't come in.

"I'm in here," she called, thinking he must be looking for her.

A hand holding a long dagger pushed through the tent flap, followed by a scruffy, gap-toothed man. Sage knew all the Norsari by sight, and this face was not one of them, yet it was familiar. "Who are you?" she asked, taking a step back.

Somewhere outside there was shouting. The man waved the knife and advanced on her. "You will come with me," he said in a harsh voice.

In the better light she recognized the style of his cloak and the royal crest on his collar identifying him as a stablehand. That was where she'd seen him.

"I said come!"

Sage seized a porcelain bowl with her right hand and flung it at the man's wrist, immediately following with one from her left aimed at his head. The dagger went flying from his hand, and the second missile hit his skull with a satisfying *thunk*. She was already hurling more things at him—scissors, bedpans, wads of dressing—anything she could get her hands on, but she was running out of things to throw.

With a yell, he lunged for her as she kicked a trunk of medicines between them, knocking his feet out from under him. He fell forward, hitting the tent pole. Sage dove under a table just as the structure came down around them. She scrambled for the side of the tent and crawled under the edge. Once outside, she rolled away and into a crouch, one hand on the hilt of her dagger.

The man was thrashing wildly under the canvas, screaming. A moment

172

later Sage realized why—the lantern had also fallen and set the tent on fire. The noise was bound to draw his friends to the area. Snatching an iron skillet from the rack behind her, she sprinted at the flaming lump and slammed it down on what she thought was the man's head. With a loud *crack* the lump flattened and was silent.

Sage dropped the pan and drew her dagger as she turned in a quick circle, looking around. The area was deserted. Light and noise were coming from the other side of the camp, and she ran toward it, knife in hand.

51

A SMALL OPEN area was lit by several torches. About thirty men surrounded a dozen Norsari and three squires, holding them at sword and spear point. Half the Demorans were still armed, if only with knives. Lieutenant Gramwell stood among them, blood streaming down the side of his face. Sage hid behind a tent to watch as six more bleeding and limping Norsari were tossed into the cluster of Demorans. They must have been some of those standing guard.

"Where is the last boy?" someone said.

"Lenis and Ullya are looking," another answered.

"We only need the prince." A tall, cloaked man pushed through the Kimisar and addressed the Demorans. Sage caught a glimpse of arms tattooed with swirls that looked strangely familiar. "Give him to us."

In response, the Norsari formed a tight circle around the three squires. "Come and take him," one said.

Some of the Kimisar looked ready to accept the challenge. Their leader held up a hand. "We will not harm him," the man said. "You have my word."

A couple of the Norsari spat on the ground to show what they thought of his promise, but Sage had already seen enough to know Nicholas was not among the three boys in the middle. They must have hidden him somewhere or gotten him out of the camp. There was nothing she could do against so many, but she needed to get to Alex and tell him what was happening. She backed away and skirted around the circle of light and to the closest pen. Over the backs of several horses prancing around in nervousness, she spotted one that was saddled.

The gate was on the far side, so Sage sheathed her knife and pried one of the top rails from its post and dragged it aside. On the second rail she only got one side down before the anxious horses began to make for the gap. She smacked the nearest one on the rump and sent it flying out. Others followed, and Sage waited for several to pass before darting into the pen to get to the saddled one. She had her hands on the reins and one foot in a stirrup when something swept her other foot out from under her and dumped her on the ground. The sharp point of a halberd was shoved into her face.

"Sage!" gasped Nicholas. He pulled the weapon back and grabbed the horse's lead to keep it from running off, then helped her to her feet, whispering urgently. "They're after me. Lieutenant Gramwell told me to make a run for it, but then I heard what was going on. I can't just leave them!"

"You can and you will," she said. "They're making a stand so you can get away—we can't waste it." The loose horses would hopefully cause a diversion and break up the crowd surrounding the Norsari. "Get on the horse."

"Come with me, Sage," Nicholas begged. "Please."

Combined, the two of them probably only weighed as much as a fully armed soldier. "All right," she agreed. Sage pointed to the staff in his hand with its small ax and hook under the spear tip. "Is that all you have?"

Nicholas nodded. "It's all I could find in the dark, and even it's broken." He held up the lower end so she could see the last couple feet had splintered off, making the weapon only as tall as him.

"It's better than nothing," Sage said. "You swing it, and I'll drive." The horse was saddled for someone much taller, and she mounted with difficulty. Once she was upright, she took the halberd so Nicholas could get up behind her. Then she swung the horse around, an idea taking shape. Her boot slipped out of the too-long stirrup when she gave the horse a kick, and she had to clamp down hard with her thighs to stay on. They sprinted through the camp, heading for the fire she prayed was still burning at the medical tent.

175

Luck was with her again; the fire was still going and had spread to the supply tent next to it. Sage nudged the horse around, squinting through the smoke for what she wanted. There—and close enough that it might work. She had to hurry—it sounded like they'd been spotted.

"What are you doing?" said Nicholas. "We need to go!"

"Calling for help." Sage directed the horse to back up against a short stack of casks containing lamp oil. "Make him buck, Nicholas."

"What?"

"Poke him in the ass and make him kick, dammit!"

Nicholas swung the halberd around, and the horse whinnied and bucked, breaking at least one of the small barrels open and sending several flying. Sage barely managed to stay on as the prince whiplashed into her from the movement. She caught a glimpse of men rushing at them, bows raised. Then she and Nicholas were flying out of the camp and into the night, the orange glow of a raging fire lighting up the sky behind them.

52

THEY MADE IT through a brief shower of arrows, but Sage and Nicholas were less than two hundred yards out of the camp when the horse suddenly reared up, screaming. As Sage clutched the mane to stay on, the prince slipped off the back with a cry and then a grunt as he hit the ground. The horse went back to all fours, and Sage urged it forward, yanking the reins around to keep it from trampling Nicholas. "Are you all right?" she called, searching for what had spooked the horse.

"I think so," he answered. "But the horse was hit."

Sage felt around on the side the horse was favoring until she found the arrow buried in its thigh. How deep it went she couldn't tell—the shaft had been broken off by Nicholas's tumble. Hot blood spilled over her hand as she tried to get a grip on it enough to pull it out. The horse screamed again, its hind leg buckling. Sage threw her leg over the withers and dismounted, trying to soothe the beast with gentle words. She reached for the arrow again, but now her angle on it was even worse.

"We've lost our ride," she told Nicholas. "And they'll be on us in another minute. Can you run?"

"I think so." The shadow that was the prince lurched to its feet. "Ow. I think my wrist is broken or sprained."

"We'll deal with it later. I'm just glad it wasn't an ankle."

Nicholas wobbled a little. "Yes, well, now that I'm standing my knee doesn't feel so great, either."

Sage looked back at the fire that was probably consuming all the

Norsari's supplies. She felt bad about that, but it would definitely serve its purpose. "Captain Quinn will be here soon. We have to stay hidden until then."

The halberd lay on the ground, its staff broken again so now it was as short as an ax. Sage picked it up and jabbed it at the limping horse to urge it farther down the river path. Then she pulled Nicholas's arm over her shoulder and helped him into the woods. After a few uphill yards she set him down and went back to cover their tracks as best she could. Not a moment too soon she dodged off the path as three men came running down it. They carried no torches, and they missed any signs that were left and continued past her. It wouldn't be long before they caught up with the wounded horse.

Sage crawled back to Nicholas. "Give me your wrist." The prince held out his left arm, and she gently felt along it. No bones sticking out, but it was swelling rapidly so it was difficult to tell. Nicholas whimpered, and she whispered an apology. "How's the knee?" she asked.

"Better now. I can probably run."

"Not yet."

The sound of weapons clashing came from the east, in the direction help should come from. Half a minute later the noise ceased. Sage put a finger to Nicholas's lips and closed her eyes to concentrate on listening. A horse was coming toward them—an unwounded one. *Spirit above, please be who I think you are.*

Light from the distant fire reflected off a drawn sword. The rider was moving swiftly but cautiously, and her eyes had adjusted enough to recognize the dark form through the trees. Sage stood and ran down the hill before he could pass. "Alex!"

"Sage?" The relief in his voice was too much, and she cried as she threw herself at him after he dismounted. He felt her all over. "Are you all right?"

"Yes, I'm fine," she sobbed. "Nicholas is, too. We're all right." She was babbling now.

"Your arm is covered with blood."

"It's the horse's," she explained, trying to bring herself back under control.

"I found that horse. Several Kimisar, too."

"There's more back at camp," she said. "They're after the prince."

"How many?"

"Couple dozen, sir," answered Nicholas, sliding down the hill behind her. "At least."

"Cass is a few minutes behind me, bringing a platoon. I came ahead." He still held her with his free arm. Sage leaned into him, savoring the closeness. Alex was here. Everything would be all right now. "Did you set that fire?" he asked, looking down at her.

"Yes."

"Good job."

There was genuine pride in his voice. "Alex," she began. "About everything—"

"Not now, Sage." The heat of his body vanished as he released her, but at least he didn't sound angry. "They're coming at us from all sides. I need to get the two of you out of here."

"Where?"

"The river," said Nicholas. "The boat isn't far from here."

Alex nodded. "Good idea." He handed his horse's lead to Sage. "I go first. You stay back in case I run into someone."

They made their way back down the path quickly, Nicholas grunting a little from keeping up. Apparently his knee was worse than he'd thought. The boat was easy to find in the firelight reflecting off the river, but it was in plain sight from the camp. It wouldn't be long before someone saw them.

"Get in." Alex jammed his sword in the soft ground to free his hand and began untying the rope. "It's dark and smoky. Just lie low and let the current take you."

He wasn't coming with them. Sage tried not to panic. "Where should we stop?"

"Use your judgment. Better too far than too close, though."

179

Nicholas tossed the broken halberd in the boat and clambered in. Sage waited until he was seated before climbing in behind him. Shouts echoing from the forest and camp told her they'd been spotted. The rope came loose, and Alex tossed it in the boat. When he reached for the bow to push it into the current, she placed her hands on top of his.

"Alex."

He looked up into her eyes. There was fear, but all for her and none for himself. Alex shoved the boat out into the water as shadows bearing weapons came running down the slope behind him. At the last second he lifted a hand to her neck and pulled her face to his, kissing her desperately. Her free hand slipped around his neck and gripped his hair, and then she was sliding away with the momentum of the boat.

"Go," he whispered.

She nearly fell out reaching for him, but the prince pulled her back by her belt. Alex waded up the bank to Surry and pulled his sword from the ground. Quickly, he mounted and turned to face the men closing in.

Smoke over the water enveloped them, but Alex was still visible. Sage clutched the sides of the boat as it reached the center of the river and picked up speed, carrying them deeper into the haze as the number of Kimisar around him grew. To her right, downriver, Norsari approached on foot, Casseck in the lead on his stallion, but she didn't know if Alex could hold out that long. The boat turned with the current, and she lurched to the other side to keep from losing sight of him.

Alex's sword flashed, but now Casseck was almost there. Sage raised up to her knees, straining to see as the boat began to pass around a bend.

The last thing she saw was Alex tumbling backward and off his horse, an arrow buried halfway into his chest.

53

ALEX HIT THE ground hard, but he'd had enough practice throwing himself off a horse's back that he knew how to land without breaking anything. Surry responded to his sudden shift in weight by stepping to the opposite side, clearing an area on the ground. Within seconds he was on his feet, his back pressed into the mare's flank. Mounting the horse had been stupid—it made him a clear target, but thankfully he'd seen the archer in the trees in time. A dozen Norsari ran onto the beach, cutting their way through the Kimisar.

He waved to his friend, and Cass grinned in relief, having seen him fall. They fought their way to each other as waves of soldiers poured into the fight. At some signal Alex couldn't see or hear, the Kimisar turned as one and scattered into the woods.

Casseck trotted up to him, shaking sweat from the blond hair matted to his scalp. "I think it's over. From what I saw before we left, they're running out there, too."

"It was all a diversion to get Nicholas," said Alex. "I found him and Sage and put them on the boat and sent them down the river. We'll go find them at first light."

Cass nodded, and then grinned wryly and pointed at Alex. "You are the luckiest son of a bitch I've ever seen."

Alex lifted his right arm to see what his friend was talking about. An arrow dangled from his jacket, the head jammed into a metal ring in the leather below the armpit.

"Impressive, though I doubt he was aiming for that spot." Alex bent the shaft and broke it off, tossed the fletching aside, and reached for Surry's reins so he could remount. "Come on," he said. "We've got a mess to clean up."

∞⟡∞

Alex held the torch high and kicked charred canvas aside, looking for survivors and the supplies he would need in tracking Sage and Nicholas down. They'd found six bodies so far, not counting two by the river, but none were Demoran. Confident as he was in his Norsari, it struck him as strange. It was as if the Kimisar had *avoided* killing.

A glimpse of fabric made him stop. Bending over, Alex pulled out an undergarment that could only have been Sage's. A flush crept up his neck as he glanced around, verifying he was in the spot her tent had stood. He pushed the tarp aside and inventoried her things. There wasn't much—she'd traveled lightly. Alex pried up the table and found her open trunk and an untitled leather-bound ledger. Curious, he picked up the book and opened it.

Pages and pages of her handwriting in Demoran, Kimisar, and a language he didn't understand, phrases circled and underlined, notes in the margin. After that, it was words and phrases in Demoran and the third language paired up, with comments on grammar. Then she'd moved on to attempts to build her own sentences. *I've been studying old Casmuni trade agreements and treaties for weeks.* He'd believed her when she said it, but seeing her work was something else entirely. It was brilliant.

One last section contained a dated account of all Sage had learned and observed as well as some of her conclusions. Corporal Wilder in particular had been a wealth of information. Though it contained nothing personal, he could sense her increasing frustration. The last entries were written during the desert mission.

Darit and Malamin had been the names of the Casmuni he'd captured. She and Nicholas had "shared water" with them and talked. The desert men said they lost their companions in the sandstorm, and while they were headed for the border, they were adamant that they had not and never would cross it. There were no more notes after that.

Under the back cover was a folded piece of parchment that looked like a letter. Alex opened it to find one of his own to her from months ago. He remembered this one, remembered panicking the moment the dispatch left with it, because he'd written it in the throes of longing, and surely his words would be too much for her. When she'd never mentioned it, he'd assumed it was lost.

The worn creases told him it had not only been read, but read often.

> In 812 days I will hold you to your promise to be mine. In most cases you are the stubborn one, but on this I refuse to negotiate, for nothing is more vital to my survival, you must understand. And when I say over and over how I want you to be mine, it is only because I am already completely yours.

Fresh tearstains smeared the ink. She'd been reading it last night.

Alex shoved the book and letter into his jacket and called for Casseck to gather three squads of volunteers. Sunrise was over an hour away, but he wasn't waiting for it.

54

THE SOUNDS OF battle had died away long ago. Sage kept her head low, clutching the sides of the boat as it rocked and fishtailed in the current. The image of the arrow striking Alex in the chest, of him tumbling backward, played over and over in her mind.

Alex was dead.

Maybe he could survive the wound. Maybe the arrow hadn't struck his heart, maybe it had missed vital organs.

But she'd seen how far it had gone in—halfway *through* him, meaning it had slipped between the ribs. If his heart was pierced, he would bleed out, or worse, bleed into his lungs, and he would drown in his own blood. If only the lung was hit, breathing would become impossible as it collapsed.

It all ended the same, with him dying, gasping and alone, as his enemies closed around him. Without knowing that she understood. That she was sorry. That she loved him.

Somehow the tears wouldn't come.

She had no concept of time until the river of the stars faded with dawn's approach. Nicholas was curled into a ball in the bottom of the boat, dozing restlessly, his swollen hand cradled to his chest. The wrist needed to be bandaged, but she let him sleep. As soon as there was enough daylight, they'd find a place to go ashore and camp to wait for Alex to find them.

Reality punched her in the chest.

No. Alex would never come for them. And Casseck and the others wouldn't even know where to search, but the Kimisar might. She and Nicholas were on their own.

She gazed down on the sleeping boy at her feet. Alex had died for his prince. If necessary, she would do no less.

⤟✦⤞

Nicholas squatted by the fire and warmed his hands as Sage searched the riverbank for smooth stones. She pocketed over a dozen and headed back to the prince. "Are you hungry, Nicholas?"

"Aren't I always?" he said with a weak attempt at humor.

She tried to smile back, but she couldn't. "We'll stay here until they find us. We can forage until then."

"I don't have anything but the halberd and my knife," Nicholas said apologetically.

"That's all right, I have my sling. Fancy some squirrel?" Other than some flint and wadding, the sling was the only thing she'd had in her belt's pouch. Sage laced the knotted leather strips between her fingers and pulled a stone from her pocket. "I'll be right back."

Sage stepped into the trees and returned ten minutes later with a black squirrel and tossed it at Nicholas's feet. "Skin it, and get it on the spit. I'll go find a couple more."

As she turned back to the forest, a shout came from across the river.

Nicholas dropped the squirrel and jumped to his feet. "They're here!" He waved his uninjured hand in greeting.

Sage lunged at Nicholas's raised arm. "Wait!" She looked around. They were too exposed, but she hadn't wanted to stray far from the boat, as it would be both a beacon to the Norsari and the fastest means of escape, should they need it.

Two men stood on the opposite shore, pointing to them. Three more men appeared upstream. Weapons came out.

"I don't recognize any of them," said Nicholas.

Sage scooped up the halberd and shoved the prince toward the boat. "Run!"

55

"THEY ARE GETTING back on the river, Captain!"

Huzar burst out of the trees just as the two boys pushed the boat off the opposite shore and jumped in. Damn.

Everything had gone as planned until the fire started. Suddenly there were horses everywhere, and someone saw the prince and another boy riding away. Sometime during the pursuit, Quinn appeared and put the prince and his companion on a boat and sent them downriver.

Then the Norsari arrived, and Huzar ordered his men to fall back. Once he understood where the prince had gone, Huzar left without waiting for the full casualty report. None of it would have been in vain if he could get to the boy before the Demorans.

The Kimisar captain led his squad along the river, following as swiftly as they could, catching occasional glimpses of the boat through the trees.

Another squire was with the prince, which was good. Huzar wasn't about harming children, and an extra hostage could be handy. The boy could be sent back to Quinn, where he could explain how the Kimisar had been stranded and that they only wanted to go home.

Huzar had left the Norsari in chaos, but they couldn't be far behind, and there were more soldiers on the road, maybe a day away. The Kimisar were outnumbered and cornered. There was no going back now, no more chances to hide. If Huzar couldn't capture the prince and force Quinn to listen, it was only a matter of time before all his men were dead.

Downstream, the river bent in a U, and if they hurried, the Kimisar could get ahead of the boat. In his excitement, Huzar shouted orders in his own language as he ran.

Several of his men spread out on the bank, waiting for the boat to come around. One put an arrow to the string as the boat came into view.

No!

Huzar called to the archer not to shoot. His second-in-command held the bow taut as he looked back at him, obviously disagreeing. It had been he who ordered the Kimisar to aim at the prince last night as he fled on horseback, and Huzar had been furious. They were lucky the boy hadn't been hit.

From the corner of his eye, Huzar saw the other squire stand up in the boat and wave his arm in a tight circle. Too late, Huzar realized what he was doing and shouted a warning. His second looked back at the boat just as a rock smashed into his face. The half-drawn arrow released, arcing weakly into the water, well short of the now-dead man's intended target.

With a start, Huzar recognized the boy with the sling.

And he was no boy.

56

SAGE DROPPED BACK into the boat and lay flat. They may not have wanted to shoot her before—she'd heard a shout from somewhere that made the man with the bow hold his aim—but they probably wouldn't hesitate now. A splash in the water nearby made her peek up. A man was swimming toward the boat.

No, two men. Fear of archers vanished.

"Grab the oar!" she yelled to Nicholas. "Hit him when he comes close!" The river was deep and the rocks at the bottom were slippery. As long as the men were in the water, she had the advantage.

The two men shouted a count to each other before lunging from opposite sides at the same time so the boat wouldn't capsize. Nicholas stood up on his knees, awkwardly swinging the oar around with his one good hand, and brought it straight down on the man closest to him. He lost his balance and fell back in the boat.

Sage jabbed her own oar at the other man like a short spear. He grunted but held on. Flipping the oar over, she slammed it down on his fingers. One hand slipped but the other kept its hold. She dropped the oar to draw her dagger from her belt and stabbed his other hand. His fingers splayed out, releasing his grip, but he was pinned to the side of the boat. Sage wrenched the knife free, and he slipped into the water with a garbled cry.

The boat listed violently with the lost weight, throwing her on top of Nicholas, and his oar went flying into the river. Sage's knife clattered to the bottom of the boat as she caught the prince by his tunic before he tumbled overboard and pulled him away from the man grabbing at him.

A wild fury rose in her. These men wanted Nicholas. They'd harmed and possibly killed many other soldiers. Her friends.

They had killed Alex.

Sage snatched the knife up and launched herself at the man now half in the boat, bringing the weapon down, striking him above where the neck and shoulder met. The dagger was buried almost to the hilt, and she pressed back to lever the blade forward. The man clutched at his throat, knocking her hands away. They struggled against each other to pull the knife free but only succeeded in driving it in deeper and under his collarbone. Sage pushed him back to get a better grip on the handle, and she saw his face for the first time. Saw his fear and agony.

Saw the life in his eyes go out like a candle.

Then his weight carried him over the side, and the knife was too deep for her to pull out before he twisted away, taking it with him.

57

ALEX KNEW SOMETHING was wrong the minute he saw the dying fire. It smoldered near the shore, a half-made spit and a dead squirrel lying next to it. The squirrel had been killed by a stone from a sling. All signs Sage and Nicholas had been there, but they'd dropped everything and abandoned the camp.

He followed running footprints back to the shore, where the bottom of the boat had left grooves in the sand.

No signs of anyone in the area around them. Across the river Cass waved his arms for attention.

"What do you see?" Alex called to him.

"Lots of men, moving fast over here. Two to three hours ago," came the answer.

"Gather your team," he shouted back. "We're going after them!"

58

THERE WAS ONLY one oar left, and Sage used it as a rudder, directing the boat into the swiftest currents. Nicholas gripped the bow with white knuckles as he looked ahead to warn her about rocks. They'd hit one waterfall before entering the Beskan Gorge, but it was only about five feet high, thanks to the rain-swollen pool at the bottom, and they managed not to capsize, though they were nearly soaked.

Every once in a while, Nicholas glanced over his shoulder at Sage, like he didn't recognize her. At first she thought it was shock. Likely he'd never seen a man die before.

The man on the boat had been the second man she'd killed—third, if the archer she hit was dead—but the first she'd really experienced. The first had been last year, in a desperate struggle for survival while she was on the point of blacking out—she *did* black out, and he'd bled to death while she was unconscious.

Alex had once confessed he was terrified all the lives he'd taken in battle had made him a monster. She'd assured him he was nothing of the kind, but as she recognized the look on the prince's face, she truly understood Alex's fear. Nicholas was scared. Of her. He looked at Sage like she was a monster. Perhaps she was.

She and Nicholas were safe in the canyon for now. High rock walls protected them from attack, but offered no shelter. They would need to eat eventually, too. Sage saw lizards and a few decent-sized rodents, but she didn't dare stop. If their pursuers were smart, they'd try to catch her and Nicholas when they emerged on the far end. Their only chance of getting away from the Kimisar was to stay ahead, but beyond Beskan lay the impassable Yanli Gorge. She and Nicholas would have to leave the river at some point, and when they did, they would be in Casmun. The question was how deep into Casmun the Kimisar were willing to follow them.

As the sun slipped outside the canyon's rim above, Sage made a decision: they would steer to the shore as soon as possible and forage for a few minutes before continuing downriver. As long as there was enough light to see, they'd stay on the water, but when they did stop, lighting a fire would be too risky. It would be a cold night.

Sage shivered in her damp clothes as they continued through the shaded canyon, praying they'd reach the south end before sunset.

59

ALEX'S LUNGS BURNED, and his legs begged for respite, but he would not stop. Every step was one step closer to her, to Nicholas. They found a place where the river plunged several feet, but there was no sign the boat had been wrecked. As the sun sank lower in the sky, Alex and his Norsari reached the entrance to the Beskan Gorge.

The sides of the river rose high, the water rushing into the narrow opening between stone walls. He paused to check for signs Sage and Nicholas had stopped, even for a few minutes, but found none. Across the river, Cass and his team combed the opposite bank for similar signs. He used hand signals to report over the river's roar echoing out of the canyon. *Nothing.*

Rest and drink water, Alex signaled back, and gave the same instruction to the men around him.

Cass waved to him again with a report. *One dead Kimisar, several miles back. Stone in head.*

Alex grimly acknowledged the message. Sage and her sling. He deduced the Kimisar were following along, probably harassing Sage and Nicholas enough that they didn't feel safe stopping, but she'd nailed one of them. Good for her.

He looked into the gorge. Beskan would provide Sage and Nicholas several hours of safety from the Kimisar, but little chance to relax. Alex would kill for a boat of his own right now.

Sergeant Lance approached and offered some dried fruit and venison, left over from their ill-fated trip into the desert. Most of the Norsari's provisions had been lost in the fire. Alex looked around at the dozen men who'd kept up with him over the last five hours. They looked tired, but determined. Good men, all of them. He'd never been so proud to be a commander.

"Drink up and fill your canteens," he said. "It's not over yet."

60

SAGE STEERED THE boat to the right shore, where a tangle of trees extended south. When they'd exited the gorge, a blast of hot desert air hit them, which felt good after so many hours of shade and damp, but her anxiety shot up at how exposed they were. It was another hour before she felt secure enough to land. This area had promise—a fallen tree leaned out and created a natural eddy and a place out of sight from the other shore.

She and Nicholas jumped out in shallow water and towed and pushed the boat onto the sandy pebbles. The first thing they did was find a place to relieve themselves. When they regrouped, Nicholas described a tree with some kind of fruit hanging from it, but it didn't sound like anything Sage recognized as safe. A bird's trill made her grab his arm. She wasn't sure the source was an animal.

As if on cue, a man wearing a scarf wrapped around his head and loose tan clothing stepped out of the trees, leveling a bow and arrow at them. Sage swept Nicholas behind her and looked around. There had to be more.

Six additional men revealed themselves, holding various weapons. The leader of the group she identified immediately by the way everyone deferred to him. As she met his eyes, he swept his head scarf back, revealing the narrow white scar across the forehead of a familiar face.

Sage raised her hands to show she wasn't armed. "*Basmedar*, Darit Yamon."

"*Basmedar*, Saizsch Fahler." Darit smiled ironically. "Though from the look of you, I think your fortune has been bad," he said in Casmuni.

"We are agreed," she replied. Eyebrows went up at her use of what was probably a formal and antiquated phrase.

Darit said an unfamiliar word, and the men around them lowered their weapons. He addressed her again. "Is your bad fortune due to your help to us?"

Sage shook her head. "Kimisar attacked us."

The Casmuni leader didn't look as though he quite believed her. It probably did seem awfully convenient. She wasn't sure she had enough words to explain.

One of his companions shouted and pointed at the river. A body had drifted into the eddy pool.

Sage took a step toward it, and weapons went up. After a glance at Darit, she continued to the water's edge. Wading into the river, she grabbed the man by his arm and dragged his body onto the shore.

She recognized the soldier even before she rolled him onto his back. The hilt of Alex's dagger still protruded from his throat, his face frozen in an expression of desperation. Bile rose in her throat at the memory of taking the man's life.

Darit walked up behind her. "Your work?" he asked, pointing at the knife.

"Yes," she said. Sage pulled the dagger out and wiped it on the dead man's shirt, then tucked it back in its sheath on her belt and stood to face Darit. "More will come soon."

Darit gestured for his men to lower their weapons, but noise from the west made them turn in that direction instead. Another Casmuni man burst from the trees, shouting and pointing upriver.

His meaning was plain: the Kimisar were coming. At Darit's nod, two men left the arc around Sage and Nicholas, and followed the man back into the forest, weapons in hand.

Darit stared at the dead Kimisar for a few seconds, then looked back to Sage, who had gone to stand by Nicholas again. He nodded as though making a decision. "Come with us," he said. "We will protect you."

"What is he saying?" Nicholas asked.

"He's offering us protection."

"What do we do?"

She doubted the Casmuni would force them, but the better choice was obvious. It would be several days before the Demorans found her and Nicholas. *If* they found them. "We go with them," she said.

61

HUZAR'S TEAM LOST precious time crossing the river, but their prey would be foolish to stop on the side they'd been attacked from. The Kimisar were famished, exhausted. He began to worry that if they caught the prince, they wouldn't be able to hold on to him. Huzar's only chance of getting home was slipping through his fingers like sand.

Damn that woman. Not for the first time, he wondered what role she'd played at Tegann, other than killing Dirai, his black-tailed hawk—the last means of communicating with the men he'd been separated from last summer. Now she was back. Capable as Demoran squires were, the young prince would probably have faltered on his own eventually, but she drove his escape. If not for her, they'd have him, and Huzar wouldn't have left the bloody mess of his second-in-command behind.

Shouts ahead. Had the Demorans gotten around them? Three of his men came running from the trees. They stopped and bent over, hands on knees as they tried to catch their breath.

"Casmuni!" one finally managed to gasp.

"A half mile ahead," said another. "Attacked us."

The third man fell to his knees, clutching a bloody hand to his thigh.

"Are they following you?" asked Huzar.

"No," said the first man. "They went back where they came from. There must be more."

Huzar's hands clenched into fists. To be so close to his goal only to meet another obstacle. "And the prince and his companion?"

"No sign we saw, Captain, and we lost Gispan."

Though he thought things could not get worse, Huzar was proved wrong by a yell from behind. Demorans had been sighted along the rim of the gorge. The only thing that offered mercy was the setting sun and the promise of another moonless night.

Failed. Huzar had failed.

He looked up into the eyes of the men who awaited his command. "We must withdraw. Let the Demorans deal with the Casmuni."

62

ALEX PRODDED THE corpse with his foot. Dead about a day. The cause of death was obvious—his throat was ripped open, but the lack of blood told Alex it hadn't happened here. He crouched down and fingered the wound. It was a clean, narrow cut made by a blade about the length of his handspan. Could have been any dagger, but Alex would have put money on one with a black-and-gold hilt.

Casseck approached from behind. "The trail from that fight back there led into the desert. Three to four men, at least one was wounded. From the blood, it was yesterday evening."

Alex nodded as he pushed to his feet. They'd lost a lot of time last night. He hadn't wanted to stop, but he'd been near collapse from not having slept in over two days, and it became too dark to track anymore. The Norsari took shelter near several large boulders at the east end of the canyon and slept for a few hours. As soon as the twilight was enough to see by, they were on the move again. Three miles downriver, they came across bloody footprints and trampled foliage. Cass had taken a team to investigate, but Alex had continued along the river until he found the boat and the dead man.

His friend barely glanced at the body; it had been dragged out of the water and was obviously incidental. "So they stopped here. Then what?"

Alex pointed to an arc of heavy footprints in the sand. "They were surrounded." He moved to where she'd faced them, standing between Nicholas and about eight men. Sweet Spirit, she was brave.

"Then she and Nicholas went this way." Alex followed her steps into the trees. Tracks in dry sand were difficult to interpret, but he was able to determine she wasn't running or stumbling. When her footprints and the others reached the edge of the vegetation, they narrowed into a single line leading southwest, into the dunes.

While the order of events was a little confusing, the conclusion was obvious. Sage and Nicholas had been found by Casmuni and gone with them into the desert. They hadn't put up a fight, but he trusted her to have made the best decision at the time.

As he watched, a strong wind swept across the sand, beginning the process of erasing the only clues he had to find her.

"What are your orders, Captain?" said Casseck.

Uncle Raymond would want Alex to go after Nicholas, but the Norsari with him had brought very little food along, thinking they'd be gone only a day. It would take at least two days to get provisions from the camp. Thanks to the fire, there might not even be enough to gather until Colonel Traysden arrived. With the prince now in the hands of the Casmuni, Alex losing command was inevitable, but it was nothing compared to losing her.

Somehow that gave him a tremendous sense of freedom.

"You're going back," Alex said finally. "Inform Colonel Traysden of everything that's happened and turn command of the Norsari over to him."

"What about you?"

"I'm going after them." Alex pivoted to address the Norsari gathering behind them. "I need all the canteens, every scrap of food you men have, and two volunteers."

63

DARIT LED THEM through the sand well into twilight before stopping in a copse of trees surrounding a spring of clear water. The sun was high overhead when Sage woke the next morning, though she lay in the shade. Nicholas was sprawled on the sand nearby, still asleep. She groaned and stretched, noticing the smell of cooking drifted across the pool. Malamin sat by a small fire, stirring a pot that was the source of the delicious scent. He smiled at her and touched his forehead with his fingers in greeting, and she returned the gesture.

Sage tossed the blanket aside and headed for the spring to wash her hands and face, then rinsed sleep and desert grit from her mouth. Her stomach begged for food, but she made herself drink first. When she stood, Malamin held up a small bowl, and she tripped over her own feet in her eagerness to accept it. The meat in the stew appeared to be from some kind of bird, almost chicken-like in taste, and the grain swimming in the broth resembled barley. She drank it down, pausing only to accept a spoon. Nothing had ever tasted so delicious.

As soon as she finished, her bowl was refilled, and she picked out a piece of the meat. "What this?" she asked.

"*Vargun*," he answered, producing a flat board on which a leathery skin was drying. Malamin smiled at her surprised expression. In all their years of living outdoors, Father had never suggested eating *snakes*. Sage shrugged and raised the bowl in salute before digging in again. First time for everything.

She finished her second helping much slower and forced herself not to ask for more. Her stomach was already protesting after being empty for so long. Darit and several others returned, carrying a few desert hares. Nicholas sat up and looked around like he was trying to remember where he was.

The Casmuni tossed the rabbits to Malamin, who pulled out a knife and started skinning, then went to the pool to drink and refill their waterskins. Darit approached her and touched his fingers to his forehead as Malamin had and offered her a hand up. "Saizsch," he said solemnly.

"Darit," she said, putting her hand over her heart. "I wish thank you," she said in Casmuni. "For our safe."

He smiled at her awkward speech. "I am well thanked. Please come with me now." Taking hold of her arm, he gently pulled her in the direction he'd come from. Nicholas made to follow, but she shook her head. The Casmuni brought her to the edge of the trees where two of his men stood on either side of a third man on his knees. At Darit's nod, the bound man's gag was loosened.

The man dressed and looked like a Demoran, but from the hate in his blue-gray eyes, she knew he was Kimisar.

His clothes were wet with the blood of a wound in his side, and her hand unconsciously went to the knife on her belt.

"Why did you attack us? Why did you pursue us?" she demanded in her own language.

"I am only returning the favor," he answered. "One enemy to another."

He spoke Demoran. Very well, too.

She gripped the handle of her dagger. "Why were you in Demora?"

He sneered. "We came on invitation. We remained because of betrayal."

"Is Kimisara planning an invasion?"

"How would I know? I've not been home in over a year."

Sage blinked. "You've been here"—she remembered *here* was not actually Demora anymore but continued—"since last year? Why?"

The man snorted. "Do you think your king would let us leave?"

"Why did you attack the Norsari camp?"

The man turned his eyes away.

"Answer me."

"I will not." He looked back to her. "I am loyal to my captain."

The vision of Alex tumbling backward off his horse flashed in her mind. Sage didn't even realize she had her knife out and was reaching for the man's throat until Darit caught her from behind and pulled her arms back, lifting her off her feet. She screeched and fought him as the other two men yanked the Kimisar away from her. The weapon was stripped from her fingers, but Sage twisted out of Darit's hold and lunged for the prisoner again. Before she got two steps, Darit swept his leg out and knocked her off her feet. Within seconds he had her pinned to the ground.

"Stop!" Darit shouted in her ear. "You must stop!"

"Get off of her!" Nicholas tackled Darit from the side, but the Casmuni didn't let her go, and they rolled and tumbled together in a tangle of arms and legs. By the time they were pulled apart, Sage had a bloody lip, and Nicholas's tunic was ripped completely open. She sat sullenly, glaring at the Kimisar man, who was lying on his side several yards away, looking shaken.

The prince clutched his bound wrist. "Are you all right?" he asked Sage.

"Yes, fine." She licked sand out of the gash on her lip and spat. "You?"

"If my wrist wasn't broken before I think it is now."

Sage looked up as Darit stood over her, offering her a waterskin. She accepted it and rinsed out her mouth while he knelt beside Nicholas to examine his arm.

"It is not well to let words affect you so much, Saizsch Fahler," Darit lectured her over his shoulder. "I promise you his threats will come to nothing."

Sage sipped water. "He made no threat," she said.

Darit glanced at her. "Then you deserve your injury. Only children respond to taunts." His expression lightened a little as he turned back to Nicholas. "But you may tell Nikkolaz he did well in coming to your aid."

After rebinding the prince's wrist with a splint of stiff palm leaves,

204

Darit offered Sage her knife. Alex's knife. She put it back on her belt, resisting the urge to trace her fingers over the initials. "You do not fear I will harm the man?" she asked.

Darit shrugged. "I think if you want to kill him, you will not be stopped by lack of a weapon."

64

SERGEANT MILLER AND Private Wolfe were his volunteers. Both men had been in the desert with Alex the first time, for which he was glad—they already knew how to walk in the sand and conserve water. They'd left camp without head scarves or tents, so they improvised by wrapping their heads in undershirts donated by some of the men who'd returned with Casseck. As for tents, they did without, but luckily they found a small spring with a handful of short trees on the second day, and they were able to refill their canteens and take shelter during the hottest part of the day. The trees were a kind Alex had never seen—their leaves opened like paper fans to be larger than an archery target. Alex stripped several dead leaves down to their thick, arm-length stems to use for fuel. The Demorans walked through the night, but when they did stop to rest, it was damn cold and the fire was welcome.

Their luck ran out on the third day.

He and the two other soldiers had spread out to where they could see each other well enough to communicate if they saw something nestled in the dunes between them. As a consequence, Alex couldn't be sure when exactly Sergeant Miller disappeared, but it was a full hour after noticing Miller was gone that he and Private Wolfe established that he'd vanished without a trace. Wolfe claimed to have heard what sounded like a scream. At the time, he'd thought it was one of the desert hawks they occasionally saw.

Sage would've known the difference.

After their fruitless search, Alex and Wolfe spread apart again, though not as far as before. Not that it mattered. It was nearly sunset when Wolfe shouted for attention. Alex ran at him, calling for him to wait, but Wolfe wasn't moving as Alex had initially thought—he was sinking into the sand. While still fifty yards away, Alex's boots sank over his knees within two steps. Alex crawled his way back in the direction he'd come as Wolfe's cries became weaker and weaker. By the time Alex was on solid-enough ground to stand and turn back around, Private Wolfe was gone, swallowed by the sand.

For a long time Alex sat there, terrified to move, hoping against hope that Wolfe would emerge, clawing his way out, or that Miller would appear over a nearby dune, having only been lost. He wasn't much for praying, but he prayed then, asking the Spirit to pass on to them how sorry he was for leading them to their deaths. Losses in battle were easy to bear in comparison. Those lives were currency spent to achieve an objective; these were like being robbed.

The right thing to have done would have been to have waited—waited for supplies, waited for permission, waited for more information. He deserved to lose his command, but given the chance, he'd have done everything the same, though he would have done it alone.

Eventually, Alex continued southwest—the only direction he knew to go in, worrying every step would be his last. Sergeant Miller had been carrying their one water sling, and Alex was down to one empty and one partially full canteen. When night came, he hunkered down between dunes for a few hours and lit a fire. With nothing left to burn, he resorted to tearing the leather-bound cover and a few blank pages from Sage's ledger. He should've rested, but instead Alex read and reread the letter she'd kept. She must have turned to it dozens of times in the last weeks for reassurance that he loved her. He would never give her a reason to doubt him again.

The heat of the fourth day brought hallucinations. Sometimes he thought Miller and Wolfe were walking next to him. Other times it was Sage. In both cases he wanted to cry and beg their forgiveness, but his eyes were too dry to make tears. Twice he thought he saw a spring like the first one, but neither was real. Alex stumbled from hill to hill, each time telling himself he would go just one more. His head throbbed with every step, and he began staying along the ridges of the dunes to prevent the cramps that seized his feet when he walked downhill.

At some point he started hoping the sand would swallow him, too.

The sun sat low and red in the sky when the black tops of trees appeared, silhouetted against the horizon. In a corner of his mind, he knew it wasn't real, but the part that kept him walking believed it. If he pulled the makeshift scarf off his face, he could smell the greenery. He didn't need his jacket, either. Alex left them both in the sand behind him. His legs were cramping. If he removed his boots, he'd be able to walk better. The sand was pleasantly warm under his feet.

The sword belt was slowing him down, too, and he struggled to undo the buckle with fingers that didn't want to bend. His trembling legs suddenly gave out, and he fell, first to his knees and then forward onto his face. Alex tried to push himself up, but his arms shook so violently he barely rose enough to turn his head out of the sand to breathe. He felt he was sliding down the side of a dune though nothing around him changed.

Sliding into sleep, that's what it was. He hadn't slept in so long.

Alex closed his eyes and let the darkness take him.

65

DARIT'S GROUP TRAVELED outside the heat of day for the most part, and Sage's sense of direction told her they didn't take a straight path. The hours of walking in sand were brutal, but she was strangely grateful for the concentration required for each step—it kept her from thinking about Alex. When they stopped to rest, she was so tired she dropped instantly to sleep, but it never lasted. Bad dreams always woke her after only a few hours, and then she couldn't stop the thoughts and memories. Sage would pull her legs in tight to her body and rock back and forth as wave after wave of grief swept over her. She never cried, though, just as she hadn't when Father died.

Late in the second day, Darit stopped for several minutes and frowned over the dunes, which had settled into smaller hills in the last hour. All the Casmuni shifted nervously as they waited. At last, Darit shook his head and unfastened a long rope from his shoulder and handed it down the line. Everyone took a position on it with their left arm entwined—except the Kimisar, who grasped it with both bound hands—and Sage and Nicholas followed their example.

After about a mile of walking, Malamin, fourth in the line, took a step and sank to his waist before anyone could react. At his cry, everyone turned and braced their feet as best they could in the shifting sand and pulled the rope taut. The man called Yosher unshouldered another rope and made it into a loop that was thrown around Malamin, who pulled it tight across his chest.

With a quick, rhythmic count, the Casmuni heaved Malamin from the sand trap and dragged him away. For a full minute they lay flat, spreading their weight over as large an area as possible, gripping the rope and watching the sand for signs of another collapse. At Darit's direction they pushed to their knees and crawled away. When he judged it safe, they stood and walked to a place they obviously felt wasn't as dangerous, though Sage couldn't see how it was any different from where Malamin had nearly disappeared.

Nicholas's hands were still shaking. "That happened so fast," he whispered.

Sage nodded, trying to work out how such a thing would be created. She handed the prince the waterskin Darit had given them to share and walked to Malamin. He looked as shaken as Nicholas as he removed his boots and dumped sand from them. She squatted next to him and picked up the boot he'd dropped, running her hand along the bottom. It felt cooler than she expected. Darit stood over her as she rubbed sand from the sole between her fingers. It was damp.

She cupped a bit in her hand and held it out for both men to see. "*Drem*," she said, using their word for water.

Darit nodded. "Water flows beneath the sand."

Fascinating. "How do you know where?" Sage asked him.

Darit wiped sweat from his brow before pointing to his nose and sniffing. "I smell it."

He helped her to her feet and gestured for her to follow him. With his left hand wrapped in the rope, he led her back the way they'd come. Yosher held the other end of the rope as she grasped Darit's free arm tightly. When he halted, he breathed deeply and indicated she should do the same.

She smelled only sand and heat. Standing in a spot Darit half expected to sink into the ground unnerved her. Sage closed her eyes and breathed again.

Moisture. It was barely there, but in the arid wind she could distinguish it like a thread of blue woven into a length of red cloth. Her eyes snapped open, and she found Darit smiling a little.

She waved at the area where Malamin had fallen. "How is it called?"

"*Dremshadda.*"

Watersand.

As she and Darit made their way back to the group, Sage sent a prayer to the Spirit that no one from Demora would try to follow them.

On the fourth day of walking, a brown spot appeared on the horizon around noon. When Darit pointed it out, a small cheer went through the band, and instead of stopping as before when the sun was high, the pace of travel picked up. As they drew closer, Sage noticed a regularity to what she'd first assumed was an outcrop of rock. It was, in fact, a group of tents clustered around an impressively large oasis, though Sage admitted to herself it was only the third she'd encountered so her experience was limited.

Sentries appeared and greeted Darit and his men with hands to foreheads followed by clasping arms up to the shoulder. They cast curious looks at Sage, Nicholas, and the Kimisar prisoner but asked for no explanation, and the group continued onward to the camp.

She smelled horses, iron, and cooking as they approached. The dun-colored tents were sturdy against the almost-constant wind, but nothing appeared permanent, not even the low growth of plants. Other than the horse paddock she caught a glimpse of between tents, there were no herd animals, leading her to conclude this wasn't a nomadic group but a traveling camp, probably military in nature, if the heavy presence of weapons was any indicator.

What Alex wouldn't give to see all this.

No, Alex would never see anything again. Suddenly Sage couldn't breathe.

Darit paused to look at Sage where she'd stopped. "Are you well, Saizsch?" he said. "You need not fear."

Nicholas, too, wore concern on his face. Sage took a deep breath and continued walking. "I am well" was all she said.

Darit took them to what appeared to be an equal in rank, judging by their greeting. They spoke rapidly, and though Sage had believed her Casmuni to have improved quite a bit in the last few days, she was instantly lost. One word Darit threw in her direction caught her attention: *filami*. Friend.

The man sent another off with a verbal message and called forth several more to take care of the prisoner. When his eyes settled on Sage, she tensed, but he only nodded and turned back to Darit and resumed their conversation. She felt like she was deliberately left out, yet there was a polite air to her exclusion.

When the messenger returned a few minutes later, Darit looked at her thoughtfully. "I will take you to wash and find some clean clothes," he said, speaking in a slow manner for her benefit. "Please follow me."

He led them to a tent with an open side. The men they'd traveled with were in its shade, scrubbing themselves at large basins of steaming water. Darit raised his arm to indicate Sage and Nicholas should join them.

The prince didn't hesitate, but Sage stayed where she was. "With that man you called me your friend."

"Of course I did." Darit looked at her in confusion. "You have not shared water yet."

Apparently there was more to the ritual than she'd realized. Her lack of knowledge now could get her into trouble. "I understand this not. Please tell me like I am a child," she said.

"We do not speak or use names until water is shared. I thought you knew this."

Thank the Spirit she'd shared water before trying to introduce herself the first time. "Then . . . you called me your friend . . ."

"Out of custom." Darit smiled. "But if you are asking if we are friends, I think yes."

His words comforted her more than anything else he'd done over the last four days. "Am I permitted to share water with others?" she asked. Maybe there was a message in that she hadn't yet.

Darit nodded. "Yes, but first you must share with Palandret. After you are presentable, you will dine with him."

Sage was about to ask who that was when her mind separated the name into two words: *Pal andret.*

My king.

66

CASMUNI CLOTHES WERE as comfortable as they looked—she moved easily in the loose garments, and they kept her skin cool while absorbing sweat. Sage wore her own boots, though, and fastened her belt and knife around her waist. The left side felt unbalanced without her second dagger. She assumed Darit still had it, but she'd been afraid to ask for it back.

At sunset Darit led them to the massive tent at the center of the camp. Sage pulled Nicholas to her as they followed Darit past two guards standing outside the curtain that acted like a door. Inside, the air was cooler and brighter than she expected, thanks to several horizontal vents in the peaked ceiling. The noise level dropped as well, absorbed by ornate tapestries hanging vertically around the outer walls, creating a sanctuary from the bustle outside. A low table had been laid out with quality but light and practical plates and flatware. Sage wasn't sure what she'd expected, but it was something more exotic than the standard forks and spoons she was used to; it was almost disappointing. From the scents wafting from the covered dishes, however, the food was less likely to be so.

Darit halted about ten feet from a kneeling man, who didn't appear to react to their presence, giving Sage time to study his profile by the light of the low lamp beside him. His skin was sun-bronzed like most Casmuni, but while the hair colors she'd observed ranged in shades of cedar, the king's wavy hair and close-clipped beard were nearly black as ebony. A long, embroidered coat was tucked behind him, which differed from the loose breeches and jacket tunic she'd come to think of as Casmuni styled.

On his left side a curved sword peeked out from the coat. Calloused hands rested lightly on his thighs as he sat in the center of a worn indigo carpet with his eyes closed.

After several seconds, the king—for she assumed that's who he was—opened his eyes but did not look at them. "I hear my friend has brought guests," he said.

"*Da, Palandret,*" answered Darit, bowing low.

Without further acknowledgment, the king stood and stepped off the carpet, then bent over and picked it up. Gold stars had been woven into the rug's faded blue-violet background, giving it the appearance of the night sky. He hung it on a pair of hooks with care, like it was precious to him, and at last turned to face them.

He wore no crown or symbol of royalty she could see, other than perhaps the gold embellished belt and the jeweled hilt of his sword. The long jacket hung to his knees, but he matched Lieutenant Casseck in height, though not in thinness of build. In the light, his eyes were a deep shade of green, reminding Sage of dried seaweed. With purposeful strides, the king came to stand just beyond arm's length of them. Sage tried not to fidget and hoped Darit hadn't omitted anything in his instructions.

The king studied her with an expression of dismay. "Has my friend brought me a pair of *wendisam*?" he asked. Sage had no idea what *wendisam* were, but it didn't sound good. "They are but boys."

Darit's mouth twisted up in what Sage had come to know as his ironic smile. "If My King would speak to them, he would see they are anything but."

The king raised his eyebrows and looked back to Sage and Nicholas. As Darit had bowed the first time he spoke, Sage crossed her arms over her chest and lowered her head; Nicholas followed her lead. "*Bas medari,*" she said, choosing to go with the older, more formal greeting.

His expression was even more surprised when she looked back up. "They speak Casmuni?"

Four days among the desert men had improved her grammar, pronunciation, and vocabulary, and she understood much more than she could speak, but that wasn't enough. "Very little," she answered.

"My friend is modest," said Darit, and Sage blushed that he'd called her his friend more than from the compliment.

The king's eyes had never left hers. "And a woman." He now looked her up and down.

Sage ground her teeth a little and reminded herself the Casmuni did not think it polite to speak directly to someone they hadn't shared water with.

As if also remembering this, the king gestured to his left and a servant appeared, holding a silver tray with a chalice and pitcher. He calmly took the cup and poured water into it, then looked her straight in the eyes as he took a long drink before extending it to her. Sage took a trembling step forward and accepted the chalice without breaking eye contact. Darit had described most sharings as casual, but when one met a king for the first time, all formality was observed.

The Casmuni king didn't reach for the cup when she was finished, which Darit had told her meant she was to hand it to Nicholas. It also meant the prince wouldn't be addressed except through her, but she was glad to have them assume she was of higher rank. Nicholas took his sip and handed it back to Sage, and she offered it back to the king.

The king replaced the chalice on the tray and extended his hands to her, palms down. "You are welcome in my tent," he said formally. "I am Banneth, the seventh of that name."

Sage warily reached out, placing her fingers under his, and he grasped them gently. "I am well welcomed," she said awkwardly, hoping that would work. "I am called Sage Fowler."

The king struggled to say her name as Darit had, then gave up and released her hands. "I am sorry I cannot say it correctly."

"It is nothing." She extended an arm to the prince. "This is Nicholas Broadmoor," she said, giving him her uncle's surname. Banneth clasped one of the prince's hands briefly and stepped back.

Now what?

Nicholas's stomach roared audibly, and the king smiled. "Yes. I think we should eat."

67

THE TABLE COULD have seated six, but there were only the four of them. Sage was invited to sit at Banneth's left hand, with Nicholas beside her and Darit on the king's right. The two men were casual and comfortable with each other. It was obvious they were close friends, and she was gladder than ever she'd helped Darit and Malamin escape.

Darit gave an account of his mission, though Sage only understood sporadic words. His report sounded very thorough, and Banneth ate and asked questions, casting occasional looks at Sage and Nicholas.

"Saizsch gave me this," said Darit, now speaking slowly for her benefit. He pulled out her dagger and offered it to Banneth. "As a sign of friendship and to aid in our escape."

The king accepted the knife and unwound the leather strips on the hilt. She'd used the ones on Alex's knife to bind Nicholas's wrist, so now it was obvious the daggers matched. Banneth ran his thumb over the golden *SF*. "Saizsch Fahler," he said, pairing her name with the letters.

There was room for a *Q*, but it would never be there now. The food in her mouth suddenly tasted like ashes.

"I do not think she knows what it meant," Darit said.

Sage's eyes flicked back and forth between the two men. What unknown custom had she breached?

Banneth looked amused. "I assume you will not accept," he said.

Darit chuckled. "No."

The king turned to Sage, suppressing a smile that reached his eyes nonetheless. "Giving one a weapon means you are friends." He held up the dagger. "Giving a gift with your name on it like this proposes marriage."

Sage choked, spitting crumbs all over her plate. Nicholas pounded her on the back until her coughing subsided. When she could finally breathe, she drank all the water in her cup to avoid looking at Darit or the king.

Banneth handed the dagger back to her. "Don't ask," she said in response to Nicholas's confused look. Face flaming, Sage jammed the weapon on her belt. "I have much to learn about Casmun."

"As I have much to learn about Demora," Banneth replied. He paused thoughtfully. "Are you familiar with any other tongues?" he asked in Kimisar.

Before she could debate how to respond, Nicholas's head jerked up, his eyes wide, giving himself away. Sage took another slow sip of water from the cup Darit had refilled. "Yes, I am," she said in Kimisar.

"I take it no one asked," said Banneth with a glance to Darit, who looked shocked. "And it was not something you wished to reveal."

"I chose to leave it unsaid," she answered.

"Wise as well as brave."

She felt herself blush again. "I do not know all my friend here has told you about me, but I do not consider myself either wise or brave."

"I assure you he said nothing bad."

Sage's mouth twisted up on one side. "But not all of it was good."

Banneth chuckled. "Good people are boring."

"Yes, they are."

"I'm sure you have many questions," said Banneth. "Please ask. I will answer."

"So I may return the favor?"

The king smiled wryly. "Of course."

"Are we your prisoners?"

He shook his head. "No, you are my guests."

She wasn't quite ready to believe him. "What do you plan to do with us?"

"That I have not decided," he said. "I do not yet understand what your presence means." She tensed a little. "But should you wish to leave, I will not stop you."

That meant little considering the desert between her and home. "I thank you for your hospitality."

"May I ask questions now?"

She nodded. "Please . . . except first, how may I call you?"

Banneth thought for a moment. "*Palandret* is traditional. But I am not your king. Would that cause offense to say?"

"No, Palandret."

Banneth nodded, then went straight to business. "Why were you in Casmun?"

The question no doubt referred to both times, but Sage decided to address only the second. "We were running from a Kimisar attack. We escaped, but they pursued us, and we continued into Casmun out of necessity."

"You are the only survivors of the attack?"

Sage flinched. "No, most survived."

Green eyes shifted to Nicholas. "Why do the Kimisar want your young friend?"

Sage's stomach somersaulted. Somehow Banneth had figured out Nicholas was the valuable one. Her right hand drifted toward the hilt of one of her knives.

Darit tensed. "My King," he whispered in Casmuni. "I have had to restrain her before."

The king seemed unafraid as he looked her straight in the eye. "If your friend is worth chasing, worth dying for, you understand my need to know his importance."

Thank the Spirit Nicholas was silent; it allowed her to think. Sage combed through every interaction she'd had with Darit. Nothing she said now could contradict what he'd seen. "They wanted him for ransom," she said, starting with what she suspected was the truth.

Banneth nodded. "But not you."

"No."

"You are not brother and sister, then?" The king glanced at Darit.

Here was an out—apparently that was what Darit had assumed. She'd introduced the prince as having a different last name, however. Either they hadn't noticed or she was being tested. It was highly unlikely the Casmuni knew what her botanical name implied—or that they even knew sage was a plant—but it gave her an idea. "Different mothers," she said. "He is the heir, but I am nothing."

"I see." Banneth seemed to understand she was saying she was illegitimate. "And what is he heir to?"

"Land, mostly." A roundabout truth.

The king nodded again. "Why, then, were you and Nikkolaz in the company of soldiers?"

Sage should've anticipated that, but she'd not counted on being questioned in a language she could speak. She racked her brain for what Darit had seen while a prisoner. What must he have learned or suspected about Alex and the mission into the desert?

Alex. The thought of him hit her like a blow. Suddenly she could think of nothing else.

"I am learning to be a soldier," Nicholas said abruptly.

"Let me handle this, Nicholas," Sage snapped in Demoran. Her mind still felt like it was stuck in the mud, but the prince's words were like a rope she could grasp on to and pull herself out with.

"Sage snuck into my training to watch over me," he continued, unperturbed. "She's always following me like I need her protection."

Now she regretted teaching him Kimisar so well. Sage seized his uninjured arm without taking her eyes off Banneth. "Enough," she snarled. "Not another word, Nicholas."

"See what I mean?" Nicholas said. She applied pressure to his wrist, and he whimpered but finally shut up.

Sage tried unsuccessfully to smile. "Do you have any younger brothers, Palandret?"

"No," Banneth said, green eyes sparkling in amusement. "Only a sister."

Sage brought her hands back to the table and made herself relax. "Would you like to trade?"

The king chuckled. "We can negotiate."

❧

The Casmuni king created a space for them in his tent, adding to the image of their treatment as guests, but it didn't escape Sage that it also meant they were heavily guarded. The moment they were alone, Sage grabbed the prince's elbow. "*Never* do that again, Nicholas. I have reasons for not telling them the truth, foremost being your safety."

"I know, I just had an idea that explained everything." His brow wrinkled in concern. "And you seemed to be struggling."

Sage rubbed her forehead. "You were lucky," she said. "*We* were lucky."

"You have to admit I pulled it off pretty well, though," Nicholas said proudly.

He had. The prince had saved both of them when her mind had failed. She sighed. "Just promise to consult me first next time, please. No surprises."

Nicholas nodded. "No surprises."

He sat down on the blankets and cushions that were apparently meant to be his bed, and Sage settled in the area designated for her. The Casmuni king had a partitioned space on the other side of the tent. "What do you think of our new friends?" she asked.

"I like them," Nicholas said. "Food's not bad, either."

"Trust you to appreciate that."

"Will you sleep tonight?"

Apparently he'd noticed how little she'd slept on their journey. "I'll try."

"Good. You look tired."

Sage grimaced. "Which is a nice way of saying I look like shit."

He grinned as he lay down and drew a woven blanket up to his chest. "Yes."

"Twerp." She sank back on a cushion and turned away, unhooking a knife from her belt to keep handy.

Alex's knife. Her inner vision swam with the image of his face, tense with anxiety, as he pressed it into her hand back at Tegann. *Remember what I taught you.* He'd loved her then, even as she rejected him out of anger and spite.

His last actions showed he'd never faltered in that love. She would never have a chance to prove her betrayal had been out of love, to save him from the consequences of his actions.

Sage squeezed her eyes shut as she gripped the dagger. Alex had died in protection of the prince. Now the only thing that mattered was making sure it hadn't been in vain.

68

THERE WAS A fire in front of him, the light of the dancing flames penetrating his consciousness. Alex struggled to open eyelids that felt as rough as sand. His mouth was parched, but not as badly as he'd last remembered. He wore only a shirt and breeches from the feel of it, and both were wet, as was his hair. Alex rolled to his back and groaned with the pain of a hundred cramping muscles.

Hands appeared on either side of him, and Alex was too weak to resist as they raised him into a sitting position. Something was put to his lips, and water—warm but blessedly wet—trickled into his mouth. He swallowed with difficulty; the back of his throat felt melted shut.

After a few sips, the water was pulled away and poured gently over his face, and Alex was finally able to open his eyes and see. It was night, and he lay in the shelter of a grove of trees. The faces of two men swam into view. Casmuni.

Apparently he wasn't dead. Yet.

The waterskin was again brought to his lips, and he instinctively tried to grab it with his mouth and suck on it to bring the water faster, but they pulled it away. "*Remoda*," one of the men admonished.

Alex didn't understand the word, but took it to mean he was to drink slower. He nodded and the water came back. After a few minutes, they took it away and laid him down, this time against a soft pile of something. "More," he begged them. "Please."

They shook their heads and left him, shortly replaced by a third

Casmuni holding a bowl. This man sat beside Alex and patiently fed him a thick, orange liquid. Between spoonfuls, Alex looked around, counting ten men coming and going around the fire. At least two watched him like it was their job, and all were armed with daggers and curved swords. The soup was made from some kind of stewed fruit, a bit like a tart peach, and when it was gone he only knew he wanted more. Another few sips of water was all they would give him.

His stomach full, Alex's eyelids drooped with the need to sleep—real sleep this time, not just unconsciousness.

The last thing he felt was his wrists being tied together.

✲

Twice before daybreak he was half awakened and given more water. When the sun came up, Alex was feeling nearly human again.

Throughout the day, they fed him doses of the tart concoction, which had a bizarre, herbal aftertaste from something the cook started adding. Alex had to trust that the desert men were experts at treating his condition. He was certainly feeling better—the muscle cramps had abated, and he wasn't always thirsty. By evening he was permitted to eat a few solid foods. Afterward they took him to a pool of water at the center of the trees where he was allowed to wash himself, at least as well as he could with his hands tied.

Early the next morning, Alex was given as much water as he wanted to drink and some of the thick porridge the rest of the men ate for breakfast. He had to drink his portion rather than use utensils, as they wouldn't untie him, though he asked. With some trepidation he watched them pack up the camp. Would they make him walk barefoot and bareheaded, or would they leave him here? He wasn't sure which would be worse.

Then Alex saw his sword belt among their things. He couldn't remember if he'd gotten it off before collapsing, but if they knew it was his, it marked him as a warrior. No wonder they didn't trust him. The man he'd picked out as the leader of the group approached, carrying an armload of leather clothing. They'd found his abandoned jacket and boots. Alex wondered how far he'd gotten without them.

223

Everyone looked impatient to go, and thankfully they untied him long enough for him to dress himself. Though he knew it wouldn't matter after a mile of walking, Alex took a little extra time shaking sand out of his socks to give his chafed wrists a respite. Before putting on the head scarf made from Casseck's shirt, he tore a few wide strips of fabric from it and wrapped them around his wrists, then offered his hands to the man waiting to bind him again. Demoran army policy was not to be a compliant prisoner of war, but these men had saved his life, and he was grateful.

When all was ready, they returned one of his canteens to him—empty; he had to go to the spring to fill it—and headed into the rising sun.

69

BANNETH ALLOWED SAGE and Nicholas to roam the camp freely, but she knew their every move was watched. They spent the first day orienting themselves and watching the posted guards. She had no desire to escape at the moment, but she had to be ready, just in case. All the tents were set in an orderly manner, and Banneth's was by far the grandest. Most were large enough to house four to six men, though, and the preferred design was circular, around a central pole. They radiated from the spring-fed lake, which was round, but the wave of the dunes made the area of plants grow in a teardrop shape.

Shortly after sunrise on the second day, Sage and Nicholas witnessed Casmuni combat exercises. They stood on the edge of the training circle, observing the men spar without weapons. She watched in awe, unconsciously adjusting her feet in the sand in imitation of the stances.

Banneth slipped up behind them, but her attention wasn't so focused that she didn't see him approach. She turned and bowed with her hands crossed over her chest, and Nicholas followed her example.

Before the king could say anything, she waved her hand at the pairs in the ring. "This is beautiful," she said in Kimisar, glad the shared language gave her more words to use.

His eyebrows shot up. "*Beautiful* was not the word I expected."

Her gaze was drawn back to the fighters. "The moves are smooth like water, but fast like lightning."

"Demoran fighting is different?"

"I cannot speak for your weapons fighting, but with respect to this, yes. Our fights are . . . heavier. Does this make sense?"

Banneth nodded. "It is a style we call *tashaivar*. It roughly means *whip strike* for its lightness, flow, and speed."

"*Tashaivar*," she repeated. "A lovely name." This time she used Casmuni words.

The king stepped into the training ring and offered her his hand. "Would you like to learn?" he asked, also in his own language.

Sage didn't even hesitate. Banneth led her a few steps away from Nicholas and took a fighting position. She stepped up beside him and mirrored it, then looked back to the king's unreadable expression. "Let us begin," he said.

⤝⤞

Her willingness to learn opened some kind of door within Banneth. He spent the whole morning teaching her the basic stances and moves of *tashaivar*, as well as the words for them and the body parts they involved. She also picked up the terms for *quickly* and *slowly*, *pointed* and *blunt*, *forward* and *backward* and *sideways*, and several others.

When the training session broke up, Banneth led her and Nicholas around the camp, giving her more Casmuni words for things they saw. He was a natural teacher, unable to hide his satisfaction in helping her understand. When they stopped at the horse paddock, Banneth explained that soon the semi-permanent pen would be all that was left of the oasis. Sage silently theorized the spring was fed by an underground river flowing from the mountain snows of the Catrix to the west. Perhaps it also created the *dremshadda*, the watersand they had encountered.

"The spring here is the largest and will remain for several more weeks," he said in Kimisar. "But it is not the only one we must rely on to cross the desert."

"Where will you go from here, Palandret?" she asked.

"To Osthiza, the capital city. It lies many days to the south and east."

"And us?" she ventured.

226

He looked down at her. "It would please me that you should come with us to Osthiza. As my honored guests."

Honored guests. A euphemism for prisoners. That was what she and Nicholas were, for all they were well treated.

She hesitated for so long that Banneth spoke again. "Darit can attempt to take you back to where he found you, if that is your wish."

"Attempt?"

"As the springs fade, the *dremshadda* expand in unpredictable ways," the king explained. "Every day the journey becomes more dangerous."

It wasn't the drying springs so much as the *dremshadda* that made the desert impassable. "I would not wish to ask Darit to risk his life twice more for me," she said, meaning it.

"A true friend would not," Banneth agreed. The king was trying to make it seem as if they would go with him by choice, but whether that was for his benefit or theirs, she wasn't sure.

In the end, it didn't matter. There was no other option.

Deep down she'd known it would be almost impossible to return right away, but Sage looked away to hide the moisture gathering in her eyes. "We are not important enough to be honored guests," she said at last. "But we will accept your hospitality."

Nicholas had moved out of earshot and was stroking the nose of a dusty bay. Banneth stepped closer to Sage and lowered his voice. "Do not be afraid to accept this honor, Saizsch Fahler. It is for your protection but also because I do believe you are important."

Her stomach twisted in anxiety. "Important how?"

"I have long wished to reconcile our nations," Banneth said. "While I hoped for an ambassador or a prince to open talks with, I will not waste what I have been given to work with."

He already had one of those. To change the subject, Sage gestured to the horses. "Shall we ride, then, to Osthiza?"

Banneth nodded. "We do not take horses into the dunes due to the risk of *dremshadda*. Men are light enough to have a chance of escape, but a horse can be buried to its neck in a matter of seconds. To the south the ground is firmer." He looked her up and down. "Can you ride?"

"I can, assuming the horses are taught similar control."

"And Nikkolaz?"

"Better than I," she said. "When do we leave?"

"As soon as my last patrol returns from the west. They are already later than I expected, but then so was Darit." Banneth looked at her pointedly. "I wonder if they, too, ran into Demorans and Kimisar."

Either were likely to know Nicholas's true identity. Armed Demorans could ruin the innocent image she was trying to build around her and Nicholas, but if the patrol brought Kimisar . . . Sage scraped a bit of dirt—or was it blood?—from the hilt of Alex's dagger with a sick feeling. The man Darit captured had refused to speak. She wondered whether she'd be willing to silence a Kimisar who wanted to talk.

70

THE JOURNEY EAST was mostly silent, as far as Alex was concerned. The Casmuni spoke among one another but rarely addressed him. Miles of featureless desert and hours of silence gave Alex little to focus on outside his thoughts, which were mostly of her. He had to believe the Casmuni Sage followed would have avoided the sinking sand.

The number of tracks she'd met with was about ten, the same as this group. Alex hypothesized they were both patrols of some kind, which meant they would go to a central camp or village. Whether he was being taken to the same place depended on what kind of presence the Casmuni had in the desert. He couldn't imagine anyone living in this harsh an environment permanently, but he'd thought the same about the tiny mountain hamlets high in the Demoran Catrix.

In the late afternoon of the second day, Alex's group crested a large dune and looked down on a lake of clear water, shining like a diamond in the center of an eye-shaped sea of green. The Casmuni started down the hill with a spring in their step, and Alex couldn't help catching their enthusiasm. The distance was greater than it looked, however, and night had fallen by the time they reached it. Armed sentries met them about a mile out, clasping arms and greeting as friends did. No one addressed him.

Half the oasis was occupied by a camp, which Alex immediately recognized as military and non-permanent in nature. Almost everyone they passed wanted to greet the men he'd traveled with, like they'd been waiting for them. Every time they paused, Alex looked around, both observing what he could and searching for signs of Sage or Nicholas. Most of the ten peeled off and disappeared in the sea of canvas, but Alex was directed toward a grand tent nestled in the middle. He'd meet the commander of the camp right away, apparently.

The ground inside was covered with rugs and warmly lit with lanterns, though the air was cool. A meal was being cleaned up from a low table, where four people had recently dined, judging from the pillow seats around it. The tent was large enough to house many, but there was only a lounge area with several cushions. A single partitioned section had a curtain that had been swept aside while a servant moved around within, preparing what looked like a bed. He saw no one outside the servants. For several minutes he and two of the men who'd found him waited.

Alex was nearly asleep on his feet, but he wouldn't show weakness by asking if he could sit. Finally a tall man entered the tent, and everyone within stopped what they were doing and bowed. Like the Casmuni who had brought Alex, the man wore a single curved sword. If he was anything like the others, he also had several smaller weapons hidden in his clothes.

The man whom Alex had identified as the leader of the group bowed and then spoke rapidly for a few minutes. Making a report.

As he was ignored, Alex took the time to study the tall man before him. He'd known enough royalty in his life to know a prince when he saw one, even without the fine trappings of the tent. The jeweled sword and scabbard he wore were not merely decorative—their quality told Alex they were crafted for hard and frequent use. His clothes were finely made, but loose and somewhat damp. Water dripped from his uncovered black hair, as though he'd come from washing. Alex thought of the lake and hoped he'd get a chance to visit it, too.

When the report was over, the prince stepped in front of Alex to peer at him. Alex met his green eyes with a steady gaze. Fear was natural in his situation, but it was not to be shown. "One armed Kimisar in my land is curious," the man said in Kimisar. "Two is a disturbing pattern."

Alex knew his surprise showed on his face. He'd not expected to be able to communicate beyond gestures and the few phrases he'd learned.

Sage's notes in his jacket contained many translated Casmuni words, but he hadn't dared take them out in the last two days.

Also, the Casmuni had assumed he was Kimisar, and he wasn't the only one they'd found.

Alex's mind raced. The Kimisar who'd attacked the Norsari camp wore Demoran clothing. If the Casmuni had captured another Kimisar, his complexion, dress, and weapons would've been similar to Alex's own. The assumption he was also Kimisar was natural. Sage and Prince Nicholas, however, had been wearing very different clothes—she, that long tunic, and he, a squire's uniform—and they were both fair skinned and lighter haired.

"Why did you come to Casmun?" the prince demanded.

No matter Alex's nationality, the Casmuni considered him a threat. If he identified himself as Demoran now, it might make the Casmuni prince suspicious of Sage and Nicholas when they arrived. If they arrived. Alex was also afraid of being recognized as the Demoran soldier who'd entered Casmun and kidnapped two men.

Alex looked away. Saying the wrong thing could be fatal, and not just for him. It was better to be disassociated from Sage and Nicholas, at least for now. Sullen and silent, that's what he'd be.

The prince exhaled heavily and spoke a few words in his own language. Alex half expected to be struck, but they only turned him around and escorted him out. He was taken to a tent not far from the large one, where another man lay on a rug to one side, his hands and ankles in chains.

The Casmuni now took Alex's canteen and searched him for weapons again, still not finding the pages of Sage's book tucked into the lining of his jacket. He didn't know if they'd be confiscated, but he had no desire to find out. The ropes on his wrists were removed and replaced with shackles like the other man wore. They were a little looser on the chafed areas and also allowed him to separate his hands by several inches.

Once he was secure, Alex and the other man were left alone, which struck him as sloppy, but his chains were staked to the ground, and outside, the camp bustled with activity. He'd have a hard time escaping, even with the lock pick he had in the sole of one of his boots. And if he did get away, where would he go?

Alex shifted into a more comfortable position on the rug they'd given him and looked the other man over. His hair was black as Alex's own and his complexion as tanned, though it was difficult to tell, as filthy as he was. Alex imagined he looked just as bad. The clothes the man wore were Demoran in style with military attributes. It wasn't difficult to deduce this was the other Kimisar they'd picked up.

The man's blue-gray eyes were clouded with fever. "Where did they find you?" he asked in Kimisar.

"In the sands. You?" Alex replied in the same language.

"Near the river. They came out of nowhere." He suddenly looked hopeful. "Why were you in the desert? Did the captain send you after me?"

The man assumed Alex was part of the same unit, meaning the Kimisar either had large numbers or hadn't worked together much. "No," he said. "I was tracking the prince. I lost him, though."

The man stared at the roof of the tent as it waved with the desert wind. "I should've stayed in that mountain village," he said with a sigh. "I had food, I had work. I might have had a girl someday."

I heard a bunch of Kimisar came through Jovan last year . . . They raided some and disappeared. "Is that where you were?" Alex asked. "In the mountains?"

He nodded. "For the whole nine months. Never saw anyone else until the captain called us back together. How about you?"

Things were making sense now. The Kimisar had been trapped on the wrong side of the mountains, so they'd dispersed and hidden in the general population. "I wandered a bit. Wintered in the valley. Didn't see much of anyone else, either." Alex leaned back on the tent pole and pointed to the man's side. "What happened to you?" His clothes had been rinsed some, but they'd obviously been soaked with blood.

"Happened when they caught me," the Kimisar said bleakly. "Hurts like hell, but the bleeding finally stopped."

"May I see?" Alex scooted closer, and the man shrugged and opened his jacket and raised his shirt. A sickly sweet smell came from the oozing wound in his side. Alex shook his head. "Looks bad. I think it's infected."

The man shrugged apathetically and dropped the clothing back over it.

"Have you showed the Casmuni?" Alex pressed. "They treated me."

"And you let them?" The man looked disgusted.

"I was unconscious most of the time." Alex shifted from what had become a dangerous topic. "What's your name?"

"Gispan Brazco. You?"

"Armand Dolan." The first was a common Kimisar name, and the second was a town in Tasmet.

They talked into the night, and Alex learned more of what the Kimisar had been doing for the past year. Waiting, for the most part. Their captain, a man named Malkim Huzar, had taken command of them after last year's failed action in Tasmet and ordered them to hide until things calmed down. When the Norsari had been formed, Huzar decided they had no more time left and called the Kimisar together.

"Were you with him when he left the false trail south last year?" asked Gispan, yawning widely. His words were coming slower and slower.

Alex shook his head, not wanting to risk giving incorrect details. "No, but I heard it confused the hell out of the Demorans."

"It did, though that's not hard, is it?" Gispan laughed, then winced and breathed deeply, his hand over his side. His red-rimmed eyes closed. "I will say one thing in their favor—their girls are pretty. Least the ones that aren't wanting to kill you."

Alex didn't have a chance to ask about the story behind that statement. Gispan was asleep.

71

SAGE AND NICHOLAS made their way back from the lake, wearing fresh clothes and feeling cleaner than they had in months, despite not being allowed to use soap in the water everyone drank from. She and Banneth had been trying to convince Nicholas to venture with them into deeper water when a messenger appeared and called the king away. Sage gave up coaxing Nicholas and floated on her back, working dirt and sand out of her hair while the prince scrubbed himself with a rough cloth in the shallows.

Two guards stood outside the tent, which told her Banneth was inside. They didn't try to stop the Demorans from entering, so either the message was delivered, or it wasn't anything they couldn't know about. The king sat alone at the low table, studying a map. Nicholas gave him a quick bow and went straight to their sleeping area.

"Is everything well, Palandret?" she asked in Casmuni. "You left so quickly."

Banneth glanced up. "Yes, it is well. The last patrol returned, and I received their report."

Sage held her breath for several heartbeats. "Did they find anything of concern, My King?"

"Nothing you need worry about," said Banneth. He looked back to the map. "You should get some rest. We leave in the morning."

72

ALEX WAS ROUGHLY awakened at sunrise and handed a bowl of porridge. He sat up and started shoveling it into his mouth before he was fully awake. The Casmuni guard had a little more trouble with Gispan, but eventually he woke. As the Kimisar moved, Alex caught the smell coming from his wound. It wasn't just festering, it was actively rotting.

The guard wrinkled his nose, so he must have also caught a whiff of it. He looked unconcerned, though. "My friend needs help," Alex tried to tell him.

The man didn't seem to understand him, and Alex pointed to Gispan's clothing, which was wet from the seeping wound.

"Let me be," said Gispan, bringing the spoon to his mouth. Alex remembered how the Kimisar didn't like that he'd accepted treatment.

"But you'll die," Alex insisted. He might even die if he was treated.

"You think I don't know that?" Gispan took two more bites and held out the bowl to Alex. "I'm not hungry."

"Do you think less of me for wanting to live?" Alex asked, taking the bowl.

"No," said Gispan. "I have nothing to go home to. Most of my family died in the famine, and the rest in the wildfires on the plains last year. That's why I volunteered to go into Tasmet. You obviously have a reason to live."

After breakfast the tent was taken down around them, and Alex could now see the entire camp was breaking. Horses were being loaded, but

Alex saw no wagons. He and Gispan would either ride or walk. Alex suspected the latter, and he was correct. They were chained to a heavily burdened nag near the end of the caravan. Alex watched Gispan warily. He wasn't sure the Kimisar would last long.

Just before they started moving, a Casmuni approached, carrying Alex's canteen and a waterskin for Gispan. Rather than hand them to the prisoners, the man dropped them on the ground in front of them and walked off. After that first day, the Casmuni had been strangely distant when they gave him water, and Alex wondered if there was some kind of message in that. He picked up both, thinking Gispan didn't need anything to weigh him down.

The Kimisar was talkative as he limped along, telling Alex all about his home and family, about the girl he'd set his eye on in Demora, and his love of woodcarving. Most people might assume he was merely lonely after days with no one to talk to, but Alex recognized it for what it was: a dying man realizing all his experiences and thoughts and feelings would die with him. Gispan would feel better if he knew his memories would live on with another person, and so Alex listened.

When Gispan collapsed in the late afternoon, despite having drunk all his water and most of Alex's, the Casmuni paused to redistribute the nag's load on other horses, then slung him over the animal's back. It had to be a painful position, but fortunately the Kimisar was unconscious.

They reached a small oasis in late afternoon, and a few tents went up, including the large one, but most men opted to sleep outside. Alex sipped from his refilled canteen as he sat next to Gispan and watched the stars. Funny how the sky was the same as at home, only shifted. The Northern Wheel sat lower on the horizon, but the stars turned around it just the same.

When the Kimisar woke, Alex tried to get him to drink, but he refused, saying he probably wouldn't be able to keep it down. The entire side of Gispan's clothing was wet and crusted with blood and fluid from his gangrenous wound. Alex didn't dare try to pull anything away to look—he knew what he'd see, and there was no reason to cause additional pain.

Exhausted as he was, Alex stayed up all night, listening to Gispan's labored breathing. A few times the sound stopped but then continued several seconds later. As the sky began to lighten in the east, the Kimisar suddenly opened his eyes. Alex scooted closer so Gispan could see him. "Do you want some water?" he asked.

"Yes," Gispan rasped through parched lips, and Alex gently poured a little into his mouth. "Thank you, my friend," he whispered.

"I will not forget you," Alex said, giving the man the last reassurance he needed.

Gispan turned his face up to the fading stars. "I wish they'd just let that woman kill me," he said. "Then I wouldn't have had to spend my last days walking through hell."

Alex sat straight up. "What woman?" The Kimisar didn't respond, and Alex swung his feet around and stood on his knees over Gispan to shake his shoulders. "What woman, Gispan? When?"

Gispan never answered.

⊶⊷

Alex insisted on burying Gispan himself. The Casmuni gave him a shovel but kept a close eye on him throughout.

Before Alex had even joined the army as a page, his father made it a point to teach him that enemy soldiers had thoughts and desires like any Demoran. Alex's first real fight came as a squire, at the age of fifteen, and the experience of killing a man had made him want to give up soldiering entirely. His father told him that was as it should be; taking the life of another human being should never be easy. Then one of Alex's friends died at the hands of Kimisar, and he felt the need to avenge him. After that, each death he delivered was progressively easier. There was always one more enemy to fight, one more injury to repay.

In the years that followed, he lost count of how many Gispans he'd sent to the Spirit without thought or care. One for each shovelful of sand now, perhaps, each one taking him deeper into the pit that was his soul.

As he dug, Alex played Gispan's last words over and over in his head.

I wish they'd just let that woman kill me. Then I wouldn't have had to spend my last days walking through hell.

When people were dressed for the desert with their heads covered, it was often difficult to tell, but Alex had identified a few women in the caravan. Gispan could've been referring to one of them, yet none of the women were outfitted like the Casmuni fighters he'd seen, so Alex doubted any had been in a patrol group. *My last days*, he'd said. He'd only walked one day with Alex, and it must have taken several to get to the camp in the first place. Whoever wanted to kill him tried before he arrived.

I wish they'd just let that woman kill me. If someone had merely argued for his death, Gispan wouldn't have understood the conversation, so there must have been an actual attempt on his life. Had this woman been the one to injure him? Alex hadn't looked close enough at his wound to guess how it had been made, nor would it be worth trying now, after so long. The wound had been around ten days old, though. It was entirely possible Gispan had been picked up by the Casmuni group that found Sage and Nicholas.

Which meant Sage had tried to kill him.

And if Gispan had been brought to the Casmuni prince's camp, so had she.

238

73

THE PATH BANNETH'S caravan took wandered to stops at various springs but steadily took them southeast. When the king asked Sage what she knew of Osthiza, she truthfully answered *nothing*, but then she paused. *Thiz* was the word for spring, and *os* was seven. After thinking a moment, she asked if the city was built around seven springs.

Banneth appeared pleased by her deduction. "Yes. Are your cities named in similar ways?" he asked in Kimisar.

"Some of them," Sage replied. "But Demora was created by uniting three distinct cultures—four if you include Tasmet now—and the languages mingled and created a new one. The original meanings of many names were lost over time."

"Our people would lament such a loss. They would consider it a corruption of what was pure."

"You must not like cake, then."

Banneth blinked at her for a moment. "I think you must say that again. There is a misunderstanding."

Sage briefly pulled her lips between her teeth. "Eggs are tasty. Sugar is wonderful. Oils and flour and spices are good, too. If cake is considered a corruption of their purity, then your country is missing out."

The king threw back his head and laughed, a deep, throaty sound. She knew he had a sense of humor and had seen him smile on many occasions, but this was new to her. No one else reacted as though the king's behavior was out of the ordinary, though, so he must not always be the solemn ruler she'd come to know.

He refocused on her, his eyes bright and merry. "Your point is taken, Mistress Saizsch."

She started to grin back when a memory of Alex hit her hard. They'd been riding side by side on the way to Tegann last year, and she told a story and he laughed so hard he nearly fell out of his saddle. Not only that, but then *she* had laughed, probably for the first time since Father died. It had taken her more than four years and Alex's friendship to recover.

Alex had been gone less than three weeks. How could she have been almost happy, even for a moment?

Sage abruptly turned away and feigned fixing a buckle on her saddlebag. For the rest of the day, she hardly spoke.

On the tenth day of travel, there was a noticeable shift in the caravan's mood. She heard laughter and jokes she could translate if not always understand, and even the horses seemed to be dancing in delight. Banneth brought his bright bay stallion up next to the sand-colored mare she'd been given to ride, looking cheerful.

"Are we near Osthiza?" she asked him in Casmuni. Thanks to her earlier study and three weeks of immersion, her grasp on the language was fairly strong, though her grammar was still clumsy and her words occasionally wrong. "Everyone is happy today."

Banneth pointed ahead, to the east. "That is the Protector's Gate. The city is half a day beyond. We will dine in the gardens of Osthiza tomorrow."

Sage squinted at the two towers of stone in the distance. "But the gate is too far to go before night." The shadows were growing long already.

"We will ride until midnight to camp in the shelter of the gate," he said. "There will be songs and dancing tonight, and few will sleep."

"How long have you been away from your city?"

"Over three months I have been gone." The king put his right hand on his hip and pulled the reins in closer, body language Sage had learned to associate with preparing to have his question rebuffed. He also switched to Kimisar, meaning the conversation was likely to be complex. "You said before that Tasmet now belongs to Demora? It was not so in our last dealings."

Events of fifty years ago were nothing Sage felt had to be hidden. Briefly she explained how Demora became tired of Kimisara's constant attacks staged from Tasmet, not to mention desiring the strategic value of the Tegann and Jovan Passes. King Raymond's grandfather had begun the campaign that eventually ousted the Kimisar and forced them back. "The land is poor for farming, but there are quarries and mines. Mostly it serves as a buffer between us. The army keeps a heavy presence there."

Sage had planned to say more, but her stomach twisted. Tasmet duty had been Alex's primary job before he was assigned the Concordium escort last year, which he'd been rather bitter about until it became obvious he had a real threat to deal with. And of course it was how they'd met.

She would not think of it.

Banneth held his braced posture. He probably thought she'd cut herself off to prevent saying something strategically important. "You were with the army. Does Demora have eyes on other areas that may increase its comfort?"

She knew what he meant, but she feigned confusion to gain time. "Palandret?"

He cleared his throat. "Recovering lost citizens is an excellent excuse to send a significant force into Casmun." His green eyes focused only on her.

Sage couldn't even be sure Demora knew she and Nicholas were with the Casmuni. If the Norsari had captured the right Kimisar, they might have learned enough and followed the river to the boat and the body next to it. Whether they would've drawn the right conclusions from there was uncertain.

She pressed her lips together before answering. "Palandret, I can promise if Demora does come for us, they will be armed and ready to fight. To be otherwise would be foolish." Banneth gave a short nod of acknowledgment. "But I have no reason to believe Demora wants to expand here. The taking of Tasmet came only after all other options were exhausted."

Banneth's fingers tapped a beat on his sword belt. "You said *if* Demora comes. You seem uncertain."

"I am uncertain. Nicholas and I may be presumed dead. Or they may believe the Kimisar have us."

The king looked thoughtful. "I am sorry for your family, but we should hope for either of those. Then when you are returned next year, it will be a happy miracle."

His hand relaxed and moved to rest on his leg. Sage was glad the questions were over because she'd become stuck on the phrase *next year*. If the Demorans had no idea where Nicholas was, his return would indeed be a happy miracle. If they did know, however, they would come to retrieve him much sooner.

And when they did, they were likely to bring an army.

74

THEY KEPT ALEX outside all the time, other than when the caravan paused to rest under lean-tos in the heat of the day. There was never a good time or place to read Sage's notes or to pick the locks on his chains, and Alex wasn't sure attempting to escape was a good idea yet anyway. He'd be spotted right away, and with horses to run him down, the Casmuni would catch him in five minutes.

Gispan's last words and the possibility of Sage being with the group haunted him. Alex obsessively searched the line ahead every time it came into view, but it was always so far that he couldn't focus on the riders in front. In the evenings he scrutinized every person who passed near him.

What would he have done if he did see her or Nicholas? Alex wasn't sure. But if he could know they were safe, it would give him some peace. Maybe then he could make a plan to get them out of here.

After ten days, the caravan stopped in the shadow of two great pillars of stone. They must have been within a day of their destination because a bonfire was built in the center of the camp, and every piece of firewood they carried was thrown into it. No tents were set up, not even the grand one. Instead, everyone pitched lean-tos around the fire, and at last Alex had a chance to study all the faces without head scarves.

And there she was.

Alex nearly sobbed with relief, then wiped his eyes and took in every detail. She sat cross-legged on a large rug directly across the fire from him, by all appearances unharmed. Though her face was flushed from sun and the heat, there were shadows under her eyes as she gazed blankly into the flames, reacting little to those around her. The Casmuni prince sat on her right, but she didn't seem afraid of him.

Nicholas was on her left, looking positively cheerful, though he threw an occasional concerned glance at her. Both wore Casmuni clothing; it was easy for Alex to imagine their own clothes had been ruined in their escape. The two princes conversed with Sage and each other periodically, and then she'd respond—never looking upset or worried, but she never smiled, either. Alex knew the look on her face. She'd worn it the first time she'd spoken of her father's death, when she struggled to talk about what she'd buried for so long.

What had happened to make her wear it now?

Alex wanted to stand up and shout her name, to see her run toward him across the sea of Casmuni and throw herself in his arms, but two observations stopped him.

First, Sage wore two daggers on her belt, and Nicholas, too, carried a knife. If she'd made an attempt to kill Gispan and the Casmuni had stopped her, Sage's capacity for violence was known. Yet she sat next to the prince, armed with not one but two weapons—the second of which must have been returned to her by the men she helped escape. The Casmuni trusted her, and Alex didn't dare associate himself with her now.

Second, on the other side of the Casmuni prince sat the familiar man with a scarred face who had every reason *not* to trust Alex.

75

WHAT SAGE THOUGHT was a pyramid of rock in the distance proved
to be a terraced city. From the Protector's Gate, everything looked as
brown as the land between them, but as they drew nearer, a mixture of
reds and greens began to separate from each other. The red came from
the sunburned stones the city was built with, and the green was an abun-
dance of plant life. She'd never seen a place so obsessed with gardens.
Every window had some sort of plant hanging from it.

Banneth had told her Osthiza existed entirely on the springs it was
named for, and the overflow was used to grow crops. The Kaz River
was still several miles farther east and south, and the land between
expanded in a delta of green fields from the heavy stream that flowed
out of the city. Otherwise the surrounding land was desert, leading Sage
to believe the gardens were not merely decorative—they must produce
food, too. Scattered groves of date palms and at least one orchard grew on
the lowest wide terraces, and the air was laced with the scent of their
blossoms even at this distance. Sage closed her eyes and breathed
deeply. The desert had its own stark beauty, but trees would always be
first in her heart.

Banneth watched her from the side as they rode. "Are your cities so
green?" he asked in Casmuni.

"Yes and no," she answered. "Our cities are places green does not
intrude, rather than one of the few places it can grow."

The king nodded. "Farther south there are forests as wet as the desert is dry. Cities there are the same as yours, a haven from nature."

A group of mounted soldiers approached from the city. Once Banneth's traveling party was positively identified, several riders returned to Osthiza at speed and the rest escorted them to the gates. They passed through the reinforced archway and the lower terrace, and began the long, winding path up the hill to the domed palace at its peak. The king rode at the caravan's head with Sage on his right and Nicholas between them but slightly behind.

Greenery hung down over every wall, grew from every roof. Sage's hands were drawn to touch the vines and leaves within reach. After so many weeks of desert and rocks, to be among living things again was like coming up from under water.

The people of Osthiza must have been used to seeing their king come and go. They moved out of the group's way and cheered and bowed, but otherwise didn't disrupt their routines and business. Children rushed up to offer flowers and fruit to the king and his riders, but they hesitated to approach Sage or Nicholas. By their Northern Demoran coloring alone, it was obvious they were not Casmuni.

Banneth reached over and tugged her headdress down. The short wisps of hair she could see were much lighter after several weeks in the sun. She must look as blond as Queen Orianna to them. At the king's gesture, Nicholas also pushed his hood back, revealing the light, coppery shade of his own hair.

"Was that wise, Palandret?" she whispered as the children around them fell silent and gaped. "To show them who we are without warning?"

Banneth waved and smiled to the growing crowd. "They were already talking and speculating. Best to let them see." He turned to her. "I do not want anyone to think I am hiding you."

Whether or not it was his intention, Sage was reminded she and Nicholas were the first Demorans these people had seen in three centuries. She represented her country, and first impressions were crucial. Her posture straightened, and her mouth curved into what she hoped passed for a smile.

"Thank you," Sage said, accepting the flower one child finally dared to approach with. "How lovely. You are too kind."

She never knew sitting straight and waving could be so exhausting. By the time the sloping road leveled out, Sage's arms and back wanted to wilt like the flower in her hand. Banneth led their party into a courtyard of marble columns with a wide staircase leading into the palace. Halfway up the steps stood a young woman with her hands folded across the stomach of her crimson dress. Her long, black hair fell in waves down her back to her waist. She wore a regal and dignified expression, but its effect was somewhat lessened by the child bouncing at her elbow.

The riders stopped and began to dismount. The king was barely off his horse when the little girl, who looked about eight or nine, came flying down the steps, the train of her white gown floating like a sail behind her. "Bappa!" she yelled, throwing herself into his arms.

Sage was too tired from her fake smile of the past hour to resist the real one that suddenly spread across her cheeks. It felt good.

Banneth caught his daughter and lifted her up as the woman in red came down the steps in a manner of stately exasperation. When she reached the bottom, the king extended his free arm to her, and she stepped into his embrace. "Brother!" she said. "I have missed you so."

Banneth kissed her cheek. "And I you." He squeezed them both for a few seconds, then groaned but did not set the child back down. "You are getting too big for me to hold."

The woman, a *chessa*—princess—if she was Banneth's sister, stepped back and pursed her lips. "I told her this, but she will not listen."

"I don't know who she learned that from," Banneth said, tugging the little girl's russet-brown braid, and both princesses scowled at him. "We have guests." He turned and gestured for Sage and Nicholas to come forward. Sage had been staring openly at the domestic scene, thinking the king was full of surprises. She'd known about a sister, but the daughter was unexpected.

"Yes, I know." The woman waved to a servant waiting off to the side, and he rushed over, carrying a tray.

247

Water was quickly poured and shared, and names given. Banneth's sister was Alaniah, but after exchanging looks with her brother, the princess told Sage to call her Lani. The girl was introduced as Reza. Now that Sage knew their relationship, the resemblance was obvious; Banneth and Lani had the same straight nose and coal-black hair, and Reza had her father's smile.

"You are most welcome here," Princess Lani said. "I look forward to hearing about your land and your journey."

"As I look forward to telling," said Sage.

Lani jumped a little. "You are a woman." She looked her up and down with wide eyes. "I'm sorry I did not see that."

Sage blushed. "My own clothes were . . ." Bloodstained? Torn? Soiled? "Too hot," she finished.

The princess had eyes the color of moss and earth, framed by thick, black lashes, and they lit up, showing much more interest and curiosity than before. "You must tell me about Demoran clothes, but first come." She turned to lead them up the steps. "There are rooms being prepared for you."

They all followed Lani, Banneth carrying Reza, who chattered so fast Sage couldn't understand more than a few words. Something about teeth—the princess pointed to a gap in her mouth—a sword, and wine. The last was said with a disgusted face. Apparently she'd tasted some and was not impressed.

"Lani," said Banneth when Reza paused for breath. "Our guests will stay in Hasseth's and Tamosa's rooms."

The princess stopped in the middle of the steps to stare at him, her mouth dropping open in a perfect O. "I have baths ready in the east wing," she protested.

"It is little trouble to move them," he said.

Lani glanced at Sage with wide eyes, then turned back to the stairs. "As you wish" was all she said.

Banneth leaned closer to Sage. "Hasseth is my son. He is away at school."

He did not say who Tamosa was.

76

ALEX HAD BEEN worried how the people on the streets would react to a chained Kimisar prisoner, but once inside the city gates, he was shuffled to walk surrounded by fighters on horseback. From inside his cocoon, he saw and heard little that wasn't several feet off the ground. They wound their way up to the top of the hill, taking a path that kept the journey from being steep, but made it very long.

He was not led into the palace, but rather under it. Prisons didn't frighten him—they always had weaknesses. Escape might finally be possible, but he wouldn't leave without Sage and Nicholas.

Yet he'd not counted on such a clean prison. Alex was stripped naked and his head and much of his body shaved. Then he was dusted with a vile powder to kill any lice that might remain. His clothes were tossed onto a cart and taken across the antechamber to a furnace. He felt the loss of Sage's notes and the letter more than that of the lock pick in his boot. It was almost like losing her, but there was nothing he could do.

They gave him patched breeches and a lightweight shirt, which Alex took his time in putting on to keep the shackles off for a few more minutes. Without his boots or the cloth strips tied around his wrists, his arms were bleeding and his ankles swelling with bruises by the time he reached his cell. The straw pallet in the corner looked fresh, and he sank down on it as the bars were closed and locked behind him.

Maybe he should've revealed himself. Sage and Nicholas were in the palace above, by all appearances being treated well. If the Casmuni trusted them, their word could set him free. Or their association with him could shatter that trust. It mattered little now. Even if he could make the guards understand he was Demoran, there was no guarantee they'd tell anyone else. Their job was to hold him. Who he was didn't matter.

Alex leaned against the wall and closed his eyes. Tonight he would rest. Tomorrow he'd decide what to do.

"Kimisar." A rough whisper interrupted his doze.

"I'm asleep," Alex replied in Kimisar.

"They said you were caught near Demora," the voice said.

"I was," Alex mumbled, his words thick with sleep. "So what?"

"Are you one of Captain Huzar's men?"

The name had Alex swimming for the surface in his consciousness. "Yes, you?"

"No, but I knew him years ago."

Alex forced his eyes open. "How did you get here?"

A man slouched against the bars in the cell across from his, studying Alex with sharp, golden-brown eyes set over an oddly delicate-looking nose. "We came on a mission. Won't be here much longer."

"Execution?" Alex's heart pounded at the thought. Most Kimisar spies in Demora ended up on the block, and vice versa.

The Kimisar shrugged. "Something like that. You got a name?"

"Gispan. You?"

"Stesh." He pointed his thumb at a lump sleeping in the cell adjacent. "That's my brother Kamron." He shifted against the bars. "So what has Huzar been doing over there?"

Briefly Alex described how the Kimisar captain had scattered his company for months and drawn them together to make an escape once the Jovan Pass had cleared of winter snow. He left out the plan to use Prince Nicholas as a hostage.

Stesh snorted a little. "Always the hero. Couldn't just leave those idiots who got themselves trapped."

Still playing the part, Alex bristled. "Says the man lying in prison."

"I don't expect anyone to come after me if I fail."

"How did you know Huzar?" Alex asked.

"We joined the army together at sixteen," said Stesh. "Parted ways five years ago when I went into the *dolofan*. Haven't seen him since, but his noble sacrifice of going back for you men didn't surprise me at all."

Dolofan were spies and assassins. No wonder Stesh expected to be executed. Alex had never had a chance to speak to one like this. "I wanted to be a *dolofan*, too," Alex said. "But they wouldn't accept me. Never found out why."

"I can answer that just by the look of you," said Stesh. "You're one of those fools who thinks honor means something." He leaned his head back and closed his eyes. "Just like Huzar."

77

SAGE ALMOST COULDN'T believe the quarters they were given. While hot water was being carried in, Princess Lani showed her around the apartment, which included its own washroom with a bathtub set into the floor, a dressing closet the size of Sage's room in Tennegol, and a sitting room that could be closed off from the bedroom. Light blue and gold tapestries covered the walls, giving the rooms an airy feel, and the wide bed was adorned with an embroidered silk coverlet. Sage's hostess led her through a set of gauzy curtains and outside to a private patio that overlooked an enclosed manor house–sized garden. Around the edges of the courtyard, several other marble porches peeked through tangled vines of jasmine.

Lani pointed to one across the way. "That one is to my rooms."

If Nicholas was given the prince's quarters, it wasn't a surprise to learn they were being housed in the royal family's own wing, but it was disconcerting to see. Either Banneth wanted to honor them, or he wanted to keep an eye on them. Or both. After Lani's initial reaction to Banneth's order, Sage didn't dare ask who Tamosa was or had been, but from the opulence of the rooms and the absence of Reza's mother, it wasn't hard to guess.

While Sage bathed, Lani disappeared and returned carrying a dress in a similar style to what she herself wore, with long draped sleeves and a square collar, but the color was a pinkish-orange Sage knew would make her look sickly. She wondered if Lani had done that on purpose until the princess scrunched her lips to the side as she looked at her and apologized, saying it was probably the only dress she had that would remotely fit her.

Lani had given her clothes from her own wardrobe. The princess was a little taller and far more shapely, though. Sage expected to spend the entirety of dinner shifting her outfit to keep the neckline from hanging so low, but Lani produced a golden sash to help secure it.

"What are Demoran dresses like, Saizsch?" the princess asked as she tied a knot that somehow looked like a rosebud.

She hadn't worn a dress since Tennegol. Alex had liked the dark-blue one best.

"Um." Sage struggled to push the thought out of her mind and find something within her grasp of the language. "Skirts are much . . . bigger. And women often wear what is called a corset." She gestured to her waist. "It makes the middle look small and holds you straight."

"I would not need that," Lani said loftily.

The prince entered from a side door that connected their rooms, his copper curls slicked down with water. His formal outfit was much like the one Banneth had worn when they met him, but Nicholas was swimming in the knee-length jacket and its high collar.

"You are both ready," said Lani, nodding her approval. "Someone will be here shortly to take you to dinner, but if you will excuse me, I still have my own preparations to make." She swept out gracefully, making Sage wonder how in the world she could add to her appearance.

"What now?" said Nicholas. He looked like a little boy wearing his father's clothes. Together, Sage suspected they looked like lost children, but maybe that was better. They didn't look threatening.

"I want to see your rooms," Sage said, and he led her back the way he'd come. The door between the suites had a lock, but only on Sage's side. She inspected his rooms, memorizing all access points.

"Do you not trust Banneth?" Nicholas asked her.

"It's not necessarily him I'm concerned about," she replied, pushing on the wall for signs of hidden doors. "Princess Lani said something that made me think not everyone here is happy about our arrival." She turned around and saw the prince had gone a pasty color. "Spirit above, Nicholas, I'm just being cautious."

"It's not that," he said. "I was remembering what you said on the road, about how I could be negotiating treaties in a few years."

The smile she returned felt as good as the one earlier. "I don't think you'll be negotiating the treaties that come from this directly, but what you do and learn will have a huge effect on everything, maybe for the next hundred years. Present yourself well and learn all you can."

Nicholas closed his eyes and shuddered, clenching his fists. Sage stepped closer and put an arm around him. "You'll do fine. Don't worry."

"I'm scared," he said. Tears began to stream down his cheeks. "I can hardly understand anything people say and the food is strange and the clothes are itchy and—"

"I thought you liked the food."

Her feeble joke didn't help. "I want my mother, Sage," Nicholas sobbed. "I want to go home."

In only the last month, the prince had gained an inch on her, which had made it easy for Sage to forget he was little more than a boy, and a sheltered one at that. All things considered, he'd held up pretty well until now. "I'll get you home, Nicholas," she said. "That's a promise."

"What if they won't let us leave?" He sniffed and wiped his nose on his gold-threaded sleeve. "What if they find out who I really am?"

"I've been thinking about telling them, but let me make that decision." Sage stepped back and straightened his jacket, forcing him to look her in the eye. "As for not letting us leave, we'll deal with that when it happens. I'll get us home. Just trust me."

78

BESIDES THE KING and Princess Lani, two council members were present at dinner. They sat on either side of Banneth, discussing matters of state. Sage was across from Nicholas, who had apparently recovered his appetite, and next to the minister of war, a pompous, piggy-eyed man who reminded Sage of her uncle William—with less bathing.

Lani sat at the opposite end of the table from Banneth, now wearing a necklace that complemented the golden glow of her skin and sparkled with rubies as red as her painted lips. From the way her eyes rested on everything in the room except the minster of finance, Sage suspected most of Lani's appearance was aimed at him. Not that Sage could blame her. Though he was probably twice Lani's age, he was fit and handsome, with graying hair that gave him an air of wisdom and gravity. Definitely preferable to the man next to Sage, who kept looking at her and sniffing like there was something rotten in her dress.

As neither minister had shared water with Sage or Nicholas, however, Lani was left to entertain them. Sage had to remind herself the Casmuni were actually being polite by ignoring her, but at one point she said something to Lani about how odd it felt. "I can see what you mean," said Lani. "But the whole council will share water with you when you are presented to them."

Sage glanced nervously at Nicholas. "When will that be?"

"The day after tomorrow," replied Banneth from the head of the table. The two ministers sat back a little to stay out of the conversation. "Tomorrow Lani will take you into the city to find some clothes. Darit will take Nikkolaz."

Sage didn't like the idea of separating from Nicholas, but if she trusted anyone, it was Darit.

"Of course," said Lani brightly. "We will go right after the council meeting." She turned to Sage. "Tomorrow morning the council meets to go over all Banneth has missed."

Banneth cleared his throat. "I meant you should do this instead of attending the council."

Lani froze, her eyes darting to the minister of finance. "I have presided over all the sessions in your absence. I should be there."

"Our guests should be properly outfitted, and Minister Sinda and I have just discussed funds for it. You love shopping. Go." Banneth waved his hand dismissively. "It will only be mundane updates and audits."

"That is exactly why I should be there," Lani insisted. "What if something is missed?"

Sage leaned back in her seat, feeling awkward. This was the second time the pair had almost argued in her presence.

The finance minister spoke up. "I can personally assure Palachessa that nothing shall be omitted."

Lani met his eyes, and many unspoken words passed between them. Apparently, the attraction wasn't entirely one-sided. Then the princess tossed her head. "It seems I am not wanted," she said, going back to her food. "Just remember who gave me permission to spend tax money on clothes."

The ministers sat forward again and resumed their conversation with the king, but Sage now had better reasons to study the man on Banneth's right. By the time the dessert of zara fruit in cream and cinnamon was served, Sage was certain Lani and Minister Sinda had shared more than water.

After Nicholas was settled for the night, Sage went for a walk. Her primary intention was to see where the outer doors of their quarters led, but she also wanted to see how the king's guard would react to her wandering the palace halls alone. Having been here only a few hours, she could easily claim she was lost.

High windows were set under the arched, two-story ceilings. During the day they allowed hot air to flow out, but now the moonlight pouring in reflected off the white stone walls, illuminating the passage without torches. At first Sage avoided guards, wanting to finish a sweep of the passage that wrapped around the royal family's rooms and private courtyard. Her count of the doors against the ones she'd seen in her and Nicholas's rooms indicated at least one set in each led into other places—most likely servants' passages. She made it all the way to the far end without being seen, but on the way back she heard voices and prepared herself to look lost. The voices didn't come toward her, though. Sage debated whether to approach or wait for the conversation to end.

She was near Princess Alaniah's rooms, and one of the voices was feminine, so Sage crept a little closer. Lani had been friendly enough, but when Sage identified the second voice as Minister Sinda's, she decided interrupting them might not be ideal, especially when the princess's tone turned angry.

"You didn't even try, Dev," she said, her voice straining to stay low. "You have always insisted I be there. Yet now I don't seem to matter."

"No, Lani, you matter more than anything," Minister Sinda answered in a pleading voice, sounding very different from his confident baritone at dinner. "I just have to agree with him right now, don't you see? I need to be on his good side before I ask him for what we want."

Lani sighed. "I suppose this meeting isn't important for me," she admitted.

"I think this is actually a good thing," he said. "Getting to know this foreign woman better can only help your brother."

"Will I see you in the afternoon?" Lani asked hopefully.

Sage was now close enough to see the shadow of Minister Sinda pressing Lani up against the wall. The *chessa*'s hands were on his jacket collar, holding him close. Sinda shook his head, and Sage backed away from watching and just listened.

"I'm auditing the prison accounts, remember? Because of the council meeting, I have to go in the afternoon."

"There is a new Kimisar down there. Banneth brought him in with the Demorans."

Sage hadn't seen the man Darit captured since their arrival at Banneth's camp. She'd almost completely forgotten about him.

"Really? General Calodan would be interested in talking to him," said Sinda.

"You should tell him, then. It could make him like you better."

"We've been on better terms lately, but that's a good suggestion."

"That reminds me," said Lani. "My maid said she heard from his manservant that he's planning to retire."

"Calodan?"

She must have nodded. "I can think of someone worthy of taking his place."

"I have a job already."

"Not for much longer, if I have my way," the princess said. There was a long pause followed by a sigh.

Sage's face grew hot. This was definitely not a conversation she wanted to be caught overhearing.

"Someone is coming," whispered Lani.

Oh, no.

"I'll leave," said Minister Sinda.

Lani's reply was a little breathless. "I have a better idea."

Sage heard a door open and close. Then silence. She slowly released the breath she'd been holding and clasped her trembling hands. That had been close.

Heavy, boot-clad footsteps echoed down the curved corridor. The regularity indicated a guard. Sage jumped out of the shadows before it could look like she was hiding. A few seconds later, a man carrying a spear and wearing a curved sword came around the bend, and the relief on her face was genuine.

"Can you help me?" Sage threw out her hands in appeal and so he could see she had no weapons. "I cannot find my room."

79

THE CELL BLOCK was empty other than Alex and the two Kimisar. Alex managed to sleep a bit before Kamron woke, then he spent a good hour telling the brothers about Gispan's family and where he'd grown up, which fortunately was far from their home. They knew the places Gispan's memories described, however, and Alex's account of the wildfire that killed Gispan's family seemed to seal him as genuine in their eyes.

Stesh told him Banneth was the name of the prince of the Casmuni camp, and he was, in fact, the nation's king. The Kimisar were glad to hear he'd returned to Osthiza. Perhaps death sentences required royal approval, as they did in Demora. The pair had been here for over a month, which was probably why their imminent execution didn't faze them anymore. A man waiting for death could only care for so long.

Alex also recounted Huzar's actions for Kamron. He, too, was unimpressed. "Should have just waited a few more months. Now he's brought the whole Demoran army down on his head."

"Why should he have waited?" asked Alex.

"Once the south pass has dried up, King Ragat will march through and take Demora from behind," Stesh said, referring to Kimisara's ruler, who'd been on the throne for over forty years now. "Of course, Huzar's actions put troops in our way. Jackass."

Alex shook his head. "Jovan is sealed tight. I doubt our army can get through."

Stesh cocked his head and drew his brows down. "We mean the pass here, in Casmun."

Alex had a vague sense there was another pass through the Catrix, but he knew little else. It was safe to assume if Casmun and Kimisara hated each other enough to send assassins, the pass was heavily guarded. Alex feigned puzzlement. "That one would be even harder to cross. They'll have to fight through Casmuni first."

"Not if they get out of the way," said Kamron with a grin. He resembled his brother in the color of his eyes and most other features, except the nose. Kamron's was crooked from a previous break, while the daintiness of Stesh's was apparently a source of brotherly teasing. Both were paler than the average Casmuni, which might have explained how they were caught.

"Enough talking," said Stesh. "The more we babble, the more likely we are to be overheard." He pointed to the grate in the ceiling that let in light and air.

The two men retreated to the back of their cells and sat side by side, talking quietly through the bars. Alex lay back down, though he was unable to sleep.

He knew the Demoran army was strained and how few defenses were on the east side of the mountains. That was why the king had been so concerned by the evidence of Casmuni intrusions. If he was going to pull resources from Tasmet, it had to be absolutely necessary.

Despite what Kamron said, though, it was unlikely many forces would be brought across the mountains to chase Huzar, especially if Lieutenant Casseck and Ash Carter were able to convince Colonel Traysden what was really going on. That left the Tenne Valley wide open for an invasion force from the south, hugging the mountains until it was past the Casmuni desert.

Letting the Kimisar army march through Casmun was dangerous, however, even if that part was uninhabited. Once the supplies required to get thousands of men across hundreds of miles of barren land were through the mountains, there was nothing to stop them from heading

261

for the Casmuni capital instead. Risk aside, King Banneth's imprisonment of Alex, Gispan, and the *dolofan* coupled with his honoring of Sage and Nicholas went against that idea. His sympathies were clearly Demoran.

He'd been gone for months, however, and the *dolofan* had been captured several weeks ago. If Kimisara couldn't barter passage, maybe they only needed to distract Casmun long enough to get through. An assassination would easily accomplish that. Fortunately, the men had been caught.

Something wasn't quite right, though. Stesh and Kamron were too unconcerned about failing their mission. Rather, they acted like it simply wasn't complete yet.

The more Alex thought about it, the more he felt sure there was a traitor within Casmuni high circles. Someone stood to gain from Banneth's death, and that someone would release these men when the time was right. By holding the Kimisar in prison, they were already inside the palace perimeter.

The king of Casmun was about to be murdered, and there was no way Alex could warn him.

80

DESPITE HER INITIAL objections to shopping, Princess Lani walked through the marketplace with a bounce in her step. She linked arms with Sage and led her through the streets and into a dizzying array of shops. As quickly as she was met at the doors and offered the latest items and styles, Banneth's sister must have been a common sight and a free spender, Sage thought. Sage herself wasn't much for shopping. She was more interested in the city itself.

The rooftop gardens, she learned, weren't just for food and decoration; they provided natural cooling for the homes and businesses. Abundant water from the seven springs ran beneath homes in canals and along gutters in the streets, providing both waste removal and additional cooling.

"Do you always ask so many questions?" Lani said after she'd finished explaining the network that delivered the soiled water as fertilizer to the fields between the city and the river.

"Yes," Sage replied. "But you know so much."

"Attend as many council meetings as I have and sewer facts will be drilled into your head," the princess said dryly. "I think half their time is spent explaining everything like I can't remember the ten times they told me before. Men love to hear themselves talk."

Sage had never attended such a high meeting, but Alex said almost the same thing about them.

Alex.

The thought of him hit her so unexpectedly, she stopped in the middle of the street.

"Are you well, Saizsch?" Lani looked at her with concern. "Your face is white as a zara flower."

Sage wiped cold sweat from her forehead. "I am well. My thoughts were not pleasant." She pushed them from her mind. "But you have remembered me to ask about your exclusion from the council today."

Lani's expression changed, anger making the green in her eyes dominate the brown. "If it weren't for Minister Sinda, I would still be on the outside of matters, but when I came of age last year, he insisted I be allowed to attend. He said it was only right, as I was now able to make decisions in Banneth's absence."

No wonder she admired the man. "Minister Sinda sounds like someone I would like," said Sage.

Lani relaxed and smiled. "Once you have shared water with him, I know you will."

"His looks are good, too, I think," said Sage slyly.

Jealousy flashed across Lani's face. "He is too old for you."

"Really?" Sage said innocently. "I am only one year younger than My Princess."

Lani realized Sage was teasing and scowled at her. "How did you know about us?"

There was no way Sage would admit what she'd overheard last night, but she had observed the attraction at dinner. "The true question is how My King could *not* notice," she said. "But I was learned to see such things."

"Learned?"

"At home I worked for a *matchmaker*"—Sage used the Demoran word—"a woman who creates marriages."

Lani's brow furrowed. "I thought you were Nikkolaz's sister."

Oops. Sage needed to be more cautious about what she said. "Yes, but he gets all the land so I must work." Lani nodded sympathetically, and they continued along their way, Sage telling the princess more carefully chosen details about her background and learning much about Lani herself.

"You train in combat, too?" the princess asked as she straightened the shoulders of a dark-green dress on Sage in a shop. The outfit was similar to the one she'd worn last night, but the color and fit were much better. "You should join Reza and me in the afternoons."

Sage blinked in surprise. *Tashaivar* didn't seem like a very princess-like thing to do, and she said so.

"I have studied *tashaivar* since I was six," said Lani. "When a girl has no mother, it is considered a sign she should be raised with more masculine care." She cocked her head to the side. "You lost your mother at an early age. Is your custom not similar?"

Sage shook her head. "No, I am unusual."

The princess stepped back and giggled, putting her hand over her mouth.

Sage frowned. She must have chosen a word that didn't mean quite what she thought. "I just said I am not shaped correctly, didn't I?"

Lani burst out laughing. "Yes, you did!"

81

ALEX STRETCHED AND exercised within his cell, working off some of his restlessness while trying to keep the shackles quiet for the Kimisar sleeping across from him. Stesh said they typically slept during the day, no doubt waiting for the night they'd escape and carry out their mission. Judging from the cycle of meals, it was now afternoon. The man who fed them hadn't responded when Alex spoke to him in Kimisar, so he likely didn't speak the language. Alex had no way to tell anyone what he knew.

The door down the passage opened, and a man strode toward them carrying a torch. When he stopped between the occupied cells, Stesh looked up from his straw mattress. "Is it tonight?" he asked lazily.

The man answered in Kimisar. "No, I need a few more days. Plans may be changing."

It was him, the traitor. Alex shrank back against the wall, trying to be invisible.

Stesh sat up, suddenly wide awake. "I don't like the sound of that."

"You will do as ordered," the Casmuni man said. "But your target is the same. My targets may have changed."

The Kimisar looked unconcerned once more. "Decide who you want blamed already and let us out. Kamron needs a bath."

The man ignored him and turned to face Alex. "You're the one brought in yesterday?" he said in Kimisar.

Alex squinted against the bright light. "I am," he answered.

The hand that held the torch wore several rings with large stones. Alex could barely see his knuckles. "Why were you in the desert?"

Stesh answered for Alex. "Gispan says he was in Demora for the past year."

"That does not explain why he came to Casmun."

Alex swallowed. "I was pursuing two Demorans."

The man brightened. He pulled a ring of keys from his belt. "Come with me, I wish to discuss them."

He wanted to know more about Sage and Nicholas so he could frame them for Banneth's murder.

Stesh had stood and moved to the front of his cell. "I'm sure our friend can tell you many, many things about Demora." His teeth glittered in the torchlight, making him look like a predator. "And if he doesn't want to, we'll know why."

The man glanced back with the key half turned in the lock. "Why would that be?"

"Because he is not Kimisar."

Alex's heart skipped a beat and then began pounding in his chest. What had given him away? The Casmuni frowned at him. "Demoran?"

"Either that, or he has become Demoran in the last year. He wouldn't be the first." Stesh spat in disgust.

The sound of the tumblers of the lock falling into place echoed through the room.

Alex charged out of the cell, slamming the Casmuni against the bars across the way. The torch dropped into a puddle and sizzled before going out as Alex swung the chain linking his wrists at the man's head. In the sudden darkness, he half missed and nearly lost his balance. He turned and ran for the main door, but the chain between his ankles wasn't long enough, and the Casmuni man had almost caught up with him as Alex burst out the door.

The guard outside jumped from where he leaned against the wall, but Alex was already down the corridor, going back the way he remembered arriving from. They wouldn't understand him, but speaking in Demoran might get their attention. "I need to speak with the king!" he shouted.

Something low to the ground snapped out and caught the chain linking his feet, and he crashed shoulder first onto the stone floor. Three men were on him in a second, punching and pinning him down. He saw the blow coming and knew what it would do. Alex opened his mouth to scream his last hope of getting them to listen: her name.

"SA—"

82

THERE WERE NO good choices.

Huzar could surrender to the Norsari and the force that had joined them, he could attempt to push his way through Jovan and then Tasmet and back to Kimisara, or he could try to make his way through Casmun to the southernmost pass.

His men were broken and lost, and the Demorans might have treated them with mercy if Huzar hadn't just tried to kidnap their prince. The Norsari returned without the boy, and it didn't matter if he was now in Casmuni hands, the Kimisar would be blamed for his loss. Even the option of returning to the places and employments that sheltered the scattered Kimisar in the past year was gone.

As for Jovan—*Shovan*, he reminded himself, as he was no longer hiding among Demorans—it would be sealed even tighter now that the Demorans knew the Kimisar were here. If by some miracle they made it through, the last he'd heard, the Demoran army's headquarters were based in the fortress on the other side. He'd be leading his men straight into the hornet's nest.

That left Casmun.

Huzar ordered everyone to disperse and make their way nondirectly to the area south of the Kaz River's first major fork by the full moon. The tactic worked—the Norsari were left chasing so many ghosts that the Kimisar were able to stay one step ahead. Then Huzar led the remaining 141 men into the foothills of the Catrix and followed the mountain range south. The terrain made for slow going, but the Demorans didn't pursue them.

By the tenth day, Huzar had forgotten what it felt like to walk on level ground, to take a step without wondering if the earth would slide away. Water was scarce in this Spirit-forsaken place. In a few spots, melted snow trickled down the mountainside but most had dried up for the year, and only small rodents and scrubby bushes survived the arid steppes. The starving and bedraggled lot behind him had been further reduced by a tenth. His lost were buried in the shifting slopes of the Catrix, several by nature itself. The most recent rockslide had covered its victims, which was a relief at the time; he'd noted their names and moved on. One hundred and twenty-five remained of the original company, but he'd fought shorter battles with greater casualties.

That's what this was: a battle.

And every footstep he heard behind him was a victory.

83

ALEX PUSHED THE *boat into the water as Kimisar closed in from behind.*
When he tried to climb in, she pushed him away. I don't need you to protect me.

Alex shook his head. Let me in, there's room for all of us.

I can do this myself. *She shoved him again, and he stood with his hands*
up in surrender as the boat slipped away. To her horror, she realized she had a
bow in her hands and an arrow aimed at his heart.

I love you, *he whispered.*

She let the arrow fly.

⚜

Sage woke screaming, seeing only darkness. Then, remembering where
she was, she crawled off the low, wide bed without fully untangling from
the blankets. Once free, she stumbled to the door open to the outside. The
cool air hit her sweat-drenched nightshirt, refreshing her a little but not
enough, and she ran across the patio and was sick in the decorative
plants at the bottom of the steps.

She sat back and wiped her face with her sleeve. So much for Banneth's
garden. Sage rested her cheek on the cool stone of the knee-high wall. Was
there protocol for vomiting in your host's flowers?

"Saizsch?"

Her eyes flew open. "Palachessa?"

Lani stepped out of the shadows, pulling a silk dressing gown around her. "Are you well?"

Sage lurched to her feet and found her knees were too shaky to hold her. An arm slipped around her for support. "I'm sorry to wake you," she mumbled, turning her face away. "I had a bad sleep."

"I was already awake. Come, I will take you to the fountain."

Sage let herself be half carried to the center of the courtyard, where a six-foot-high fountain bubbled. Lani set her down on the wide marble edge of the pool and produced a metal cup from somewhere. "Rinse your mouth."

Sage gratefully accepted and obeyed, spitting into the grass off to the side, then drank what remained in the cup.

"I thank you, My Princess."

"I need no thanks. It is what friends do."

A day of shopping and pleasant conversation—under orders—did not a friendship make. Even a few hours in the training arena later did not, especially when one was with a princess. Sage trailed her fingers in the fountain, afraid to ask if Lani meant the word.

"Who is Ah'lecks?" Lani asked.

Sage froze. "How do you know that name?"

"You were saying it in your sleep. Then you screamed it."

Sage pulled her hand back from the water and fiddled with her cup.

"Is he your lover?"

"No," said Sage. "Not anymore. And we never . . ." He'd wanted to wait. There was to be no doubt that he married her because he wanted to, not because he had to.

Lani glanced over her shoulder in the direction of her rooms. "I think I would cry and scream, too, if I lost someone I loved." There was a long pause. "Why did you part?"

Sage had resisted saying it until now. "He is dead."

"I am very sorry." Lani reached across and put a hand on Sage's knee. "How did it happen?"

When Charlie had died, Alex blamed himself, and Sage had never understood why until now. Even if the duke had been the one to cut

Charlie's throat, it was Alex's decisions that had put his brother in that room. Sage looked down at her hands. "I killed him."

"You what?"

"He died escaping Nicholas and me to Casmun."

Lani shook her head. "That does not mean you killed him, Saizsch."

Maybe not physically. "I lied to him. Right before the battle, I admitted my betrayal." Why couldn't she cry? "I killed his heart," she whispered.

"No," Lani said firmly. "He gave his life for yours. How can you doubt his love?"

"I don't doubt," Sage said. "But he knew not I loved him still. He knew not I was sorry."

Lani was silent for a few moments, then she scooted closer to Sage. "Do you know who Tamosa was?"

"Was she Banneth's queen?"

"Yes," said Lani. "It was an arrangement neither wanted."

"Then why married him to her, or not call for a wait?"

"You made marriages in your own country; you know why such unions are made." Lani folded her hands on her lap. "I think he was afraid to act against the council. I was only six years, so I saw this through the eyes of a child, but looking back, I understand better what that time was like. Our father and two older brothers died in the year before, and our mother only a few weeks after his crowning. He was young and frightened and alone."

Banneth had been third in line for the throne. "He expected never to be king?"

Lani shook her head. "He was to be a scholar, at the school where his son now studies. I barely knew him, but suddenly he was all I had." In the starlight Sage could see Lani grimace. "I think this is why he still treats me like a child, despite that I am half a mother to Reza."

The princess shifted uncomfortably. "I do not know the arrangements in your country, but here it is unusual for a king and queen to have separate rooms. They obviously did their duty, but to the council it was another excuse to pressure him. Even after Tamosa's death, they pushed

273

him around. Sometimes I think he would leave for months at a time, visiting corners of the country, just to get away."

"Is that why he went in the desert this year?" Sage asked.

"Yes and no," Lani answered. "It has long been Banneth's dream to make peace with Demora and reopen trade, but the council resisted and turned people against the idea. Dev—Minister Sinda—told me all about it. My brother's solution was to make his yearly journeys to the place where he might 'accidentally' make contact with Demorans."

Sage's stomach turned over. She and Nicholas were far more important than she'd realized. Their presence was a threat to a council unwilling to lose the power they'd wielded for years. Everything the Demorans did or said could be used to undermine the king. "I would like to help Banneth," she said.

"Me, too," said Lani. "But he does not make it easy."

84

LANI WAS DISGUSTINGLY cheerful the next morning. She came into Sage's rooms and hopped onto the bed. "Wake up!" she chirped. "You're being presented to the council today. You have to get dressed."

"The meeting is after breakfast," Sage protested, pulling the covers over her head.

"Yes." The princess yanked the blanket down. "Which is why you must be ready before then."

Sage let Lani haul her to the wardrobe full of dresses that had been delivered last night. Apparently Lani had taken it upon herself to purchase everything Sage had looked at for more than two seconds.

"You want to look humble," Lani said. "But not fragile."

"I think you forgot that style yesterday." Sage yawned as the princess sorted through the bright fabrics.

Lani pulled a light-colored dress out. "I absolutely did not," she said, holding it up for approval.

Sage grimaced. "It's pink."

"So is your face," said Lani. "They match." Sage continued to glare at the princess until she shrugged and put the outfit back. A few seconds later she pulled out a blue dress that was so light it was almost white. "This will make you look less pale."

Sage rolled her eyes. "Fine."

Lani not only shooed away the maid and dressed Sage herself, she combed and styled her hair. No one had done that for Sage but Clare, the first time being when they were on their way to the Concordium. Sage let herself sink into the misery of missing her friend. It was safer to think about Clare than anyone else.

Even with the short length, Lani managed to weave Sage's hair into a braid that hugged her head like a crown, then moved on to paint her face. Suddenly Sage could bear it no longer; it had all become too much like preparing for her disastrous interview with the matchmaker. "Enough," she said. "I'm not a doll."

The princess frowned but didn't force the issue. When Sage went to put her daggers on her belt, however, Lani objected. "You're not going to a fight, Saizsch."

"You're wearing one." Sage pointed to the curved knife at Lani's waist. Most Casmuni carried one at all times, as a tool more than anything.

Lani pressed her lips together. "Just one, then." Sage relented, and they went to breakfast together. Eating improved her mood enough that she thanked the princess. There really wouldn't have been enough time to prepare afterward. Lani took her by the arm and led Sage to the council chamber, Nicholas trailing behind them like a stray puppy.

The meeting began with the sharing of water, though it was done in a businesslike fashion, with a cup merely passed around the table. The king introduced her as a scholar of some renown, and she flushed. Nicholas must have put him up to that. With the exception of Minister Sinda, the council members did not appear impressed.

"What is it you study, Mistress Saizsch?" the minister of roads asked, twisting his waxed mustache. "Fashion?"

Beside her, Lani scowled. "Just because I like pretty things doesn't mean I cannot grasp dull subjects," she muttered.

"Does Palachessa have something to say?" The minister frowned at Lani like she was a disobedient child.

"No, forgive my interruption."

"Mistress Saizsch?"

Sage cleared her throat. "I am a student of languages and history." At least, that was what was relevant at the moment. "Thus I arrived in Casmun with a grasp on your speech."

"And your little boy?"

Her lips twitched with the urge to smile, as Nicholas probably understood that. "My brother isn't much for studying."

"How did you come to be in Casmun?" asked a man whose title she'd forgotten.

Sage recited a story with enough truth that she couldn't be caught in a lie. "We were fleeing a Kimisar attack. A boat was our best chance to escape, and we came into your territory. We were still being chased, so we accepted Casmun's protection. Your nation's generosity saved our lives, and for that we will be forever grateful."

"How convenient that My King was in the area," the minister said sarcastically.

"Our record of springs across the desert hadn't been verified in decades," said Banneth smoothly. "I was doing the minister of roads a favor."

"Saving life is always fortunate," added Minister Sinda. "That it brings a chance for our nation to learn and grow is equally fortunate."

When he turned his head, Sage saw a large bruise on the side of his face. The back of his head also had a swollen area and a long vertical scab. The injuries looked recent.

"What is it Mistress Saizsch wishes to accomplish now?" asked the minister of war, once again sniffing like he smelled something foul about her.

"We only wish to return home as soon as possible," she said. "Our family would repay your efforts twice over."

"The effort would be considerable," said the minister of war with a sneer.

"Consider how our nation looks if we make such an effort to return our guests," said Minister Sinda. Sage thought Lani would burst with pride beside her.

"Very well," said the man who was equivalent to a lord chamberlain. He'd spent the whole proceedings looking bored. "We will discuss the matter and decide what resources to commit." He waved his hand. "Thank you for your attendance today."

Sage stood and bowed, and Nicholas did the same. "I thank you for your consideration," she said.

"Princess Alaniah, you are also excused."

Lani's face reddened with anger, and Minister Sinda's hand on the table clenched into a fist, his knuckles curling under the large rings of state he wore. "I may be able to contribute to the meeting," she said. "As I have been attending them for many months now."

"As I recall, you missed our last session to visit shops in town," said the minister of war dryly.

"I was asked to do so by the king," Lani retorted.

"She was attending to the needs of our guest as only she was able," added Sinda.

The chamberlain's thin mouth twisted in an ugly smile. "Spoken by a man who knows about attending to a lady's needs."

All the color drained from Sinda's face. Lani flushed scarlet. "I wish to stay," she said. "My presence harms nothing." Her eyes went to Banneth for support, but the king only shook his head slightly. She held his gaze for a dozen heartbeats, then shoved her seat away from the table and stormed out the door so fast Sage and Nicholas had to run to keep up.

85

OUTSIDE AND WELL away from the chamber, the princess allowed herself to explode. "The nerve of that man!" She picked up a potted plant and hurled it against the wall, where it shattered. A servant rushed to clean up the mess. "'You are excused, little girl,'" Lani said in a mocking voice. "'Why don't you go shopping, little girl?'"

"That's not exactly what he said," Sage said carefully.

"No, but it's exactly what he meant."

Lani frowned at the floral victim of her rage. "I am sorry for your trouble," she told the man on his knees, sweeping up the dirt. "When that is repotted, you may put it in my room. I will care for it in apology." He bowed his head in acknowledgment.

Sage smiled wryly. "Will you share water with it and give it a name?"

"Maybe I will." The storm had passed. Lani grinned and plopped down on an upholstered couch under a colored glass window. "Did you see how Dev fought for you, and how angry he was on my behalf?"

Sage had appreciated Minister Sinda's efforts, but she'd also seen Lani's secret romance wasn't quite as secret as she believed. "I saw," she said, taking a seat beside her friend. "I was glad to have a smile among so many frowns."

"I cannot wait to marry him. Then I will not be shut out of council meetings and important matters."

"How will that help?" asked Nicholas, who had followed them. His

Casmuni speech lagged far behind his understanding, and he spoke slowly and awkwardly.

"Because then . . ." Lani hesitated. "As the wife of a council member I will have more standing."

"I saw not other wives," the prince said. "You are princess. There is no higher but queen, and there is none now."

Lani frowned, and Sage saw Nicholas had a good point. Lani and Minister Sinda's love might be genuine, but the princess was a bit blind on what she stood to gain.

"Nicholas," Sage said. "Will you excuse us?" The prince shrugged and left.

"Lani," she said quietly. "How far has your relationship with Minister Sinda gone?"

Lani blushed a little. "Don't be such a *taku*, Saizsch. I'm going to marry him."

After overhearing Lani and Sinda, Sage wasn't surprised, but it still complicated things. As for being called a *taku*—an overbearing grandmother—she'd been just as willing if Alex had ever wanted . . . Sage cut that thought off before it could gain traction. "What power does a chessa's husband have?" she asked.

"Not more than Dev already has," said Lani. "He will actually have to resign his current position as minister of finance. It is a conflict of interest to have two royals with direct access to the treasury."

"Will he leave the council?"

Lani nodded. "Yes, but I have plans for him." She leaned toward Sage and lowered her voice. "General Pig-face will be retiring soon. All I must do is plant the idea in Banneth's head that Dev is the man for the job. Minister of war is traditionally held by the king's brother or uncle, anyway. Pig-face is only there because our brothers died." She sat back. "Of course, Dev has no idea that is my intention."

"I think what Casmun needs is a princess on the council," said Sage. "As Nicholas said, there is no woman higher than you."

Lani smiled thoughtfully. "Perhaps what Casmun really needs is a queen."

Sage didn't like the look on her friend's face. "What happened to Minister Sinda?" she asked to change the subject. "His head was hurt."

"Oh, you didn't hear about yesterday!" The princess brightened. "He was auditing the prison's weekly accounts when a Kimisar man tried to escape, but Dev stopped him. He was a hero," she boasted.

"You have Kimisar prisoners here?"

Lani nodded. "Two spies caught last month and one who was brought in with you."

"Can I see them?" Sage asked.

"I don't see why not."

86

LANI LED SAGE down several winding staircases to the lowest levels of the palace. The air became damp and cool, and they frequently had to lift their skirts to step over puddles in the corridor. "It doesn't drain well," said Lani, pointing to one. "The stones are worn from use, and that traps any water that drips from the ceiling. Perhaps we should fill them with cement, or carve grooves so the water can flow out."

Lani was much cleverer than she gave herself credit for.

Eventually they came to a landing with several guards. The princess waved her hand, and they stood aside. Sage followed, thinking Lani knew her way around the prison as well as she did the marketplace. "Do you come here often?" she asked.

"I inspect when Banneth is gone," Lani answered. She walked up to a man who looked to be in charge and spoke with him briefly. He bowed and led the way down more steps and tunnels until they came to a guarded door. Within was a large room with metal bars running down either side of a central aisle. Lani swept past him with a thank-you.

The only occupied cells were at the far end. As Sage and Lani approached, both prisoners lifted their heads from the straw mats they slept on. In spite of the dank conditions, the prison was generally clean. The guard came running up behind Sage, carrying a torch to supplement the dim light coming through a grate in the ceiling. "Stay back, My Princess," he called. "These men are dangerous."

Lani rolled her eyes at Sage. "And I thought these men were here for a picnic."

One of the prisoners stood and walked to the front of his cell. "Princess, ay?" he said in Kimisar. The man looked at Lani with disdain. "I think I understand a few things now."

The other man sat up and squinted at Lani in the same way. Neither man seemed bothered by their surroundings, like they had become a way of life.

Lani ignored them and addressed the guard. "Where is the third man?"

"Haven't seen him since yesterday," said the prisoner before the guard could answer. "Heard him a few times, though."

The guard coughed and rubbed his throat. "He needed extra restraint."

"Have you seen enough of them?" Lani asked Sage, who nodded. Something about both men made her skin crawl. "Take us to the third man," Lani told the guard.

Sage stepped aside so Lani could go first. The Kimisar called out to her. "Ay, Demoran girl." Sage looked back over her shoulder without thinking. The man met her eyes and winked. "I hope you like it down here."

She couldn't get out of there fast enough.

A few turns down the hall, the guard stopped before an iron door. "He's in here, Palachessa."

Lani stepped up and slid a narrow horizontal window open to look inside.

Sage stood on her toes next to her. The tiny room was completely dark except for the slash of light from the opening in the door. "I can't see anything," she said.

At her voice there was movement within the chamber. A shadow shifted and chains rattled. Though she knew she was safe, Sage jumped back. "He can barely move."

"It is necessary," said the guard, closing the window with a rusty screech.

The chains rattled again, weakly, and Sage took another step away from the cell. "Surely he can be restrained in another way."

"That man nearly escaped again last night, after his first attempt with Minister Sinda in the afternoon. He injured two guards and almost killed a water boy."

"He would be better treated if he behaved," said Lani.

It was one thing to know such monstrous men existed, but it was quite another to see what had to be done to contain them. Did such conditions make them more vicious, like caged fighting animals? "Perhaps he was desperate," said Sage.

The princess frowned. "Saizsch, this man was part of the attack that killed Ah'lecks, no?"

Sage twisted her hands as the image of Alex falling off his horse played in her mind. Lani was right, but the room was little bigger than a coffin. Just the thought of being shut inside made it difficult for Sage to breathe. "How much longer will he be kept in there?" she asked.

"That is not my decision, mistress," the guard said nervously.

Lani pursed her lips. "I can order him moved." She raised an eyebrow at Sage. "Is that what you wish?"

Sage thought of the bruises on Minister Sinda's face and of a terrified little boy being held hostage. Even considering that, the man's treatment made her queasy. Or perhaps it was guilt for having tried to kill him herself. "Yes?" she said, unsure.

The princess turned her gaze to the guard, who shifted his feet and hesitated before responding. "I want to obey My Princess, but I must also answer to my superiors."

"I understand," said Lani magnanimously. "You will relay my order, then, and if the head guard disagrees, he has until sunset to personally explain to me why."

The man bowed, looking relieved. "Yes, Palachessa."

Sage glanced at the iron door, feeling a strange pull. The man would be put in better conditions by nightfall. She wondered if he'd heard and understood their discussion. Probably not. Maybe she should say something to him. But what?

"Are you satisfied, Saizsch?" asked Lani. "Or is there more you would like to see?"

The underlying purpose of speaking to the man would only be to make him grateful to her and make herself feel better. Sage turned away. "I have seen enough."

87

ONCE HE THOUGHT he heard her voice, as if through a thick fog. Then it was gone.

Alex's escape attempt yesterday afternoon was unsuccessful, but when they'd caught him he didn't go down without a fight. The Casmuni traitor had questioned him for hours, but he could barely focus on account of the pain—he'd fielded one too many punches to the gut in the confrontation.

Alex tried to resist the interrogation, acted like an ignorant foot soldier and gave inconsequential information, dragging his answers out as long as he could to put off the next blow. Admitting he was Demoran now would be a death sentence.

That night, when it was over, he'd almost escaped by grabbing the guard who came to feed him. The man had no keys, but the one who ran in to assist him did. Alex got them off his belt while both guards gasped and choked on the floor next to him—nothing permanent, just enough to incapacitate them while Alex unlocked his shackles. He got six turns in the corridors before running full-force into a boy carrying two buckets of water. By the time Alex scrambled to his feet, he was surrounded, and the boy cowered on the floor in front of him.

He didn't resist, not wanting the boy to be hurt. This time they put him in a room so cramped he couldn't have turned around even if all four limbs weren't chained inches from the walls. Alex drifted in and out of consciousness, dreaming of Sage, until the ringed man returned, and suddenly the only thought that had sustained him was dangerous.

Because now the questions were about her.

Knowing Sage, she'd made herself valuable. She'd gotten close to the king and could therefore be used by this man. He wanted to blame her for the king's murder, which, for all Alex knew, had already taken place.

"Who is she?"

Alex was blindfolded, hanging by his wrists from the ceiling, but he'd learned to sense the shift in the air just before he was struck, and he tensed. "I don't know!" he cried out when the initial wave of pain subsided. "Captain Huzar never told me." Alex still clung to his Kimisar identity, believing it was his only chance of getting out alive, his only chance of keeping her alive.

"What did your commander want with her?" The pain of the shackles faded under a fresh assault.

"He never said." Alex's ribs were so bruised he could barely breathe. "I was only following orders."

"Liar." The man forced Alex's chin up. "You expect me to believe you crossed *dremshadda* and miles of desert on your own without knowing why?"

Harsh light leaked through the underside of the blindfold, making his eyes burn.

"She was incidental," he gasped. It was hard to think of her as unimportant when she mattered more than anything to him. "I was only after the prince."

Through the pounding in his head, he realized what he'd said, but it was too late.

For a moment there was silence in the room. No movement, no breathing.

Then, "What prince?"

88

THE COUNCIL HAD made no decision by the next morning. Sage was restless, studying maps of Casmun, trying to estimate how long it would take to get home by the long way. Lani dragged her out of her room for *tashaivar* in the afternoon, saying Sage needed to stop brooding. The exercise helped, but only for a few hours.

At dinner, Lani peppered her with questions about the marriages she'd helped arrange while apprenticing for Darnessa Rodelle, the high matchmaker of Crescera. The princess cast frequent looks at her brother, no doubt beginning the process of softening him to her desire to wed Minister Sinda. Sage tried to support her friend but stuck to political marriages. It was too painful to speak of love matches, which were more common in Demora than people thought. Her own parents had spurned the system and chosen each other, but so had Alex's—though according to official records, they were matched and wed nine months before his birth.

Late that night she returned to her maps, unwilling to go to bed until she was too tired to dream.

"Mistress Saizsch?"

She stood from where she leaned over the table and dropped her distance-measuring tool. "Palandret?"

"May I enter?"

"Of course, My King."

Banneth parted the gauzy curtains leading to the patio and stepped inside, nervously. "You are looking at maps?"

"Yes." Sage pointed to her charcoal marks. "I was trying to determine how soon we could be home."

"Are you so eager to leave?"

"No. Yes." Sage sighed. "I feel welcome here, but it is not our home, and I want our family to know we are safe."

Banneth nodded to the map. "They will know soon enough."

Relief washed over her. "The council has agreed to send us home?"

"No, Saizsch." Banneth shook his head. "The Demorans are here."

"Here?"

"Well, actually, they are about here." The king pointed to a spot in northeast Casmun, along the old trade route. "In four or five days, they will arrive in Osthiza."

Merciful Spirit, that was swift. They must have realized where she and Nicholas had gone within days. "That's good." Sage tried to sound casual. "How many are coming?"

"Four hundred soldiers, plus an ambassador and his party."

Oh, no.

"That's quite a number." Banneth tilted his head to the side and looked at her with piercing green eyes. "It makes me believe you and Nikkolaz are more important than you have told us."

Sage felt cold all over despite the warm night. "Palandret—"

"I am not angry," Banneth said. "I understand why you might not wish to say. And I owe you an apology. I have known about the Demorans for two days."

"Does the council know?"

The king nodded. "I told them after you left with Lani. It was why I did not want her to stay. She would have told you, and I wanted time to think."

"How did the council think on it?"

"The minister of war is not happy, as you can imagine," Banneth said. "He is urging a military response. Others are fearful. They question your true purpose in coming here."

"We were fleeing for our lives," Sage insisted. "I never lied about what happened. The Demorans don't want a fight, I promise."

"And I believe you." Banneth suddenly looked nervous. "Lani and I have been discussing ways to show our people they have nothing to fear, which brings me to my reason for visiting tonight." He held up a finger, then stepped out to the patio briefly, and returned carrying a belt and *harish*—a curved Casmuni sword. "This is for you."

Sage had wielded practice swords in *tashaivar* lessons, but the quality of this *harish* made them look like trash. Her eyes roved over the finely wrought scabbard and hilt. They were simple in decoration, and she wondered if that was in deference to her personal style. Her fingers itched to touch the weapon and test its balance, which no doubt matched its beauty.

The king offered it to her with a timid smile. "It is the finest steel in Casmun," he said. "A weapon fit for royalty."

Sage's mouth was suddenly dry. "I am not royalty, Palandret."

"This I know." He paused. "I have one for Nikkolaz, too. These gifts will show my trust in you."

He held it up for her to take, and Sage nearly snatched the sword from him, so eager was she to have it. She held her breath as she drew the blade out. The song of it sliding from the scabbard fell to a whisper once it was free. Banneth gently took the belt from her left hand and stepped back as she swung the *harish* experimentally. Its blade was so smooth and sharp that the air seemed to part in front of it visibly, like fabric. The balance was perfect.

"Oh," she breathed.

The golden glow of the lamps reflecting off the blade made it look like it was crafted of light itself. She admired it from several angles, dimly aware of Banneth removing her belt and wrapping the new one around her waist. The difference in weight drew her attention back, and her left hand felt for where her daggers usually sat. Notches in the leather assured her there were places for them as well. She smiled shyly at Banneth. "Shall we try her out tomorrow in the arena?"

The expression he returned was serious. "There is something I would ask you, Mistress Saizsch."

"Yes?" Sage said, distracted by the sword again.

"When the Demorans depart, will you consider staying?"

She lowered the sword, Banneth's words striking a strange chord within her. "You wish me to stay as ambassador?"

"No, Saizsch," he whispered. "I would have you stay as my queen."

89

HE DID NOT pressure her to accept, merely stated his reasons for proposing marriage: it would protect her and make a statement to his people that the Demorans were to be welcomed, he felt she had the knowledge and wisdom to use the position wisely, and—most importantly—it would create a union between Demora and Casmun neither nation's councils could ignore.

His last words, however, shook her most.

"I do not love you," Banneth said softly. "And I know you do not love me." He looked down. "I know, too, about Ah'lecks, and how your heart is broken. My heart was once broken the same way."

He *had* loved Queen Tamosa, but she hadn't loved him. Sage took a step backward, clutching the sword against her chest. "And yet My King asks."

His gaze came up again to meet hers. "I dare to think you might not wish to return to Demora, as your Ah'lecks is not there, and you can see the goodness that can come from staying."

Alex wasn't the only person she cared about in Demora—there was Clare and the queen and the princesses, and even Darnessa and the extended family she'd left behind in Crescera. Yet in a way she'd lost them, too. King Raymond and Ambassador Gramwell would depend on her in future negotiations, not only in language, but in the friendships she'd built. By the time Sage returned to Demora, everyone else's lives would've moved on, including Clare's, and there would be no place for her. It would never feel like home again.

"And what of your feelings, Palandret?" she managed to say. "Can you enter a second marriage without love?"

Banneth smiled tentatively. "I admire and respect you, and I am easy in your company. I hope someday we might find affection. If nothing else, I believe we can be content with each other."

Sage could almost hear the matchmaker's voice in her ear, whispering the same. She would say this kind of match—one where many people had a vested interest in its success—often had better chances of happiness than ones made for love or passion.

"I—I will have to think," she stammered.

He nodded. "It is not a decision to be made lightly, but if you accept, we should proceed at once." He blushed a little. "I have two heirs, as well as Lani, so we need not have children unless you wish to. You may stay in these rooms."

"After the first night," she whispered hoarsely. "After it is permanent."

It was only ever supposed to be Alex.

Banneth's flush deepened. "Yes."

Sage looked down at the weapon in her hands, suddenly afraid it bore a personal mark. The king stepped closer and pointed to a place on the hilt. It was blank, like the place on her dagger for the Q that would never be there.

"I will carve my name here, but not until you agree," he said. "If you do not, it is still yours to keep."

She trembled all over. "I will consider all you have said."

Banneth reached up to her face, framing it with his warm hands. "As my queen, there is nothing I would not give you, should you ask for it," he said.

Still no words would come, but the king seemed to understand.

He leaned down and kissed her forehead. "Good night, Saizsch Fahler."

Sage stood unmoving for several minutes after Banneth left.

He wanted her to be his queen.

He didn't love her, which was a relief, but she couldn't ignore what else he'd said.

By all standards, it was a good match with tremendous potential. They'd enter the marriage fully knowing it might never grow to love, but they were compatible as friends, and children were not necessary. Even Darnessa, who pulled the strings of power in marriages all across Demora, could not have plotted a better political match.

Sage shut her eyes and held the *harish* to her chest. Even having arranged several successful marriages during her time with the matchmaker, she'd never considered marrying a man she didn't love, and she didn't love Banneth.

Yet she was considering this.

Alex, forgive me.

And what kind of life would this be? Surely not terrible. Banneth would never misuse or mistreat her.

But Alex.

She would be Lani's sister and Reza's mother. She could have children of her own and raise them alongside Lani's, but that would be her choice.

But Alex.

Soldiers sacrificed their comfort, their time with family, and sometimes their very lives for the good of many thousands of strangers. She might not have the skills to fight for peace on the battlefield, but this she could do.

Alex. Alex. Alex.

Alex was dead.

He had died for *her.* How could she even consider betraying him like this?

When I say over and over how I want you to be mine, it is only because I am already completely yours.

She could never love anyone like she loved him, but Alex wouldn't have wanted her to waste away, mourning and missing him so much she might as well have died, too.

He had died so she could *live*.

Her hands tightened around the hilt of the sword.

Alex.

I'm yours.

I am.

I always will be.

The textured grip pressed painfully into her palms as she choked back a sob.

But you're gone.

90

SAGE FORCED NICHOLAS to attend *tashaivar* lessons the next afternoon, not wanting to be alone with Lani, who apparently had been the
brains behind Banneth's proposal. She hadn't decided what to do, but
with perhaps only three days left before the Demorans arrived, there
wasn't much time left to give him an answer.

"Isn't this a girl's way of fighting?" Nicholas complained, looking at
Sage, Lani, and Princess Reza standing with their instructor, a gray-haired
woman Sage had learned to fear a little bit.

"Just because women learn it does not mean it is only for them," said
a familiar voice.

Sage turned to find Darit and the king joining them, dressed to spar.
It had been only a few days since Sage had seen Darit, though it felt much
longer, and she hadn't realized how much she missed him. He smiled
warmly as he clasped her right shoulder, and she returned the gesture.

"It is well to see you again, Darit."

He smiled. "And you, Saizsch. Your language is much improved." Darit
gestured to the arena. "I have come to see what else you have learned."

Banneth had brought the sword he'd spoken of for Nicholas and
worked mostly with him, keeping a respectful distance from Sage, but
not avoiding her, either. She doubted he'd speak of last night unless she
did, or until the Norsari were on his doorstep.

"I did not know Demorans chopped so much wood," Darit said with
a wink to the king.

The prince shot Sage a questioning look, and she couldn't help but smile. "He's not being literal, Nick," she said in Demoran, using the short name that had crept into her use over the past few days. "You fight like you're chopping wood."

He scowled back. "I fight as I was trained to fight. And I was quite good for my age, you might recall."

Banneth and Darit were watching with patient annoyance, and she switched to Casmuni. "You must unlearn Demoran swordplay to master this style."

Demoran swords were longer and heavier, used for hacking, blocking, and pounding more than slicing and deflecting. The Casmuni *harish* complemented the fighting style of *tashaivar* with its speed and smoothness, often striking and then retreating back to a starting point before advancing—if advancing at all. Many movements were designed to end a fight before it truly started.

The king gave her a slight nod of thanks. Nicholas's frown remained. "It works against the Kimisar. It has been many years since Casmuni battled them. Will their style defeat them?"

Sage blushed at the prince's rudeness, but Banneth only looked thoughtful. "You have a fair point," he said. "And a good teacher is also a constant student, so I am not above learning what you may have to teach. Would you do me the honor of instruction?"

He may have said that to please Sage, but Nicholas didn't consider the request beneath its surface. He waved the *harish* to emphasize its light weight. "It has been several years since I forged a blade," he said, referring to the blacksmith training all pages went through. "So I would need help, but I can design and make Demoran-style swords with your permission."

Banneth brightened a little. "That may not be necessary, if Kimisar weapons are as similar as you say. We have two taken from our prisoners in the desert."

Sage waited until Banneth had instructed a servant to fetch the captured weapons before speaking. "Two prisoners, Palandret? I was only aware of the one Darit brought with us."

The king smiled a little wryly. "A second came in with the last patrol. Given how Darit said you reacted to the first, I did not think it wise to inform you at the time. The first died on the journey, from his wound."

That second man, then, was who had been chained in the cramped room.

Sage waited with Banneth for the servant to return, carrying two belts and swords obviously longer and heavier than he was accustomed to. He stopped before the king and held them up. Banneth gestured for Nicholas to choose, which the prince did eagerly, opting for the slightly smaller one.

The king took the second and slid it from the scabbard, stretching his arm awkwardly with the straight blade.

"This will do nicely," Nicholas said as he whipped the sword around, displaying the competence and comfort he didn't have with the *harish*.

But Sage's attention was focused on the weapon in Banneth's hand.

She knew that sword, knew the simple but elegant design of the hilt and crossguard, knew the way it felt pressed against her ribs in stolen moments.

Banneth looked impressed. "Fine balance for the weight—" He broke off as he caught sight of her. "Are you well, Saizsch?"

A dull roar began to build in her ears. "Where did you get that sword?" she whispered.

Nicholas glanced to them and then the sword. His eyes widened.

Banneth offered it to her. "Is it a design you recognize?"

The roar was now deafening. Sage wrapped her fingers around the hilt and took the weight with hands that shook. The last time she'd seen this sword, Alex was holding it as he fell off his horse into a crowd of Kimisar.

"Where did you get this?" she asked again, louder.

She swayed a bit, and Banneth reached out, ready to catch her. "The Kimisar brought in with the last patrol carried it."

Even with an arrow in his chest, Alex wouldn't have let it go easily. In her mind she saw a man holding Alex down with a foot to his chest, making it even harder for Alex to draw his last breaths, waiting until he had no strength, no resistance, no life.

Sage tore her eyes away from the sword to meet Banneth's concerned gaze. "You promised me anything I wanted, if I accepted your proposal."

His eyes widened. "I did."

The fire of emotion was suddenly stripped from her like she'd plunged into an icy river, leaving a hollow, brittle shell. Sage raised the blade between them, making him flinch.

"I want this man's head."

91

GUARDS WERE COMING. Swiftly. With a purpose.

Alex turned his head on the straw pallet. It had been three meals since the ringed man last visited—his only way of judging the passage of time—and after that interrogation he'd been moved to a different cell, though he was too battered to appreciate it much. He dared to hope the man was done with him. The footsteps stopped outside his door, torchlight streaming through cracks. Apparently not.

The door opened, and he squinted against the brightness, eyes watering. Then the light was blocked by the guard who carried the keys. Alex's arms and legs were unchained from the wall and reshackled to each other, and that's when he knew what was happening. They were taking him to his execution.

Adrenaline flooded through his veins, making him awake and alert. Though everything hurt, Alex didn't think anything was broken except maybe a couple ribs. He let the guards pick him up and drag him out the door, all the while twisting and moving to loosen joints and muscles. The chains on his ankles were a hindrance, but he exaggerated their effect, hoping to lull the guards into a false sense of security.

He wouldn't go without a fight.

"Where are you taking me?" Alex demanded of each guard in turn, using it as an excuse to look around in imitation of the wild fear he forced himself not to feel. None answered, and that fear threatened to break free when they turned away from the directions he knew led outside. A hood was yanked over his head, and Alex fought panic as the darkness closed around him.

A minute later he felt the sun on his skin, and he couldn't help thinking for a moment that he was going to die without ever having seen it again. Without seeing her. But sunshine meant he was outside, which meant the best and possibly only chance he had of escaping. He would not waste it.

Alex braced his feet and rammed his shoulder into the man on his right, then spun around with his hands together, swinging the dangling chain in a circle. The metal vibrated to his wrists as it hit another guard in what sounded like his head. Alex yanked the hood away and reflexively shielded his eyes against the glaring light. He was outside and in a clear area. He had a chance.

A guard came at him, and Alex opened his arms and leapt to grab the man around his neck and into a hold. Keeping him upright, Alex used the leverage to kick his chained legs up at another guard, but the man he held went down, and Alex was forced to release him. He lunged for the hilt of a sword, but when he pulled, the blade was too curved to come straight out of its scabbard. In that second of hesitation, the remaining guards were on him. He fought with every ounce of strength he had, but there were too many.

Something pressed on his neck, and Alex's vision dimmed, then burst with colors as his mind fought the blackness creeping in from the edges. He stopped fighting. The only thing worse than dying was dying while unconscious.

The pressure eased a second before Alex would have blacked out, and his head exploded in pain as the blood was allowed to flow again. All his fresh injuries rushed into his awareness, doubling the agony.

"Sage," he gasped, though he couldn't put much force into his words at first. "Sage Fowler. I need to talk to the Demoran, Sage Fowler."

As his voice rose in pitch and volume, someone yanked his head back and pulled a gag across his mouth. Dizzy with pain, he felt a strange gratitude that her name was the last thing he'd ever be able to say.

92

BANNETH WATCHED HER with his characteristic silence. Lani had taken Sage's side immediately and now stood with an arm around her waist. Nicholas, however, wouldn't stop pleading for her to wait.

"Sage, you don't know why he had the captain's sword. Maybe he found it."

Sage focused on the direction they expected the man to arrive from. "He had Alex's *belt*, Nicholas. His belt and dagger. He stripped them from Alex's body after he killed him or while he was dying."

"You don't *know* that!"

"I know what I saw."

"Sage, this isn't you. *Listen to me.*" He grabbed her arm, and Sage shook him off.

Commotion from nearby kept Nicholas from arguing further. Several guards appeared, half dragging a chained man with his head down. The only things clearly visible were his dirty prison breeches and the stubble of black hair on his head.

Banneth frowned and moved to meet them. "What happened to him?"

The Casmuni leading the way carried a wide executioner's *harish* at his waist. He stopped before Banneth and bowed. "He attempted to escape, Palandret. We had to subdue him."

Four of the guards were visibly bruised and bleeding. The rest were disheveled and had obviously been in a fight. Banneth raised his eyebrows as they pushed the man forward and he slumped to his knees in the dirt. "Impressive. How close did he come to escaping?"

"Closer than I would like to admit, Palandret."

Sage couldn't get a good look through the guards around him. They maintained an alert and ready posture though the man swayed like he would pass out any minute. Her hands tightened on the hilt of Alex's sword to steady their shaking. "Will we do it here?"

He must have understood her because the prisoner's body jerked and twisted at her words. The guards around him immediately moved to restrain him again, but he continued to thrash, grunts and muffled yells escaping from his gag. It took six men to pin him to the ground, and still he struggled. She wondered how he could breathe. "Let's finish this," she said.

Banneth shook his head. "I will give you what you ask, Saizsch, but he has the right to know the reason for his death. He must also have a chance to speak his last words."

Lani rolled her eyes and made a noise of disgust. "I doubt this man gave Ah'lecks the same courtesy."

The king looked back at her sharply. "Then that is a difference between us and them I am happy to have."

Lani opened her mouth to argue, but Sage shook her head. "My king is right."

Alex would've approved. When it came to mercy, however, she doubted Alex would have shown any if he was now facing the man who had killed her.

A guard went to fetch a bucket of water. Sage stared at a spot on the ground. Did she want to look him in the eyes? It felt cowardly not to face the man whose death she was demanding, but she didn't want the image of this man to pollute Alex's memory. She'd never be able to think of one without the other.

"I hope he begs for mercy," Lani murmured, her arm tightening around Sage.

Sage glanced at the man through the bodies holding him down. Soon his blood would stain the sand, and his body would rot in the criminals' graveyard outside the city. Wild dogs would dig up his bones and devour what the desert did not. He deserved it.

Yet somehow the thought did not bring her peace.

The water arrived, and the guards rolled the man over. He didn't resist; Sage wondered if he was still conscious. Darit squatted next to the prisoner and poured a dipper over his blood-and-dirt-covered face.

"Wait," said Banneth, coming forward. "Why is this man so damaged?" The king pointed to the prisoner's torso, which was visible where his shirt had come up. The exposed skin was almost completely covered in bruises.

"He had attempted escape twice before, Palandret."

The men moved so Banneth could see better. "I have a hard time believing all this was necessary," the king said, shaking his head.

"What does it matter, brother? The man is about to die," snapped Lani.

"It matters a great deal if this happened in my prison." Banneth crouched and lifted the shirt higher to trace a raw mark across the man's rib cage. He stood, looking angry. "I must find out who has done this."

Darit used a wet scrap of cloth to wipe the man's face. "We will have to ask him and investigate."

"More delay." Lani stomped her foot. "Can't you see how this hurts Saizsch?"

Darit sat back suddenly. "Palandret, I know this man." He looked up at Sage. "He was with you in the desert when I was taken. He is Demoran."

Nicholas knelt beside Darit to look. "Bleeding hell, Sage."

"Is Darit right?" Sage took a step toward them, trying to understand how that was possible. "Is he a Norsari? Do you know him?"

"I can't— I can't—" The prince was shaking his head, unable to find words even in Demoran. "It's not possible— It's not—" He leapt to his feet and met her as she came closer. "Sage, oh my Spirit!" He grabbed her shirt and shook her.

"Who is it, Nick?" Sage twisted around him to see.

"It's Captain Quinn."

93

SHE COULDN'T STOP staring at him, even hours later.

Alex's head rested on a cushion at one end of the bath while the rest of him floated just below the surface. Rather than rub his bruises and lacerations with salves, the Casmuni healers had put the curatives in the water to soak into his wounds and skin. Sage cleaned dirt and blood from Alex's face as gently as she could and treated what wasn't underwater. Even heavily dosed with pain medicines, he'd flinched away when anyone but Sage touched him.

Banneth watched from the opposite side of the bath. "I am more sorry than I can express, Saizsch," he said.

"I know," she whispered.

"He did not tell us he was Demoran. Why would he not do that?"

Sage had been mulling over that for the last three hours. "I think he was worried Darit would recognize him, and you would be angry for what he'd done." She looked across the water at the king. "Though it's difficult to imagine him being treated worse."

"Again, I am sorry." The king sighed. "But you are right. And my anger and mistrust would have fallen on you as well, once I knew what he was to you."

"Perhaps he was afraid of that, too." It was easy to imagine Alex enduring imprisonment to protect her from his association, especially if he'd been able to see that she was safe.

Around midnight, the healers moved Alex to Sage's bed, where they bandaged what they could. Once again, Sage was the only one who seemed to be able to touch him without causing pain. Fortunately, none of the cuts or abrasions were very deep, and other than the ones from his last-minute escape attempt, his injuries were a few days old and healing on their own. His shaved hair made the wounds easier to clean, as well. The bruising would be more difficult to recover from—almost his entire torso was mottled with blue and purple, including clusters of three round marks in a row. She'd have to force Alex to move around when he woke.

Darit knocked and entered. "It is done," he said. "Gispan Brazco is dead."

That was the name Alex had been listed under in the prison, and Banneth had decided everyone should believe he'd been killed in an escape attempt. Those who knew better—Lani, Nicholas, Darit, the healers, and the guards present at the time—had been sworn to secrecy until Alex's torture could be investigated. Lani had grumbled that she couldn't tell Minister Sinda, but the king insisted the perpetrator would be easier to find if he didn't know he was being hunted.

Banneth nodded his thanks to Darit. "We will start first thing in the morning."

"What about what he said?" asked Sage. When Alex had been unbound, he'd babbled about the king and an assassination. He'd only calmed down when Sage assured him Banneth was alive and well. Then the pain medicines had taken over, rendering Alex unconscious and leaving them to speculate over his words. "He said there were *dolofan* in the prison."

Darit shook his head. "The manifest has no such prisoners listed."

"But they are there," Sage insisted. "I've seen them. Two men in an otherwise empty cell block. They've been there for weeks." She didn't want to think about how she hadn't looked close enough to see the third Kimisar prisoner was Alex. It was her fault they hadn't found him sooner.

"I will look again in the morning, but if they are in the prison, that is the best place for them."

Banneth nodded. "And we cannot keep Ah'lecks in this state." He

306

stood and stretched, then addressed the healer in the corner of the room. "I will get some rest. You will send for me as soon as he wakes."

"Yes, Palandret."

Both Banneth and Darit left, and a few minutes later, the healer was dozing in the corner, effectively leaving Sage alone. She sat on the bed and took Alex's hand in hers. After weeks of imagining him cold and lifeless, it was a miracle to feel his warmth now.

He was alive.

He'd come for her. After everything she'd done, he'd still come for her.

She stroked his hand, wanting to kiss him more than anything, but too scared to touch his battered face. Pink tinged the eastern sky when Alex's eyes suddenly opened.

"Hello."

Sage's head jerked up. He smiled and blinked lazily, still dazed from drugs they'd given him. All the emotions of yesterday came crashing over her, and her eyes flooded with tears.

He frowned. "You're crying again. Why are you crying?"

"I thought you were *dead*, Alex." She wiped her cheeks with her sleeve, but the tears kept coming. "I thought I'd never see you again."

"Well, here I am," he said, his face relaxing back into a half smile.

"And look at you." She sniffed. "What did they do to you?"

"Some of it I deserved," he said, wincing as he stretched his cheeks and mouth. "I thought I was on my way to an execution, so I put up a fight."

Sage choked back a sob. "You were. They showed me your sword and said a prisoner had it. I thought he'd taken it from you after he— after he—" She stopped, panic threatening to take her at the thought of what she'd almost done.

"And you demanded my execution." Alex's shoulders shook in quiet laughter, some of the fog clearing from his eyes. "Promise me you'll never change, Sage."

His reaction only made her cry harder. "How can you laugh about that?"

"Because it didn't happen. Everything is funny when you've just cheated death."

That wasn't the only thing that hadn't happened. Sage put her hand over his heart. "I saw the arrow," she whispered. "It knocked you off your horse. How on earth did you survive that?"

Alex looked puzzled for a moment, then he placed his hand over hers. "I saw the archer and dove down. The arrow hit under my arm, lodged in my jacket. Didn't even nick me." He squeezed her hand gently. "I had no idea you saw that. I'm so sorry you suffered all that time."

"I deserved it," she said, pulling her hand back. "I lied to you and defied you in front of everyone."

He shook his head slowly. "You did the right thing when I was wrong. You stopped a war I nearly started." Alex glanced pointedly around the room. "Apparently you've gained the trust of the Casmuni royal family, and you kept Nicholas safe." He paused, looking guilty. "He is safe, right?"

"Of course." Sage gripped the bedclothes with tense white fingers. "But none of that makes up for what I did to you. I was too stubborn and wrapped up in myself to see beyond what I wanted."

"You seem to have forgotten that I was acting like an ass. And that's putting it mildly." Alex closed his eyes and took a deep breath. "Sage . . . What I went through back at Tegann, when I thought I'd have to choose between—"

"I know. Cass told me."

"*I* should've told you." He exhaled heavily, and when he reopened his eyes, they were bright with tears. "But that's why I was so afraid to have you with me. If it's a choice between you and everyone else, it's you." Alex's bandaged arm shook a little as he raised it to touch her cheek. "It's always you."

"And I only made it worse," she insisted, though she leaned into his caress. "I took your worst fear and made it real."

"Are we going to fight now about who was at fault?" His hand dropped to her neck, and he slipped trembling fingers into her cropped hair. "I'd just as soon never ever argue with you again. You can choose my meals and underclothes for the rest of my life, and I'll never complain."

"I'll hold you to that." Sage laughed as she wiped the last of her tears away, then put her left hand on his chest again, reveling in the strong pulse beneath her fingers. All traces of the pain medicine had left his eyes, leaving them clear and bright.

He was here. He was alive.

He was hers.

"I love you," she whispered.

"That," he said, pulling her down to him for a deep kiss, "is the best thing I've heard in months."

94

ALEX COULD'VE KISSED her all day, but at some point the sound of someone clearing his throat made her look away. The Casmuni king stood in the doorway to what looked like a garden, averting his eyes politely.

Sage helped Alex sit up and propped pillows behind him, but just the effort of being upright was exhausting after a few minutes. His mind was clear, though. Before the Casmuni king could ask any questions, Alex thanked him for taking care of Sage and Nicholas. "You saved their lives," he said in Kimisar. "For that I will be forever in your debt."

"Perhaps you can repay it by explaining what you said yesterday," said the king. "But first things first." He deliberately picked up a chalice from the table by the bed. After drinking from it, he offered it to Alex.

Sage had told him the king would do this, and it was important. His arms trembled from even holding the cup, but Alex took a sip and handed it back.

"Now," said Banneth. "You must tell us all that has happened."

Alex started with events the king already knew of, in hopes of establishing himself as honest. When he described his first escape attempt in the prison, Sage sat up straight on the edge of the bed, eyes wide.

"Did you see the man enough to recognize him?" asked Banneth.

"I only saw him that once. After that my eyes were covered," Alex answered. "But I feel if I saw him again, I would know it."

The king shook his head as he paced the room. "He might be only a middleman. That could lead nowhere, but we will investigate." He stopped in a patch of golden sunlight. "What did he want to know from you?"

"He wanted to know about Demora and Sage and Nicholas. I think he wanted to blame them for your assassination."

Banneth frowned. "That makes little sense. This plot was in the making long before I met Saizsch and Nikkolaz."

"From what I heard, it was a change of plans—a target of opportunity," said Alex. "Was there anyone on the council who was hostile to them?"

"Only about three-quarters of them. The most outspoken being the minister of war, but his job is to be suspicious of foreigners."

Sage had still said nothing, but Alex could tell she was frantically trying to work something out.

"Maybe we can reverse the line of thought," suggested Alex. "Who could have been the original enemy to blame?"

"Are there any councils without power struggles?" Banneth shook his head. "The minister of roads hates the minister of trade, and the minister of war hates the minister of finance. The chamberlain hates everyone." The king went back to pacing.

Alex took a deep breath and winced. "All right. Who stands to gain from your death? Who inherits the throne?"

"My son Hasseth, who is nearly eleven."

Alex felt he was on the right track. "That's too young. Who would be appointed regent?"

"Traditionally it is the minister of war, who is often the brother of the king, and therefore the heir's uncle." Banneth stopped and gazed into the garden thoughtfully. "But my sister also has claim. Lani is of age, and rules when I am gone. She is also popular with the people."

That was the third time the minister of war had been mentioned. "Who is the war minister's enemy again?" asked Alex.

"Minister Sinda," said Sage, her face pale.

Banneth nodded. "Yes, that is a good lead. The finance minister has been supportive of opening talks with Demora. He and General Calodan have been at odds for years."

"No," she said. "I mean Minister Sinda is the traitor."

The king stared at her. "Dev Sinda has been your biggest champion since your arrival."

Sage looked like she wanted to cry. "I know, but it all makes perfect sense."

95

SHE HADN'T WANTED to believe it when Alex described hitting the man with his chains as he tried to escape. Dev Sinda had a wound like that, but it could have been from subduing Alex as Lani had bragged. Sage didn't want to jump to conclusions, especially since Sinda had been openly supportive of the king, Lani, and the Demorans. For Spirit's sake, he'd gotten Lani into council meetings and given her more power.

But that had given him tremendous influence over Lani. The princess may have been old enough and have the right relationship to Hasseth to be appointed regent, but if Sinda married her, he had significant claim to both minister of war *and* regent. Framing General Calodan would make his post vacant and ripe for Sinda to step into as the young king's uncle. If Lani's youth and relative inexperience were considered an impediment to being named regent, her husband was an alternative she might not object to. Even if he was somehow excluded from both offices, Sinda could still wield power through his wife.

However, Lani had said Calodan—or General Pig-face, as she called him—was planning to resign. Sinda didn't need to get the minister of war out of the way anymore, but his retirement would almost certainly be delayed by dealing with the approaching Demoran force. If Sinda "uncovered" Sage's and Nicholas's guilt in Banneth's murder, he could use it to ensure the resignation of the military commander who'd let it happen under his nose—and line himself up to succeed the general. Additionally, the princess would be heartbroken at Sage's betrayal and depend on Sinda even more.

The third piece had been the absence of the Kimisar *dolofan* in the prison records. Minister Sinda audited the prison accounts weekly, according to Lani. He had every opportunity to erase their official existence, not to mention access to treasury funds for bribing anyone who saw too much. When he heard about Alex, Sinda saw him as a gold mine of information he could use to undermine and frame the Demorans.

Banneth wasn't convinced. "You said Kimisara would do this in exchange for passage through the mountains to attack Demora," he said to Alex. "Only the minister of war or the king could give the order for the garrison at the pass to stand down. That implicates General Calodan."

"Unless that was also arranged to frame him," said Sage. "Sinda could forge the order to make it look like Calodan had issued it. If he's bribing prison guards, he can pay the right people to have it done."

"*If* he's bribing prison guards." The king sighed and rubbed his forehead. "I can't decide whether you are trying to grasp at sand or if I am. Everything is circumstantial."

"I would recognize him if I saw or heard him," said Alex.

"It doesn't matter if I believe you; I can't arrest a high-ranking council member over an assassination that hasn't been attempted on the word of a foreign prisoner," said Banneth. "I need proof."

"We may get some from the *dolofan* when Darit finds them," said Sage. "But perhaps we can find some detail Sinda knows but should not." She looked to Alex. "When you were . . . questioned, what did you tell him?"

"I told him about Nicholas." Alex's face had gone parchment white under his bruises.

Her eyes widened and darted to the king. "I never told anyone who he is."

"I think you should tell me now," said Banneth, folding his arms.

Sage held Alex's gaze for a few heartbeats and took a deep breath. "Nicholas is a prince. He is the youngest son of the king of Demora."

"I see." Banneth drew his brows down. "What does that make you?"

"I am a tutor for the royal children. Nothing more."

The king turned his green eyes on Alex. "Is she speaking the truth?"

"In a strict sense," Alex admitted. He smiled at her lopsidedly. "But she is everything to me." Sage rolled her eyes as she blushed.

Banneth sighed. "Very well. If we can get Sinda to admit he knows this, as well as a confession from the *dolofan*, that will be proof enough."

"What about Princess Lani?" Sage said. "We can't let this surprise her."

"You say she's in love with Sinda." Banneth shook his head. "If you had difficulty convincing me—and I am still not fully convinced—imagine how she will react. It will be a shock no matter when she learns."

Sage wouldn't budge. "The longer you wait to tell her, the more humiliating this will be, and the more public. If you leave her out, she will never trust you again, but most importantly, she deserves to know."

Alex didn't hesitate. "I agree with Sage."

"You don't even know my sister," said Banneth.

"It doesn't matter," said Alex. "She deserves to know."

❖

Lani didn't want to hear it. She screamed at Alex and threw vases at the wall.

Banneth was silent, waiting for his sister's rage to run its course. When Lani finally collapsed on the floor, weeping, the king knelt by her and took her in his arms. "The betrayal is worse for you," he said. "I know your heart is broken."

"I don't believe it," Lani sobbed. "He could not do this. I don't care what they say." She looked up with eyes as green as Banneth's. "Prove it, Saizsch. If you can."

Sage glanced to Alex, who'd watched most of the conversation without understanding what was said. "Come here, then," she said to Lani.

The princess stood and strode to Alex's bedside as Sage lifted his shirt to expose his chest. She pointed to the lines of three bruises all over his body, and Alex winced as he rolled to his side to show more on his back. "Who wears rings that would do this, Lani?" Sage asked quietly.

Lani spun around and ran for the patio, but Banneth caught her arm. "You will not leave this room, Alaniah."

"He was going to ask you for my hand tonight, Banna," Lani cried, fresh tears falling down her red cheeks. "Today was supposed to be the happiest day of my life yet."

"Then nothing has happened that cannot be undone," he soothed.

Lani looked at Sage then. Banneth was wrong. Sage went to her friend and wrapped her arms around her. Lani had always seemed taller than Sage, so overwhelming was her presence, but now Sage realized they were the same height.

"I thought I had something real," Lani whispered.

"Someday you will have it, Lani," Sage whispered back. "I promise."

After a few minutes, Lani pulled herself together and turned back to Banneth and Alex. "What do we do now to prove this to the council?"

"We bring the *dolofan* to them," said Banneth. "In their questioning we try to get Sinda to admit what he knows. If that fails, we will reveal Ah'lecks, but his words could be turned against all the Demorans, so that will be a last resort."

"Will it be enough?" Lani asked.

"It doesn't matter," said a voice. Everyone turned to face Darit, who stood in the doorway to Nicholas's room. "The *dolofan* are gone."

96

ALL THINGS CONSIDERED, Alex thought Banneth took the news that two assassins were loose in the palace rather well.

"We know their plan," the king said, switching back to Kimisar for Alex's benefit. "That means we are ahead."

"Yes, but catching them in action only catches them," said Lani. The princess's Kimisar wasn't quite as good as everyone else's. "I think confession unlikely."

"Then perhaps we should make Sinda think he has succeeded," said Sage. "See how he acts and who he blames." She looked to Banneth. "What would be the first steps after the murder of a king?"

"Besides shutting down the palace and searching for the culprit? The council would be called into session to declare the new ruler."

"How soon?" she asked.

"As soon as the death is discovered."

"Even in the middle of the night?"

Banneth nodded. "Even so, but I would think there would be no reason for my body to be discovered until morning."

Sage bit her lip. "He will be prepared for that timing, so I say you should be found in the middle of the night. It gives us a slight advantage."

"Agreed, but how do we do that? Have the guards hear a disturbance and investigate?"

Sage gave the king an odd look. "Perhaps I can discover it. That will play right into his hands. It could make him overconfident."

Banneth threw a furtive glance at Alex before replying to her in Casmuni. She nodded, turning pink.

"Just a damn minute, Sage," interrupted Alex in Demoran. A horrible suspicion was growing in his gut. "Why would you be in the king's bedroom in the middle of the night?"

"I wouldn't," she answered quickly. "But if we tell Sinda at dinner that Banneth proposed to me, then I can legitimately discover the body sooner rather than later."

A sound idea, but it had been thought of too quickly. "*Did* the king propose to you?"

Her face was scarlet. Though he wouldn't have understood what Alex asked, the king answered in Kimisar. "I asked Saizsch to marry me two nights ago."

Alex looked back and forth between the two of them. "And what was the answer?"

"It was no," said Banneth.

❧

After they'd developed a plan for that evening, Alex had to rest again, though he refused the healers' strong recommendation that he take their formula to sleep better. Wonderful as that fog had felt, a clear mind was more important. He also suspected Sage hadn't slept in weeks, and Alex convinced her she wouldn't hurt him by curling up beside him. In truth, it was painful when she bumped or brushed against him, but having her close was worth it.

It was late afternoon when he woke alone. Everything hurt again, and his joints didn't want to bend. Alex was used to injuries, though the last time he'd been nearly this bruised all over was during his early page days, when a squire had openly questioned Lady Quinn's faithfulness to Alex's father. Officially he'd been disciplined and had a talking down from Colonel Quinn himself, but unofficially, he and the boys who'd joined in to help him were given extra rations for a week.

He was stretching and working things loose when Sage came in from the garden, dressed in what looked like riding clothes with a Casmuni

318

sword belted at her waist. She was sweaty and disheveled but cheerful, explaining she'd been learning some kind of fighting with Princess Lani, who'd needed to work off a lot of anger.

"How do you feel?" she asked, sitting on the bed and leaning down for a kiss. "A lot of the swelling in your face is down."

"Better now that I've seen you again, but very sore," he admitted.

Sage looked over some of his bandages, touching him more than she probably needed to, but he didn't complain. "Do you want to stay here tonight? Banneth was worried you wouldn't be up to it."

"I think another bath will do me good." He'd been unconscious for most of it, but last night they'd kept him in a medicinal bath for several hours.

She stood and began unbuckling her sword belt. "I'll call for it, but me first. Even I can smell how bad I stink."

Alex pushed himself upright as she headed toward the bathing room. "You know that tub is large enough for both of us," he called.

"Don't tempt me."

An hour later, he was soaking as Sage prepared for dinner with the king and Minister Sinda. After Alex assured her he was covered, she walked in the room, wearing a forest-green dress with draped sleeves. The style hugged her slender figure and left much less to the imagination than the full, billowy outfits Demoran women wore. "Please tell me you're bringing that dress with you when we return to Demora," he said.

She smiled and sat on a stool next to him. The scent of orange blossoms and jasmine washed over him. Not the lavender and sage he was used to, but it didn't bother him as much as he might have thought. "What shall I tell Banneth?" she asked. "Are you well enough to help? No one will think less of you if you aren't recovered."

Did she really expect him to hide in her room while assassins were in the palace? "I'm fine," he assured her. She nodded and twisted her hands in her lap, biting her lip. "Trust me, Sage."

"It's not that," she said. "It's . . . well, it's . . ." Sage took a deep breath. "Banneth wasn't quite honest when he said I'd turned down his proposal."

"I see."

"But I hadn't said yes, either," she rushed to say. "I promised him an answer in a few days."

"Sage—"

"He only wanted to assure our safety and force the council to talk to the Demorans when they arrived, rather than fight."

"Love—"

"He doesn't love me. It was purely political, for peace. He told me we didn't have to have children."

"Sage—"

"I only considered it because I didn't want to go back to Demora if you weren't there."

Alex had already made peace with the idea, given that she'd thought he was dead. He sat up and brought his face close to hers. "I wouldn't have blamed you for saying yes, Sage."

She blinked, tears collecting in her lashes. "Is that truth?"

"Truth," he whispered before kissing her long and hard. She looked like she needed it. Alex sat back, trying not to wince, and added, "If you'd still said yes after you'd found me, *then* I'd be worried."

Sage wiped her eyes and laughed. Sweet Spirit, he'd missed that sound. He'd never do anything to make it go away again. "All right. I have to leave. The healers will bandage you this time." She stood, and he was free to admire her again.

"You're only wearing one knife," Alex said, hissing in pain as his torn and bloody wrists slipped back into the water.

"Lani says two look ridiculous when wearing a dress." She fingered the letters on the hilt. "It's yours. No matter how much I hang on Banneth tonight, I've got your initials at my waist."

Alex frowned a little. "But you normally carry two."

"Yes, so?" She cocked her head to the side.

Realization dawned on her, and Alex nodded. "Maybe we should consider changing our plan slightly."

97

SAGE WAS IMPRESSED by Lani's composure throughout dinner. When Minister Sinda took her hand to kiss it in greeting, the princess traced her fingers over the distinctive stones he wore in his rings with a flicker of anger in her eyes, all traces of doubt swept away. After that she smiled and giggled through the first two courses, casting her eyes on him every few minutes and playing the giddy bride-to-be. The wine may have helped.

As for Sage, her anxiety wasn't difficult to disguise as nervousness over Banneth's coming announcement. Twice he reached for her hand, and she flushed and tried to look back doe-eyed. Sinda frowned slightly each time.

Banneth had suggested leaving Nicholas out of the evening, saying it only increased the chances something would be given away, but Sage was unwilling to let the prince out of her sight. If Alex was right, there might be an opportunity while they were at dinner to catch one or both of the assassins. She didn't want to risk something happening to Nicholas while Alex and Darit were busy. Banneth needn't have worried, though. Nicholas played his role well.

When Sinda asked Banneth if he could marry Lani, she blushed and then cried when the king granted his permission. The princess's limit, however, was reached when Sinda went to kiss her. Lani turned her cheek to him.

"Don't think you can take liberties now," she said teasingly as she met

Sage's eyes with a different look entirely. Sinda kissed Lani chastely and returned to his seat.

Banneth cleared his throat and took Sage's hand again. "I had not thought to say anything yet, but now seems opportune." He raised Sage's fingers to his lips and looked at her in a way that made her wonder if he'd been truthful when he said he didn't love her. "This afternoon I asked Mistress Saizsch to marry me."

Nicholas cheered and jumped up to kiss Sage on the cheek, then went to shake the king's hand while Banneth looked genuinely puzzled at the gesture. In the corner of Sage's vision, Sinda tensed, then recovered and smiled. Lani beamed at him. "Isn't it wonderful, Dev?"

"Most wonderful," he replied, raising his glass. "I wish Palandret all the happiness I expect to have." He took a sip without waiting for anyone else to join his toast. "When does My King intend to tell the council?"

"Tomorrow," said Banneth. "With the Demorans coming, I wish to proceed as soon as possible." He glanced at Sage meaningfully. "The sooner this union is cemented, the better for both nations."

Sage flushed and looked away. Sinda's smile widened.

For the rest of the meal, they discussed when the weddings should be held and who should be involved. Minister Sinda insisted no money for his and Lani's should come from the treasury, that he would bear the cost himself.

The hard gleam in Lani's eyes told Sage she was tallying every minute of his betrayal for repayment.

98

ALEX NESTLED BEHIND an ornate tapestry in the dark corner of Sage's dressing room, thinking how funny it was to have such a decorated closet, when he heard the door to the servants' passage open in the next room. He flexed his hands a few times before going perfectly still and waited for the shadows to go through her room, searching. Not finding what they wanted, the *dolofan* came into the dressing room and began touching and pressing fabrics and items lying around.

"Here," one whispered in Kimisar. He slid Sage's second dagger from under a pile of silk.

Alex recognized Kamron's profile as he made a face. "You win. I'll go secure our escape route."

Stesh tucked the knife in his belt. "I'll wait in the garden where I can see when he puts the lamp out."

"Don't get caught, little brother." Kamron flicked his ear. "I won't save your pretty little nose this time."

The Kimisar made an obscene gesture and slipped out the door. Kamron stayed behind, poking through Sage's things and tucking a few pieces of jewelry in his vest. Alex had been worried about losing the man while following him, but Kamron's greedy delay meant Alex was able to take him down right there.

After using several of the silk scarves lying around to bind the Kimisar, Alex poured a triple dose of medicinal tea on the man's gag. Then he dragged the limp body out of the room and back into the servants' corridor. About halfway there Alex realized he'd overestimated how much his body could take. Though brief, his struggle with Kamron had exhausted him and undoubtedly set some of his healing back a few days. He had to rest every few feet, and it took much longer than expected to reach Banneth's room.

Originally Alex had planned to be there, waiting with Darit, but when he'd seen Sage dressed for dinner and wearing only one knife at her waist, it occurred to him how she could be blamed, and he decided to wait in her room. Darit's relief was plain on his face when Alex finally appeared.

"I had to admit, there was a part of me that did not trust your honesty," the Casmuni told Alex as he took the Kimisar's legs and helped carry him into the bathing room.

Alex wasn't insulted. "I have much to atone for with you, Darit," he said. "Especially as you saved Sage and my prince." Darit only nodded. Once the Kimisar was set against a wall and his restraints rechecked, Alex collapsed in a corner. The next thing he knew, the king had returned from dinner.

"Saizsch is in her room," Banneth said, gently shaking Alex's shoulder. "She will wait for you to return before coming here."

Alex rubbed the sleep from his eyes. "Where is Darit?"

"He left after the guards saw me speak with him. That way he has an excuse to be close when my body is found." The king pulled a familiar black-handled dagger from his jacket. "Saizsch sends you this."

"Thanks." Alex used the wall to help him stand and accepted the weapon. On the opposite side of the room, Kamron was still unconscious, his half-open eyes glazed with the effects of the sedatives.

Banneth watched Alex walk around to loosen his muscles. "I know you are risking your life now for Saizsch and Nikkolaz," he said after a few silent minutes. "But this is also for me, and I am grateful."

"I, too, have much to be grateful for," said Alex simply.

The king hesitated. "I would have treated her well, but I knew that she would never care for me like she cares for you."

"I know this." Alex paused to offer Banneth a smile. "That is why I am not angry. Besides"—he looked away because there was a small part of the situation that *was* painful, even if he didn't want to admit it—"I cannot blame you for seeing her worth."

Darit returned then, and Banneth went about preparing for bed as though nothing was wrong. A manservant helped him undress while Alex and Darit stayed out of sight. Once his man was dismissed for the evening, Banneth settled cushions under the bedclothes to make it look like he was there, extinguished the lantern, and slipped back into the bathing room. He'd wanted to stay in the bed as bait, but both Alex and Darit considered that too dangerous. They took places in the corners of Banneth's silent bedchamber and waited.

Alex almost missed the man's entry. The assassin came in with a breeze that rippled the sheer curtains leading to the patio. Dark as it was outside, the king's chambers were darker, giving Alex and Darit a slight advantage. The moon wasn't up, and Stesh cast no shadow as he glided, wraithlike, into the room. Despite the Kimisar's intentions, Alex couldn't help admiring the man's stealth.

Stesh had his back to Darit's corner, and as he approached the king's bed, the Casmuni eased away from the wall. Alex was in his line of sight and didn't dare move. There was a low hiss as the assassin slid Sage's knife free of the sheath. One hand reached for the lump on the bed.

The hand froze and the man stepped back.

Darit was still halfway across the room. Before Stesh could turn around, Alex leapt from his corner, resisting the urge to throw his knife—they wanted him alive. The assassin reacted instantly, hurling the dagger in his hand at Alex, but Alex was already diving down to the carpet. His intention had been only to give Darit a chance to get closer. A burning stripe across his left shoulder told him he'd been grazed by the blade. The impact on the floor was far worse, and Alex nearly blacked out from the pain as he rolled into the side of the bed, clutching his bleeding arm.

By the time Alex had recovered enough to stand, Darit was struggling with Stesh on the other side of the bed. For a moment he hesitated, unsure which man was which in the darkness, then the pair separated.

Darit's sword swung out and Stesh deflected it with a curved dagger. Alex flung his knife at the Kimisar's hand, knocking it away, and Darit sliced around. Stesh dropped to his knees, clutching his middle. Darit kicked him over and stepped on his neck to hold him down as Alex slumped on the bed, gasping.

"Palandret," Darit called softly. "It is finished."

99

SAGE SAT IN her room, trying not to vomit from the coppery smell of blood all over her nightdress. It reminded her of waking up drenched in the blood of the first man she'd killed. The man who formerly owned this blood wasn't dead, though. At least not yet.

She looked down at her hands. The blood on them was actually Alex's. Everything had gone as planned except Alex had been hurt again. He claimed it was just a scratch, but to him, "just a scratch" meant a half-dozen sutures. Currently he and the *dolofan* were hidden in Lani's dressing room, the least likely place anyone would look for the king's assassins, especially since everyone believed they were already caught. Some of the guards who'd been present when Alex was discovered were with him to watch over the Kimisar. She hoped he was getting some sleep.

Once everything was in place, Sage had run screaming from Banneth's rooms and across to Lani's apartment, and Lani, in turn, raised the alarm. Darit had been the first on the scene, after the guards in the outer passage. Because Darit was the king's close friend and lead rider, all the guards had obeyed him when he ordered the palace locked down. Only council members were permitted to enter the gates, and they were escorted straight to the meeting chamber. Some got a detour to look into the king's room, but no one was allowed to get close to the body, lest they discover it was still breathing.

Minister Sinda arrived in the middle of it all, neither too early nor too late. Lani had thrown herself at him, sobbing, and Sage suspected she enjoyed smearing as much blood on him as possible. Upon learning it was Sage who discovered the body, he'd ordered her and Nicholas confined to her quarters and the garden searched. She wasn't surprised when the bloody knife was found buried in the flowers near her patio. After all, she'd chosen the spot.

The four guards in the room imposed silence every time she'd tried to speak to Nicholas, who looked terrified. Though he'd known since dinner there was some sort of ruse going on, Sage hadn't explained everything, only assured him in their own language that Banneth wasn't dead, for all he was lying in his bed covered in blood. The council meeting was in full swing by now, and she expected to be called and accused at any minute. She hoped it would be soon. Much as she disliked wearing all this blood, the king had to lie in it.

As the sun rose, Sage began to feel agitated. They'd wanted this resolved by dawn, before the people in the city had a chance to hear the rumors of Banneth's death. Sinda was likely dragging this out to create maximum panic. Finally, she and Nicholas were called before the council and prodded by guards with spears all the way. They stood before the long table, still wearing their nightclothes, with over a dozen hostile faces staring at them. From the far end of the room, Lani flashed an icy smile.

Minister Sinda stood and addressed everyone, making a long speech about how their nation had nursed two vipers to their chests, that he himself had been deceived by their innocent appearance and swayed by their beloved king's good but naive intentions. Sage remained calm throughout, taking Nicholas's hand when he began to tremble. She let Sinda say everything he wanted. His elaborate knowledge and story would only work against him once they were proved false when Banneth simply showed up alive.

Sinda finished his speech and turned to the Demorans. "What have you to say for yourselves?"

"You have no proof," answered Sage.

"Where were you last night?" Sinda demanded.

"After dinner with you and the royal family, I stayed up late with

Princess Alaniah. As you may recall, you asked the king for his permission to marry her. We had much to talk on."

The faces around the table looked to one another in surprise. Apparently that hadn't been mentioned this morning. The minister had probably wanted to wait until he was the hero, when the news would've gone over well.

Sinda was unfazed. "I recall another event from that dinner, do you?"

"Dessert was orange custard."

"*Do you find this amusing?*" Sinda bellowed. She'd rattled him by not behaving as he'd expected. "The king is dead!"

She blinked innocently. "We hadn't gotten to that part yet."

Lani put her face in her hands and sobbed, but Sage suspected she was actually laughing.

"Our beloved king told me that he had proposed marriage to you."

Sage nodded. "Yes, he did." Heads reeled again in shock. "But why would I accept, only to kill him?"

"I don't know," said Sinda. "Perhaps that was your entire purpose in coming to Casmun, to seduce our king and get close enough to assassinate him. It was you who 'discovered' his body in the middle of the night."

"And yet, I did not kill him," she said. Alex believed the *dolofan* would have no reason not to identify the minister as their conspirator, but it couldn't be depended on, or that the council would accept their testimony. Sinda had to admit what he'd learned about Nicholas—and how, if possible—in front of everyone so Alex's later testimony would ring true. The question was whether he wanted to hold that back for other purposes.

Sinda gestured to a guard who came forward and set a bloody dagger on the table. The golden *SF* glittered in the sunlight streaming through the window. "Is this your weapon?" Sinda asked.

Sage barely glanced at the knife. "You know it is."

"It was found buried in the royal family's garden, between your quarters and the king's."

"That proves nothing," she said. "It could have been put there to blame me." Sage was actually enjoying herself. The only thing she felt bad about was Nicholas's fear. She squeezed his hand in reassurance. "I gain nothing from the king's death. As you pointed out, I have lost my chance to become Casmun's queen."

"You act incredibly unconcerned, Mistress Saizsch." Sinda turned to face the council. "Is that because you know your country is coming to your rescue? Is that why four hundred Demoran troops are on their way to Osthiza right now?"

Sage saw her opening to turn the focus on Nicholas a little. "If so, it would appear they are a little too late to save my brother and me."

Sinda snorted. "Your brother?" He looked back to her. "Or your prince?"

A ripple of murmuring broke out among the council. Nicholas paled even more, and Sage squeezed his fingers again. The less she said, the more Sinda would have to reveal what he knew.

"I learned this in questioning the Kimisar man who followed them into Casmun," Sinda told the men around the table. "Something General Calodan could not be bothered to investigate, I might add." The minister of war's face went purple with rage, and Sinda raised an eyebrow at Sage. "Do you not deny Nikkolaz is the son of your king? That he was sent into Casmun to give your country an excuse to invade?"

"Those are two questions with different answers."

"You will answer for your treason!" shouted Sinda.

Darit had been standing by the double doors to the chamber; now he turned around to unbolt them.

"I committed no treason, Minister," Sage said, dropping Nicholas's hand and stepping forward. The room was so riveted no one noticed the doors opening. "Unlike you, I have no duty to Casmun or its king."

His face triumphant, Sinda shook his head. "No, but you will stand trial for the king's murder. As will Nikkolaz."

The familiar silhouettes in the doorway brought a smile to Sage's lips.

"That will be rather difficult," said Banneth.

100

THE ONLY THING better than Minister Sinda's face when he saw Banneth was when he recognized Alex standing beside him. They strode into the room together, Alex three steps behind the king, as the council erupted in shouts. Several ministers fell out of their chairs and to their knees, thanking the Spirit. Sinda's complexion took on a greenish cast, which only worsened when Lani came to stand by Sage.

Banneth had cleaned up and changed, looking imposing and in complete control, unlike anyone else in the room. When the chaos had died down and everyone was back in their seats—except Sinda, who was rooted to the spot—the king called the council to order.

"Gentlemen," he said, then paused to nod to Lani and Sage. "As the full council is present, I invoke an emergency judgment trial, for the good of the nation, that we may resolve this matter quickly and decisively."

No one objected. Sage imagined they were still too shocked to understand what was happening.

"At any time, any member may call for a judgment that will end the proceedings if the vote is unanimous in favor of guilt or innocence. The accused is allowed to call any witness in his defense until such a judgment is made."

"Palandret," said the minister of roads weakly. "Who is on trial and what are the charges?"

"Dev Sinda stands accused of treason, conspiracy, and attempted assassination of a sovereign. I am sure we could add bribery, but those will do."

"I object," said Sinda, finding his voice. "I will never vote in favor of my guilt—this trial is nullified."

Banneth had anticipated that. "The minister of finance is engaged to marry the Princess Alaniah. By law, such a close relationship to the royal family removes him from his post. Dev Sinda is no longer a voting member of this council."

Before Sinda could protest that a full council no longer existed, Lani spoke up. "I nominate Darit Yamon for the vacant position of minister of finance."

"As king, I have the right to make an interim appointment," said Banneth. "Darit Yamon, do you accept?"

Darit bowed. "Yes, Palandret."

"So be it."

Guards appeared on either side of Sinda, stripping him of the knife he carried and searching him for more weapons. Sage was speechless at how well coordinated everything had been.

"Now," said Banneth, taking his seat at the head of the table. "I suggest we begin with my first two witnesses, as one isn't likely to live much longer." The doors were opened and four guards entered with the *dolofan*. At the look of hatred from the Kimisar clutching his bloody stomach, Sinda panicked and bolted for the door, but the guards were faster. In one last stroke of justice, it was Alex who produced a set of shackles to hold the accused.

The first and only vote was held an hour later.

❖

Casmuni law required a full day between sentencing and execution. Two mornings later, Dev Sinda was led to the block in the market square in front of the prison. Though Lani looked calm and regal as ever, she was on the verge of collapse, and Sage had her arm around her friend's waist to support her.

The charges of conspiracy, treason, and attempted assassination of a sovereign were read aloud and the verdict and sentence announced. Sinda stood silently, his shackled wrists hanging in front of him. His unkempt hair and lined face no longer looked handsome and distinguished, but rather cold and calculating.

Banneth stepped forward, and the crowd sighed in audible relief. Despite the immediate shutting down of the palace, rumors of his assassination had spread quickly, and people were glad to see for themselves they weren't true. "Do you have anything to say for yourself?" the king said.

Sinda then turned his eyes to Sage and Nicholas. "Do give the Kimisar my regards when you return home."

The *dolofan* had failed, but the smug look on Sinda's face made Sage sick to her stomach. "Wait!" she shouted in Casmuni.

The executioner froze with his harish in the half-begun swing and looked to Banneth, who held up his hand to indicate he should halt. Sinda rotated his head from the block and looked up at her. "Yes, my dear?" he said mockingly.

"You sent the order for the garrison to stand down as soon as you thought the king was dead, didn't you?" she said. "The pass is open."

Or it would be within days.

Sinda only smiled. "*Bas medari*, Saizsch Fahler."

He turned to resettle his neck on the block. "Let's get this over with."

333

101

THE DEMORANS ARRIVED in Osthiza that evening to find a city in an uproar. Banneth was organizing as many troops as possible to march the next morning for the pass to the west. The distance was far, but the desert ground was solid enough that a road linked the capital to the fortress. Seven days was considered the minimum time needed. Banneth planned to do it in fewer than five.

The king was busy, so Sage, Nicholas, and Alex rode out to meet the Demorans as they set up camp on the plain outside the city gates. Ambassador Gramwell was there as Sage expected, but she was surprised to see Clare next to him. Alex stepped up to Colonel Traysden and saluted formally before requesting permission to report. While he explained everything to the ambassador and officers, Clare filled Sage in on what had happened on the Demoran side.

That Sage and Nicholas went into Casmun was known within a day. When Alex and two volunteers had gone into the desert after them, Casseck returned to a camp occupied by Colonel Traysden, who assumed command of the Norsari. While dispatches went flying to the capital, the Demorans pursued the Kimisar to the foothills of the Catrix, where they crossed into Casmun, and the Norsari did not follow. Extra troops came across Jovan in case the Kimisar came back, but the Norsari and the unit Colonel Traysden brought headed for Vinova, anticipating permission from Tennegol to go after Nicholas the long way around. As soon as they had the authority, the ambassador and almost all the soldiers at Vinova headed south. Thanks to what Sage and Clare had learned, the Demorans never considered trying to cross the desert.

Everyone finished their stories at about the same time, and they all stood looking at one another for a minute. Colonel Traysden cleared his throat. "Captain Quinn, I hereby formally return command of Norsari Battalion One to you. It was my honor to serve as commander in your absence."

Alex saluted, and Sage could see he was holding back tears. The colonel returned the salute, and the moment was over.

"So, Captain," said Traysden after the officers took turns shaking Alex's hand and welcoming him back. "When do we leave for the pass?"

∞❖∞

They returned to the palace with Ambassador Gramwell, Clare, their retinue, and the news that the Demoran soldiers would march with them in the morning. Banneth took one look at the Demoran horses and insisted on providing Casmuni mounts for the officers, saying the lighter, slender breeds they rode would be more reliable on a journey across the desert. Alex looked a little insulted, but he acknowledged the Demoran horses were exhausted from pushing so hard to get to Osthiza.

Lani offered her white stallion to Sage, and when that was translated for Alex, he shook his head. "You're staying here with Nicholas."

Sage crossed her arms. "Who's going to choose your meals and underclothes if I'm not there?"

Alex opened his mouth to protest, then clamped it shut and exhaled through his nose, frowning.

"I'm going to have to watch you ride away for years, Alex," she said, stepping close to him and lowering her voice. "I'll be damned if I do it when I don't have to." She put a hand on his crossed arms. "I'll stay back from the fighting, I promise."

He sighed. "Is this the wrong time to tell you how much you remind me of my mother?"

"Is that an attempt to dissuade me?"

"Only if it works," he said, dropping his arms and planting a kiss on her forehead.

Ten minutes later, Clare committed to coming, too. "Sage can't be out there alone," she said. "Think of her reputation."

Alex rolled his eyes, but didn't even try to object.

They left at first light, but instead of heading directly for the road west, Banneth led them south, to a mountain of stone on the horizon. Outside an entrance carved into the rock, a wagon was being loaded with clay pots sealed with wax. Each time a vessel was put down, a man wrapped cloth around it, presumably so they wouldn't bang against one another while riding. "What's this?" Sage asked Banneth.

"Come, I will show you," he said, dismounting. "Bring Ah'lecks and his top men."

Sage signaled to them, and they gathered around a pot that had cracked and been set aside. Banneth picked it up carefully and gestured for everyone to stand back, then dropped it on the ground so it broke open. Among the shattered pottery was globs of what looked like apple jelly. The king poured a little water in his hand and sprinkled it over the mess. When the drops touched the jelly it sizzled and flamed for a few seconds.

"It is an ancient weapon most Casmuni do not even remember we ever possessed," said Banneth as Sage translated. "Water is what makes the flame. You must never touch it. Even the sweat on your skin is enough to set it off." The king took another step away from the pot and jelly and squeezed a stream of water on it. Flames leapt up, making everyone jump back. As they watched, the heat of the fire melted the sand and stone around it into black glass.

"We call it *dremvasha*," said Banneth.

Waterfire.

"Is it made with oil?" Sage asked, and Banneth nodded. "So if you put this on water, it will float and spread?"

"Yes." Banneth slung his waterskin back over his shoulder. "It was done once before, many years ago. The devastation lasts to this day."

Sage watched the liquid jelly slide down the glass until it reached more sand, which it melted in a lengthening trail. Corporal Wilder had described the desolate canyon on the border with Casmun as steep and smooth with sides like jagged broken glass. Deadly. This was what had done that. "Yanli Gorge," she whispered, and Banneth nodded.

Alex looked at her questioningly, and she explained to him and the others. He shook his head in awe. "Sage, the oldest maps labeled Yanli as a plain. That gorge wasn't just melted, the entire thing had to have been formed by this. All forty miles."

As they mounted their horses and moved on with the loaded wagons, Sage looked back to see the flames were still burning.

102

THE CASMUNI AND Demorans arrived at the pass five days later to find the fortress built into the cliff abandoned. For now, Alex and Banneth were less concerned about where those men had gone than with setting up their defense. The king led the way through the gap in the rock wall, which was only wide enough for five mounted men to stand across. A few dozen yards beyond that, however, the passage suddenly widened into a bowl-shaped area large enough to hold about a thousand men before narrowing again.

Alex studied the curved edges of the bowl. The almost-perfect circle didn't look natural. At his question, the king replied that it had been deliberately mined as a quarry centuries ago to form the shape. The idea was to create a place for the first line of defense. If that failed, the invaders still had to go through the Neck, as the outer narrow gap was called, where the Casmuni would have a second chance to defeat them with the land.

"But that means the men fighting in here can be trapped, unable to retreat," said Alex.

Banneth nodded. "That is the trade we made for two places to stop the enemy—one place that may also stop us. But the loss would not be great. Only a few hundred."

It was a good space to fight with the number they'd brought, but there was no one outside the pass to back them up. "Do you think we made it in time?" Alex asked. His biggest fear had been arriving only to see the tail end of the Kimisar army, headed north.

Banneth gestured to a spot on the ground where the sand had a flowing look. "The river here has only recently dried up. If they had passed through in the last week, we would see it there."

Next to them, Colonel Traysden nodded his agreement. He'd come along with his own unit, which was small for his rank, but he made no move to interfere with how Alex commanded the Norsari. "Where do we use the waterfire?" Traysden asked.

The king led them out of the bowl and deeper into the pass, where it was wide enough for ten armed men to walk abreast. After about a quarter of a mile the pass had several snakelike bends. He stopped and pointed up to the rock ledges partway up the almost-sheer sides of the canyon. "Here, I think. If we can drop enough fire on their heads while they are backed up trying to enter the bowl, perhaps they will retreat."

Alex nodded. Not a bad plan for ten to one odds.

103

SAGE AND CLARE were left to themselves while the soldiers prepared. The number of men seemed pathetically small when Sage considered how many thousands were likely to come through the pass. More Casmuni soldiers would eventually arrive in support, but if the Kimisar came in the next three or four days, the force here was all there was between them and Demora.

Crates were constructed to hold the pots of *dremvasha*, and they were hauled up and along a ledge that ran the length of the pass about forty feet up. Barrels of water were placed nearby for setting the waterfire ablaze. Scouts ventured deeper into the pass, looking for signs of Kimisar on the march, but between the narrowness and frequent bends, it was difficult to see ahead in most places. Depending on how fast the messengers could run, there would only be a few hours' warning.

Alex was almost healed from his time in the dungeon, which was a relief, as he would've fought no matter his condition. He told Sage and Clare that when the time came, their place was at the high watchtower of the fortress, and Sage fully intended to obey that—when the time came.

Their second day passed slower than any she could remember. Every noise made them jump, and her hand ached from constantly gripping the hilt of her sword. The men, too, were irritable and snapped and argued over the most minor of slights. Lieutenant Casseck had to break up two men before they came to blows. When night fell, she sat under the stars with Alex in the bowl, ready to fall asleep on his shoulder from being so tense all day. "Is it always like this?" she asked. "Before a battle?"

"Pretty much," he said. "It's why some men charge in to a fight when they're at a disadvantage. They're too impatient to wait for the better moment."

"Thinking before I act isn't my strength," said Sage. "I don't think I'd make a very good soldier."

Alex nuzzled her hair with his nose. "Love, you are one of the bravest, fiercest people I know." He kissed her head. "And that is truth."

There were few higher compliments he could offer. Sage wasn't sure she had the kind of bravery needed on the battlefield, though.

Alex suddenly leapt to his feet, nearly knocking her over. Shouting echoed out of the pass, and all around them soldiers were standing up, including Lieutenant Gramwell, who'd been sitting with Clare not far away. Alex helped her up, and she resisted the urge to hold on to his arm in case he needed to draw his sword. Two men came flying out of the gate of stone. One dropped to his knees, panting, and the other bent over and vomited from running so hard.

"They're coming," the man on the ground gasped. "They'll be here by sunrise."

Everyone was moving in a matter of seconds. Alex swept Sage close with an arm around her waist and kissed her. "This is it," he said. "Go to the fortress. Watch everything. If we fail, you and Clare have to get back to Osthiza and tell everyone what happened."

"You mean just *leave* you here?" Sage cried.

"Yes." He pressed his forehead to hers as orders were shouted around them in two languages. "Promise me, Sage. I can't focus down here unless I know you'll be safe."

She nodded reluctantly, and he kissed her again, slowly this time, like he had all the time in the world. Then Clare was pulling on her hand, and they were running to the horses already being saddled for them. Sage led the way back through the Neck, hearing the reports of readiness behind them. Outside the canyon, they hooked around to the right and into the shelter of the fortress. She didn't want to leave the horses saddled—it felt like expecting defeat—but she'd promised Alex they'd be ready to flee.

By the time she and Clare made it to the top of the tower, half the stars had faded. Rows of troops spread out in the twilight below, looking pathetically small, even in the contained area of the bowl. Beside her, Clare's face was parchment white and her mouth drawn into a thin line. "I wish I hadn't come," she muttered.

Sage was about to answer her when the glow of flames could be seen reflecting off the stone walls leading into the pass. Was it the *dremvasha*? That should've been too far to see.

But no, it was torches carried by the lead rank to light the way through the dark canyon. The first Kimisar burst into the open area, appearing surprised to find opposition.

The Casmuni and Demorans charged.

❖

For the first hour, the Kimisar made little progress. Every time they gained a few yards into the bowl, the allied fighters drove them back again. Sage could see their side rotating men, having them peel away from the fight to let the fresher rank behind them take over. The sun peeked over the horizon, shining light into the battlefield through the Neck.

If the *dremvasha* was having an effect, Sage didn't see it.

"Sage." Clare tugged on her arm, but Sage was glued to the battle, trying to pick out the one figure she cared about most. "*Sage.*"

"What?" she snapped, harsher than she meant to.

The fortress's watchtower was built to see both into the bowl and outside the pass itself. Clare pointed at the flat plain below. "Who is that?"

Sage squinted at a column of figures approaching from the north, along the slopes. It couldn't be reinforcements—no one lived in that direction. Sage led Clare down the steps of the tower to where they could look out a window and not be seen by the advancing group. The first of the new arrivals reached the mouth of the canyon, and after a brief discussion, several entered the pass. A few minutes later they returned and others gathered around them.

"Come on." Sage went lower to find a better place to look out at the men, and Clare followed.

"They look like Demorans," Clare whispered, and Sage nodded in agreement. Their clothes were definitely Demoran in style, but everything was worn and filthy, like they'd come a long way.

Sage crept closer to the window until she could overhear them talking.

Kimisar.

They were discussing what they'd seen in the bowl, concluding whoever had their backs to them were fighting their countrymen. Several wanted to join in.

Sage tried to make a quick count, getting lost twice at a hundred as they shifted around, but she was sure there were more than enough to cause a major problem. The Casmuni and Demorans weren't expecting danger from the east. With the rising sun, they wouldn't even see the Kimisar coming until they were right behind them.

"What do we do?" whispered Clare.

104

HUZAR HAD TRIED to make it to the pass before dawn, hoping for the chance to sneak in under cover of darkness. As he and his men approached, he saw no light coming from the fortress in the rock, as if no one was there. Seeing nothing to stop them, Huzar decided to continue even as sunlight poured over the horizon.

The sound of shouting and metal on metal echoed out of the entrance to the pass, and he sent a few men in to investigate. There was fighting in the round area beyond the narrow opening. That must be where the men manning the fortress had gone—to stop Kimisar coming through the pass. Huzar's numbers were few, barely over 120, but the Casmuni were trapped in the bowl. If he came in from behind the main battle, the Kimisar could wear the Casmuni down on two fronts. He discussed it with the men around him, and they were all eager to join the fight.

This was what real soldiers did—not ally with traitors, not take young boys hostage. They didn't die under rock slides. They faced their enemies and fought like men.

Huzar was organizing the company into columns and instructing them how he wanted them to spread out, when a scream interrupted him. A white horse came flying around the fortress wall, ridden by a Casmuni man waving a sword. The Kimisar instinctively scattered out of his way, and the rider flew into the pass.

Shit. Just as the Casmuni weren't looking behind them, Huzar had been complacent about who could sneak up on the Kimisar. The rider hadn't attacked, though—he was going to warn the Casmuni inside.

Huzar had lost the element of surprise.

105

ALEX ROTATED TO the rear ranks of the allied soldiers, taking the chance to catch his breath. Gramwell was next to him, leaning on his sword and panting.

"Where's the damn waterfire?" Alex said. "I haven't seen any sign it's being used."

"Want me to go look?" asked Gram.

"Maybe you should." The whinny of a horse made Alex turn around. Out of the golden light streaming through the pass came a rider on a white horse. He headed straight for Alex and skidded to a halt in front of him.

"Alex!" Sage shouted down at him. "Thank the Spirit!" She sheathed the sword she was carrying.

"What the hell are you doing here, Sage?"

She waved a gloved hand behind her. "Kimisar," she gasped. "Coming from behind."

"Where the bleeding hell did they come from?"

"I don't know," she said. "But there's over a hundred."

Alex grabbed the man next to him. "Turn around! Turn everyone around! They're coming from behind us!" Soldiers began to react, forming a rear line. "Sage, you need to get out of here!"

"I can't," she said. "Not till all those Kimisar come through."

She was right. Just then a Demoran came running toward them, calling for Captain Quinn. "Over here!" he shouted back.

A man from the *dremvasha* detail collapsed in front of Alex. "Sir, the waterfire! There was a rock slide. It's half-buried, and so are most of the men. We can't use it!"

"Here they come!" someone yelled, and dozens of Kimisar came running out of the sunlight.

Sage kicked the horse to get behind the line of fighting. Alex followed, keeping himself between her and the Kimisar. "I heard what he said about the *dremvasha*!" she shouted over the noise, and pointed to the path up the ridge. "I can't go back—let me go help up there!"

Alex held her gaze for a pair of heartbeats, then nodded and grabbed Lieutenant Gramwell beside him. "Go with her, Luke!"

Sage yanked the reins around and took off for the canyon.

106

SAGE ABANDONED LANI'S horse when the ground became too steep for him to climb and scrambled up the side of the bowl on her hands and knees. From the ledge, she paused to look down on the battle below. The Kimisar coming from behind had changed the whole dynamic.

She ran along the ridge and into the canyon mouth, trying to ignore the forty-foot drop on her right. The air became thick with dust, and the stone vibrated under her feet with the rhythm of the soldiers passing below. That must have set off the landslide. Sage pulled her head scarf up to cover her face and stepped over an arm sticking out of a pile of dirt and rock. At the last second, she stooped to brush her fingers across the dead man's palm, whispering a quick prayer.

Several soldiers were ahead, digging with hands and makeshift tools to free a crate of *dremvasha* half-buried in the hillside. The crate came free, but it was full of dirt now, too. A pair of men dragged it toward the ledge, and the earth began shifting to fill the new hole. Sage screamed for them to get out of the way as the hillside came loose and pushed the crate over the edge, along with one of the men. Watching him tumble made her dizzy enough to turn away and hug the slope behind her.

When the dust settled, Sage was on one side of a vertical scar across the hill, while three men on the other held on to the last crate, which had been ripped open. She looked down on the Kimisar below. *Dremvasha* and pottery lay strewn on a newly formed hill, and the Kimisar ran over and around it. There was no sign of the man they'd lost, and she hoped for his sake he hadn't survived the fall.

Every few seconds another rank of Kimisar passed, faster than before, headed into the narrow entrance to the bowl. The only way to end this was to cut off the supply of invaders entirely.

Sage looked back to the men on the other side of the rockslide. "Throw it all out!" she shouted, and waved.

Clay pot after clay pot went over, the sounds of shattering pottery lost, for the most part, in the movement below. The only thing left was the water, which was on her side. Sage turned around to find the barrels of water half-buried. She began flinging rocks away with her hands, grateful she still wore her riding gloves.

One of the men on the *dremvasha* side called out, telling her to break them open rather than dig them out. Sage reached for her sword, but the soldier shouted again and stretched across the scree between them to hand her an ax. Yes, that was probably better. Sage reached back, but she couldn't quite grasp it, and he had to toss it to her.

A quick glance assured her the last of the *dremvasha* would be on the ground soon. Sage gripped the ax with both hands as she turned back to the barrels and took a horizontal swing.

The blade bounced off, jarring every bone in her body, and she nearly lost her footing. Setting her feet, she tried again, this time aiming at a downward angle. A few heavy splinters came off, but it was better than nothing. Again and again she hacked at the barrel, sometimes switching to an upward angle to make the opening that was taking shape wider. When she felt she'd weakened it to the last few blows, Sage climbed over the barrels to the other side. Once the water was released, she'd only have a few seconds to get the other barrel open before the canyon below went up in flames. She worked the second as she had the first, until she felt sure a couple more hits would have it spraying water over the ledge.

Sage stopped for a moment to look back the way she'd come. Lieutenant Gramwell was flying down the path, covered in dirt and blood. "Kimisar coming behind me!" he shouted. "Run!"

"I can't!" she yelled. "I have to get these open!"

Gram stopped and took in the situation, then nodded. "All right, do it! I'll hold them off!" He turned and set his feet, gripping his sword with both hands.

If she wanted to escape, she needed to be on the other side. Sage scrambled over the barrels again to where she'd begun, then raised the ax to break open the one on the opposite side. After three hits, the barrel burst open, pouring water from the hole in its side and onto the *dremva-sha* below. Sage was positioning herself to finish the second when Gramwell staggered back against the barrel, gasping, his face gray.

Sage screamed his name and dropped the ax to grab him before he fell over the edge, soaking one leg of her breeches with water in the process. The left side of his body was wet with blood, and as she hooked an arm around him and heaved him to her side, she felt a warm wetness soak through her sleeve.

So much blood.

What had happened? There were no Kimisar on the path she could see. Sage propped Gramwell against the steep hill and felt around his body, finding an arrowshaft buried almost to the fletching under his rib cage. The angle told her it had come from the valley below. There was light and heat at her back as the *dremvasha* ignited, and she prayed to the Spirit whoever had fired the arrow would be caught in its rage.

"Be still," she told Gramwell. "I'll get you out of here."

But the depth and the blood told her there was nothing she could do. She was sure the arrow had pierced his lung, and probably also his heart.

"I can't— I can't—" he gasped, blood bubbling on his blue lips.

There was no place to lay him down, so Sage pulled his hands up to his chest and pinned him upright against the slope. He took a rattling breath, struggling to fill his lungs with air. The pool of blood beneath him expanded.

"Clare," she said, her face hovering over his. "Think of Clare."

"Cla-Clare," Gramwell choked, spitting blood.

"Yes. Think of how much you love her."

And she stayed with him until he could think no more.

107

HUZAR RAN AROUND a bend in the path and stopped short at the wave of heat and light coming from the canyon below. In the rocky slope, a half-buried barrel poured water from a split in its side, but rather than extinguish the fire below, it seemed to add to it. What kind of weapon was this? He gripped his sword and took a few more steps, looking for the bronze-haired Demoran he'd scuffled with a few minutes ago. On the other side of the barrels, the boy on horseback he'd followed out of the bowl stood straight and faced him. Huzar froze in shock as he recognized him. Her.

He'd seen her first outside Tegann, when she'd climbed a tree and struck down his hawk with a sling. He'd thought about shooting her then; he'd had a clear shot, but something had stayed his hand. Perhaps it was because she reminded him of Ulara, the sister he'd lost three years ago in the famine. In any case, she was relatively harmless.

Or so he'd thought.

She'd used the same weapon to take down his second-in-command as they pursued the prince along the river. Barely minutes later he'd watched her defeat two of his men as they tried to climb into the boat with her and the prince—one killed, one badly wounded. And despite all that, he was glad he'd spared her the first time because, Spirit shield him, that kind of courage was rare. This woman and Captain Quinn had been his two greatest obstacles in the past year, and he could bring himself to hate neither.

Now she stood before him in Casmuni clothes, her short hair flying in tangles around her face, the left side of her body covered in her companion's blood, a fierce look in her eyes. And Huzar hesitated.

In that moment of hesitation she drew the curved Casmuni sword from her belt and swung the blade around in a fiery arc reflecting the light below. She struck the barrel of water in front of her, and it split in half, sending gallons of water over the ledge in one rush.

Fire exploded below, so intense Huzar took a step back.

Triumph gleamed in the woman's eyes, but the loss of weight in that barrel and the other leaking next to it changed everything. The slope shifted, the earth moving toward the edge, no longer held back by the mass of the contained water. At least one more barrel went over the ledge with it, and Huzar knew whatever was happening below was now beyond anything anyone could stop.

The woman scrambled to get out of the way, and Huzar watched in horror as she climbed on top of the sliding land mass, clawing desperately at something to pull herself up with but finding nothing until she, too, went over the edge.

108

THE FALL OF forty feet was considerably less thanks to the landslides, but it was still quite a distance.

Sage landed on her hip, her left hand thrown instinctively out to catch herself as her right curled around to protect her face. Her left sleeve and pant leg were drenched in blood and water, and when she tumbled down the mound of earth, she rolled over several shattered jars of *dremvasha*, which burst into flame as it touched the moisture on her clothes. She expected to feel heat, but there was none, only pain.

Get out get out get out

When she'd hit the ground, she knew which way was the shortest path out of the fire, but as she screamed and writhed, she lost all sense of direction, all sense of dignity.

Don't touch anywhere else

It would only get worse if she got more of it on her. Sage lunged in the only direction that seemed possible to move in and nearly fainted from the wave of agony. Screaming gave her an anchor in consciousness, gave her the energy to lunge again.

And again.

And again.

A tall figure stood on the edge of the fire around her, on her. Casseck. He reached out a gloved hand, and she rolled and threw her good arm at him, and he grasped it and yanked her out.

The flames followed her from the river of fire as he dragged and rolled her across the sandy ground. Some of the jelly smeared and extinguished briefly before reigniting.

Hands on her waist, jerking her breeches down. Half the cloth had burned away and the rest melted to her skin. She cried out as they came apart. Her sleeve was already gone, but Cass tore the edges of that off, too. And her glove. The thick glove came away, and she saw it was on fire, but it had protected her wrist and hand, though they were blistered. Somehow they hurt more than—

Through a haze of pain, Sage managed to focus on her leg, which was red as raw meat but still had ashy patches of fabric on it. She reached for one with her right hand, thinking to peel it off, when Casseck grabbed her to prevent it.

"I just want to get it off, it doesn't hurt there," she told him. Those places were islands of calm in the sea of agony that was the left side of her body.

And then she saw her left arm, and it was close enough in her pain-blurred vision to see the same patches that were not, in fact, black cloth but charred skin.

She felt no pain there because there was nothing left to feel.

Sage looked back down to her leg, where the skin bubbled and blistered, and fresh waves of pain washed over her. Then she cast herself into the ocean of it and let the depths swallow her into their blackness.

109

AFTER THE LANDSLIDE, everyone had stood still, shocked by the explosion of flame and light and heat. But Alex had only one thought: Sage.

He kept no count of the men he killed or maimed to get to her. Most were fleeing, not fighting, but he made no distinction as he cut his way through them. They were obstacles, nothing more.

Casseck was already there, bent over Sage near a river of fire flowing out and around a huge mound of dirt and glass. Alex fell to his knees beside her and took everything in. Cass had already stripped away the affected clothing, though Alex suspected most of it had burned off. Her left arm and leg lay exposed, red and blistered with sickening patches of black, but she didn't look in danger of burning more. He felt her neck, praying for a pulse, and found it, shallow and rapid. Alive but unconscious, which was better for her.

Flames spewed from the top of the pile of earth. The stones themselves seemed to be melting, though it was hard to tell through the waves of heat. Molten streams advanced slowly, sputtering out of cracks between the rocks near the base. He needed to move her, but how to pick her up? If he cradled her on her left, he would grind against her wounds, but he could shelter them better. From the other side he'd still have to hold her, perhaps centering pressure in places that would damage her further.

"I need a blanket," he shouted to Casseck. His friend pushed to his feet and ran. Alex put his arm under Sage's shoulders and pulled her up and against him, putting his mouth to her ear.

"I'm here, Sage," he whispered. Her back arched, and her eyelashes fluttered against his neck. "Stay with me. I'm getting you out of here." He pressed his lips to her soot-smeared forehead.

Spirit above, it was just like Charlie—

The sound of a sword being drawn from a scabbard made him look up. Casseck stood between them and a Kimisar fighter dressed in Demoran clothing. Swirling tattoos decorated his exposed forearms. The man raised his hands, palms out, then slowly reached up to push the hood of his cloak back. He wasn't very much older than Alex himself, but he looked much wearier. His brown eyes looked past Casseck to Alex cradling Sage, and there was recognition, though Alex couldn't recall ever seeing this man before.

"Get back!" Casseck shouted through the roar of fire and smoke. They didn't have more than a minute to get Sage out of here.

The man shook his head and pulled his hands around to undo the clasp at his neck. Slowly and deliberately, he shrugged off his cloak and held it out. "Take it," he said in Demoran. "Carry her away."

The Kimisar was armed with knives at his belt, so Cass reached for the cloak without lowering his sword. As soon as Casseck had it, the man retreated, hands in the air again, until he faded into the smoke.

Alex didn't even consider that it might be a trick, but Casseck never turned his back on the spot where the man had vanished as he brought the cloak to them. After a moment's hesitation, he jammed his sword in the ground and spread the rough cloth next to Sage.

Alex grabbed an edge and pulled it under her torso and rolled the rest of her onto it so she lay on her uninjured side. Then they folded the end around her, making a hammock. Alex grabbed his sword and stood, and they lifted her together.

"This way!" he shouted, tugging his end. Casseck followed him into the smoke.

110

SHE LAY AT an angle, so her weight rested on her right side and her back. Her left side was almost too painful to comprehend. It both throbbed and stabbed with a thousand daggers. Yet it was better than the first time she woke, when they'd been cleaning sand and dirt from the wounds. Her jaw still ached from biting down on the leather strap they'd put in her mouth. She'd screamed and thrashed at first, until she became aware of Alex holding her against him where he could. He was whispering in her ear, trying to soothe her, but his own choking sobs were impossible to hide. She focused on his voice and managed to quiet down and also stopped fighting, other than the twitches and jerks she couldn't help, and tears from Alex's face fell and mingled with hers.

Now a moist fabric lay over her body to keep her wounds from drying too much. Most of the outside of her leg, her hip, and the middle section of her arm had been burned to huge, painful blisters that ran into one another and burst before sloughing off, leaving weeping rawness behind. A spot on her thigh and another on her calf, plus one on her upper arm, had burned to the point of charring. Her hand, though, protected by her thick glove, had only been comparatively singed. She only ever looked at her burns once. That was more than enough.

Alex took almost exclusive care of her, being gentle when she needed it, but also tough when she resisted. Every few hours he spread a pungent, oily balm over her burns, murmuring apologies for hurting her, but she no longer needed the strap to get through it. Twice daily he forced her to stretch and move her arm and leg in multiple directions, saying it was necessary to keep muscles and tendons and skin limber. During those exercises she unleashed torrents of obscenities at him, but he only smiled and told her she needed to be more creative. Every hour he made her drink water and broth—laced with sedatives, she was sure.

Clare was often there as well, stroking her hair as Alex washed away the dead skin every day. Her friend's face was drawn and pale, and her red-rimmed eyes never focused on Sage, even as she talked to distract her from Alex's work. Despite the haze of pain and medicines, Sage was never able to forget Lieutenant Gramwell or how he'd died, but she didn't know how to tell Clare how sorry she was.

"Did we stop the invasion?" she asked Alex one day.

Alex nodded. "Once the army was severed, most of the Kimisar scattered. I don't think Casmun or Demora needs to worry about an invasion through here for many, many years. There's a wall of black glass blocking the way, thanks to you."

Another time she asked about Gramwell, but she wasn't surprised when Alex said they hadn't found him. He was probably buried under the wall of melted stone.

Her beautiful sword, too, was gone. She was the only one bothered by that. Banneth said he'd have a new one made as soon as they returned to Osthiza. "Like your friend, it perished in saving us, and there is no greater honor," he told her.

That sentiment wasn't likely to console Clare.

It was almost two weeks before Banneth and Alex agreed that Sage could be moved. They traveled slowly for the benefit of the wounded, of which there were many. All told, over a dozen Norsari had been lost either on the ridge or in the bowl, plus ten other Demoran soldiers. Banneth would be leaving behind about forty of his own men, and Sage cried for a day when she heard Darit had survived, but lost his left arm.

Before they put her in the wagon, Alex wrapped her burns in bandages for the first time and helped her into an outfit Clare had tailored to cover her where her skin could be touched. It was an awkward-looking affair that laced in strange places to make it easy to get on and off, but it was better than the blankets that kept slipping. Until they were moving, however, Sage hadn't appreciated being as still as they'd kept her. The constant rocking of the wagon set off waves of pain reminiscent of the first few days, and after an hour she begged for more of the opiates Alex had been weaning her off of. Alex frowned but allowed it.

By the tenth day of travel she needed higher and more frequent doses to keep the pain at bay, and she'd grown to like the hazy hours when she didn't have to think or remember what had happened. When Sage asked for a sedative that night after they'd stopped and Alex refused, she screamed at him. He tried to gather her in his arms, and she fought him until the pain was too great, and she collapsed against him, weeping.

"I'm sorry," he whispered as he rocked her. "I shouldn't have let it go on as long as I did, but I couldn't stand to see you in pain."

"Then let me have it," she sobbed. "I want to forget."

Alex looked stricken. "Forget what, Sage?"

"Gramwell, Charlie . . ." She kept going. "The guards in the barracks, the men on the river, the Kimisar in the pass—I killed them all." Alex said nothing but continued to hold her. "And me," she finished.

"You?"

It was selfish. She was alive, and she should be grateful, yet that wasn't how she felt.

He kissed the top of her head. "You'll heal, Sage. It just takes time."

Sage didn't want to say it, but she was in too much pain to stop the words. "I'll be scarred all over."

"Yes, probably." Alex's lopsided smile was belied by the tears in his eyes. "You'll have me beaten for battle wounds. I don't know if I'll be able to live that down."

She tried to laugh, but instead the fears and emotions she'd drugged away for the last weeks came rushing in at once, demanding to be felt. Sage could only cry uncontrollably as they hit her in wave after wave.

Alex remained silent but held her to him even after she fell asleep, exhausted.

111

THE NEXT DAYS ran together in one long, terrible stretch of time. She was dimly aware that Alex insisted on stopping for her, but Banneth and Clare and most of their group moved on. The only pain relief Alex would let her have was that which came from the burn salve he still applied several times a day, and it wasn't nearly enough. Her mood swung wildly between rage and depression, and very little of what she ate she kept down. She tried appealing to Casseck, but he shook his head sadly and sided with Alex.

No one would listen, so Sage screamed and threw fits and lapsed into sullen silence for hours. Or she lay weeping, too sad to even lift her head.

At times she was so cold she shook as though caught in a blizzard. Then suddenly she would be gasping with heat, sweat soaking her hair and dripping into her wounds, burning like molten lead.

And there was pain. Always pain.

Pain that itched and pain that stabbed. Pain that rolled like thunder and struck like lightning. Her skin felt like it was sewing itself together or crawling with insects. They tied her hands and feet together like a slaughtered hog to keep her from scratching.

Nightmares, too, came.

She dreamed of fire, of being trapped under a melting wall of black glass. One night she dreamed of cutting her burned limbs off and of the look of horror when Alex saw her. Yet even in her nightmares, he never left her, and he was always there when she woke, hoarse from screaming.

Once she saw her father, or thought she did. He walked into the camp and sat by the fire without looking at her, even when she called out to him. Then Alex came over and forced her to look in his eyes while she tried to tell him what she saw, and he insisted she was wrong. When she looked again, Father was gone, and she cried all night.

Then one morning she woke feeling clearheaded and alert—and hungry. She carefully pushed herself into a sitting position, wincing with the pain, and looked around. They were camped at the base of two stone columns—the Protector's Gate. So they were near Osthiza.

Alex lay nearby, a bucket she remembered vomiting into repeatedly near his head. There were dark circles under his eyes and dirty trails of tears on his cheeks. Movement by the smoldering campfire caught her eye, and she saw Casseck squatting next to it, coaxing it back to life in the gray light of dawn. He jumped a little when he saw her.

A few seconds later he was untying her wrists and giving her a cup of water to drink. "How are you feeling?" he asked quietly.

"Like a newborn foal," she answered. Her hands wouldn't stop shaking, but it was different from how they'd shaken and writhed for the last few days. It felt cleaner somehow. "What happened?"

"We had to let the medicine work itself out of your system. I've heard of it being done with those recovering from severe injury, but it's quite different to watch it happen." Cass glanced over at Alex. "He never left your side."

Memories surfaced in her mind, but she wasn't sure which were real and which were hallucinations. "Did I ever hit him?"

Cass smiled ruefully. "Once or twice. Mostly you scratched. But with your injuries it was hard to restrain you too much."

Her cheeks burned with shame. "How long did it take?"

"This is the eighth morning."

"*Eight days?*" She dropped the cup and put her hands over her eyes, her left arm throbbing with the movement.

Alex stirred and sat up, instantly awake. "What's happening?"

"I think she's finally out of the woods," Cass said, refilling the cup with water.

Alex crawled toward her, and Sage reached out to touch the streaks of red on his face and neck. She had done that. "I'm sorry," she sobbed. "Oh, Alex, I'm so sorry."

"No, no," he said, pulling her carefully into his strong arms, the way he'd learned to do over the past weeks. "It's over, love." Alex rocked her and stroked her hair as he kissed her again and again. "I'm just glad to have you back."

112

THEY STAYED IN Osthiza two more weeks. By then most of Sage's burned skin had grown over, shiny and pink—and itchy as hell. At least she was wearing full clothes again. She still craved the relief of the opiates they'd given her. Twice she'd broken down crying. Alex stayed with her when that happened—never judging, just holding her tightly and whispering that he knew she was strong enough to get through it, telling her over and over until she believed it, too.

Clare avoided her most of the time—so much that for the first two days after Ambassador Gramwell, Colonel Traysden, and Nicholas left for Vinova, Sage had thought she went with them. She'd been afraid to ask, not wanting to admit her friend had left without saying good-bye, but on the third day, Clare appeared in her doorway. Sage was sorting dresses and trying to decide which to take back to Demora. At the sound of Clare clearing her throat, Sage looked up in surprise and dropped her handful of silk. For a half minute they looked at each other awkwardly, then Clare strode in and stopped in front of her.

"I hate you," she said. "I hate you because you lived and he died. I hate you because he died saving your life. I hate you because you still have Captain Quinn and I have—" Clare choked. All Sage could do was stand there as her friend fought to bring herself under control. "Lani told me to say all that. She said it would make me feel better."

"Do you feel better?" Sage asked.

Clare shook her head as tears spilled down her cheeks. "I feel worse now because I don't mean it. I'd miss you just as much as him. More."

"Clare, I'd do anything to bring him back. If I thought I could go there and dig him out with my bare hands, I would."

"I know," said Clare, sniffing and wiping her eyes. "I'm sorry."

"You have nothing to be sorry for."

"How can you be so forgiving?"

Sage sat on the edge of the bed and shifted her dress around the sensitive skin on her leg. "Because I understand. When Father died, I hated everyone, even those who took care of me."

"How long did it take for you to get over it?" Clare whispered.

"Years. Sometimes I think I'm still not over it." She squeezed Clare's hand. "But it really didn't get better until I talked about him with friends. You're way ahead of me."

❧

Banneth threw a banquet for Sage's last night in Osthiza. Lani had all Sage's favorite foods prepared and wanted to talk the whole time about Sage and Alex's wedding plans.

"Lani, it's still almost a year and a half away." Sage glanced nervously at Clare, whose grasp of the Casmuni language was good enough to understand what they were talking about.

"I think I will come visit you next summer so we can plan it." Lani tossed her long black braid over her shoulder.

"You are welcome in Demora anytime, but it gets very cold in the winter."

"Then I will have to find someone to keep me warm," said Lani airily. She cast her eyes on Lieutenant Casseck, who was eating at her right hand, completely unaware of what had just been said. Sage nearly choked. Lani shrugged. "I'm in no rush, though. Demoran men can't marry until they're twenty-four anyway."

"That's only Demoran *army officers*," Sage gasped after she swallowed her mouthful.

"Same difference," Lani said, taking a sip of wine. She caught Casseck's eye and smiled. He blinked in surprise and smiled back, oblivious.

Banneth leaned closer to Sage and spoke in a low voice. "I suggest you teach that one more than *please* and *thank you* before we meet again. Otherwise she will talk him into something he doesn't understand."

❧

The journey north was uneventful. Banneth accompanied them until they reached the last major town along the Kaz River. From there, they headed north to Vinova, but Ambassador Gramwell wasn't there, so they rested briefly before pushing to the Jovan Road. Over dinner at an inn one night, they were met with a number of dispatches from Tennegol.

Alex passed out dozens of scrolls to the men with him. Every Norsari received a commendation from the king, and Sage and Clare had ones specially addressed to them. Alex read Sage's over her shoulder from his seat next to her on the bench while she blushed and nudged him away with her shoulder.

"Not bad for an eighteen-year-old," he said. "Of course, I had two or three of these by your age."

"You did not!"

He grinned and kissed the tip of her nose. "No, I didn't."

"What are the rest of the messages about?" she asked.

"Let's see . . ." Alex dug through the satchel. "The last two have seals of official orders rather than those fancy ribbons. For me and the Norsari here, and—" Alex broke off as he saw the two silver pins attached to the scroll.

Sage leaned over to look. "Promotion to major, huh? Not bad for someone your age."

Alex shook his head. "It's unheard of." He pulled the pins off and stuffed them in his pocket. "Don't tell anyone. I can't even wear them anyway since I don't have a uniform. They'd look really strange with this." He gestured to his Casmuni breeches and vest.

"What's the other one?" Sage asked.

Alex squinted at the writing on the outside of the second scroll. "This one's yours. Uncle Raymond has plans for you, apparently."

"Interesting," Sage said, taking it. She broke the seal, and a smaller, unofficial-looking note with three distinct handwritings fell out. Sage opened it first, finding a personal letter from the queen and the two princesses.

> Dearest Sage,
> I can never express my gratitude for what you have done in protecting my son from harm. He has told us the story many times, and we all look forward to hearing your more modest account of events, but I suspect that will have to wait. You have more important duties now, which will serve the realm as a whole, but we will miss you all the same. Please remember that if there is anything I can do for you, you need only ask, as I am forever in your debt.
>
> Most Sincerely,
> Orianna March Devlin

The other paragraphs scrawled at the bottom were from Rose and Carinthia, begging her to remember them fondly, with a heavy hint from Rose that she was more than willing to visit, should Sage feel lonely. They were all referring to what must be on the official scroll, which Sage now realized she should've read first. A knot formed in her stomach as she unrolled a royal proclamation.

> Following the permanent retirement of Ambassador Lord Gramwell, Mistress Sage Fowler is hereby requested by His Majesty, King Raymond II, to serve as Ambassador to the Nation of Casmun, effective immediately, representing the crown in matters concerned with opening and establishing trade routes and laws, judging matters of Demoran citizens in Casmun, representing Demoran interests, and

maintaining open and clear communication between our
nations. For the time being, the post shall reside at the
Fortress of Vinova near the boundary of the two lands,
and all honors and necessities shall be provided for the
office and its duties.

Signed,

H.M. Raymond II

Sage froze with the letter in her hands. The honor and trust of the
position were dizzying, but her heart sank, and she looked up with tears
in her eyes.

Alex had his mouth scrunched to one side as he read his orders.
"Pretty much what I expected. Back to the capital for more recruits and
then out for training. He wants to expand the Norsari to a full battalion
by next summer. Must be why the promotion." He handed the orders to
Cass and frowned at her expression. "What's wrong?"

"He's named me ambassador to Casmun."

"But that's wonderful," Alex said, grabbing the paper to read it himself. His face fell as he read it. "Vinova," he whispered.

Sage shook her head. "I'm not going with you."

Casseck was reading the Norsari's orders aloud to those in the tavern
to great enthusiasm, but neither Sage nor Alex paid the noise any attention. Without a word, Alex took her by the hand and led her upstairs to
her room, then bolted the door behind him and wrapped her in his arms.

"I thought we'd be together until at least Tennegol," she choked.

Alex rubbed her back and laid his cheek on top of her head.
"Me too."

"I hate this!"

"I know, but it's too late for me to take up farming now."

Sage laughed weakly and wiped her eyes on his shirt, breathing
him in. Spirit above, they only had hours left.

"The decision is yours," Alex whispered. "But you can turn it down.
You've already given so much."

She snorted. "You know I won't. Not when the kingdom needs me."

"Both kingdoms need you, yes. I know. It was just wishful thinking." He continued holding her against him.

"I'll keep Clare with me—I ought to have a companion, and she knows so much already. She can't be sent back to her father. He's awful. He'll have her married off to someone else within a month."

"I'll tell Uncle Raymond. I'm sure he'll be fine with it."

"And Alex?" Her fingers curled around folds in his shirt. "Stay with me tonight. Please. We only have a few hours left."

He swallowed. "All right. Just promise me . . ."

She nodded. "I'll be good, I promise."

"Well." Alex smiled crookedly, and her heart skipped a beat. "I wouldn't mind if you were a *little* bad."

EPILOGUE

A FEW DAYS AFTER the battle, Huzar led all the Kimisar survivors he could gather across the southern pass. He'd approached the Casmuni camp alone, after it was all over, carrying a makeshift flag of truce, and asked for Captain Quinn. When the Demoran met him, he recognized Huzar immediately and called for his cloak to be brought to him. That had been the last thing Huzar expected, but he accepted it with a thank-you.

"No," Quinn had said. "Thank *you*."

Huzar folded the cloak over his tattooed arm. "Will she live?"

A ripple of pain had passed over the Demoran's features. "We can only hope right now. She's strong, though."

Huzar smiled a little before clearing his throat. "I've come to request the release of my countrymen, that they may return home."

Quinn crossed his arms. "And why should I allow that?"

"Please," Huzar said simply. "We're only soldiers following orders. Surely you can understand that." He waved an arm back at the pass. "The threat is gone. Let us go home."

Quinn eyed him for several seconds. "Your Demoran is quite good."

"Yes, I've spent a great deal of time in your country."

Quinn raised an eyebrow. "Apparently so."

Huzar looked down at his hands. "We were abandoned and stranded by your D'Amirans. Everything I've done in the past year was to return to Kimisara. I could not call myself a commander if I didn't always do my best to bring my men home."

Finally Quinn had nodded. "I will speak to King Banneth."

In the end, the Casmuni king turned the prisoners over, and Huzar led them and the other survivors he'd found back into Kimisara, expecting to return to a nation in even more ruin than when he'd left almost two years ago, but there was nowhere else to go. At least he could not be expected to return to war. Most of the army had dissolved once word got out that King Ragat had been tossed from his horse and trampled in the rush to get away from the molten river of fire.

Huzar and the survivors traveled slowly, carrying many wounded. They skirted the smoldering wall of black glass by using the rocky ledge above, but then followed the canyon through the mountains, not even bothering to set a rear guard. At the end of the pass, they found a supply train that had been abandoned and scavenged. As no one of higher rank was present, Huzar took responsibility for releasing the Kimisar with him from their military obligations.

He then allowed himself a couple days to rest and scrounge supplies from the wreckage of the wagons before setting off with a few companions. Harvest time was approaching, and surely the place he should be was home. Three days out, he was met on the road by royal troops. When they learned who Huzar was and where he'd been, they escorted him to the seat of the local barony, where regional judgments were made.

For the first time in his life, Huzar was faced with royalty. Nearing thirty, Queen Zoraya had been half her husband's age and still had the bloom of youth, with gold-bronze skin and hair so black it almost had a sheen of blue. Up close, one could see the lines in her face from the strain of years of barrenness, and then having only one child to shield her from being disposed of as Ragat's two previous wives had been. Her son was now only five, and heir to a land of ashes.

"My husband's ministers do not see fit to tell me all that has happened," she said, gripping the arms of the chair set up as a makeshift throne. "Perhaps you can shed some light on events."

Huzar told her everything that had happened since he'd left Kimisara. Though he knew nothing about the man, he heaped praise on King

Ragat and his bravery in battle, but the queen snorted and rolled her eyes. When his tale finally ended, Zoraya stood and paced in front of him on the dais.

"You've been a most loyal son of Kimisara, Captain. I can never truly repay either the service you've rendered or your honesty to me now."

"I live only to serve, My Queen," he said.

She stopped in front of him. "You must understand how precarious my position is. My son is king, and I may be regent by law, but I am flouted at every turn by those would usurp my position and take power for themselves."

"What is it My Queen wishes of me?"

"The country is recovering from the famine, but the king's death and the failure of his campaign may throw it back into chaos. I need to project strength and create stability. I need men of honesty and loyalty." She held out her right hand, her sapphire-blue eyes piercing his soul. "May I count on your service?"

Huzar stared at the bejeweled rings on every finger of the queen's smooth hand. "May I first ask what My Queen plans to do? Forgive me, but I cannot see where a mere captain can assist."

The hand dropped. "I will first sue for peace with Demora and Casmun. This fighting must stop. You, who have such wide knowledge of both nations, will attend this process, but you will be loyal to me, not the ministers or generals. I need your help to keep them from going behind my back and undermining my goals. Now." She raised her hand again. "May I count on you?"

Let this end. Let this be done.

Let me go home.

Huzar trembled as he knelt and took the hand she offered, kissing the four-pointed star of Kimisara on the ring on her middle finger. "Until death, My Queen."

ACKNOWLEDGMENTS

This second book was much harder than the first, but I stuck it out, and you, dear reader, stuck with me. I'm honored. A special thanks to reviewers who were kind but held me accountable on many levels, and to the fans who emailed me in the middle of the night. Oh, and the fan art . . . I can't believe what people have made! For me! (Dang it, there's dust in my eyes.)

As before, big props to the Father of all, and my personal heavenly cheerleaders, Dymphna and Francis, though to paraphrase St. Teresa, I really wish y'all didn't feel the need to prove to me that I could handle this much stress. *Deo gratias.*

My publishing angels on earth are led by the best agent that ever waded through the slush, Valerie Noble, who swept away the cobwebs, untangled plot threads, and talked me off of metaphorical ledges in addition to all the normal contract stuff. I'm sorry I said you were short. I thought you knew I had no tact. Then there's Rhoda and Nicole—I'm finally not hyperventilating when we talk on the phone. Thanks for your patience in the deadlines I missed and the steaming mess of a manuscript I had to clean up. I promise to learn from my mistakes. I bow to copy master Alexei Esikoff; and Natalie, you made not one, but two beautiful covers. I can't wait to see the third.

Last time, I didn't get a chance to thank all the wonderful Fierce Reads people who gave me the life-changing opportunity to tour with them. Brittany, Amanda, and Ashley especially made everything wonderful. I think of you ladies with heart-eyes. My tour buddies Taran Marathu and Scott Westerfeld were both intimidating and fun to hang with, and I learned so much from both. I only wish I lived in that parallel universe where Kristen Orlando was able to make it. (Read her books, y'all, even if Reagan's boyfriend is a West Pointer. No one's perfect.)

The circle of readership was much smaller for this book due to time constraints, but it includes the old friends Kim, Caroline, Amy, Kammy, Dan, El Deeferino (since you're not into the whole brevity thing), and the Class of 2017 Debut support network, plus some new friends, especially the lovely dragon writer Laurie, who inspires me with her enthusiasm, her resilience, and her ability to disconnect from social media for long chunks of time. Thanks to Mom for bragging about me all forty years of my life, and Dad for teaching me how to stab people. Special shout-out to Doctor Kate, who provided lots of gross info on burns. All my wonderful friends and family who supported me with little messages and gifts, came to see me on tour, and told anyone about me who would listen: there are way, way too many of you to name, but you have all been more important to my sanity than you'll ever know.

There were two special readers who took the time to help me get the things right that I never would have seen: Ashley Woodfolk and Joshua Gabriel Lontoc. I am eternally in your debt.

As much as I talked about suffering through this, I didn't keep the suffering to myself. I'm generous like that. So to my kids, I'm sorry for ignoring you and knowing more about imaginary people's lives than your own these past few months. I'll make it up to you, but don't ask for Chick-fil-A or pizza because you'll get plenty when I'm working on the next book. Thank you for telling everyone how cool you think your mom is.

And Michael. It's funny how I can't find adequate words when it's your turn, but fortunately we're psychotically linked so you always know what I'm thinking, which is usually that I need a nap. I love you.

ERIN BEATY

What did you want to be when you grew up?
I wanted to be an astronaut or work for NASA. I went to Space Camp four times as a kid, earning the money to go every time. It's also why I chose the Naval Academy—most astronaut alumni of any school. Plus it was tough and I wanted the biggest challenge, figuring if I could get through USNA, I could do anything. Things didn't work out space-wise for several reasons beyond my control, but I don't re-gret any of the choices I made that led me to this life, which now includes writing. At least two of my kids have their eyes set on working in the space program, though, so the returns on my choices are decent in that respect.

When did you realize you wanted to be a writer?
I always wanted to be a *competent* writer, so I worked at that and was consequently always voted to do group lab reports, but I had it in my mind for thirty-plus years that I was an engineer, not a storyteller. I resisted writing until I got an idea that wouldn't go away, and in putting it down, I realized writing a book *is* engineering. Worlds and plots are complex systems, and that's my bread and butter. Forces are exerted from all directions. Everything has to be

logical and supported and parts have to move smoothly. It takes a lot of trial and error. I have no idea when I realized I wanted to be a writer, but I realized I actually *was* one when I was thirty-seven. For the record, that's not old.

What's your most embarrassing childhood memory?
Oh, hell no. I will take that to the grave.

Did you play sports as a kid?
I tried just about every sport as a kid. Basketball was a big love; it was what you *did* growing up in Indiana (that and going to Steak 'n Shake at every opportunity). I ran cross-country and track and played tennis in addition to basketball, but I was never the star of any team. Middle-level at best. I was in it for the love and the fitness. It's not technically a sport, but through high school I was also a flag twirler with the marching band. Lamé, spandex, and sequins all the way, baby!

What was your first job, and what was your "worst" job?
I detasseled corn for a couple summers, starting at age thirteen. It was rough, exhausting work but decent money, especially if you worked overtime. (And by decent money, I mean $4.25 per hour.) It also had me learning how to fill out 1040-EZ tax forms on my own the next spring. During the school year I babysat, sometimes seven kids at a time, worked at a home daycare, and also had a weekly paper route. At seventeen, I started working at Discovery Zone, which was like a Chuck E. Cheese's—that was everything from making pizza and washing dishes to repairing game machines to hosting birthday parties to cleaning up body fluids. Space Camp (see above) made it all worth it. After

that was the navy, which was all sorts of awesome, though not all the time. No job is.

My "worst" job was probably answering phones for Omaha Steaks, which I did for extra holiday cash while I was writing and revising what would become *The Traitor's Kiss*. The place was actually awesome, as were the perks, but I underestimated my phone anxiety. I went home and threw up after the first day. After a couple weeks I was okay with it, but I'd rather detassel corn again.

Where do you write your books?

We currently live in old naval base housing, and my writing space is a tiny room that used to store confidential material and files. It's wired with at least two different alarms and the windows are barred and there are blackout curtains, but it's cozy, and I'll miss it when we move. In the last house I had a card table in a guest room, and before that it was a corner of a dining room-turned-office. Sometimes even here in my little nest I need a change of scenery, though, so I'll go to a coffee shop, but even just moving my laptop to the bed or living room for a few hours is enough to make me more productive.

Do you ever get writer's block? What do you do to get back on track?

Since I tend to binge-write for several days straight, I often get burned out, but it only takes a day or two away for me to reset. I do puzzles and watch TV and movies that either drain or sustain the emotions I want. When I'm blocked on what to do or can't straighten a tangled plot, I call my agent or editor and babble incoherently for an hour or so. That usually works, even if they don't say a word. Otherwise, I've found writing things out by hand unlocks creative centers in my brain, and there's ample medical evidence that that's a real neurological phenomenon. Scenes I write in notebooks change much less in revision than anything I type first. Typing is much faster, however, so I get the best of both worlds by recording snippets of ideas by hand and outlining a plot on Post-its I can move around and replace as necessary, then typing like mad.

Unlikely alliances are forged
and trust is shattered in the stunning
conclusion to The Traitor's Trilogy.

Keep reading for an excerpt.

1

FOR SOMEONE WHO hated fighting, Clare was getting pretty good at it. Sage now had to break a sweat to defeat her friend, which was impressive today, given how cold it was. The massive stone walls of Vinova, Demora's outpost fortress, offered shelter from the winter winds that swept across the eastern plain but did little to hold in warmth. Repelling invasion and resisting siege had been first in the builders' minds. Now that the southern nation of Casmun was opening diplomatic talks, it was the location that mattered for Sage's position as ambassador. Self-defense was important for life in general, however, and so Sage insisted her best friend and companion train in combat.

Clare's face contorted into a scowl of concentration as she gripped a lightweight sword in one gloved hand. Her eyes narrowed over the shield on her left arm, but that wasn't what Sage was watching.

Beneath her knee-length skirt, Clare's boots shifted in the dirt, and Sage unconsciously leaned to the right, bracing her own feet on the frozen ground, still waiting for the movement that would give her friend away. Rare was even the most seasoned warrior who could attack without some warning in body language. At not quite seventeen, Clare was nearly two years younger than Sage, and she'd begun her training only a few months ago.

It was a sharp, slight movement a split second before Clare lunged that gave her away, but it was enough. Sage met her on the left and blocked the swing with her shield before catching Clare's sword with her own, lifting the blade up, around, and back down. The motion drew them up against each other as their hilts locked. This time Sage left herself open to a countermove.

"What are you forgetting?" she asked, bearing down until the tip of Clare's sword touched the ground.

In response, Clare pivoted and rammed her shield into Sage's exposed side.

Your shield is also a weapon.

Sage grinned as she fell back, but her friend didn't smile as she jerked her head to toss her thick braid over her shoulder. Her brown eyes flashed in silent challenge, and her slight frame trembled with something other than cold. "You don't have to keep telling me," Clare spat.

She was angry now. Which meant things were about to get interesting.

Rage was useful in a fight—Sage knew that firsthand. It heightened the senses and brought strength and endurance, but she'd also experienced the recklessness that easily took over. Clare's lack of control could force Sage to react in a way that might hurt one or both of them.

"Anytime now," taunted Clare, her words muffled behind the shield.

Sage moved several careful steps to the right, forcing Clare to adjust her stance and give herself more time to think. *What would Alex do?*

The thought of him brought an involuntary smile to her lips. Last year Sage had lashed out in anger while sparring with Alex, and he'd disarmed her and smacked her rear end with the flat of his blade in a single move. Alex wouldn't escalate this. He would stay methodical, meeting her at her level, never forcing her back too much but never conceding ground, either.

Clare was waiting for her to make a move. Sage shifted to walk to the left side, twisting her curved sword in a lazy arc, briefly reflecting a ray of sunlight that had escaped the blanket of clouds above.

Her friend didn't take the bait. She was in control right now, but it wouldn't take much to tip that balance.

Sage began running through a series of basic arcs, slices, and parries, stripping her movements of the personal style she'd developed over the last year and a half. She imagined herself as the clock in the chapel tower—gears and pendulums and arms rotating but anchored firmly from the center and therefore restricted and predictable. The only sound was their heavy breathing and the steady clash of metal on metal.

With only the slightest twitch in warning, Clare broke from the rhythm, countering a parry with a slash across Sage's leg close enough to catch the fabric of her breeches. Clare's eyes widened in shock, but Sage didn't acknowledge it, refusing to leave enough time for fear to get ahold of either of them. Their sparring dropped all feel of formality and rote practice. Even if neither truly wanted to hurt the other, it suddenly felt *real*, and they danced around each other with intense concentration and vague smiles.

Sage pressed Clare hard, slowly draining the reservoir of rage. Her friend managed to hold her temper in check, and there were no damaging hits to either side other than a few earsplitting shrieks as swords grazed across shields.

After nearly twenty minutes, the fire was spent. Sage rested on a bale of hay outside the horse paddock, fiddling with the hole in her breeches. The cold had begun to make itself known again, starting with her nose. Next to her, Clare's breath frosted in the air between them as she slowly came back down from the exertion. Every few seconds she cast a guilty look at Sage's leg, but Sage studiously ignored her concern. She didn't think the skin was cut, though it was hard to tell with gloves on. Either way, her friend shouldn't feel bad about it.

"I think your clothes give you an advantage," Sage said casually. "It's harder to see what your upper legs are doing. Makes you less predictable."

"Finally, something I have over you," Clare said, pulling her skirt down as far as it would go. The hose she wore underneath was thick enough to hide the shape of her legs, but she was still self-conscious. There was no bitterness in her voice, though, only weariness, which was good.

Sage shivered and ran a hand over her head, pressing down the hair that had escaped the short horsetail in the back. She could tell by her shadow that she looked like a half-drowned cat. Clare's mahogany braid was flawless, as usual. "We still have time for a bit of *tashaivar*," Sage said, glancing at the angle of the sun.

Just then the chapel bell tolled, its pulses echoing off the bare stone of the fortress and its surrounding walls, declaring three hours past noon. Clare hopped up, energy restored. "No, we don't."

Sage groaned inwardly, but a deal was a deal—Clare submitted to Sage's combat training and Sage took lessons from her friend in diplomacy. Besides, a hot bath was what she needed now. Cold had seeped into her toes, and the dampness under the Casmuni-styled clothing she wore for sparring chilled her skin. The loose breeches and jacket were meant for desert wear and dispersed body heat quickly. Though her teeth had begun to chatter, Sage volunteered to put Clare's weapons away so her friend could clean up first.

Clare was done by the time Sage entered the dressing room connecting their suites. When they'd taken up residence at Vinova several months ago, Sage had worried at the cruelty of putting her friend in rooms meant for the wife of the ambassador stationed at the border stronghold. After all, Clare was supposed to marry the son of the previous ambassador, Lord Gramwell, who was expected to be an emissary in his own right someday. She'd spent nine months living with her betrothed's family, preparing for the role.

It would never happen now.

A Kimisar arrow may have killed Lieutenant Lucas Gramwell, but Sage could never forget that he'd taken it in protection of her. Clare didn't blame her, except perhaps in her worst moments, which—thankfully—were becoming more rare. And it wasn't as though Sage had come through the battle unscathed. She and Clare spent many nights sleeping in the same bed, comforting each other through nightmares. Now they occurred maybe once a week, and more often it was Sage who woke screaming and thrashing.

In waking hours, Clare's episodes of anger usually sparked over something trivial and then simmered below the surface until they burst forth in the middle of training, over dinner, or during a diplomacy lesson. It was a reaction Sage herself had experienced after her own father's death six years ago, so she didn't judge her friend harshly. Time was the only thing that could truly heal either of their wounds.

Sage loosened the laces of her jacket with her right hand as she dipped her left into the bathwater. Just right. She shed the rest of her sweaty clothes and hopped in. Clare rolled her eyes as water splashed onto the polished wood floor, but Sage barely noticed as she ducked under the surface and pulled her short, sand-colored hair free of its leather tie. The left side of her body tingled with a sensation stronger than an itch, but she ignored it and lifted her head out of the water, reaching for the bottle of hair tonic.

"We're almost out of this," said Sage, pulling at the cork with her teeth to avoid taking her left arm out of the water. The scents of orange and jasmine wafted from the open bottle.

"Let me get that." Clare finished tying the bodice of her simple gray dress and moved to help Sage get the last of the hair tonic out. Rather than just dab it on Sage's wet hair, she began to lather it, too. She often did such things, finding quiet ways to make up for losing her temper. Sage didn't think the silent apologies were necessary, but they made her friend feel better.

"When did you last hear from Major Quinn?" Clare asked casually, as if she didn't know. Bringing up Sage's betrothed was another way of smoothing roughness between them.

At the mention of Alex's name, heat crept into Sage's cheeks, and she tried to reply just as casually, "Two days ago."

"How is the training coming along?"

Alex commanded the Norsari, Demora's elite fighters. Last spring the army unit was reestablished twenty years after having been disbanded. As it turned out, the initial company had been ready just in time to face a Kimisar force coming through the southern nation of Casmun. Now the Norsari were being expanded to a full battalion. The increase had been planned from the beginning, but now it was a necessity. Kimisara's king, Ragat, had been killed at the Battle of Black Glass, and no one in Demora knew what the combination of warm spring weather and a new ruler would bring. Whatever it was, the Norsari would be at the front lines. As would Alex. Sage tried not to think of the added distance and danger as she gently rubbed a washcloth over the pink-and-white scars on her leg. "They'll be finishing up their seventh week now."

Clare used a small pitcher to rinse Sage's hair. "Will he be able to visit?"

Sage shook her head and wiped suds from her eyes. "He can't afford to be away that long." The training camp was over a hundred and fifty miles to the west. At best, it was four days of hard travel to Vinova and another four back, and the winter weather didn't help. "Maybe when they've finished in another six weeks."

Yet she knew he wouldn't. Alex couldn't justify such a trip in the face of his responsibilities, especially considering they weren't married—and he was restricted from marrying until age twenty-four. Sage frowned thoughtfully and counted the days from midwinter in her head. Then she smiled.

His birthday was tomorrow. They had only a year left to wait.

2

AN HOUR LATER it was Sage's turn to scowl. How could eating be so complicated?

"Today you have an earl from Reyan on your left, a lower Casmuni prince on your right, and I am a Demoran countess," said Clare from her seat across the table, which was spread with more dishes, utensils, plates, and goblets than Sage could keep track of. "The earl only speaks his own language. I speak Reyan and Demoran, and the prince speaks Kimisar and Casmuni. Whom do you address first and in what language?"

Diplomacy gave Sage headaches and even a few nightmares. At least Kimisar weren't in the mix. The best Demora could ever hope for with them was an uneasy truce and constant denials that any of the raids in Tasmet were from their country. Reyan was a longtime ally, but the relationship with Casmun was still new. The nations' royal families wanted it to succeed, but the common people on both sides were slower to change after generations of hostility. The process was delicate, especially after last summer's events.

"Have I shared water with the prince before?" Sage asked. Casmuni didn't think it polite to fully address or use names with a person they hadn't been formally introduced to.

"Yes, but it was years ago, and you aren't sure if he remembers."

Dammit, her friend was crafty. But ambassadorship could be that complicated, and not being prepared could cause disaster on a national scale. Sage never felt more in over her head than she did during these lessons. She suddenly grinned. "I'll leave you to chat with him while I address the messenger who just walked in."

Clare turned around to see Master Finch approaching with a scroll bound by a violet ribbon. "That looks unusual," she said.

Sage untied the ribbon and unrolled the parchment, then spent several minutes silently studying the words. Clare kicked her under the table. "It can't take that long to read," she scolded.

A slow smile had spread across Sage's cheeks. "I think we should change the prince on my right to a princess." She flipped the page around to show Clare it was written in Casmuni. "Lani is coming to visit."

"When?" Her friend seized the official-looking parchment, drawing her brows down as she scanned it, reading slower than Sage had. "Sooner than this summer?"

"Tomorrow."

The lesson forgotten, Clare jumped to her feet. "Spirit above, we've got to get ready!"

"Can't we at least finish eating?" Sage gazed longingly at the covered dishes and their still-empty plates. Time in the tilting yards always made her hungry. Sometimes the promise of food was the only thing that made etiquette lessons bearable.

"Are you kidding?" Clare was halfway to the door, casting a look over her shoulder that indicated that if Sage didn't come along, she would drag her. "We won't have time to sleep tonight."

With a sigh, Sage pushed her chair away from the table and followed her friend, but not before grabbing a bread roll. Or three.

∞◆∞

Sage had once seen a Norsari company march into battle on a moment's notice. That was the only thing she could compare the activity around the Vinova Fortress to over the next hours. Clare took charge of the kitchens and household matters, having food and rooms prepared.

Alaniah Limistraleddai would be the first Casmuni to set foot in Demora in over two hundred years, and she wasn't an ordinary emissary;

she was the king's sister and the highest-ranking *chessa*—princess—in the nation. "How many in her retinue?" Clare asked again.

"Twelve," Sage answered without looking at the note. "Plus sixty soldiers." That wasn't very many, considering Lani's status.

"She could've given us more warning," Clare grumbled, counting chickens plucked and laid out.

"*An ambassador is always ready to receive*," Sage recited with a grin.

Clare grimaced. "Thank the Spirit that Papa began cleaning things up when he and I were here last summer. We'd be much worse off now if he hadn't." She referred to her fiancé's father, a retired diplomat who had been recalled to act as ambassador at the Vinova Fortress near the southern border, when Demora had been preparing to reopen relations with Casmun. That was interrupted by the Kimisar staging an attack, and Sage had fled into Casmun with the king's youngest son, accidentally becoming the first Demoran they'd spoken to in generations. Lord Gramwell led the effort to retrieve the prince, escalating to the Battle of Black Glass, in which the Demorans and Casmuni fought the Kimisar and won. His only son didn't return from the fight, and once the dust had settled and the prince was returned home, the grief-stricken ambassador asked for permanent retirement.

Sage was appointed to replace Lord Gramwell and kept Clare with her, both for companionship and to keep her friend from having to return to her father now that her betrothed was dead. On paper, Sage was the most qualified person in the realm for the position. She'd learned the Casmuni language and established a good relationship with their royal family, but she was still an eighteen-year-old commoner with no formal training, and she wondered if she would be replaced at some point. Not that King Raymond had ever indicated she might be.

In the meantime, she subjected herself to Clare's lessons. Between her friend's knowledge and what she'd learned about Casmun's people and customs, Sage hoped to be worthy of the job.

Their first test arrived in a matter of hours.